DANTE'S WOOD

DANTE'S WOOD

LYNNE RAIMONDO

A MARK ANGELOTTI NOVEL

SEVENTH
STREET
BOOKS™

59 John Glenn Drive
Amherst, New York 14228–2119

Published 2013 by Seventh Street Books™, an imprint of Prometheus Books

Cover image of trees © mike_expert/Shutterstock.com
Cover image of buildings © Hal Bergman/Media Bakery
Cover design by Jacqueline Nasso Cooke

Inquiries should be addressed to
Seventh Street Books
59 John Glenn Drive
Amherst, New York 14228–2119
VOICE: 716–691–0133 • FAX: 716–691–0137
WWW.PROMETHEUSBOOKS.COM

17 16 15 14 13 • 5 4 3 2 1

Library of Congress Cataloging-in-Publication Data

Raimondo, Lynne, 1957-
    Dante's wood : a Mark Angelotti novel / by Lynne Raimondo.
        p. cm.
    ISBN 978-1-61614-718-1 (pbk.)
    ISBN 978-1-61614-719-8 (ebook)
    1. Psychologists—Fiction. 2. Blind medical personnel—Fiction. 3. Youth with mental disabilities—Fiction. 4. Child sexual abuse—Fiction. 5. Murder—Investigation—Fiction. 6. Chicago (Ill.)—Fiction. 7 Psychological fiction.
    I. Title. II. Title: Mark Angelotti novel.

PS3618.A387D36 2012
813'.6—dc22

0205   2012031725

Printed in the United States of America

To my parents

"Nel mezzo de camin di nostra vita
mi retrovai per una selva oscura
ché la diritta via era smaritta."

(Midway in the journey of our life
I came to myself in a dark wood,
for the straight way was lost.)

—Dante Alighieri, *Inferno I*
(Translated by Robert Hollander and Jean Hollander,
Doubleday, 2000)

ONE

There was no arguing with the file. Several inches thick and stamped *Confidential*, it sat on my boss's desk like a fresh indictment. In my spare time—I had a lot of it in those days—I relived the contents again and again, treating each chapter like evidence in a trial, searching for a sign that the jury was still out. But as any good lawyer will tell you, evidence seldom leads us to the truth. Even then, more than a year after the slipup that started the whole mess, after the blood tests and the endless examinations, after the weeks of waiting and the final crashing verdict, I still hadn't given up hope.

Septimus Brennan turned the pages slowly.

"Am I allowed one final appeal?"

"Not yet," he said. "When I'm done reading."

While he continued his inspection, I took a mental tour of my surroundings. A few yards to my right, a tall window illuminating a collection of carefully tended miniature bonsai. Directly in front of me, Sep bent over the file, wearing as usual a starched jacket and a tie dating back to the Reagan era. On the wall behind him, a display of African tribal masks bearing an uncanny resemblance to their owner. One of them was always scolding me with a mouth shaped like a big *O*, as though I'd just been caught stealing from a piggy bank. Or, in this case, my employer's payroll.

Sep stopped over the most recent entry. Dated less than a month ago, it ended on a typically negative note. "According to this, nothing's changed," he said, making it sound like an accusation.

I roused myself and shrugged. "You were expecting a brand new me?"

"No, I suppose not." He replaced the paper with a sigh. "But I *was* hoping for a better excuse."

"It's only until the end of the year. I promise I'll be ready by then."

"By the end of the year, I'll have to get down on my knees and beg them to keep you."

"That's a bit harsh, isn't it? I mean, with your arthritis?" Sep made a show of clearing his throat and I thought maybe I'd gone too far. "Besides," I added, "it's not like I'm guilty of extortion. You'd think I was making it all up." Beneath the desk, where I hoped he couldn't see it, my right leg was twitching like the needle on a polygraph.

"No one's accusing you of that. However . . ."

"Go ahead. My skin's pretty thick these days."

"Some have questioned your, ah, sincerity."

"Who? The tyrants upstairs?" Feigning outrage, I waved imprecisely at the file. "Have any of them bothered to read what's in there? Or were they expecting me to do it for them?"

"There's no need to gild the lily. I have the lab reports right in front of me."

"Then why are we still here?"

"I'm waiting for you to give me something I can sell. Put it in terms of a formal history if that helps."

My leg was really going now, so I crossed it over the other and pretended to study the toe of my shoe. It's an old psychiatrist's trick, one I had often used myself: asking the patient to describe himself in the third person. But knowing just what Sep was up to didn't make me feel any better about misleading him. Despite the Dr. Gillespie exterior, Sep was essentially a soft touch who had hired me two years before on the strength of my résumé, with few questions asked about why someone in my seemingly enviable position would suddenly decide to quit and start all over. In the months that followed, I repaid the favor by doing everything possible to challenge the wisdom of his decision, and while I wasn't *technically* responsible for the events that brought us together that afternoon, I still thought I owed him something better.

I sneaked another pass at my watch. It was nearing 4:00 p.m. and a shift change, when the hospital corridors would take on the urgency of a big game stampede. I figured most of the people rushing for the door would pretend not to see me, but a few brave souls, stirred by sympathy or a sense of fair play, would stop to ask how I was doing. The thought of being trapped in one of these exchanges was enough to make me volunteer for group therapy, so I gamely forged ahead.

"Very well. Our subject today—let's call him Patient M—is a forty-seven-year-old male employed as a clinical psychiatrist at a large urban teaching hospital. For the better part of a year, M has been on leave of absence following the sudden onset of a rare medical condition, the effects of which are considered by most members of society—with the apparent exception of M's employer—to impose significant restraints on the patient's lifestyle and to require a prolonged period of adjustment and rehabilitation."

I stopped and asked how I was doing so far.

"A little self-serving, but go on."

"Since that time, M has secluded himself at home and avoided contact with the community at large, except when he is putting in appearances with his social worker or relearning how to cross a street. Although M has been cooperating with his treatment regimen and is making steady forward progress, he has thus far resisted returning to work, insisting he needs more time to become accustomed to his new routines. M's immediate superior"—here I nodded in Sep's direction—"while claiming to be sympathetic to M's circumstances, has imposed a deadline for said return that M considers both unrealistic and punitive."

Sep made a noise suspiciously like a snort, but didn't rein me in.

"M has been referred to Chicago Kaiser psychiatric staff for evaluation of suspected malingering. Upon physical examination, M is found to be in general good health, apart from a neuropathology of known origin that is anticipated to persist—" I stopped again, feeling a familiar rise in my throat. "How much longer do I have to keep this up?"

"A little longer," Sep said.

"—to persist for the rest of M's life. M is observed to speak candidly about his condition, to acknowledge its frustrations without hesitation or embarrassment, and to be at ease interacting with others who resist the impulse to treat him like a toddler. Fortunately for M, he did not choose surgery as a specialty, and with certain adaptations not relevant here, should be able to resume the role of a treating physician once he and his superior have agreed upon a more suitable timetable. Done?"

"Hardly. You haven't said anything about M's psychological factors."

"M denies he has any fears about coming back."

"You don't say."

This wasn't going as well as I'd hoped. "OK. How's this, then—when pressed, M admits he is experiencing . . . some minor anxiety of a clinically insignificant nature."

"Is that the best you can come up with?"

"*Jesus*, Sep," I blurted out, more loudly than I wanted to. "Do I really have to spell it out for you?"

"Good. You're getting angry."

"Is that what this is all about?" I nearly shouted. "Getting me to admit I'm not happy about . . . this?" I steadied myself and sniffed. "I hope you're not going to start parroting that crap about the five stages of grief."

"No. But let me give you my differential diagnosis, so you'll understand why I'm not letting you off the hook."

He paused, allowing me to locate the cane that had slipped from under my foot and rolled somewhere off to the side. I retrieved it and propped it against my shoulder, hoping the picture thus presented might lead to a less protracted sermon.

He began on an uncharacteristically benign note. "M came to this hospital two years ago with glowing recommendations and a solid record of publication. M quickly lived up to his credentials, and in the opinion of a majority of his colleagues, including this supervisor, is a physician of rare skill and insight."

I squirmed under the compliment, which I took to be an effort to soften me up.

"Until the appearance of his illness, M was a diligent worker who did not shy away from challenge and at times appeared to embrace it with excessive enthusiasm." Here Sep let off a little cough. "However, M displays a sharp tendency to overrate his own judgment, and a corresponding resistance to being told what to do, which often causes him to cling to positions long after others would have been persuaded, in deference to their superiors, to abandon them." I bristled at this, but it was true. "In other words," Sep said, "he is damned stubborn."

He went on, warming to his task. "Coworkers have noted that M rarely seeks the advice of others, and when convinced he is right—which is to say, most of the time—can be rather outspoken about his views. Outside of his patients, M tends to be unforgiving of human error, which on occasion has resulted in a failure of empathy and strained relations with his peers—"

"I thought you agreed Jonathan's research was flawed," I broke in, feeling more than a little bruised by the character sketch so far. Sep was referring to an incident, a month after I'd joined his staff, in which I'd questioned the methodology of a five-year-long study by one of the department's top grant-getters. My criticisms had been justified and later vindicated by peer review, but they had earned me the eternal animosity of the study's author, whom I regarded as professionally overrated and an officious little prick.

Sep replied unperturbedly, "After you showed me why, I did. Though you could have been more tactful in making your case. But to continue, all of the aforesaid traits are indicative of an individual who values his independence highly, who prefers doing things his own way, and who would understandably feel stress, if not panic, at being perceived as—"

I knew where this was headed and cut him off again.

"'Perceived' is one way of putting it. Anyway, if that's your thinking, why does it surprise you I want more time?"

Sep said, "I'm not finished. Fortunately for M, his superior has a high opinion of M's ability to perform under adverse conditions, is under continuous pressure to meet budget goals by trimming unproductive staff, and cannot afford to let a talented younger associate—and, I like to think, friend—wallow indefinitely in self-pity while he continues to shirk work he could easily do blindfolded—"

"Very amusing," I muttered.

"—particularly when M denies any psychological effects stemming from his regrettable . . ."

I'll spare you the rest of the lecture, which went on for another thirty minutes and ended, more or less, in Sep agreeing to another few weeks, and me agreeing to think about it. Finally released from my little circle of hell, I was just starting down the hall when my old friend and partner in insubordination, Josh Goldman, bounded up to me. Josh is a short, bearded fellow with a belly that would tempt you to rub it for good luck and the smile to go with it. I'd expected that he or one of his operatives would be doing eavesdropping duty in the coffee lounge nearby so they could report on the score from time to time. Sep and I had intentionally spoken in lowered tones to keep the office gossips nimble.

"Mark," Josh said innocently, like he was just there by accident. "You're still here." His voice quickly dropped to a whisper. "How did it go?"

"Major carnage," I said. "He's threatening to call in hospital counsel."

"Septic wouldn't do that."

"I don't know. The old bastard sounded serious."

"You've got nothing to worry about," Josh assured me. "There isn't a lawyer in America who would give the OK to firing you. I can just see the headlines now."

"That *is* what worries me. You up for another cup of coffee?"

"How'd you know I just had one?"

"I can smell it on your breath."

"OK, but now that you mention Breathalyzers, you look like you could use something stiffer."

"Our usual joint?" I said, brightening at the thought.

"Where else? I'll grab my jacket and meet you by the elevator." He stopped short. "That is, unless you want me to take you over there."

I shot him my best withering look.

Getting into the elevator we bumped into Jonathan Frain—literally in my case—the guy whose study I'd trashed.

"Love the new fashion statement, Angelotti," he said, referring to the big white stick I was toting at my side. "But isn't it a bit tall for you?"

"There's a reason for that," I said, pushing past him into the car. "It's supposed to keep me from running into assholes."

When Josh and I rolled up to the Lucky Leprechaun a little later it was almost silent, in the dead zone just before happy hour. The Double L, as I call it, is my favorite dive, a traditional Chicago tavern where the Christmas tinsel hasn't come down since the elder Daley left office, the floor underfoot feels like superglue, and the management frowns on anything more exotic than Old Style. As best I can tell, it staves off insolvency only because of its proximity to the hospital where Josh and I work. Inside, the place was close and dim and smelled of old stogies, an aroma that was still hanging around long after the city council outlawed smoking indoors. It was just the therapy I needed. I let go of Josh's elbow, trailed him over to our usual booth in the back, and sidled in.

"First round's on me," Josh said. "What'll it be?"

"Whatever they're trying to pass off as bourbon today."

While Josh was off getting our drinks I stared into space and listened to the Cubs' one o'clock start on the television set over the bar. It was the usual demoralizer. A four-run lead until the bottom of the seventh, when the shortstop had blown an easy grounder up left field. In the natural order of things this was followed by two walks, a grand slam homer, and another three RBIs before the inning mercifully ended on a pop-up over the mound. The Cubs had rallied to tie the score in the eighth, only to fall behind again in the ninth. Now, with one out left to go, the score stood at 10–8, with players cooling their heels on second and third. It was the kind of game that reminded me why I'd stuck it out as a New York fan after moving to Chicago, in certain quarters an allegiance considered only marginally less belligerent than the Japanese attack on Pearl Harbor. It was only recently, in fact, that I'd felt safe wearing my '69 World Series cap outdoors again.

Josh returned some five minutes later, slid my glass over the table, and said, "Jesus sends his regards." Jesus was not an emissary from heaven, but the strapping Columbian who tended bar on alternate weeknights and worked a sideline as a sales representative for the colorful girls who closed the late-night shift. I turned in his general vicinity and waved.

"*Hola, amigo,*" Jesus called out in reply. "*¿Que tal?*"

"*Como veas,*" I said, with a shift of my shoulders. "*¿Y tu?*"

Jesus and I exchanged small talk over the chatter of Len Kasper and his fellow jesters—improbably, the Cubs had moved ahead again—while I sipped at my drink. I don't speak much Spanish, but it's similar enough to Italian that I can get by, which comes in handy when my housekeeper, Marta, periodically decides she doesn't understand English anymore. We went on until Jesus had to turn his attention to a loud group that had just wandered in the door.

"He wants to fix you up with someone," Josh said.

"So that's it. I wondered why it was taking you so long to come back with our drinks. Don't tell me it's one of his accounts. I think my Hep. B is out of date."

"No. A cousin of his. She's got a brother with your issue, so he figures she'll know what to do."

"That's disgusting," I said.

"I don't mean sex—I mean the other stuff."

"Great. So now I should seek out dates based on whether they would make good Labrador retrievers."

"Don't be like that. Jesus just wants to help you out."

"I'll bet. She's probably three hundred pounds and has a harelip."

"I don't think so. Jesus says she's a lawyer."

"Which, everyone knows, is incompatible with being fat and ugly. Besides, I don't need that kind of complication in my life right now."

"I agree with you about women being complicated," Josh said, finally taking the hint that I wasn't interested in becoming one of Jesus's experiments in noncommercial matchmaking. "You remember that orange juice we bought last weekend?"

"Sure. Was something wrong with it? Tasted OK to me."

"That's because you couldn't read the packaging. I was supposed to get the fresh-squeezed, Vitamin A and D added, low acid, reduced sugar, lots of pulp kind."

"I take it that's not what we got."

"Low acid wasn't on my list. But I was supposed to remember anyway."

Josh and I continued to chat about the intricacies of the female mind until the Cubs game ended, as I'd predicted, with a loss, and the Channel 9 Evening News came on. The lead story was a human-interest item about the birth of a baby giraffe at the Lincoln Park Zoo. I assumed this meant there were no murders, arsons, or tornadoes to pump up Nielsen ratings that afternoon. The Double L was starting to fill, and I had just turned my attention to the more interesting human-interest stories going on around us when a news flash came on. I was wrong about there being nothing gruesome to report on:

"Police are still declining to release details in the fatal stabbing of Gloria Jackson, whose body was discovered at six o'clock this morning in a DePaul neighborhood alley, the latest in a series of slayings that are already being compared to the killing spree of mass murderer Richard Speck.

"The deaths of two other nurses, also occurring in the early-morning hours, appear to be the handiwork of the same killer, who is believed to be a male in his early twenties based upon the description of an eyewitness who reportedly observed him fleeing the scene. All three victims were hospice workers at area nursing homes, and police speculate that revenge for the death of a loved one may be a motive in the killings.

"Today Jackson, age twenty-eight, was remembered by family and coworkers as a caring professional who helped terminally ill patients make it through their darkest hours . . ."

The broadcast switched to footage of Jackson's parents, who could be heard sobbing on the screen.

"Ugh," Josh said. "That could be my daughter in a few years."

I downed the rest of my drink in a gulp.

"Makes you consider how random life is," Josh continued. "You know, I've always thought that had to be the worst—burying your own child. I don't see how you ever get over it."

I mumbled something about not having an opinion.

"That's a first. Sometimes I envy you still being a bachelor. You were never tempted?"

"Who would put up with me?"

Josh laughed, a little too heartily. "I see your point. Buy us another?"

"I'll get them," I said, suddenly feeling an overwhelming need to be on my feet.

On my way over to the bar, I wished I'd come clean with him. The trouble was, I wouldn't have known where to begin.

TWO

Thirteen months earlier, I was diagnosed with Leber's Hereditary Optic Neuropathy, a disease caused by a defective gene I didn't even know existed until I woke up one morning with blurred sight in my left eye. For reasons that aren't completely understood, this gene sometimes causes a power failure in the nerves that channel information from the eye to the brain, similar to a car that's been driving along just fine abruptly running out of gas. The eyes keep on working, but the brain is getting a weak signal—or none at all. Usually the patient experiences this as a rapid loss of vision in one eye, followed a few weeks later by the other, though occasionally it happens all at once in both. The end result is nearly always blindness in the legal sense, ranging from the relatively mild (poor central acuity with intact peripheral vision), to what ophthalmologists call CF (the ability to count fingers held up at close range), HM (the ability to see a hand waved in the face), and all the way on down to NLP (no light perception or total blindness).

I first had an inkling of what was happening to me when I rose from bed, stumbled over some books I'd left on the floor the night before, and realized my depth perception was off. I began experimenting by closing one eye, then the other. When I looked out my left there was a spot in the center of what I could usually see, like a small jot of petroleum jelly had been put there. I could make out objects distinctly around the perimeter, but not through the middle. This caused me to think at first that something was trapped under my eyelid, but nothing came out when I blinked several times and my pupil seemed clear when I checked it in the bathroom mirror.

There was no pain, and I'd never had any trouble with my vision before, so I told myself it was just strain, or maybe a mild infection. The eye was watering a bit, so I picked up some antibacterial drops at the pharmacy in the building where I work and went about my usual business. As the day wore on, however, the spot grew bigger, and while I was driving home that evening I nearly rear-ended a Mini Cooper because I didn't see a traffic light turning red. The next morning, when I tested it by covering my right eye, the spot was everywhere and drained of color.

It was only then that I conceded the need for some professional attention. I was still shaken by my experience driving the night before—it would end up being my last time behind a wheel—so I cabbed it over to the office and went by the ophthalmology group on the eighth floor to ask one of my colleagues there, Bob Turner, to take a look. Turner made a joke in poor taste about how I'd been exercising my wrist lately, but got down to business when I couldn't even read the first line off the Snellen chart.

"You really can't see it?"

"Not unless you're hiding it from me."

"Fascinating," he said, sounding like Mr. Spock. "I've heard of this, of course, but never actually run across it in someone your age. I've got to get pictures."

Photographs of the back of my left eye, called the fundus, taken later that morning with special equipment, showed enlargement of the peripapillar vessels and visible atrophy of the retinal ganglia. By two in the afternoon I was in possession of blood tests confirming a homoplastic mDNA mutation at G11778—the worst kind, Turner cheerfully informed me.

"There are other mutations associated with your condition, but they don't produce as severe effects."

"Put it down to being an overachiever."

"You're sure no one else in your family is affected? Your mother never had any eye problems?"

"She died when I was an infant."

"No brothers?"

I shook my head. "I'm an only child."

"Maternal uncles? Cousins?"

"They live abroad."

He sounded deflated. "Too bad. You might want to contact them and find out. It would make an intriguing family study. I'm sure I could get government funding."

And I could donate my body to science, too. "Thanks. I think I'll pass on that. You were saying there could be further deterioration?"

With my new cyclops vision I could see Turner nodding his head. "So what happens next?"

"Well, I'd like to get you started on drug therapy right away. With your mutation the chances of a full recovery are almost nonexistent, but there have been studies in Japan showing mild improvement in patients who are started early on a regimen of vitamins and coenzyme Q10—"

"I meant with the other eye."

Turner hemmed and hawed in the way you'd expect, but eventually got to the point.

I must have surprised him by how calmly I took it. I saw no reason to tell him what I was really thinking. After the standard-issue pep talk and a pat on the back, he gave me some useless prescriptions and a pamphlet on living with vision loss and told me to phone him if I had any special concerns. Otherwise there was nothing to do but sit it out. I went home and did what any sane person in my circumstances would have. I wept and prayed and punched a hole in my living room wall, got drunk, bargained with God, slept when I could, got drunk some more, thought about killing myself—though I prided myself on never actually *needing* to call the suicide hotline—and wore myself out in many other equally unavailing ways while I waited for the other shoe to drop. Suffice it to say that it did, twenty-one days, four hours, and fifty-seven minutes later.

You may have noticed an avoidance of melodrama in the way I've laid this out. It's deliberate. In works of literature blind characters are always tragic figures burdened with heavy symbolism. Usually they are being punished for a crime that is sexual in nature, and their blinding is a dramatic affair involving fire (Edward Rochester is the poster child for this) or self-mutilation (Oedipus, Hazel Motes). Rarely have they lived a blameless existence and steered clear of bigamy, incest, and morbid preoccupation with religious issues. Readers of fiction have therefore come to expect that the blind hero will err in a major way, be maimed in a sensational fashion, and, thus humbled, undergo a spiritual transformation that will return him to life's journey sightless but filled with a new, inner light—or, in the alternative, "happy ending" version, with vision miraculously restored.

Of course, this bears no resemblance to reality. In real life, blindness occurs for no particular reason save accident or ill-luck, and often in a manner that is unspectacular, if not dull. Frequently it develops gradually, like the slow closing of a curtain. One day the individual notices he isn't seeing as well as he once did—he's tripped over a few curbstones or ended up in the wrong restroom—makes some adjustments and moves on. The adjustments add up. Large-print type gives way to magnifiers and audio books, driving a car to taxis and public transportation, until the day comes when he discovers he's no longer able to use his eyes to do the things he did before.

In my case, the process was a bit speedier, but no less unoriginal.

When people ask me what it's like, I repeat the Woody Allen joke about the miserable and the horrible. Then I explain why it's wrong. Being blind doesn't make life horrible. It simply adds a freight train of inconvenience to misery. And though I wish I could tell you that blindness made me a better person, or helped me find strength in adversity, or personal growth through suffering, or any of a number of states invented to calm the fears of those who can't imagine getting through the day without one of their major senses, it didn't. There are no special compensations that come with lack of sight, no "aha" moments when life suddenly acquires a deeper, richer meaning.

As I would go on to prove beyond a reasonable doubt, blindness did not change me. After I went blind I was still the same arrogant, uncaring, self-deceptive bastard I'd always been, with special emphasis on the next-to-last point. In fact, it took the events I want to tell you about to make me finally see how much I'd been lying to myself all along. But before we get there, I need to say a few words about how I got back on my feet, so as to dispel any skepticism that I could expose a clever killer without the aid of paranormal abilities or advanced training in the martial arts. If I can't help injecting a little humor into the account, don't be misled. For every day that I groped my way back to independence, there were two that I spent in angry frustration, swearing and throwing things around my small apartment. Pollyanna I was not. It was only when I got fed up with listening to Dr. Phil and wearing out the seat of my pajamas that I made a conscious decision to return to the living. As it turned out, this was yet another example of my bullshit, though I wouldn't realize it until it was almost too late.

I began by installing a screen reader on my computer, software equipped with synthetic speech that tells a blind person how to move his cursor to get to a desired field of text—with a keyboard, obviously, instead of a mouse—and then "reads" it to him. If you've never heard one of these things in action, imagine spending all day in an elevator that announces the arrival of each floor and points out when the door is opening and closing (as though this wouldn't be apparent to anyone with two ears) or stuck on the phone with one of those robotic hawkers of suspiciously easy credit.

My new software came with a menu of reading voices I could select from, more than twenty in fact, with names like Victor and Samantha, though to me they all sounded like Katie Couric being played back in slow motion or HAL 9000 after Kier Dullea had messed around with its circuitry. Needless to say, after the first hour of this, I was less than impressed with the wonders of technology. But I was grateful to be surfing the web again, and following a few false starts I was busily browsing all my old favorites, with the exception of certain, shall we say, indelicate URLs that could no longer be of interest to me. OK, they were still of interest, but the folks who owned them hadn't been courteous enough to make them accessible to a blind user. This is a continuous problem with screen-reading software: websites that rely heavily on graphic conventions are nearly impossible to follow. Nevertheless, with my screen reader I was able to do most of the pleasant and not so pleasant things a sighted person could do with a computer, such as keeping up with e-mail, checking the headlines for the latest disaster, and paying bills.

Naturally, in the beginning I wasn't primarily interested in listening to heavy breathing, but in gathering information about my options. Very quickly I learned there were literally hundreds of websites, list-serves, and chat rooms devoted to the special needs and interests of the blind, places where I could lurk at my leisure and hopefully pick up tips from the pros. But just as quickly I was surprised to find there was no consensus about how a freshly minted blind guy like me should go about getting himself back into circulation. In fact, when it came to learning what I would need to get by, it appeared that blind people and the social welfare agencies that served them fought over *everything*.

Take, for instance, the subject of getting around, which ought to be straightforward: you sign up for a dog or a cane and take lessons in how to use them. In my case I was sure it would be a cane—I'm not a dog person—but knowing this only landed me in a thicket of other bitterly contested issues. These included, to start, whether I should use a rigid or a folding cane. Rigid canes are more sensitive and don't fall apart easily, but they're a pain to store in tight seating areas like restaurant booths and the economy section of airplanes. Folding canes, on the other hand, can be placed in a lap or a backpack when they're unneeded, pro-viding their owners with an occasional break from always standing out in public like a Scandinavian in Tokyo. This sounded good to me until I learned on one of the more militant websites that concealing my cane would be a serious no-no, a sign I was ashamed of my blindness and still hoping to pass for normal.

Other hot buttons were whether I should learn cane travel from a blind or a sighted instructor (blind instructors, the same website assured me, were at no disadvantage in knowing when I was about to be run over by a truck), and whether my training should take place near where I lived and worked or in distant, unfamiliar surroundings (pre-sumably so that I could be scared silly and thereby develop blazing con-fidence). The list went on. All this left me perplexed and with renewed feelings of depression until I realized that with blindness, as with everything else in my life up to that point, I would just have to find my own way forward without worrying much about whether it gained me any friends.

The first decision I reached was that I wanted nothing to do with a residential program. Don't get me wrong. These boot camps for the blind do wonders for people who enjoy being part of a team and need to be isolated from well-meaning but counterproductive loved ones who are all too happy to do everything for them. But I lived alone, was by nature ill-equipped to sit through group hug fests, and had no intention, as someone in his later years, of *ever* living in a dormitory again, let alone one filled with similarly anxious adults who were being retrained in the use of knives and other sharp implements. (Woodworking, it may surprise you, is a popular offering at these schools.) Also, to be candid, at that point in my socialization I wasn't ready to accept that I belonged in a group of *blind* people. Oh yeah, I understood *I* was blind, but I still thought of it as being just like a sighted person—only one who couldn't see.

So I started my education by signing up for a Braille correspondence course, which I could take in the comfort of my own home and with a tumbler of bourbon to shore me up when I felt my spirits lagging. My social worker, Felicity, who should have been discouraged from her vocation on the strength of her name alone, advised strongly against this:

"Aren't you overcompensating?"

"You think wanting to read again shows I'm not adjusting?"

"Well, at your age . . . I mean it's going to be very difficult, close to impossible I'd say. I don't know anyone who is Braille proficient who didn't learn it as a child. And there are so many audio books available today. I'd really like to see you focus on something more positive. Have you thought about cooking classes? Many of my clients have found it very rewarding to be back in the kitchen."

No doubt those who could stand being there before. "No, thank you. Last time I checked my microwave was still plugged in."

"Or sewing. That way you could mend your own clothes."

"My dry cleaner would miss the business."

"Well, what about financial management then? The Lighthouse has a wonderful course. Being able to balance your checkbook would remind you of all the things you still *can* do . . ."

With my usual bravado I'd like to tell you that Felicity had it all wrong: that Braille was a cinch for someone like me, with years of higher education under his belt, to master. It wasn't. But after my exposure to a screen reader I was desperate to read with my own voice again, so I stuck with my lessons over the course of a few bitterly cold months in winter when it sometimes seemed as though I would have been better off trying to decipher the Rosetta Stone without the help of a translator fluent in Greek or Egyptian Demotic. Try this some time when you are alone in an accessible ATM: run your fingers over some Braille cells without looking and see if you can tell where one letter leaves off and the other begins. Like so many other things, it becomes easier and easier with practice, until one day you are skimming through books like a skater on ice, but in the beginning it felt like I'd just been sent back to first grade with Dick, Jane, and Spot.

Then, when the weather warmed up, I started working with my orientation and mobility instructor, Cherie. Cherie claimed to be congenitally blind, but I didn't believe her. One could only pick up social skills like hers during NCO training at Fort Dix. Throughout the spring and summer, Cherie pushed me through a series of increasingly complicated drills, all the while subjecting me to the Socratic Method. An example:

Cherie:	"Mark, what direction are we headed in?"
Me:	"Uh . . . not sure."
Cherie:	"Where's the sun?"
Me:	"Up there?" [Pointing]
Cherie:	"You're not pointing are you?"
Me:	"Of course not."
Cherie:	"So where is it, then?"
Me:	"Can I peek—just this once?"

Cherie:	[Exasperated exhalation of breath]
Me:	"Come on, cut a blink some slack."
Cherie:	"Slack isn't what I'll be cutting you if you don't start paying attention. Which part of your face is warm?"

By which exchange you may have gleaned that Cherie belonged to the hawkish school of cane teachers and made me wear a blindfold during our outings so I would learn to fall in love with my other senses. Our first sessions together reminded me of wilderness expeditions at Boy Scout Camp, except that I was excused from bringing a compass. Later, after I'd passed the beginner stage, Cherie sent me on scavenger hunts too, exercises in which I would have to travel alone to a store I'd never set foot in before and bring back a snack or a hard-to-recognize item. On still other occasions, we played a game in which I'd be dropped off at an unnamed location and have to find my way home without asking more than one question.

All this hilarity brought me nearly to the end of summer and my first anniversary. By then, I could cruise my neighborhood at a decent clip, get through a book with my fingers when I chose to, and had the domestic side of my life under tolerable management. Marta, my housekeeper, came every Thursday to clean up after me, though my slovenly ways were fast retreating under the harsh regime of having to search for things I hadn't put back in their proper place. Once a month, I paid a graduate student to help me out with any mail I couldn't handle by myself. On Sunday mornings, I tagged along with Josh when he did his family's grocery shopping. I'd even worked up the nerve (twice) to eat out at a restaurant on my own, which wasn't the fiasco I'd envisioned, though it's no swell time having the menu read to you by a busy wait-person who is predisposed to believe you lack the wherewithal to tip generously.

In short, when I finally got the message from Sep, whose calls I'd been ignoring for weeks, telling me that, ADA or no, I'd better get in to see him if I didn't want to be forced into alternate forms of employment, I was as ready as I was ever going to be to return to my chosen field. So why was I so resistant to going back? In retrospect the answer is obvious, but at the time I was still making up excuses.

At first I told myself it was a matter of personality: I didn't want to be labeled plucky, or spirited, or unstoppable, or any of the other cloying adjectives found in news articles about blind citizens who engage in such pastimes as skiing, or golfing, or walking in the woods. I'd become quite a connoisseur of these set pieces, similar to someone who can't help picking at a fresh scab. Three sentences in and it was always the same shocker: *"But [insert name] is no ordinary [skier, golfer, hiker] because he lives in a world of darkness. He is blind."* Blind. Wow. I was amazed they didn't capitalize all the letters, to really drive home the point of how wonderful it was these people could still put a brave face on in the morning. I vowed never to be interviewed by a reporter; none of them could be trusted to get it right or avoid going for the strained credulity angle. But it was silly to stay at home simply to rule out a headline titled BLIND PSYCHIATRIST HELPS PATIENTS *SEE* IN A NEW LIGHT, and I knew it.

Then I told myself it was fear. There was much more truth to that. Part of the trouble was my profession gave me *too* much information about the reasons people might be tempted to run in the other direction when they saw me coming. Sight is one of the infant's first sources of gratification, so it is hardly surprising that it is closely associated in the subconscious with other things that probe and give pleasure, like fingers and penises. Light is also linked in cultures the world over to the concept of the deity. So proximity to a blind person provokes a double panic in the sighted: anxiety over castration *and* permanent exclusion from divine grace. Accepting this was hard. It really did make me want to search out a monastery somewhere, say in a valley deep in the Urals, where I could devote the rest of my days to chanting and self-mortification.

But it wasn't that sort of fear either, at least not beyond what was natural for someone in my circumstances to be experiencing. It was something worse, so much worse that I couldn't stop running madly— or better yet, *blindly*—away from it until Sep put his foot down, I met Charlie and . . . well, now I am getting ahead of my tale.

THREE

Three weeks later, I was headed back to my job and even looking forward to it a bit. On my walk from home that morning I'd savored the taste of the early-autumn air, as sweet and crisp as a new-blown apple. As I neared my building on East Superior, the sun in the east was tickling my back and the locust trees were shivering in the breeze. It's around this time of year that they begin to shed their leaves, and I summoned up a nearly perfect memory of them showering down on the plaza like ochre confetti.

When I could hear the thump-thump-thump of the revolving door ahead, I stopped and fished two dollars' worth of change out of my pocket for Mike, the *Streetwise* vendor who is always stationed there. *Streetwise* is a publication put out by people who once would have found shelter in grim institutions, but are now more humanely allowed to brave Chicago winters in the open air. Mike hadn't seen me in a while, but in my Mets cap, sport jacket, and tie I must have looked the same as I always did, except for the five feet of pole I was sweeping along in front of me.

"Hey, Mike," I said, when I came up to where he was politely greeting people by the door. "What's happening?" I held out the coins between my forefingers and thumb.

Mike didn't reply and sounded for a moment like he was having an asthmatic attack.

"Mike," I said. "It's me, Mark. You remember—the guy who buys the paper from you every day."

Mike still didn't answer me.

"Come on, Mike," I said, thinking maybe I wasn't facing him properly or he hadn't seen the change. I repositioned slightly and thrust my hand out farther, with the money in my open palm. "Don't you want to get rid of your stock so you can get out of here for the day?"

More silence.

At last he said, "I'm sorry, brother."

"Sorry?" I said, as comprehension finally dawned. "Oh, yeah. Listen, there's no reason to be. I'm cool with it."

I waited for him to take the money, but he still didn't.

"Mike? Say something. *Please.*"

Another long silence, then: "I meant I'm sorry but I can't be taking your money no more."

Shit, I thought.

The rest of the morning wasn't much better.

It wasn't that my coworkers weren't trying. They avoided all of the behaviors I'd learned to expect and deal with politely (sort of) when I ventured out of my home. Nobody ignored me when I spoke to them, or shouted at me when an ordinary decibel level would do, or locked me in a half nelson to "help" me through a door. Almost everyone stopped by my office to catch up. They identified themselves by name when they greeted me and told me when they were leaving so I wouldn't be left talking into the air. In fact, they were doing such a good job of the etiquette side of things that I began to suspect Sep or Josh of having tacked up one of those "What to Do When You Meet a Blind Person" cheat sheets on the communal bulletin board. I should have been jumping for joy. Instead I felt like I'd just become the star of a documentary about interspecies cooperation, one of those programs on the Discovery Channel where humans squat on the ground and demonstrate how well they can get along with chimpanzees. Though I couldn't blame it on any one thing, I felt stupid and uncomfortable and painfully self-conscious, emotions I thought I'd banished from my blind man's repertoire after the first few times I'd needed directions to the men's room or help finding a seat on the 'L.'

By lunchtime, when Josh came to check on me, I'd barricaded myself behind a locked door and was sullenly tossing one of my Slinkys up and down on my desk. (I also collected Etch A Sketch and Wooly Willy games, but they had stopped being as much fun to play with.)

"Brought you a sandwich," Josh said, after I'd let him in.

I grunted.

"It'll get easier," Josh said.

At half past two I was ready to hang it up for the day. I had just started to pack my briefcase when Yelena, the assistant I share with Josh, knocked on my door. Yelena is as unlike Della Street as it gets, a scary bottle blonde who lives in Morton Grove with two kids by her ex, Boris, the owner of an independent town-car service. They had been at war for years. Knowing Yelena, I felt sorry for Boris and always called him when I wanted a ride to the airport. Between phone skirmishes over support payments, keeping up with her noontime Pilates, and visiting her manicurist, Yelena occasionally finds time to slip in some work for me. Earlier in the day I'd kept her busy with long-overdue filing, which always puts her in the mind-set of Lady Macbeth contemplating the inequities of her lot.

She came halfway into the room and stood there impatiently, tapping one of her trademark Manolos on the carpet.

"To bed, to bed, there's knocking at the gate," I said.

"What's that supposed to mean?" Yelena said.

"It's an old Russian saying."

"How come I never heard of it then? It's me, Yelena. I came to remind you of your three o'clock."

"Three? I wasn't supposed to have any appointments today."

"This one only came up this morning. Dr. Brennan arranged it."

"Well, you can unarrange it right now. I need at least another week to organize things around here before I can start seeing patients again."

"Dr. Brennan said you would say that."

"Did he also mention how you should reply?"

"Of course." Yelena advanced to my desk and leaned over it, probably trying to read one of the papers there. I was already beginning to see a side benefit to Braille, which was impervious to her snooping.

I said, "Let me guess. It involves something that matches your nails." Yelena's nails resemble X-ACTO knives and are always painted an incongruous shade of pink.

"Huh?"

"Pink slip," I said.

"That's pretty good. How did you know?"

"Never mind. What else did Dr. Brennan say?"

"That he was sure you would understand the importance of helping Dr. and Mrs. Dickerson." Yelena leaned in farther and I caught the scent of Obsession rising from her blouse.

"Why? Am I supposed to know them?"

"Mrs. Dickerson's maiden name is Taub. Dr. Brennan said you should look it up in the annual report if you don't remember."

I didn't need to. The Taubs were one of the wealthiest families in Chicago, whose fortune made the Pritzkers look like they'd just emerged from the steerage section at Ellis Island. Buildings named after various Taub cousins dominated nearly every major medical, educational, and arts facility in Illinois. In my own hospital's case, the Aaron J. and Lillian M. Taub Cancer Care and Research Center occupied nearly a quarter mile of prime real estate in Streeterville, the posh neighborhood sandwiched between the Magnificent Mile and Lake Michigan where my office is also located. Before my illness I'd often admired the building's gleaming façade during my early-morning bike rides along the Lake.

"The report's on my desk if you want me to read it to you," Yelena said. It was typical of her service attitude that she hadn't brought it with her.

"Thanks, but that won't be necessary." I'd already discovered that Yelena's reading style was about as gentle on the ears as a jackhammer. "I know who the Taubs are. Did Dr. Brennan mention anything else I'm supposed to know? Which branch of the family she's related to? The size of her trust fund, perhaps?"

"He said he introduced you to the Dickersons at the doctor's ball two years ago. Dr. Dickerson is a member of the surgery department."

"Here?"

"Yes. If you could see him, you'd know. The really tall one."

That jogged my memory. Nate Dickerson was one of the tallest human beings I'd ever met, nearly seven feet and easily two-hundred and fifty pounds. He'd played for the Blue Devils during college and a season or two with the Detroit farm team before getting realistic and enrolling in medical school. Being myself just a shade over five-foot nine, I felt like a Lilliputian standing beside him. He had the sort of features that would have looked doughy on someone of ordinary dimensions, but on him merely seemed carved in granite. His wife was also taller than me, dark-haired, and had the pinched look women develop from too much time in the sun or incessant worry.

"Did Dr. Brennan say what they wanted to consult me about?"

"No, just that they were bringing their son with them."

"All right," I said. "Have the son wait in the reception area when they arrive. I'll see the parents first."

Yelena didn't leave and seemed to be waiting for something. "Is there anything else?" I asked peevishly.

"I hate to ask, but . . ." This was Yelena's standard lead-in to a request for unscheduled time off, usually having to do with the misfortunes of a cousin who had just been caught attempting to smuggle one of the fruits of the new Russian economy through O'Hare and now needed Yelena's help with the INS officials who wanted to deport him. Yelena always had the good sense to seek Josh's approval first, and to present her case as a *fait accompli* that only a heartless overlord would refuse. I had been meaning to give Josh a talking to about his susceptibility to dominatrix persuasion.

A little after 3:00 p.m., Yelena showed the Dickersons in.

"Doctor? Nate and Judith Dickerson," Nate greeted me as he advanced seismically into the room.

I got up and came around my desk. "Call me Mark. We met once, though I don't expect you'll remember."

"Oh, but I surely do," Nate said, seizing my arm and bending it like a twig. "In fact, Judith and I were just talking about the occasion. It was at the annual physicians' event two years ago, wasn't it?" His voice boomed down at me like Zeus from Mount Olympus. He paused and added apologetically, "I was sorry to hear about your illness."

I was about to reply when Judith interjected: "Nate—where are your manners? I'm sure he doesn't want to be reminded of it."

I had begun to say, "Well, thank you, but—" when Nate cut back in.

"Darling, the man knows he's blind. He's not going to fall to pieces because I mention it."

"Not *blind*," Judith corrected. "Visually impaired." She said it like only the class dunce would have made such a mistake.

"There you go again. Who gives a hoot what it's called?" Nate said.

"He does. Don't you?" Judith said to me.

"I hadn't really given it much—"

"See," Nate said, "what have I been telling you?"

"Well, if he doesn't care, he should. Labels are important."

"Putting a pretty name on something doesn't change the fact."

I was starting to feel like the ball in a Ping-Pong tournament.

"Perhaps we should sit down," I said, offering them seats in the area to the left of my desk, where I have a sofa and two armchairs set up across a coffee table. The Dickersons continued their volley while they settled themselves down. I retrieved my Braille slate from my desk and took a place on the couch opposite them.

"It's because of your attitude that Charlie has such low self-esteem," Judith was saying.

"That's your mantra, isn't it?" Nate bandied back. "All the world's ills would be solved if people could just feel good about themselves. Besides, the boy seems fine to me."

"How would you know? At the office every day until midnight when you're not flying across the country to make speeches at one of those ego-fests you're so fond of. Anything you can do to avoid being home." I recalled from somewhere that Nate Dickerson had achieved fame as a cardiologist and was in demand on the medical lecture circuit.

"You never seem to mind the income my speaking engagements bring in," he parried.

"Let's not get started on money," Judith retorted. "It was humiliating for you, wasn't it, having to rely on mine when you were first starting out. But that's water over the dam. We're talking about role models here."

It went on like this for several more minutes during which the Dickersons hardly seemed to notice I was there. I began to wonder why Sep had sent them to me rather than to one of my colleagues who specialized in couples therapy. I listened, trying to pick up hints about why they had come and getting nowhere. Finally I made a big *T* with my forearms and said, "OK. Much as I don't mind being paid for doing nothing, I assume you didn't come here just to reenact *Who's Afraid of Virginia Woolf?* in my presence."

Nate was instantly chagrined. "Hell," he said. "I apologize. We shouldn't be wasting your time with our squabbles."

"That's all right. My secretary mentioned you'd brought your son along. Charlie, is that his name?"

"Oh!" Judith said quickly, rising from her seat. "I almost forgot he was outside. Poor baby. He's probably terrified sitting all alone in that strange room with everyone staring at him. I should go to him."

"Sit down," Nate commanded her. "No one could possibly tell there's anything wrong with him. He looks just like any other kid his age. He'll be fine by himself."

At last, a clue. "How old is Charlie?" I asked.

"Eighteen," Nate said.

I started to take notes, using a small device called a stylus to punch cells into the stiff sheet of paper attached to my slate. "Why don't you tell me some more about him?"

"Well," Judith began. "He's very good natured and, of course, quite advanced in comparison to his peer group."

"Not again," Nate groaned.

"Well, he is. You've always belittled what we've been able to accomplish with him, his therapists and I, that is, since you've never bothered to get involved. It's his pride, you know," Judith said, leaning in close to me. "He's never been able to accept that any son of his could be—"

"*Retarded*," Nate said, also leaning in as if to shove Judith aside.

"Please," Judith said, making it sound like two syllables. "I've asked you never to use that word."

"But that's what he is."

"He is *not*."

"What shall we call it then? Delayed? Developmentally challenged? Tell us, darling, what is the officially sanctioned euphemism this week?"

"Really, Nate, I resent—"

"I'll tell you what it should be. Retarded. Plain and simple."

"Why don't you just say he's an imbecile, while you're at it," Judith snapped back.

Nate said, "Better an imbecile than some asinine expression to sugarcoat the fact that he has the mental age of a three-year-old. To hear you talk it's as if Charlie lives in some Lake Wobegon where all the idiots are above average."

I inferred there was some unresolved conflict here.

"What is his IQ?" I asked, venturing into the fray.

"He's borderline normal," Judith said.

"Bullshit," Nate said. "Last time we had him tested he barely made forty-five on the Wechsler Scale."

I pulled up a mental picture of the DSM-IV discussion of intellectual impairment. An IQ between 40 and 50 would place Charlie in the moderate category of mental retardation, with the intelligence of a six- to nine-year-old. It was far from the mild disability Judith claimed, but not quite as bad as Nate had made out.

"Does he have Down's Syndrome?" I asked, taking an educated guess.

"No," Nate said. "Fragile X. Do you know it?"

I remembered what I'd read about this, too. Although Down's Syndrome is more noticeable because of its distinctive physical characteristics, Fragile X is actually the leading cause of inherited mental retardation in the general population. The incidence is about one in 4,000 births. Like me, the Dickersons had hit the genetic jackpot. I began to feel some sympathy for them.

"I don't need it explained to me," I said. "Is Charlie the only family member affected?"

"Yes," Nate said. "After he was born I put a stop to having more children."

"Over my objection," Judith added acerbically.

I wrote for a moment in my notes. "What are his living arrangements?"

"He lives with us," Judith said. "I would never lock him up in an institution. This isn't the Dark Ages, you know."

"Of course," I said, thinking that Judith probably had trouble letting him out of her sight. "I was just asking whether he was making any progress toward being on his own, say in sheltered housing. What about his education?"

"He attended a public elementary school until he was fourteen. Under the law, he's entitled to full support until he's twenty-one."

"Is he in high school now?" I asked.

"I'm afraid that wasn't an option for him. He's still reading at a second-grade level," Judith explained.

"She means he can recognize stop signs," Nate said. "And count to ten."

"He knows his multiplication tables up to four."

"Practically ready for calculus," Nate groused.

"What about vocational training?" I asked. "Is he able to be employed?"

"If you call bagging groceries at Jewel employment," Nate said.

"We're working on that," Judith countered. "Task concentration is still a bit of an issue."

"So what *is* he doing at present?"

Judith answered, "While I'm at work during the day he attends an adolescent daycare facility called the New Horizons Center. That's why we're here."

"Oh?" I said.

Judith paused in the style of a method actor and said, "I think someone there is molesting him."

FOUR

"Judith!" Nate exploded. "We have no proof of that. Haven't I explained the trouble you could get us into by throwing around that kind of accusation? With your family's millions we'd be sitting ducks for a libel lawsuit."

"Not if it's true," Judith said with authority.

"You don't need to worry about lawsuits here," I said. "Whatever you tell me will be held in strictest confidence. I take it you don't share your wife's concern?" I asked Nate, turning in his direction.

"I do not," Nate said staunchly. "It's complete nonsense."

"Then why are you here today?" I said.

I heard him shift in his seat. "I don't know exactly. Since I haven't been able to talk my wife out of her fantasies—"

"They're not fantasies—" Judith started in.

Nate kept going, talking over her "—I thought we ought to have someone with a proper background talk to Charlie. So I called Sep Brennan. He said you're an expert on post-traumatic stress and level-headed enough not to jump to any rash conclusions."

I made a mental note to thank Sep for tossing me a softball my first day back. I didn't like this situation one bit. Allegations of child molestation are notoriously difficult to substantiate or disprove, as the McMartin preschool trial and similar scandals had shown. The likelihood of a false accusation was even greater with a mother as protective as Judith, who also seemed to have something to show her husband. On the other hand, I knew that the intellectually disabled were at special risk for abuse by caregivers, and I cautioned myself not to dismiss her concerns too quickly.

I turned back toward Judith. "All right. Let's talk about what has prompted this fear. First, has Charlie said anything to raise it?"

"No," Judith said, "but he's been upset, waking in the middle of the night and crying himself back to sleep. It's not normal for him. He's usually very content."

"Is he wetting his bed?"

"Certainly not," Judith said, clearly offended. "He hasn't soiled himself since he was five. Though he does need to be reminded sometimes. To go, that is."

"Has he been able to say what's causing him to wake like this?"

"No," Judith said. "I've asked but he just shakes his head. When I push him further, he starts crying again."

"How long has this been going on?"

"A few months now. Three or four, maybe."

"Besides the nighttime waking and crying, have you noticed any other unusual behaviors?"

Judith reflected on this. "Not really," she said.

"Anything to link the waking episodes to," I stopped and consulted my notes, "the New Horizons Center? For example, resistance when he's being dropped off there?"

"I'm not with him then," Judith said, adding apologetically, "I often have to see my clients early in the day so I can't take him to the center myself."

"What sort of work do you do?"

"I'm a genetic counselor at the Mercy HMO on Division."

"How does Charlie get to the center, then?"

"Well, Nate is always too busy to take him"—I could picture the daggers she was throwing at him then—"so he takes a bus provided by a state agency. It's only a few blocks' ride. His babysitter walks him to the corner of our block, just off Fullerton, and he waits for it to come."

"All right. How about when you're leaving for the day? Any protests or disobedience that might indicate he's feeling anxious about going to the center?"

"No," Judith conceded. "He's always liked it there and still seems quite happy in the morning when I kiss him good-bye."

"And when he comes home? How does he seem then?"

"He's always ravenous when he gets back, just like any other teenager."

"So he's eating normally," I said.

"His appetite's never been better."

So far there seemed to be nothing connecting the nighttime crying to anything at the New Horizon Center. "Mrs. Dickerson," I said, "I have to confess that I'm puzzled about why you think your son's distress is related to the center."

Nate jumped back in, "See, what did I tell you—"

I shook my head firmly to ward him off. "Is there something else you haven't told me?"

Judith answered, "Well, as I said. He's never had any trouble like this before and . . ."

I waited for her to go on.

"It's that *woman*." She hissed the word like a polecat in heat.

"Which woman?" I asked.

"Shannon. Shannon Sparrow. She's an art therapist at the center— or claims to be. Judging by the trash Charlie brings home, I don't see much 'therapy' going on there. In fact, I don't even understand why she was hired. Though she is very popular with the students. Of course, you'd expect her to be, given her looks and the way she dresses. Completely inappropriate. I can't believe no one has spoken to her about it . . ."

I let Judith rattle on while I took further notes. Shannon Sparrow was relatively new to the center, at the time employed there a little over a year. She was in her early twenties, a recent graduate of the state university system and a native of southern Illinois. Judith described her as "a farm girl with overdeveloped udders" who had migrated north with ill-disguised intentions of landing a husband in the big city. According to Judith, Shannon was "one of those breathless blondes" whose fashion sense ran to Juicy Couture (I didn't know exactly what this was, but the name conjured up images of a *People* magazine reader), Victoria's Secret (this needed no explanation, but I wondered how Judith knew), and "those wretched boots from Australia" (presumably Uggs). In addition to poor taste in clothing, Shannon had "issues with boundaries" and was always hugging and patting her students in appreciation of their artistic efforts, which she supervised several afternoons a week. Judith knew this because she'd asked to sit in on one of Shannon's classes after another parent had hinted at "excessive physical contact." Judith's dislike of Shannon was palpable and she went on with these and other complaints for a good ten minutes while Nate remained silent, resigned, I supposed, to letting her have her say.

I asked Judith whether she had ever personally observed Shannon touching Charlie in an improper manner.

"Of course not," she replied. "If I had evidence of that sort I would have gotten her fired immediately."

"So as best you know, their physical contact has been limited to the hugging and back-patting you've described?"

"Yes. But it's out of line, especially with the young men, who might not understand and begin to develop . . . feelings."

"Do you think Charlie has developed 'feelings' for Shannon?"

"I couldn't say. I only know he talks about her all the time."

"As though he had a crush on her?"

"Perhaps," Judith sniffed. "Though I can't imagine why," she added, inconsistently.

I put myself in the position of an eighteen-year-old male with a healthy libido and decided it was possible, likely even, if Shannon was as Judith described. "Have you discussed this with Shannon's superiors?" I asked.

"Yes," Judith said. "I've had several meetings with Alice—Alice Lowe is the center's director—but so far she's refused to do anything about it."

I made a note of Alice Lowe's name. "Did Ms. Lowe state her reasons?"

"Only that she hadn't personally observed any unprofessional conduct and couldn't possibly launch an investigation without something more to go on than my suspicions. Of course, all the woman cares about is the center's reputation. It would shut down in an instant if anything like this came to light."

Which was precisely why it was so important to be cautious about leveling accusations. So far all I'd detected was the anxiety of an over-protective mother toward a potential rival for her son's affections. I asked Nate if he had anything to add. "No," he sighed with an attitude of long-standing martyrdom.

"All right," I said. "I'd like to talk to Charlie now. I need to warn you that while I did do a fellowship in post-traumatic stress disorder, my practice is primarily adult psychiatry. All I'm going to do today is ask a few questions and observe Charlie's reactions. If I see anything that warrants follow-up, I'll refer you to a specialist. But before I meet Charlie, could you describe his appearance and general health?"

According to his parents, Charlie was a tall boy, six-foot-three and on the slender side, with no physical limitations apart from small motor clumsiness. He took swimming and karate lessons, and participated in an area baseball league sponsored by the Special Olympics. His health was good. He'd had surgery the previous year for a deviated septum and come through with flying colors. He had no allergies or food sensitivities they knew of, was on no antidepressants or medications except for a mild dosage of Ritalin to help control hyperactivity, and had never been treated for a psychiatric disorder before. Nate said he was attractive in appearance, though he had the longish face and prominent ears typical of Fragile X males, with dark brown hair and gray eyes. Judith said all her friends agreed he was the most beautiful boy they'd ever seen.

I showed the Dickersons to the door and asked them to have Yelena bring Charlie in.

"Hello, Charlie," I said, rising to offer my hand when he entered. I noticed a slight shuffle to his walk as he came up, and his palm was sticky where it met mine. "My name is Mark. I'm a friend of your parents. Would it be all right if we talked a few minutes?" I didn't tell him I was a doctor right away for fear it would cause hypervigilance, a common reaction when the intellectually disabled are thrust into novel situations. I wanted him to be as relaxed as possible so I could develop a baseline for his reactions before we tackled any sensitive topics. I asked if he'd like to sit down.

"OK," he said hesitantly. "Where can I sit?"

"Why don't you take the couch there and I'll take one of these chairs." I reached over to flip on my tape recorder. "Do you know what this is?" I asked. I didn't hear anything but his breathing, which was adenoidal and coming fast. "Are you nodding your head?"

I still didn't hear anything except breathing.

"Charlie," I said. "You are going to have to do something special for me when we're together. Do you know what *blind* means?"

"Uh-huh."

"What does it mean?"

"It means . . . I think . . . I don't know."

"OK," I said. "That's good. It's important for you to tell me when you don't understand something I've asked. Do you wear glasses?"

"Sometimes. When I play baseball. I go on Saturday. Do you like baseball?" Charlie's voice was hoarse and he spoke in a rushed manner, like a train hurtling down a track, a speech affect known as cluttering.

"I like baseball very much. What happens when you take your glasses off?"

Charlie giggled. "I can't see the ball."

"Right. Well, being blind is like never being able to see the ball. Or the baseball field. It's like having your eyes closed all the time." That wasn't strictly true in my case, but it was easier for him to understand. "It means I can't see you," I explained.

"Can't you wear glasses?"

"Glasses are for people whose eyes just need a little help. Mine don't work at all. Do you understand?"

I didn't hear anything so I assumed he was nodding again.

"Did you just nod your head?"

"Uh-huh."

"See? I missed it. Go ahead, nod again."

Charlie giggled some more.

"Still didn't see it."

Charlie laughed even more heartily. "You're like James," he said.

"Who is James?"

"One of my friends. At school. He likes monster trucks, too. We watch DVDs in the morning. Only I have to tell James which ones they are. He has those things in his ears. Sometimes he doesn't understand me and I have to talk really loud." To illustrate the point, Charlie's volume rose. "Really, really loud," he barked.

"Well, my ears work just fine, so you can speak in a normal voice. But you do have to try to remember to speak all the time, not just shake your head yes or no."

I got his agreement to use the tape recorder and then asked him to tell me about monster trucks. We moved from there to baseball and his other interests, which included *Star Wars* characters and Spiderman. Like many Fragile X youngsters he could speak on certain subjects with great precocity—he knew whole plots from his favorite movies—but had difficulty recalling what he'd done the day before or even on more memorable occasions like birthday parties and holidays. He also had trouble with sequencing, putting events in proper chronological order. His attention span was very short, so we covered a lot of subjects before I judged him comfortable enough to raise the subject of the New Horizons Center. His breathing had slowed to the point where I couldn't hear it anymore and he wasn't moving as much in his seat. I started with questions about his daily routines.

"What time do you get to the center in the morning?" I asked.

"After breakfast. When the bus drops me off."

"Do you have a watch?"

"Here," he said.

"Where is the little hand pointing when the bus comes?"

"Eight," he said.

"And the big hand?"

"Twelve," he said.

"So what time is that?"

"Eight o'clock!" he exclaimed proudly.

With prompting, he could tell me that the bus brought him to the center's door at 8:30. We moved on to favorite activities, what he liked to eat for lunch. Then I asked about his teachers. "Do you like them?"

"Uh-huh. But not Mrs. Logan. She gives us food in the cafeteria. She's mean. Her mouth goes like this."

I know exactly what he meant. "Cafeteria ladies always have mouths like that. What about the other teachers? What are they like?"

A few answers later he mentioned Shannon.

"Tell me about her," I said.

"She has long hair. She teaches art. She likes my paintings. She doesn't shout when James spills his paints. James is my friend. He likes monster trucks, too."

I let him go on a few more minutes about James before steering him back to Shannon. "Is Shannon your favorite teacher?" I asked.

"Yes," he said. "Dean is my favorite, too. He's my teacher at gym. But not Miss Best. Miss Best is not my favorite." Miss Best, he explained to me, was his speech therapist.

I returned to Shannon a few more times during the next fifteen minutes, but aside from Charlie's observation that she smelled "like pretty soap," I didn't discern any preoccupation with her, much less anxiety. We'd now come to the tricky part. Truth is always a fluid issue with children, and, though technically an adult, Charlie would have the same difficulty separating imagined events from real ones, along with a strong desire to please me. I started by asking him whether he had been feeling sad about anything lately. He mentioned the death of the family cat.

"Did your cat die at home?" I asked.

"No. Mom took her away. In a special box. To the vet. She had to go to sleep then. She won't wake up anymore. Mom says that's what death is. You go to sleep and don't wake up anymore."

He stated this matter-of-factly. Nonetheless, my antennae were up. "Never waking up again—is that something that worries you?"

"No. We have a new kitten now. His name is Scooby Doo. I picked him out. He jumps like this."

"I meant Charlie, do *you* ever worry about not waking up?"

He was quiet.

I decided I had to be more direct. "Charlie, your mom says you've been waking up at night. Is that right? Remember, I can't tell when you nod your head."

Charlie squirmed in his chair, which I took for a yes.

"Do you know why you are waking up?"

He remained quiet.

"Charlie, is there something you're afraid of at night? It's all right to tell me. I'm a doctor, maybe I can help you."

"A doctor?" he said, hopefully. "Like at the hospital? They fixed my nose. I had an operation. After that it stopped hurting. I got to sleep in a special bed. And drink smoothies. I don't like it when it hurts."

"Nobody does. That's why it's so important to tell adults when you are hurting. Is there something that's been hurting you since your nose was fixed?"

Another long silence.

"What is it, son? What's been hurting you?"

Still no response. I waited.

Finally he said in agitated rush, "My wee wee. I mean my penis. That's what Mom says to call it. It's not polite to call it a wee wee. It's for going to the bathroom not for anything else. I'm not supposed to play with it." I noticed Charlie was breathing more rapidly again and he was bouncing in his seat.

"Charlie, are you telling me your penis hurts?"

"Mmm."

"When?"

"When I wait too long to pee and have to hold it in. And—" he stopped.

"And other times too?"

"When it gets big."

I asked him when this was happening.

"At night. In bed. My pajamas stick up—like this. I don't like it. It won't go away."

"Charlie, do you understand why your penis gets big?"

I got no answer.

"Is that why you've been crying?"

"It won't go away," he repeated, beginning to whine. "I want it to but it won't."

If he hadn't been so upset I could have laughed, it was so simple. Boys Charlie's age and younger get erections all the time, often from something as minor as a stray thought. By the time they're in their midteens, they've learned how to control these episodes, either by directing their attention elsewhere or by masturbating in private. But Charlie had been trained by Judith never to fondle his genitals and had no idea what was happening to him. It was no wonder he was crying himself back to sleep. At first he seemed anxious to be discussing the matter with me, but after I'd assured him that all boys, and even grown men like me, shared his problem, he seemed to relax and became voluble again.

We talked a bit about body parts and reproduction so I could gauge how much he knew. He understood penises were for making babies as well as urinating, but couldn't explain how the "seed" got from the father to the mother. We covered "good" touching and "bad" touching but he seemed utterly ignorant of both, informing me with some indignation that he needed no help going to the bathroom. Once he had seen pictures of naked women in a magazine under Nate's bed, but they reminded him of Lisa, one of his classmates, who was always pulling down her panties and saying "nasty" things like "lick my cunt!" There were other female classmates at the center whom he liked better, but none of them was pretty enough to ask out. He was waiting to get married before he kissed a girl.

Later, I would replay our conversation over and over, trying to see what I'd missed. But at the time all the answers I was getting to my questions seemed to point toward a single, innocent explanation.

When I was finally satisfied there was nothing else I could learn from Charlie, I thanked him and told him I hoped we would meet again. He was as sweet-tempered as his mother had said, one of the sweetest human beings I'd ever met, and when he left me that afternoon a part of me I thought I had safely buried envied the Dickersons their son.

When Charlie's parents returned, Nate immediately said, "Well?"

Judith piped in right away, "It's that girl, isn't it?"

"Wait, wait," I said, holding up my hand like a traffic cop. "Let's sit down again."

I started by asking them if Charlie had received any sex education during his schooling.

"It was available," Judith said, "but I asked that he be removed from the class. I didn't want him getting any ideas."

It was the only time I felt anger toward her. The risk of abuse for someone like Charlie comes as much from being kept in the dark as from being easily influenced, and I was astonished at Judith's excuse, which fell right into the myth that the intellectually disabled are sexually promiscuous. It recalled the attitudes that had led to the forced sterilization of retarded adults during the early part of the century, a practice condoned by Oliver Wendell Holmes's infamous dictum "three generations of imbeciles is enough." Even Charlie's mother, it seemed, wasn't immune to this type of ugly thinking.

I let it go and explained what I thought was going on. A few minutes later, Nate was chuckling.

"I think I understand what's needed," he said. He sounded almost gleeful.

"You don't mean—" Judith said.

"There are other options," I said quickly, to forestall another round of bickering, "including doing nothing at all. Charlie's weeping apparently hastens the end of the erections. We could just leave it at that, though he'll continue to experience discomfort. A frank discussion of what's happening to him, along with some fatherly modeling, would relieve the stress he's feeling and lessen the possibility he'll seek advice in the wrong places. I'd also recommend taking him to an urologist, to rule out a physiological disorder. I can give you a few names."

"No need for that," Nate said. "I know a good one. Well, Judith, I think we have our answer. Turns out it wasn't such a big deal after all."

Judith didn't sound convinced. "Well, if you're sure . . ." she said to me.

"Based on an hour of talking to him I'm as sure as I can be that he's sexually innocent. But that doesn't mean he'll stay that way, which is why I'd also urge you to get him enrolled in a class. One lesson from his father isn't going to be enough. He'll need simple, sustained guidance on what's safe and appropriate for him. Like it or not, Charlie has a mature man's body. Right now, he's only showing signs of curiosity, but I wouldn't bet on that being all as he gets older and comes under more outside influences."

"I'm sure I can control that," Judith huffed.

"Are you? What happens when you and your husband aren't around to watch over him every second of the day? And are you really being fair to Charlie? I'm not saying you should encourage intercourse, but pretending he's never going to experiment seems . . . unrealistic." I held back from saying I thought it would be courting disaster.

Nate said, "He's right of course, Judith. Last thing we need is for Charlie to knock some girl up." That wasn't the message I was trying to deliver, but I held my tongue, satisfied that Nate had enough good sense to keep his son out of harm's way.

FIVE

Six months went by. Fall gave way to winter: the usual Chicago affair with a series of days so short, dark, and cold that by March the sun seemed like a distant relative who visited rarely and only out of a fleeting sense of obligation. The war in the Middle East continued with equally numbing predictability. Candidates for political office scrambled for position in the polls. Another nurse was fatally stabbed by the DePaul-area serial killer the press was now calling "the Surgeon."

I busied myself with my practice, falling easily back into old habits of skipping meals and not getting enough sleep. Patients were by and large forgiving of my inability to look them in the eye—some with more interesting pathologies even preferred it—and my colleagues dealt with any unease they felt by joking with me. At times this became too much. My nemesis, Jonathan, seemed to have the web address for the most tasteless Helen Keller fare linked to his desktop. But quipping back was preferable to everyone tiptoeing around the subject, and I usually gave as good as I got.

Keeping up with journals was more of a chore than before. Even with the fancy scanner I ordered, it took three times as long as it once did to plow through the stack of dead trees that arrived in my mailbox each month. And I discovered an interesting twist to my memory: it seemed to have faded along with my sight. In my former days I had only to glance at a chart or a page in a book and it stayed in my head forever. But my eidetic prowess appeared to be tied to visual images: auditory and haptic input didn't make the same indelible impression. Though one half of my mind could still "see," often with great clarity, the things I had laid eyes on during my first forty-six years on earth, the other was now filling up with murkier data that was harder to retrieve. I think I regretted this loss more than anything else.

Still, I counted myself lucky, since my preblind memory allowed me to move around at work with relative ease. So long as someone hadn't rearranged the furniture, I could largely dispense with my cane and get by on a combination of recall and informed guesses about what the gauzy shapes around me meant. If I haven't made this clear before, I wasn't completely in the dark, though what I could see from one moment to the next varied a great deal depending on lighting conditions and how fatigued I was. In blind circles, I would have been called a "low partial." It's nothing to crow about, but to my coworkers my ability to cross a room unaided seemed well nigh miraculous and further proof of my remarkably good adjustment.

To outward appearances, then, I was making a splendid comeback.

But beneath the surface, I was falling apart. Whereas before I would have raced through a problem, reached what seemed like the best solution, and never looked back, I now dithered, procrastinated, and did everything I could to put off making a decision. I couldn't let go of the feeling I was missing something, that my judgment was off. It was the real reason for all the long hours I was putting in on little more than half the workload I used to carry. Some of my coworkers, who were experts at this sort of avoidance, praised my new cautiousness. I even overheard one of them saying it was a good thing I'd finally learned some humility. Sep, however, wasn't fooled, and toward the end of March summoned me to his office for a heart to heart.

"I'm worried about you," he said. "Maybe I did the wrong thing in forcing you back so soon."

I shrugged dismissively.

"You know," he said, "there's nothing terrible about acknowledging the heavy psychological toll of what you've been through. Relinquishing some of your former self-conceptions can't be easy."

"I'm fine with who I am, both present and past," I said. "Besides, there's no real difference between the two."

"Not from where I'm sitting. You seem altered. More wary."

"Maybe it's what people are saying about me—that I've finally bumped up against my limitations. Along with plenty of walls and doors. Is that such a bad thing?"

"Yes," Sep said. "If you let them define you. I admire what you've accomplished. Most people would have been shattered by such a setback. But I miss the old Mark. Did you notice you haven't made a single wisecrack since you walked in here today?"

"Well, I was going to disparage your tie, but I wasn't sure whether it was the one with the little ducks or the Chick Evans motif."

Sep entertained a chuckle.

"Seriously, Sep," I said. "There's nothing for you to worry about. Winter was harder this year, maybe because of the added nuisance of getting around in snow and ice. And yeah, it's been making me feel my age, but it's nothing I can't work through."

"Nuisance is how you'd describe it then?"

"OK. It's a major pain in the ass. But I'm coping. There are worse things."

Sep didn't pursue this, and after a few inquiries about routine office stuff let me go.

During this time, I hadn't forgotten about Charlie. I'd let a few weeks go by with no word from the Dickersons before e-mailing Nate to follow up. He'd responded with a tongue-in-cheek message saying that my "prescription" had been right on the mark, no pun intended. Charlie's nighttime waking had ceased; his parents had just enrolled him in an adult sexuality program offered by the Arc. I reminded Nate about the urologist and he e-mailed back that an appointment had been scheduled. There seemed to be nothing else to do but wish Charlie well. I had my own problems, as well as a slew of new patients, to occupy center stage. Nonetheless, I continued to think of him.

Two weeks into April on a Thursday afternoon, I was halfway through a tedious article on 5-HTT binding in suicidal patients when my phone rang. I waited for Yelena to pick it up, having given her firm instructions I was not to be disturbed, but she was apparently off on one of her frolics. The CID announced an outside number I didn't recognize, and I was just about to hit the Make Busy button when I decided I could use a break. When I got on the line it was Nate.

"Mark," he said. "Thank God you're there. It's Nate Dickerson." His voice cracked on the last syllable.

"What's the matter?" I said, picking up his tone. "Is it something to do with Charlie?"

"I'll say. He's been arrested."

"Arrested? For what?"

"They're saying he murdered a woman. Outside the New Horizons Center. With a knife."

I suppose I'd been primed for indecent exposure.

"Killed a woman? That can't be right," I said. "I can't see Charlie harming, much less murdering, anyone. There has to be a mistake."

"I know, I know," Nate said. "But they're saying it all the same. We were told he was found next to the victim early this morning. And . . . he had blood all over him." Nate's voice faded in and out, as if he were having trouble holding the handset steady.

"Where is he now?"

"In a police station on the near north side. We only found out an hour ago."

"No one from the center phoned you?"

"They did, but Judith was at our weekend place without her cell and I was in surgery all morning. Can you come?"

"Where?"

"To our attorney's office on Wacker. She's over in the lockup with Charlie now and said she'd like to see you when she returned."

I told Nate I'd get there as fast as I could.

When I hit the street, I could tell from all the honking and idling buses that a road stalemate was in progress. I tried hailing a cab, but there were either none available or willing to pull over for my kind of fare, and with the traffic delays walking would be faster anyway. I set off at a near jog, caning up the Mag Mile's packed sidewalks with none of my usual solicitude for other pedestrians' ankles. If they thought I looked rudderless and scurried to get out of my way, so much the better.

The day was warm for early April, and by the time I'd gone three blocks my shirt was lathered to my back and my sunglasses were sliding down my nose. I didn't wear them that often, and then mostly to shield my eyes from the sun, but that afternoon I was glad to have them for a different reason. Still, some of my worry must have showed because at the next red light a fellow stopped beside me said, "You all right, buddy? Can I help you get somewhere?" I snapped, "Do I look like I need help?" and sped into the crosswalk the minute it sounded clear, nearly getting clipped by a car making a last-minute left. "Get a dog, four eyes!" the driver shouted as he roared off. "Run over a grandmother while you're at it," I yelled back, flipping him a birdie for good measure.

After I'd crossed the Michigan Avenue Bridge I turned right and continued on to the four hundred block of Wacker, where Nate's lawyers, Wentworth, Feinstein & Shaw, had their shop in a big office building called the Acteon Center. The lobby echoed like the inside of a cathedral and a fountain gurgled somewhere near its center. "Security desk?" I asked someone passing on my right. "Straight ahead," a woman answered. I thanked her and tapped across a sea of marble to a freestanding kiosk with a high, smooth counter.

"You gotta be kidding," the guard said to me after I'd handed him my ID.

"Why?" I said. "It has a photo. A photo that looks like me." I pulled off my glasses to show him.

"This is a *driver's* license."

I pretended to smack my forehead. "Damn those guys at the Secretary of State. You'd think they'd get it right."

"I'm impressed," the guard said. "What did you have to pay them to get this?"

"The usual number of Jacksons. Look, I know this is a little out of the ordinary, but I'm in a hurry. It's a legitimate government ID. It's unexpired. I promise I don't have a sword concealed in my cane. Can't you just let me in?"

The guard didn't reply right away. I put on my dullest blind stare to help convince him I wasn't some cousin of Osama bin Laden in disguise.

"All right," he said finally. "I'm gonna trust my instincts on this one. But do yourself a favor and get a real ID. You might want to get on a plane someday." He was right. I'd known for ages this was something I needed to do, but had put off going to the DMV, an ordeal that would try the patience of Father Flanagan in the best of circumstances, let alone with all the special paperwork I figured they'd have me filling out. I assured him I would see to it soon.

"And don't go driving any sports cars," he added.

"Scout's honor," I said.

The receptionist at Wentworth, Feinstein & Shaw had been told to expect me and I was whisked speedily into a room where Nate's huge form hung quivering against the bright light from the floor-to-ceiling window.

"Nate," I began. "I'm so sorry. If this has anything to do with—"

He silenced me brusquely. "Of course it doesn't. I know my son. He was clueless about what to do before I explained it to him. I blame myself for always bowing to Judith's wishes where his education is concerned. But this . . ." he trailed off.

"I'm sure there's an innocent explanation."

"I hope to God there is. Apparently the cops are still questioning him. That's what worries me the most. Charlie's so simple-minded. Lord knows what he's told them."

I had the same worry. Charlie had spent his entire life being guided by authority figures. Getting him to admit to something he didn't do would be a cakewalk for even a rookie detective trained in interrogation techniques. "Nate," I said, moving around a large table to where he was standing and reaching up for his shoulder. "The odds are it will turn out to be nothing. He's a good boy. The cops will see that. Where's Judith?"

"She should be getting here any minute. She was out in the yard at our Michigan place when I finally got through to her. Her cell phone went missing just before she left home yesterday. You can imagine how she reacted. I told her to order a town car. I was worried about her driving all the way back from New Buffalo the way she must be feeling, but she insisted she was OK. I came over here right away when I got out of surgery. Chuck Feinstein is the family's personal attorney—maybe you didn't know Judith is related to the Taubs—"

"I heard."

"—and he got us a lawyer right away. Sharp young thing named Sanchez, ten years as an assistant in the State's Attorney's office and on the fast track to partnership here. Feinstein thinks it's an advantage to have a woman and a minority on a case like this, and she knows her way around the criminal court system like nobody else."

"Is she with Charlie now?"

"She was going to try to get a few minutes with him."

"Will they hold him?"

"Ms. Sanchez says it depends. But his being found where he was isn't a good omen."

"How do they know he didn't just happen on the victim after she was killed? What's her name, anyway?"

"I don't know that either. The police haven't released her identity and they asked the personnel at the center to stay mum until the family was contacted, though I gather it was someone who worked there."

I was about to remark on how upsetting that must have been for Charlie when Judith exploded through the door.

"Oh, Nate," she said, teetering across the room and collapsing into him. She shook there for a few minutes before noticing me. When she did, she said, "What's *he* doing here?"

"I asked him to come. Charlie's lawyer said we might need him."

Judith quickly disentangled herself from Nate and moved to within an inch of me. "I blame you for this," she spat. A drop of the stuff landed on my cheek.

"Judith," Nate said, pulling her away. "How can you say that? Unless you think Charlie's guilty of something."

Judith backed off instantly. "Of course not."

I pulled my handkerchief from my pocket and wiped my face. "Mrs.

Dickerson," I said, "I know how upset you must be. But I'm certain Charlie's in no trouble, or won't be when we get to the bottom of things."

"That's just what I'd expect you to say. Nate, do you think they have him in a cell? Oh, my poor boy!" I heard a wet sob.

I said, "Perhaps you should sit down."

"Yes, darling," Nate said. "You're as white as a sheet. Please sit, have a drink of water. You must be exhausted from all that driving and the worry. Charlie's lawyer will be back soon and we'll find out what's going on."

Nate guided his wife to a chair while I searched around for the refreshments I was sure a pricey law firm would have laid out for their clients. On a credenza against the wall there was a coffee urn, some cans of soda, and a pitcher of ice water. I poured a glass for Judith and brought it back to where she was seated. Her hand shook as she took it from me and some of the water sloshed onto my sleeve.

"When did you last eat?" I asked.

"Early this morning. But I'm not hungry."

"I wonder if there's somewhere she can lie down," I said to Nate. "Do you want me to ask?"

"No," Judith said weakly. "I don't want to make a scene. I'll just stay here. It will pass."

Nate's cell phone went off then, and he spent a few moments in hushed conversation with the caller.

"That was Ms. Sanchez," he said after ringing off. "She's in a cab coming back. She'll be here in a few minutes."

"Is Charlie with her?" Judith asked hopefully.

"No, darling, I'm afraid not. Ms. Sanchez said she'd explain when she got back. Here, give me your hand."

While we waited I took a seat on one of the leather chairs around the conference table, stowing my cane on the floor. The top was some sort of polished stone and there were legal pads and pencils arranged along its sides. I picked up one of the pencils. I was once a champion doodler and still indulged in the habit when I was by myself, but I thought the Dickersons would find it odd behavior for a blind man, so I just worried the point with my finger.

A sharp rap on the door five minutes later announced the arrival of a crowd of people who quickly filled the room.

"Hello, I'm Hallie Sanchez," one of them said, circling the table to where Judith was seated. "No, don't get up. I'm pleased to meet you, though I wish it were under different circumstances." She had a brisk, commanding air, a woman accustomed to being in charge. I pictured her in a smart business suit and sensible pumps, late thirties maybe, with a pert haircut and subdued makeup, though of course she could have looked completely different.

"First tell me how Charlie is," Judith said, rising anyway.

"He was fine when I left him. He was eating a bologna sandwich. They were getting ready to take him to Cook County jail. I arranged for him to be placed in protective custody overnight. He'll have a cell to himself and won't be exposed to the general population."

"So he won't be coming home?" Nate said. Resignation had gripped him and it was more a statement than a question.

"I'm afraid not," Hallie answered.

"But how can they do that—he's only a child!" Judith keened like a civil-defense siren. "Why weren't we called in immediately? We're his parents. We have a right to be with him!"

Hallie said evenly, "Mrs. Dickerson, your son is past his seventeenth birthday. That means he can be arrested and tried as an adult, even if he has the mind of a child. You have no right to anything."

"But isn't he entitled to any special consideration? He's *retarded*," Judith wailed.

Hallie said, "I know you're not going to like this, but in the eyes of the law the only thing he's entitled to is a lawyer. I don't want to frighten you, but there are prisons all over this country filled with retarded inmates. Charlie won't be treated any differently because he's slow. If anything, he'll be presumed guilty because of it."

She was frightening me, and I wasn't one of Charlie's parents.

Judith protested, "Surely there's someone we can call . . . Nate?"

Nate said, "We do know people, of course."

Hallie said, "Save the phone calls for now. It'll only make the cops dig their heels in further. I had a few words with his arresting officer, a detective named O'Leary. He seems like a decent sort, old school but without the usual cop swagger and not completely convinced they have the right guy, if I'm reading him correctly. He gave me a few minutes with the police reports. I've also got a call in to one of my former colleagues in the State's Attorney's office to see if we can get Charlie out on bond quickly. That's why I wanted to see the shrink you mentioned. Is he here?"

"You must mean me," I said, raising my hand. Suddenly, I could feel everyone's eyes on me.

Nate said, "My apologies. I should have introduced you two right away. This is Dr. Angelotti."

Hallie walked over to where I was seated and stood there a moment, apparently looking me up and down. I gave her my best Marcus Welby, MD smile, along with one of my new business cards, which gave my full name—D. Mark Angelotti—in ink and an abbreviated version in Braille.

"What does the *D* stand for?" she asked after a minute.

"Dante. But I never use it."

"And you're a doctor."

"According to the diploma on my wall."

I waited for the usual expressions of disbelief, but Hallie simply said, "You ever testify before?"

"Only in traffic court."

"A comedian, too. How well do you know Charlie?"

"He's not under my regular care, but I did speak to him once several months ago about some problems he was having sleeping." I didn't think I should go into the details without obtaining the Dickersons' explicit permission.

"Would you be able to state under oath that Charlie's not violent?"

"I could state it truthfully, if that's what you're asking, but I'm not qualified to be an expert witness. Normally the kind of testimony you're after would only be given after a full psychological workup by someone board certified in forensic psychiatry."

"Yeah, but right now you're all I've got. Kevin," she snapped to one of her assistants, "go find out if he needs to be a certified forensics guy to put him on the stand." Kevin scuttled out the door. Back to me: "Can you have someone fax your résumé here?"

"Sure," I said. "But perhaps you could clue us in to what's going on first?"

Hallie sighed loudly and said, "You're right. I am getting ahead of myself. Let's all sit down. Somebody get me a coffee. And a sandwich too, if there's one left in the lunch room." Another minion jumped up to do her bidding.

Hallie could only tell us what she had learned from the police reports and a brief telephone conversation with Alice Lowe, the New Horizons Center's director. Apparently, a little after 8:00 a.m. that morning, a uniformed Chicago police officer had passed on foot by the center's rear entrance, where he heard sobbing coming from behind a car parked on the opposite side of the alley. Rounding the driver's side of the car, he found Charlie hovering over the body of a dead woman, hugging his knees and crying. Judging from the warmth of the body and the absence of rigor, the woman had been dead for only a short time. A wound to the chest just below the sternum appeared to be the cause. Blood from the wound had seeped into a puddle on the ground and soaked Charlie's sneakers. There was also blood on Charlie's hands and shirt. The patrolman asked Charlie what was going on, and he replied, "She won't wake up anymore."

The officer radioed for reinforcements and several squad cars rushed in with flashing lights and sirens to secure the area. A crowd began to form. Several of the center's employees arriving for work in their cars were redirected to the streets adjacent to the center. One of them observed Charlie with the officers and alerted Lowe, who had been working in her office on the opposite side of the building and hadn't heard the commotion. She attempted to gain access to Charlie, but was told to wait to one side. The police continued to sequester Charlie while the evidence technicians arrived and began laying out yellow tape and setting up their equipment. Initial observation revealed no signs of a struggle, and the victim's handbag was on the driver's seat of the car with her wallet, phone, and keys still in it. At 9:00 a.m., Detective O'Leary approached Lowe and asked her to confirm Charlie's name and date of birth. After that he was taken in a squad car to the station house. He remained there until shortly after 1:00 p.m., when he signed a written confession admitting to slashing the victim to death with a knife.

"A confession!" Nate moaned. "That's exactly what I was afraid of."

Judith simply moaned.

Hallie said, "They do work fast, don't they? I'm sorry I can't tell you much more. I did speak to Charlie as well, but he was understandably confused by what was happening. He knew the woman was dead, which was why he was crying, but I couldn't get a coherent story out of him. When I asked him about the knife he didn't know what I was talking about. I asked for a copy of his statement but they wouldn't give it to me. By the way, can he read?"

"Not really," Judith said.

"Sign his name?"

"Yes," Nate said. "But why wasn't he allowed to have a lawyer with him before he signed a statement?"

"I'm guessing they gave him his *Miranda* warnings and he waived the right to counsel. The interrogation will be on videotape—it's a new state law requirement in homicide cases—so the cops can't lie about what happened. But they're very good at persuasion."

"You don't mean . . . ?" Nate said.

"No," Hallie said. "I'm sure they didn't touch him. They're not stupid enough to do it on tape and Charlie had no marks on him I could see. When I asked him about how he'd been treated he said the police were nice to him and gave him pop. Apparently quite a lot of it."

"Of course," I said. "Charlie would be just as vulnerable to bribes and friendly persuasion as physical intimidation. But it should have been obvious to them from the start that he's mentally handicapped. Weren't they worried about getting a false confession?"

"Hell no," Hallie scoffed. "You're a shrink. You ought to know how powerful confessions are with juries. The cops know it too, so they do everything they can to get one, no matter how hard they have to work. I've seen convictions based on confessions that were obvious fabrications—the defendant said he killed a white woman when the victim was black, or with a shotgun when the murder weapon was a hunting knife."

I said, "I've read news stories like that too, but are the police really that bad?"

Hallie said, "Not always. But they're human like everyone else and under intense pressure to get convictions. Usually the suspect has priors and they figure he's a just a scumbag who'll go off and kill somebody else if he walks, so what's the big deal? Jurors think along the same lines. Try convincing them that the defendant would admit to a crime he didn't commit."

She was right. The idea that only the guilty confess to crimes was deeply ingrained in the collective imagination. Psychologists and social scientists had been battling the perception for years, but it wasn't until DNA testing became widely available that they were able to prove their theories right.

"But Charlie's not a hardened criminal," I said. "He's a nice kid." I knew what her reply would be even before my words were out.

"To you he's a nice kid. To them he's a big, not very bright guy who was found with a dead body and blood on his hands."

"I can't believe this is happening," Nate said. From the timbre of his voice, he seemed to have aged several decades in the last hour.

"I know it seems unreal," Hallie said, "and I'm deeply sorry you have to go through this. The good news is that I'm here to help. Most people like Charlie aren't so lucky. They get talked into half the unsolved crimes on the books before they even get to see a lawyer. In any event, we'll challenge the confession, but that's not our first order of business, which is getting him out of that cell."

"That won't be a problem," Nate said, some of his fight returning. "Judith and I will put up any amount of bail."

"Unfortunately it's not going to be that easy," Hallie said. "In Illinois, judges are required to deny bail if there's strong evidence of guilt and a threat to public safety. That's where the good doctor comes in."

"If you think I can help," I said, my earlier reservations evaporating under the weight of my concern for Charlie.

"The victim is already dead, so her safety is no longer an issue. I'm not sure whether the state will claim it, but if you could testify he's not dangerous—"

"I can."

"Or a serial killer."

"He doesn't fit that profile, either."

"Good. That plus the fact that he lives with his parents and is usually heavily supervised should be enough to get him released on some amount."

I remembered suddenly what Nate had said earlier, about the victim being one of the workers at the center. Charlie's being involved made even less sense if it was someone he knew. "Hallie," I said, "do you know the victim's name?"

"Yes. I have it in my notes here somewhere." She began to flip through a paper pad while Nate, Judith, and I waited. "Here we go."

I think I must have known all along.

"Sparrow," Hallie said at last. "Shannon Sparrow."

SIX

Judith fainted dead on the spot. I didn't understand what was happening at first, only that something hard cracked the table like a bowling ball hitting an alley. "Judith!" Nate shouted. Suddenly seats were being shoved back, people were leaping to their feet, and everyone was talking over one another. Hallie dialed for the office nurse and one of the other lawyers went for damp towels and smelling salts. Nate asked for help getting Judith into a prone position on the carpet and asked for cushions to elevate her head. He spoke Judith's name over and over. I didn't offer to help, thinking I'd only get in the way.

Did it mean something that the dead woman was Shannon? I didn't want to admit there was a connection, and yet...I hastily reviewed my meeting with the Dickersons six months earlier. Judith had been insistent about her suspicions, but there didn't seem to be any concrete evidence to support them. I had questioned Charlie thoroughly. There were no signs he was being molested by Shannon—or anyone else for that matter—and the anxiety his parents had brought him to see me about ceased soon afterwards. Six months had passed, it was true, but it was fantastic to think that anything had changed, especially with Judith watching over Charlie so closely. It had to be coincidence. Charlie must have stumbled onto Shannon's corpse after she was dead, or else been a witness to her killing. Either possibility would explain the state in which he was found, which I recognized as a dissociative reaction to trauma. And his words to the police officer—"she won't wake up anymore"—were consistent with his immature concept of death, the same way he had described the passing of his pet to me. I began to relax slightly.

Judith had revived and was now weeping quietly.

Hallie said to her, "You seemed more than a little upset just now when I mentioned the victim's name. Were you and she friends?"

"Certainly not."

But Nate was quick to cut that line of inquiry short. "My wife and Ms. Sparrow had a few disagreements over my son. Nothing serious and nothing that need concern you." I took this as a signal I was to keep quiet too. Though I had some misgivings about the wisdom of holding anything back, I was professionally bound to respect his wishes.

"But Charlie knew her?" Hallie pressed.

Nate said, "Yes, of course. I'm sure Alice Lowe told you she was his art teacher."

"She mentioned the victim worked at the center, but I didn't realize Charlie was one of her students."

Hallie's questions were interrupted by the sudden ringing of her cell phone. Nate continued to comfort Judith while Hallie spoke in clipped syllables to the caller.

"OK. Uh-huh. Central Bond Court tomorrow. Yup. We'll be there. And thanks, Hector. I owe you one." She rang off and said, "Good news. Bail hearing tomorrow afternoon."

Nate asked, "Will we be allowed to see my son before the hearing?"

"No," Hallie answered. "He'll be in one of the holding pens in the basement. They'll only bring him up when his case is called, but you can watch from the spectator section. I'd advise you to go home and get a good night's rest. There's nothing you can do now except bring a check. And pray."

The Cook County Criminal Courthouse at Twenty-sixth and California occupies half a block in a neighborhood populated by *grocerias*, discount stores, and loan-shark establishments. Immediately to the south stands the huge county jail complex, cozily referred to as a "campus" by the Sheriff's Office website I'd listened to the night before.

Charlie would be housed in one of ten buildings there, in a cell with a cot, a sink, and a steel toilet. Prisoners awaiting bail hearings were transported in shackles through a tunnel that led from the complex to the courthouse, where they waited their turn to be judged in groups of a hundred or more. Hallie told me they started with the DUIs and other less serious felonies first, so we could expect to be there most of the afternoon.

I'd been in the courthouse once before, for jury duty, and remembered it as a building much taller than its neighbors, with Greek temple embellishments and an aura of hopelessness. The bleak impression carried over to the interior. Everywhere I turned there were corrections officers with thick waists and lawyers in cut-rate suits pushing steel carts overrun with files. Toward the end of the day, I was almost seated as an alternate in a capital trial. I had felt pity for the defendant, a skinny young man looking like a scarecrow in his cavernous jumpsuit, and was relieved when the prosecutor asked to exclude me, apparently not liking my replies to some of his questions about free will.

When I arrived at noon on the day of Charlie's hearing, the line to get through the security checkpoint was several layers deep. While I waited I heard babies wailing and mothers reprimanding their youngsters, loud conversations about domestic matters, the beat of hip hop emanating from headsets. I didn't need my eyes to tell me nearly everyone around me was poor. We were only a few miles south of the Loop, but travel there could have been the voyage of the *Beagle* as far as my companions were concerned. Yet no one complained of the long wait and I was treated with more friendly camaraderie than I was accustomed to. A man smelling of garlic and menthol nudged me forward when the line moved ahead, and someone else showed me where to put my phone, keys, and change at the metal detector.

The day before I'd remained at Hallie's office for several hours following the Dickersons' departure, going over the ground rules for being a witness. I was to dress conservatively, but not expensively. "If you've got a Rolex, leave it at home," Hallie told me. "Check," I replied. On direct, I was to follow her prompts and cues but not go on for so long that my answers looked staged. On cross, I was to be truthful and polite, answer yes or no whenever possible, and never, *ever* volunteer information. "And don't argue with the prosecutor," Hallie said. "Leave the arguing to me." She put me through some sample questions, showed me how I could be roughed up if I forgot instructions. My glib tongue proved to be an asset as a witness and I admit the practice session whetted my appetite for the real thing. Hallie apparently approved of what she heard because at the end she said, "You'll do."

As we had arranged, Hallie was waiting for me by the courtroom door.

"Over here, Mark," she called when I approached. I passed through a swiftly moving current of bodies to get to her.

"Sorry, I should have told you about the line to get in," she apologized.

"It did feel like *The Ten Commandments* back there, but I made it through without scars. Have you heard anything new?"

"Only that Tony Di Marco has the case and will be making a personal appearance this afternoon."

"Di Marco?"

"A former colleague. His coming down here isn't a good development. Usually they leave it to one of the junior assistants to cover bond hearings. He's a real heartthrob with the ladies—judges and jurors alike. Looks like a charming pirate. But missing the Johnny Depp heart of gold. I want you to watch your step with him. He's known for carving up witnesses like a Sunday roast."

"I'll try to stay on his blunt side."

With the proceedings not yet underway the courtroom was filled with the clamor of loud conversation. From the way the sound fed back to my ears I could tell the room was spacious and high-ceilinged. Hallie must have done her blind Miss Manners homework because as soon as we were through the door she offered me her arm. I grasped her elbow from behind and we went to the clerk's desk in front to file an appearance.

"What about him?" the clerk asked, cracking gum.

"Witness," Hallie said.

"He'll have to sign in too. Can he write his name?"

"Only if someone spells it for him," I said to no one in particular.

Hallie kicked me in the shin. "Of course he can," she told the clerk. "Another rule," she whispered to me after I'd signed and we'd moved away, "no sarcasm."

Hallie steered me to a bench in the defense lawyers' section and described the setup. Behind a glass partition to our rear was the spectator section, in which the Dickersons were already waiting. In front of us a pair of counsel tables, and farther on, an elevated bench and witness box. The courtroom was used exclusively for bond hearings, so there was no seating area for jurors. Most of the defendants would "appear" for their hearings via closed-circuit television. The monitor faced the bench and was visible only to the judge. While detainees waited for their cases to be called they were crammed into cells in the basement intended to hold no more than twenty-five inmates at a time. If they were indigent and couldn't afford counsel, they would have a minute or two to talk to an investigator from the Public Defender's office, who would take down information about their case through the cell door. Afterward it would be relayed to the single PD working the courtroom upstairs. During the hearings prisoners would be unable to communicate with their counsel, or even see them on the camera.

Charlie was lucky, in a skewed sense. Because he was being held for a violent felony he was entitled to be physically present in the courtroom for his hearing.

Suddenly a voice bellowed "All rise," and the courtroom grew hushed. The judge, apparently a heavyset man, thumped up to the dais and settled himself down. Without a minute's delay, the proceedings began.

I don't know what I had been expecting. Nail-biting drama and oratorical brilliance, I guess. But it wasn't anything like *Law & Order*. For the most part the Assistant State's Attorney spoke in a low register, as though he were a journeyman in the building trades reporting on a failed circuit breaker or clogged sink. This problem citizen will require a deposit of $500, he might have been saying. No, I'm afraid this one is beyond repair.

At the start of each hearing the prosecutor presented a brief summary of the charges, inevitably followed by the judge declaring, "Probable cause to detain. Background?" Generally, the background took all of thirty seconds. If the offense was slight and the defendant was a first timer, he walked on an "I Bond," or personal recognizance. More serious charges or a list of priors merited amounts in the four figures and upward. Most of them involved drug offenses. If the defendant attempted to say anything he was quickly silenced by the judge, whose name was Francis Connor. He didn't seem as much a harsh man as a tired one who had seen too much.

It went on this way for more than three hours, human fates decided in little more time than it takes to flip a coin. If the quality of mercy wasn't strained by what I was hearing it was only because it was already as worn and flabby as an old fan belt.

"Dickerson," the clerk called at last, followed by a case number. I snapped to attention and gripped my cane. I recognized Charlie's distinctive shuffle as he was brought in. I tried to make him out, but I couldn't distinguish him from the other dusky figures gathered near the front of the room. Hallie rose and strode over to join them. A new voice I presumed to be Di Marco's drawled, "Afternoon, Judge," from the prosecution section on my right.

"Charge?" the judge asked. "Murder two," Di Marco said. "For the record, I am tendering to the court and defense counsel a verified petition under Code Section One-Ten-Six stating that the defendant is charged with a felony for which a sentence of imprisonment without probation may be imposed and that defendant's admission to bail poses a real and present threat to the physical safety of a person or persons. State accordingly requests that bail be denied."

"May I have a few moments to review the petition, Your Honor?" Hallie asked.

"Certainly, Counsel," the judge said. The courtroom was still for a few minutes.

A rustling of paper from the bench announced when Judge Connor thought it was time to get on with things. He had started to say, "A presumption of guilt having been established . . ." when Hallie interrupted him.

"I apologize, Your Honor, but it sounded like you'd begun to rule. May I be heard?"

Judge Connor said, "You intend to contradict the State's petition, Ms. Sanchez? How? Defendant says he did it."

"Your Honor, Mr. Dickerson has an IQ of forty-five, which is well below the threshold of normal intelligence. He was held for nearly five hours yesterday before his parents were informed he was in custody. During that time there was no one to assist him in understanding his rights, nor was he permitted to contact a lawyer. When I was finally allowed to meet with him—only briefly I might add—near the end of the day, he could not explain what he was being charged with. He had no idea what he had signed and I am informed can barely read."

"Is she moving to suppress the confession, Judge?" Di Marco broke in. "Defendant waived his *Miranda* rights. And a motion to suppress is not a proper subject of a bail hearing."

"I am not formally challenging the confession at this time," Hallie countered quickly. "Not when I haven't even seen the tape of what preceded it. I can only imagine how the police got him to agree. But I *am* asking that the so-called confession be afforded little weight in considering whether the prosecution has established a presumption of guilt sufficient to deny bail. I understand the police have been unable to find the murder weapon, suggesting the victim was killed by an unknown assailant who fled the scene when my client startled him in the act of stabbing her. There is no physical evidence linking Mr. Dickerson to the crime beyond the fact that he was the first to discover the victim's body in a public alley through which scores of civilians pass each day—"

"He was found soaked in the victim's blood, Judge," Di Marco said. "And she was known to him. A teacher at his school and a beautiful young woman. It doesn't get more physical than that."

Someone tittered in the spectator seating behind me.

"Order," Judge Connor said mildly. "I have to agree with Mr. Di Marco. All we're discussing here is pretrial detention. You can raise lack of evidence at the preliminary hearing."

Hallie said, "Pretrial detention would be psychologically devastating to my client—like locking up a five-year old in Stateville penitentiary. And the State has failed to show that Mr. Dickerson is a danger to anyone, much less the community at large."

During all this I couldn't tell what Charlie was doing, only that he hadn't made a sound.

Di Marco said, "State has agreed to protective custody for the defendant. He'll be well treated. Not that he seems to lack the ability to defend himself. As for danger to the public safety, the charge speaks for itself. The defendant hacked one of his teachers to death in broad daylight."

Hallie interjected, "That's pure speculation. The State has no witnesses to the victim's killing."

"I wasn't finished," Di Marco said. "And the murder bears the same signature as others in the area that have been widely reported upon in the press—four other young women, healthcare workers, brutally stabbed on their way to work like the victim here. Police are currently doing fiber and DNA analysis to confirm their belief the defendant was responsible for these other killings as well."

Hallie interrupted heatedly. "This is the first I've heard of my client being charged for other murders. They're not even alluded to in the State's petition to deny bail."

"I only got wind of the development this morning," Di Marco apologized insincerely. "The medical examiner found the stab wounds to the other decedents' chests to be substantially similar to the ones inflicted on Ms. Sparrow—the victim here—and conceivably caused by the same instrument."

"Which wasn't found on or anywhere near my client. Really, Your Honor, the State's argument is completely improper. My client can't be held without bail for crimes he hasn't been charged with."

"I'm not suggesting he should," Di Marco retorted, "merely that the Court may properly take into consideration the risk to the community if a suspected serial killer is allowed to return to the streets to murder again. It will only take a few days to run the forensics. If there's no probable cause to charge the defendant with these other crimes, Ms. Sanchez can seek reconsideration of the court's decision. But if the defendant is freed and another young life is tragically ended as a consequence . . . well, I wouldn't want that on *my* conscience."

Hallie had just begun to offer me as a witness when Judge Connor cut her off.

"That's enough. We're not going to try the entire case this afternoon. I find the State has met its burden under the statute. Bail is *denied*."

Above the din that followed I heard Charlie asking in a lost voice, "Can I go home now?"

Out in the corridor, Hallie barely had time to hiss "That sonofabitch!" before she was overrun by a group of reporters: "Ms. Sanchez, can you confirm that your client is a suspect in the Surgeon killings? Is it true that he has an IQ of only forty-five . . ." Through the noise I vaguely perceived Nate hurrying Judith away from the video cameras and down the corridor.

I moved off to the side and tried to blend into the woodwork. I was struggling with my temper and didn't want to attract the notice of the squawking newsmen. Even in our justice system, could anyone seriously believe a retarded eighteen-year-old had carried out a series of meticulous murders and then evaded police capture for the better part of a year? Surely Judge Connor had seen through Di Marco's argument. Yet he had agreed to lock up a boy who might have been a kindergartener for all his mental years. What would Charlie do during the long hours alone in his prison cell? And worse, how would he protect himself from the company he would be keeping, hardened predators who would tag him in an instant as being slow-witted? It seemed a travesty, yet if Hallie was right, one that was repeated in courtrooms all over the country every day.

While I was making myself ill with these thoughts, a figure pulled up by my side and asked, "Are you the shrink Hallie wanted to put on the stand?"

I had no trouble identifying the speaker. It was Di Marco.

We shook hands and introduced ourselves.

"A *paisan*," he said upon hearing my name.

"*Certo. E tu sei un bastardo.*"

Di Marco paused for a long moment. "Sorry. I don't speak the lingo."

"I was remarking on what you did in there."

"Yeah, tough luck for the kid. So you're a doctor?"

"Yes."

"That's impressive. How'd you get through medical school?"

"The usual way."

"Come on," he said, giving me a nudge to the arm like we were old chums. "Don't be so modest. I was watching you. You do pretty well for yourself. But I'm surprised you don't have a dog. Or maybe you left it at home. It's all right, you know, to bring them to court."

"I don't have a dog."

"No? How come?"

"Canes are more macho."

Di Marco chuckled in his familiar way. "That's a good one. But seriously, wouldn't a dog be better? Then all you'd have to do is tell it where you wanted to go."

"It doesn't work that way. And I don't like dogs."

"Seriously?"

"Seriously."

"Well, if you don't like dogs you should get one of those things I heard about on Rush Limbaugh the other day. Hey Hallie, what's happening, gorgeous?"

Hallie, who had just come up, said, "I see you two have met."

"Yeah. I was just telling *il dottore* here about something he should be interested in. Seems some MIT students have come up with a talking cane that can actually tell a blind man when he's about to walk into a lamppost and whatnot."

"I'm sure he doesn't need your advice, Tony," Hallie said.

"On the contrary," I said. "It's a brilliant idea. Think of it—a cane that would stop me from walking into things. I'll have to keep an eye out for that one."

Di Marco said, "Keep an eye out . . .? Oh, I get it. Another joke. That's a good one, too. It's great how you people can keep your sense of humor."

"Thanks," I said. "But I don't deserve any credit for that. It's true, you know, what they say about blind people being cheerful. It's because we can't see all the ugly things you normal folks have to look at every day. Like retarded kids being sent to prison by shysters who should know better. I sure don't miss reading the newspapers."

Di Marco's tone became less pal-like. "Who *is* this guy?" he asked Hallie.

"Someone who can outdo you in the put-down department, it seems," she answered.

"You're wrong. We were just having a friendly chat, right Tony?" I gave his shoulder a tweak.

"Sure," Tony said, "and the river ain't green on Saint Patrick's Day." He turned his attention back to Hallie. "So, baby, when do you want to do the prelim?"

"After that stunt you pulled today, the sooner the better."

"Feeling good about your chances, huh?"

Hallie said, "The kid's innocent. You know it, the cops know it, and Judge Connor knows it too. But there was no way he was going to free my client after you reminded him that Election Day is just around the corner."

"I was only doing my job as a lowly civil servant."

"Lowlife is more like it."

"You would have done the same thing if you were still in the office. The retard confessed, didn't he?"

"When my expert gets through with that confession you won't be able to wipe your snot with it."

"Who? This guy here?" Tony asked, referring to me.

Some body language I couldn't make out passed between them.

Di Marco said, "Why not? If it was me, I'd use him. The sympathy factor might do you some good. How about it, Magoo?" he asked me. "Are you up for another round?"

Hallie hesitated.

I didn't.

"You're on," I said.

SEVEN

The preliminary hearing in *State v. Dickerson* took place on the last Friday in April, ironically also Good Friday. As Hallie had predicted, the State's forensics people had been unable to link Charlie to any of the earlier killings, so the charge stood at a single count of second-degree murder in the death of Shannon Sparrow. The presiding judge, a woman named Christine La Font, had made it plain she wanted the hearing to be over by midafternoon, so we got down to business right away at 9:00 a.m. Though the hearing was on defense motion, technically the State had the burden of proving the confession was legally obtained, so Di Marco went first. Hallie had theorized he would keep his presentation light, relying principally on the testimony of O'Leary to introduce the videotape of Charlie's confession and offering the State's psychiatric expert only after seeing how well I held up on cross.

At first, Hallie had been reluctant to use me, reminding me of what I'd first told her about not being a board-certified forensic psychiatrist.

"You were the one who brought up lack of qualifications, remember?"

"But, Hallie," I said, "your guys checked it out. I don't need the credential to act as a witness on Charlie's behalf."

"True, and it's always better when an expert doesn't look like he does this for a living. I'm only worried that you've developed a personal interest in the case."

"Because I believe Charlie couldn't have killed that woman?"

"No, because you and Di Marco seem to have something to prove to each other. This shouldn't be about showing who's got the bigger *cojones*."

"I'm not that childish. OK, I admit I'm pissed off about what happened at the bail hearing. But only because it was so . . . unjust. I'm good at testifying, you said so yourself, and Charlie and I already have a rapport. I want the chance to help."

In the end, Hallie had been persuaded by Nate's enthusiasm for the idea along with all the hard work I had put in reading every known article in the field about forced confessions.

"You're like an encyclopedia," she complimented me.

"You should have known me before," I said.

Together, we spent hours watching the videotape of Charlie's interrogation, with me pausing the action whenever I needed Hallie to describe what was happening on screen. We also met with Charlie a number of times. Our meetings took place in a room that had once housed the prison library but was now nearly empty except for a few stacks of mildewed paperbacks. Charlie was homesick, but he liked the food and the amount of television he was allowed to watch in the protective-custody unit. Apart from not really comprehending what was happening to him, he displayed less anxiety than I'd feared and cooperated readily with our lengthy questioning sessions. Just as we were leaving him the day before the hearing he asked whether he had done anything wrong.

"Not if everything you've told us so far is the truth," Hallie answered.

"I thought she was sleeping. I tried to wake her up. Mom says I have to be careful when I play with Scooby Doo and not be too rough."

Hallie hesitated a fraction before asking, "Were you too rough with Shannon?"

"I don't think so. I only pushed her, like this. Like when Dad is snoring in the morning and he's being too loud. I didn't mean to hurt her."

"Charlie, I've asked you this before, but I need to hear it again. Are you sure Shannon was already lying down when you found her?"

"Uh-huh."

"And you didn't see the blood until you touched her."

"I don't . . . no. It got all over me. I couldn't wipe it off."

"Tell me again why you walked to school that morning."

"The bus didn't come."

From Charlie's account and the investigation conducted by Hallie's colleagues, we'd been able to piece together a rough chronology of his movements the morning Shannon died.

Charlie was awakened at 7:00 a.m. by his after-school babysitter, who was staying overnight while Judith was away in Michigan. Nate was already in surgery and did not see his son that morning. Charlie had dressed and breakfasted on a bowl of Cheerios before being walked to his bus stop at Halsted and Fullerton, where the sitter left him to get to her other job. But the bus, due to arrive at 8:00 a.m., suffered a breakdown en route and a substitute didn't arrive until 8:25. By then Charlie had grown anxious about being late for school and set out to walk the eight blocks to the New Horizons Center on his own, following the route the bus took every day. He and one of his instructors at the center had been practicing independent travel, and he wanted to show her how well he could do, as well as avoid going home to an empty house. Along the way he became confused and overshot the center's entrance on Sheffield, ending up a block farther on, where he realized his mistake. Coming back he recognized the alley to the center's rear and tried to get in the back door, which was locked. It was not long afterward that he noticed Shannon "sleeping" in the parking lot across the way and went over to wake her up.

Di Marco was asking Detective O'Leary about this now.

"Will you describe the position of the victim's body when you first saw it?"

"She was lying face up on the ground adjacent to the driver's side of the car, here," O'Leary said, evidently pointing at a diagram. "Her arms were splayed and one leg was bent at the knee. Blood had pooled on her chest and on the ground, here."

"And what appeared to be the cause of death?"

"A single wound below the rib cage here, apparently made by a sharp blade. The wound was small with no jagged edges, from which we surmised that the instrument of death was slender and narrow, like a doctor's scalpel."

"Were there any other wounds?"

"Some faint bruising on the neck here and here, which may indicate that her assailant held her with one hand while he stabbed her with the other."

"I take it her assailant would have to be a strong person to have killed her in this fashion."

"Physically strong, yes."

"What about her personal possessions. Were any of them taken?"

"None that we could ascertain."

"Did you draw any conclusions from that?"

"Only that robbery wasn't the motive."

Di Marco had moved on now to Charlie's interrogation.

"Did you personally undertake the questioning of the defendant?" he asked O'Leary.

"No. One of my colleagues, Detective Yanowski, questioned the suspect, while I acted as an observer."

"Is that standard procedure?"

"Yes, it's required by department regulations."

"Was the defendant subjected to any form of punishment, threat, or physical intimidation at any time during the interview?"

"No."

"The defense claims the defendant did not understand his rights. Was there any indication he failed to comprehend your questions?"

"The suspect was asked repeatedly whether he understood what he was being asked and always replied in the affirmative. His answers can be observed on the DVD of the interview."

Di Marco then laid a foundation for its introduction, taking O'Leary through some recent history.

Not long ago, in response to sensational charges of police torture and a change in state law, the Chicago Police Department had installed a "state of the art" recording system in thirty-seven interrogation rooms located throughout the city. Each of the rooms had a stationary camera bolted to the ceiling in a corner, and a microphone that could pick up sounds as low as a whisper. The recording equipment was controlled by a switch located in a box on the wall outside the room. O'Leary explained how he had turned the system on while Charlie was being led into the room, and told the court about the fail-safe that prevented it from being "accidentally" switched off during the interview. A digital clock kept continuous track of the time, and when the questioning was over, a backup copy of the recording was automatically sent to a CPU at department headquarters.

"Are these your marks on the DVD recording of the interrogation?" Di Marco asked O'Leary.

"Yes."

"And is the recording a fair and accurate depiction of the events that took place while the defendant was being questioned?"

"It is."

On Di Marco's motion, the DVD was admitted into evidence.

Based on the excerpts Di Marco was now playing for the judge, there seemed little doubt that Charlie had admitted to killing Shannon.

I listened to it all again with my eyes closed, as though I couldn't bear to watch.

Yanowski, the officer leading the interview, had started off light, with the offer of a can of Coke and a promise of frequent replacements. Every time Charlie agreed with something Yanowski said he was rewarded with smiles and urged to take another sip. Whenever Charlie said he didn't know or forgot something, Yanowski grew stern and his tone demanding. Through a combination of vocabulary that was beyond Charlie's understanding, ambiguous phrasing, and outright coaching, Yanowski quickly had Charlie "remembering" that Shannon had reprimanded him for knocking over a container of cleaning supplies in her classroom:

"She called you stupid, didn't she?"

"I'm . . . I . . . I don't remember."

"Come on, Charlie, of course you do. She said you were stupid and you got angry. You don't like it when someone calls you stupid."

[Whining] "I'm not stupid."

"Sure you aren't. That's why you had to show her . . ."

He soon had Charlie describing how the murder had taken place.

"Your dad's a surgeon, isn't he? Operates on people. You try to be like him, don't you?"

"I like Dad."

"So you decided to operate on Shannon, isn't that how it happened?"

"She was sleeping."

"Sure she was. Just like your one of your dad's patients. What did you use to operate on Shannon, Charlie? Was it something you brought from home?"

"I'm not . . . I'm not allowed . . ."

"But you do sometimes, don't you? Play with your dad's stuff?"

"Mom said not to do it again. I might hurt myself."

"Where did you put the scalpel afterward, Charlie, after you operated on Shannon?"

"I don't remember. In the garbage. I have to go to the bathroom."

"In a few minutes. Just tell me how you operated on Shannon and you can go . . ."

And this:

"She was very pretty, wasn't she, Charlie?"

"I liked her."

"Did you touch her, Charlie, afterwards?"

"I wanted her to wake up."

"But she won't wake up anymore, will she? You made sure of that."

[Mumbling]

"What was that, Charlie? I didn't catch it."

"I'm sorry. I'm sorry I did it. Can I go to the bathroom now?"

It was, in every conceivable way, like taking candy from a baby.

"Defense Counsel, call your first witness."

Hallie had finished her cross of O'Leary, quickly getting him to concede that the scalpel—or whatever had been used to kill Shannon—

had never been found despite an all-out search of garbage cans and dumpsters in the vicinity, that there were no witnesses to Shannon's killing, and that the police had made at best a half-hearted effort to follow up on other theories about Shannon's death. O'Leary seemed uneasy with some of his answers but held his ground. It was now our turn.

"The defense calls Mark Angelotti, MD."

The night before, we'd rehearsed getting me to the witness stand in a practice courtroom at Hallie's law firm. When my name was called I stood and navigated around the edge of counsel table. I walked five steps ahead to the lectern on my left, which I brushed with my hand as I went past, and proceeded another five to the raised area next to the bench. The room was very still as I made my way forward to the witness box, and my taps rang out like cannon fire. After I'd climbed in and located my seat, the court reporter asked me to state my name for the record, and the bailiff swore me in.

Hallie began by taking me through my credentials, which went on for quite a while. Apparently this sort of bragging was standard courtroom procedure and forestalled objection to my qualifying as an expert. As we neared the end, I felt myself tense at what I knew was coming.

"Dr. Angelotti. I see you use a white cane. Is that because you are blind?"

"Yes," I said.

"Will you explain to the court what that means in practical terms."

"It means I have some limited perception of the things around me, but can't see any detail, such as what a person looks like."

"Can you read?"

"Not something that's printed in ink, no."

Hallie had explained she wanted to get this out in the open before the prosecution had a chance to make a big deal of it.

"And how does that affect your psychiatric practice?"

"On the reading side, very little. I have a scanner and other devices for transcribing printed material into a Braille or audio format, and in the rare instances when they don't work, my assistant reads to me."

"And in other aspects?"

"Well, naturally, it is useful to be able to observe a patient's body language during sessions, but I compensate by careful listening and other strategies, such as stopping and asking the patient to describe his posture and facial expression at various times. In many ways the patient's own perception of what he or she is doing is as significant as the reality."

We then switched to my preparation for the hearing and I began to relax a little. Under Hallie's questioning I described all the material I had gathered and reviewed about Charlie, starting in his infancy, the reports of various therapists and teachers, his IQ tests and other assessments, and ending up with his most recent evaluation by personnel at the center.

"And did you also meet personally with the defendant, Mr. Dickerson?" Hallie asked.

"I did, on several occasions."

"And will you describe your overall findings?"

"Charlie Dickerson is an eighteen-year-old male with a weighed IQ of forty-five on the Wechsler Scale, which translates into the mental age of a six- to nine-year-old child. His cognitive deficits are readily apparent from his speech, which is halting and childlike. He has difficulty understanding questions and often needs to have them repeated several times. His answers reflect his poor memory skills. He has significant trouble with sequencing—putting things in proper chronological order—and often confuses events that happened in the past with those in the present, and vice versa."

I hated to have to say such things with Charlie sitting only a few feet away and hoped he didn't understand my elevated speech. He had been very quiet throughout the hearing, and I could sense his presence only from the stertorous breathing coming from the seat beside Hallie's.

"Was he cooperative on the occasions you met with him?"

"Yes, very. Like many such individuals, Mr. Dickerson tends to defer to persons of normal intelligence, particularly those in positions of authority, and has a strong desire to please."

"What about his psychological profile?"

"I administered the Psychopathology Inventory for Mentally

Retarded Adults, the Diagnostic Assessment of the Severely Handicapped, and the Reiss Scale for Maladaptive Behavior. While none of
these tests is conclusive, the results consistently indicated a person who
is free of the factors associated with psychopathology as defined by
the leading texts in the field. In laymen's terms, Mr. Dickerson is very
well-adjusted for someone with his level of impairment and displays no
signs of depression, anxiety disorder, or other mental illness."

"So, in your opinion, Mr. Dickerson does not exhibit any traits
that are associated with violent psychosis?"

"That is correct."

"Now Dr. Angelotti, you are aware that Mr. Dickerson was inter-
rogated by police officers after his arrest?'

"I am."

"And that he purportedly waived his right to have an attorney
present during that interrogation."

"Yes. I listened to the so-called waiver on the tape."

"Have you formed any opinion about Mr. Dickerson's capacity to
give such a waiver? Please tell us first what you understand a proper
waiver to consist of."

Di Marco sprang to his feet like a jack-in-the box. "Objection.
Calls for a legal conclusion."

Judge La Font sighed. "The witness's understanding of the prevailing legal standard is relevant to the weight to be afforded to his testimony. Objection overruled. You may answer," she said to me.

"It has been explained to me that waiver of *Miranda* rights must
be both knowing and voluntary. In simple terms, the individual must
understand what he is giving up and yet still desire to do so."

"That's a better answer than nine-tenths of the bar would have
given," Judge La Font remarked kindly.

"Thank you," I said, feeling myself flush slightly.

"But don't let it go to your head," Judge La Font said. There were
laughs from the spectator section, and for the first time since taking the
stand I think I smiled.

Hallie then took me through my analysis of the "waiver," emphasizing Charlie's inability to explain any of its key terms, much less his rights as a criminal defendant, or even exactly what he was accused of. We sailed through the rest of my direct easily, with Di Marco objecting infrequently, ending up with my professional opinion that the confession had been the result of subtle, and not-so-subtle, psychological persuasion.

It was then time for my cross-examination.

I've since testified more than a few times and never failed to be impressed by the uneven talents lawyers bring to a courtroom. I guess it's no different from medicine. A diploma from an Ivy League school and a six-figure billing rate are no substitute for instinct. It's a sad truth that certain skills can't be taught. I've been on the receiving end of cross-examinations that were as dry and plodding as a mule expedition through Death Valley, and ultimately as deadly: no goal on the horizon, inadequate provisions, and a growing sense of desperation until the whole thing just fizzles out like the dying plumes of a rescue flare. It's no wonder jurors doze and judges strain not to fidget in their seats.

Di Marco, however, was a whole different story.

"You have an impressive set of credentials, Doctor," he began pleasantly enough.

I agreed modestly.

"Two residencies, a fellowship at George Washington, and a tenured position on the faculty at your former hospital, is that right?"

"Yes."

We went over some of my accomplishments there. "Your employer must have been very happy with you," Di Marco said.

"No one ever expressed any reservations about my being on staff."

"And you were there for ten years."

"Just under, but that's right."

Di Marco then made his first thrust.

"I'm curious then—why did you leave?"

This wasn't something Hallie and I had prepared for. I turned toward her, seeking guidance. She picked up my hesitation right away, and said, "Objection. Relevance."

"Sustained," the judge answered.

Di Marco pressed ahead anyway. "Was it because you were fired?"

Hallie was up in an instant, "Your Honor—"

Judge La Font said crisply, "I'll let the witness answer that one."

I took a deep breath. "I resigned voluntarily," I said, pausing and adding as evenly as I could, "for personal reasons having nothing to do with my job."

I waited to see what Judge La Font would do. Thankfully, she cut it off there. "That's all you're entitled to," she said to Di Marco. "Move on."

Di Marco couldn't possibly have known. But all the same I felt like I had been warned.

Di Marco proceeded to let the tension lapse, taking me over a few uncontested points in my testimony. I answered them easily enough, but my threat level was still on orange alert.

"So your testimony is that the defendant couldn't have competently waived his *Miranda* rights under any circumstances?"

"I can't say what he may have been able to do with proper assistance, only that none was offered or given."

"And you say the police should have recognized his 'cognitive deficits,' as you called them, immediately?"

"As I testified, Mr. Dickerson's impairment should have been obvious to even a casual observer. And he was known by the police to be a student at the New Horizons Center."

"So that should have signaled to them at once that he was an unreliable witness?"

"Yes."

"And the blood on his hands, that was unreliable too?"

"I'll object to that one," Hallie said.

Judge La Font said, "Save the grandstanding for the jury, Mr. Di Marco. It's not going to impress me."

"So what should the protocol be, in your opinion?" Di Marco asked, switching gears.

"What do you mean?"

"The protocol whenever a suspect pretends to be too dumb to

understand. Do the police have to administer an IQ test to prove he's lying?"

I wasn't going to be baited. "That's a question for policymakers to decide. I can only tell you that based upon my observation of the recorded interview and the questions I put to him afterward, Mr. Dickerson did not understand the nature of the rights he was giving up. And his IQ isn't in dispute."

"Let's talk about that. Have you ever taken an IQ test?"

"I'm sure I have. It was standard practice in the sixties to administer them to grade-school students, but the scores were never made known to me."

"Let's say, hypothetically speaking, that you had been told your score and it was lower than normal. Would that have affected your opinion of yourself?"

"Certainly."

"And your teachers' opinion of you as well?"

"Of course. That's why the practice is no longer looked on with favor. There's a danger that a low score can become a self-fulfilling prophecy. And some argue that there is a high degree of cultural bias in IQ testing."

"Leading to unreliability of results?"

"According to some researchers, yes."

"In fact, isn't it true that, according to some studies, IQ testing of the same individual can produce scores fifteen to twenty points apart?"

"Yes."

"If those studies are correct, then the defendant's purported IQ of forty-five could be as much as twenty points higher."

"Or lower," I said. "Look, if you're trying to make the point that IQ testing isn't always accurate, I agree with you. That is why current psychiatric practice looks at intelligence more in terms of deviation from a norm based upon large population studies. The results don't necessarily predict an individual's potential, but within a certain range can be useful in assessing his strengths and weaknesses relative to his peer group. In this case, though, give or take a few points, there's no question that Mr. Dickerson falls well below the threshold that would allow him to live as an adult in our society without substantial support and assistance."

Di Marco paused, rifling through his notes at the lectern as though he wasn't sure where to go next. I felt my watch for the time, certain we were nearing the end.

But Di Marco was far from through with me.

"Dr. Angelotti, may I ask how you first came to know Mr. Dickerson?"

Hallie was on him in a split second. "Objection. Calls for information protected by the physician–patient privilege."

Di Marco said, "Ms. Sanchez opened the door to privileged testimony when she elicited testimony about Mr. Dickerson's psychological profile. I have the right to follow up."

"You have a response to that, Ms. Sanchez?" Judge La Font asked.

"I . . . uh . . . no, Your Honor," Hallie sputtered.

Shit, I thought. Why hadn't I told Hallie about the Dickersons' visit? I had meant to, but evidently forgotten during all the hurried preparation for the hearing. And I'd been taught the privilege was iron-clad, disregarded only in the rare circumstance when a psychiatrist *knows* his patient intends violence toward a particular victim. Nothing remotely like that had come out in my interview of Charlie, so I'd assumed our session would be off-limits.

Apparently I was wrong.

"I'll allow it then," Judge La Font said. "Read back the question."

The court reporter did as I fought to keep my cool. I was still comfortable with the advice I had given the Dickersons, but it was all too easy to see how Di Marco could twist it into something dicey-sounding. And then there was the matter of Judith's suspicions about Shannon . . . would I have to repeat them? I remembered what Hallie had told me to do if I were caught unawares like this: stay calm and try to keep my answers as succinct as possible.

I said, "Mr. Dickerson's parents asked me to talk to him."

"I see. And was this before the arrest?"

"Yes."

"When precisely?"

"Around September of last year."

"And why did they ask you to do that?"

Hallie was up again. "Objection. Calls for speculation."

"I'll rephrase," Di Marco said.

"Did Mr. and Mrs. Dickerson say why they wanted you to see their son?"

Hallie jumped back in, "Your Honor, I fail to see the relevance of this line of questioning." She made it sound confident but I knew she was getting rattled.

Di Marco said, "It's only irrelevant if the defense has nothing to hide."

This was good enough for Judge La Font, and she instructed me to answer.

"They said Mr. Dickerson had been waking during the night."

"Anything else?"

"And that they had observed him crying afterward."

"Go on. Did they say how often this was happening?"

"An average of two to three times a week."

"And did they offer any reason why this might be occurring?"

"Mrs. Dickerson—Charlie's mother—was concerned . . . that something at the New Horizons Center was upsetting him."

"What kind of something? A relationship, perhaps?"

Hallie broke in again, "Your Honor, how long is this going to go on? He's obviously fishing. And why isn't this hearsay?"

"You have a response to the hearsay objection?" Judge La Font asked Di Marco.

"Information gathered by an expert witness at any stage of his investigation is exempt from the hearsay rules," Di Marco answered primly.

"All right," the judge said, "but I want to see where this is going soon."

"I'll cut to the chase then," Di Marco said. "Dr. Angelotti, during that first meeting with the Dickersons, did either of them tell you of their suspicion that the defendant was engaged in a sexual relationship with a caregiver at the center?"

I had no choice then. "Yes," I said.

"And that they wanted you to examine their son to confirm or deny that suspicion?"

"That's what they asked me to do."

"And what conclusions did you draw about the defendant's sexual conduct at his school?"

"I . . . I'm not able to answer the question that way."

"Why not?"

"Because I determined that Charlie's nighttime waking had a different cause."

"Which was what, exactly?"

The room was utterly silent except for the sound of a foot tapping under a table. Hallie's foot, I remember thinking. I cleared my throat, which was beginning to feel like a stopover on the Bataan death march.

"It appeared that the defendant—I mean, Mr. Dickerson—was having erections that he lacked the knowledge to . . . bring to a conclusion."

There were a few coughs from the spectator section but no one laughed.

"Are we talking about wet dreams?"

"No, merely unintended arousal."

"And is there a solution for this problem?"

"Yes."

"Care to tell us about it?"

"There are ways to . . . counteract such episodes, but . . ."

"But?"

"Mr. Dickerson had been taught never to . . . touch himself in that way."

"I see. So what did you tell the Dickersons?"

"I advised Mr. Dickerson—Mr. Dickerson *senior*, that is—to show his son how to relieve himself."

"What do you mean by 'relieve himself?'"

"Bring about ejaculation."

"In other words, you prescribed jerking off."

"Your Honor—" Hallie began.

"I'll withdraw it," Di Marco said. "But just so I'm clear on this, Doctor, your advice to the Dickersons was that the defendant be encouraged to masturbate?"

"Encouraged is putting it too strongly."

"And you didn't think there was anything remarkable about that prescription?"

"I . . . under the circumstances, no."

"Had you ever suggested such a remedy to a patient before?"

"No, but most boys Charlie's age . . . already know what to do."

"But not Mr. Dickerson?"

"No, as I said, he was ignorant of what was happening to him."

"I see."

Di Marco stepped away from the lectern and engaged in a whispered consultation with his colleagues. I took a sip of water from the glass next to me, mentally reviewing the answers I had just given. I thought I had done as well as I could. I had kept Shannon's name out of it, the only real minefield I knew of, and apart from further snide references to hand jobs, Di Marco seemed unsure where to go next. I began to breathe again.

When Di Marco returned, he said, "Your Honor, at this time I would like to tender to the Court and defense counsel People's Exhibit Number 10 for identification."

"What's he up to now?" Hallie muttered to one of her assistants as Di Marco passed some papers around.

"Yes, Counsel, what is this?" Judge La Font said.

Di Marco said with studied casualness, "Results of paternity tests, Judge."

"Paternity tests?" Hallie repeated edgily. "On whom?"

"On a fourteen-week-old fetus—"

The courtroom began to vibrate like a subway track.

"—discovered by the medical examiner during autopsy—"

With a nauseated sensation I realized what he was saying.

"—a fetus whom DNA analysis has confirmed to be the unborn child of the murder victim, Shannon Sparrow—"

Here Di Marco paused like a politician delivering a stump speech.

"—and the defendant, *CHARLES DICKERSON*!"

Pandemonium ensued.

Even now, my memory of what followed has a surreal quality, as though I were experiencing the events through the mouthpiece of a bullhorn. Time slowed to a full stop, proof that Zeno was on to something. The tiniest sounds—the ticking of a clock somewhere above my head, the rustle of Judge La Font's robes—had the painstaking clarity of a dry point etching, while the larger commotion seemed to be taking place at a great distance. Dimly I registered a deep voice—Nate's?—bellowing like an elephant. "They were sleeping together? Jesus Christ! That idiot!" Hallie, too, was shouting. "She was pregnant? Is this for real? Why am I only finding out now?" Di Marco was yelling back, also straining to be heard above the din. "Your Honor, I can explain." Judge La Font was cracking her gavel. "Order. I will have order. Everyone back to their seats. If you are not seated I will ask the bailiff to remove you." For a while, no one paid her any attention. "Order!" Judge La Font commanded once more. "This minute!"

Gradually, the collective aneurysm died down as the spectators, coaxed by the bailiff, resumed their seats and the babble of a dozen simultaneous conversations dwindled to a few pronounced whispers. I bowed my head, wishing there were some way to conceal my shock. With quiet finally descending on the room, I knew everyone's eyes were on me. It wasn't hard to guess the group judgment. Pity, disapproval, contempt: I sensed them all as easily as if I'd been watching the scene myself on a hugely popular YouTube clip. Had I been capable of any show of defiance I would have stared right back. As it was, all I could manage was a silent prayer that I might be allowed to escape, *Star Trek* fashion, in a cloud of vanishing pixels.

"What's your answer to her question, Mr. Di Marco?" the judge snapped raggedly. "Why wasn't this exhibit made available to the defense before today?"

The room was now as still as the eye of a hurricane.

Di Marco answered, "Due to the sensational nature of the evidence we ran the procedure several times to be absolutely sure of the results. I didn't think Ms. Sanchez would object, since it was she who insisted that this hearing take place at the earliest possible opportunity."

"You didn't think I'd object?" Hallie roared back. "What about the discovery rules? My client should have been informed of these results the minute they were available!"

Di Marco was unapologetic. "State has no obligation to speed up production of evidence that further incriminates the defendant, as counsel well knows."

I paid scant attention to the argument that followed, knowing only with numbing certainty there would be no stays of execution for me that morning.

Di Marco was back to me now. "Would you like me to read the DNA report to you, Doctor?"

"I'll take your word for the contents," I said miserably.

"When we left off we were discussing the Dickersons' visit to your office last fall."

I managed a yes.

"At which time his parents expressed fear that the defendant was being molested by one of his caregivers, correct?"

"That's what I testified."

"But you dismissed those fears, didn't you?"

"No," I said.

"Because *you* were convinced all the defendant needed was some sex education."

"No," I repeated in a tight voice.

"You decided 'the birds and the bees do it, so why not Charlie?'"

"That isn't what I—"

"Isn't it?"

"Masturbation isn't intercourse. In an eighteen-year-old boy it's completely harmless."

"Natural, you'd say?"

"Yes."

"Isn't it also natural that this eighteen-year-old boy, having discovered what all the fun was about, would want to get a taste of the real thing?"

"I . . . I saw no evidence of that kind of forward thinking during our session."

"Sure. The only thing you *saw* was a boy with a loaded gun who didn't know how to use it."

"No," I said again harshly.

"So you decided to give him some target practice."

"You're twisting my words."

"Tell me, Doctor, when you recommended your novel treatment program, did it cross your mind that it might unleash emotions that someone with the mental age of a 'six- to nine-year-old' would have difficulty handling?"

All I could do was shake my head.

"Emotions like jealousy and rage when the girl of his dreams decided she was tired of sex with her retarded lover and told him to get lost?"

I groped for my water. My head was throbbing like an arena in a rock concert and I could barely hold the glass steady enough to take a sip. "You have no proof of that," I said, nearly sending the glass to the floor as I set it back down.

"Don't I? Care to speculate on other ways his sperm found its way into her body?

"Objection," Hallie said meaningfully. It was my cue to stop and take a deep breath.

But I was sick of being humiliated. "Look," I said, "even if you're right, that one thing led to another and Charlie made that woman—I mean the victim, pregnant—that doesn't mean he killed her. This isn't the dark ages, after all."

"What does that mean?" Di Marco asked dangerously.

"It means that disabled adults can have sexual relationships just like anyone else. You're talking like physical intimacy between two human beings, one of whom happens to have lowered intellect, is some kind of crime."

"So you believe retarded people are entitled to have lovers?"

"Yes. Of course."

"Even with someone who can run mental rings around them."

"If they consent to it freely."

"What sort of form would that consent have to take? Would they have to sign a piece of paper or something?"

"I wouldn't go that far."

"But you'd agree with me that consent depends on all the facts and circumstances."

I had no choice but to say yes.

"And that, despite his low functioning, the defendant was capable of making that kind of important decision on his own?"

I realized then the full extent of the trap I had fallen into.

"Yes, but you can't compare it to—"

"No," Di Marco said. "I didn't expect *you* could. No further questions."

EIGHT

The next day, a Saturday, I tried to keep busy with my usual routines, starting with a ride on my road bike. It's a DeRosa, one of the most exclusive cycling machines ever built. A few hundred or so find their way into the United States every year, but I had gone straight to Ugo DeRosa's factory in Milan to get mine. I love its sleek profile and flawless construction, the endorphin high I always get after a punishing workout on its saddle. Once I rode it outdoors almost every day in dry weather. After my illness I kept it hitched to a stationary trainer in my spare bedroom. Once I got going with a fan blowing on my face I could usually imagine I was on a real road again.

That morning, though, the only image I could summon was of Charlie weeping in his stripped-down cell. Although Judge La Font had taken the matter under advisement, I didn't need a lawyer to tell me the hearing had gone badly for us. As soon as it was over Nate had found me in the hallway and snarled in my ear, "I'll see you fired for this." Hallie hadn't been much more forgiving. "You sandbagged me! Why didn't you tell me what the Dickersons came to see you about?" I could have replied that she hadn't asked, but it didn't really matter one way or the other. Charlie's fate was sealed the moment Di Marco had flourished the DNA results.

After thirty minutes of half-hearted pedaling I gave up. One of my wheels was out of true and I vainly attempted to fix it—I always did my own maintenance and had learned to make even the most complicated repairs by touch—but I kept fumbling my tools and applying too much pressure. When one of the spoke lugs snapped in half I decided I was doing more harm than good and forced myself to quit.

I wandered aimlessly around my apartment picking up articles of clothing I'd strewn on the floor during the week and trying not to feel so useless. My place was a condominium unit in a tower just north of where Lake Michigan flows into the Chicago River. It was nothing special: two bedrooms, two baths, a living-kitchen area, and a small outdoor terrace. Most of its value came from the view. I furnished it my first week in Chicago in a single trip to Marshall Field's, haphazardly choosing whatever pieces seemed to clash the least. On my salary I could have afforded something much nicer, but I was in a self-punishing mood then and didn't need the space. When I'd left my wife a few months before there was only time to pack a suitcase, and I never had the stomach to go back and claim the rest of the possessions that were mine. Apart from my books and my collections, which I had her lawyer ship, there was nothing from my past I wanted to salvage anyway.

After a time I showered and dressed and rode the elevator to the first floor. On the way down a couple entered with a dog I knew, a hulking breed that smelled like raw steak. They never did anything to control him and he always went straight for my crotch. "I wish you could see how much Hannibal likes you," the female of the pair said after I had pushed off his muzzle for the third time.

Outside, it was frigid and gray. An Alberta Clipper had roared in the night before and even though it was the first of May it felt like November. I went south along the lake path through a gale-force wind. Breakers pounded against the sides of Monroe Harbor and slapped spray on me every few feet. In a short time I was soaked to the skin and dull with cold, but it was preferable to the walls pressing in on me at home. I wandered around the museum campus and the gravel paths near Buckingham Fountain for an hour until the arctic blasts finally drove me inland. While I was passing by the Art Institute I overheard someone mentioning an Edvard Munch exhibition. It was a shame I couldn't see it. *The Scream* would have suited my mood perfectly.

By then I had developed a sliver of an appetite. The café in Millennium Park was a block away and I decided to stop there, thinking that if nothing else it would make a good warming hut. As always the place was jammed. The maître d' offered at once to jump me to the head of the line, but I turned him down. It was enough to be indoors and out of the freezing wind, with other people's voices filling my ears for company. The dollar's slide against foreign currencies had brought a wave of European visitors to Chicago that year, and most of the accents were foreign. I eavesdropped for a while on a husband and wife arguing animatedly in Italian while I waited my turn. "*Cieco*," I heard her whisper to her husband, obviously referring to me. "*Ma non sordo*," I said, giving her a tired smile.

"I thought you'd feel more comfortable back here," the maître d' explained when he'd finally shown me to a table in a distant corner. I knew what he really meant but bit down a retort. "Just wave if you need anything," he added chummily. I squeezed through the narrow space between the tables and took a seat on the leather banquette against the wall. After I'd ordered a Reuben and a cup of tea I slipped on my earphones to occupy the time. Reading at mealtimes is an old vice of mine, and I'd gotten into the habit of always carrying an audio book in my pocket so I wouldn't be stuck in restaurants with nothing to do.

Midway through the sandwich something hard ran over my foot. I jerked it away and put my book on pause so I could make out what was going on. Someone was trying to fit a stroller between my table and its closely packed neighbor.

"I'm so sorry," a youngish-sounding woman said. "They don't give you much room here and my baby is sleeping, so I can't leave it by the door. Do you mind? I'd ask for another table but I had to wait twenty minutes to get this one."

"I don't mind at all. Can I help you?"

"It seems to be stuck. Maybe if you lifted the wheel?" I reached down. What I'd thought was a stroller was really a baby jogger and the single front wheel had become lodged between the pedestal of my table and the banquette. I freed it by lifting and shifting the pedestal slightly.

"Thank you. You're very kind," the woman said. She slid onto the banquette a few inches away from me and said apologetically, "I shouldn't have taken her out today but it's so hard staying cooped up inside all day with a newborn and the only time she stops crying is when we're walking. I must have put in twenty miles with her already this week."

"She's a beautiful baby," I said politely. This didn't provoke any reaction, and I realized that with my cane hidden away on the floor I must have looked like anyone to her.

"Isn't she? She'll be six weeks next Tuesday, though it seems like an eternity since she came home. They don't prepare you, do they? For what it's really like, I mean. Or maybe it's just impossible. You have to go through it yourself to know. Before she was born my mother kept telling me they're easier to take care of when they're inside. This was when I was as big as a house and couldn't breathe at night unless I was propped up with a dozen pillows. I thought, who's she kidding? All I want to do is get this thing out of me. Now all I want to do is sleep. Do you have children?"

I don't know what made me tell her. "A son. A little older." I didn't add that I had never met him.

"So you know about babies. Listen, I wonder if you could do me a favor. I know it's a lot to ask, but I desperately need a potty break and she'll wake for sure if I move her. She only went down when we came in. Do you think you could watch her while I scoot in there? It'll only take a minute or two. I suppose you think I'm a terrible mother. I shouldn't even be thinking of leaving her with a stranger, but if she wakes again I'll never get something to eat. You seem like a nice man."

"Go ahead," I said. "I'll mind her. What's her name?"

"Anna. And I'm Kate."

"Mark." I held out my hand and she shook it.

"I'll be back in a flash," Kate said.

Almost as soon as she left, Anna's baby radar went off and she began to fuss. I felt around her blankets for a pacifier but couldn't find one. I tried to soothe her by pushing the jogger back and forth, but there wasn't enough room to move it, and when her cries became more insistent I leaned over and eased her out of the sling. She was tiny, barely the size of a kitten, and as toasty as a coal. The mingled smells of Dreft and curdled milk drifted up from her terry onesie. I brought her damp head to my shoulder and bounced her up and down on my arm, crooning a little rhyme my father had sung to me when I was small: "*Trin' trin' cavallin, sut' e' porta di Turin, sut' e' porta di Tortuna . . .*"

When Kate returned Anna was still fussing, but no longer on the verge of wailing.

"Oh, you bad girl," Kate said, taking her from me. "Crying again. Aren't you lucky Mark was here to take care of you?" Then to me: "Thank you. Again. You really are a saint. Can I pay for your lunch? It must be pretty cold by now."

"Don't even think of it. I enjoyed holding her."

Kate said, "One last thing. You are going to start thinking I'm such a pest. Is it OK if I breastfeed her next to you? Some people are bothered when they see it, especially if they're eating, and I've already imposed on you enough for one day."

I decided I had to tell her.

I was worried she'd be horrified about leaving Anna with me, but she took it well. "Wow," she said. "I can hardly believe it. You look so normal. I noticed you weren't looking directly at me, but I thought you were just shy. Wait until my husband hears about this. On second thought, maybe I won't tell him."

When the waitress came I ordered a second cup of tea and chatted with Kate while she nursed Anna and ate her lunch. I was glad for the company and in no hurry to get anywhere. Kate seemed impossibly young. Anna was her first, a surprise pregnancy who had given her parents a brief fright when ultrasound testing during Anna's third month suggested she was undersized. Kate's ob-gyn recommended amniocentesis to be on the safe side, but Kate declined. "I wasn't going to do anything about it, so what was the point?" she told me. "I didn't care if she came out with two heads so long as she was healthy." That *was* the point but I didn't say it. Maybe she felt she needed to show me how fair-minded she was.

"Those decisions are always difficult," I said. "There's no right answer."

"But how would you have felt if your parents had decided to abort you?"

"I wouldn't have known."

"Oh," she said. "I guess that's right."

We talked for a long time. Kate allowed me to hold Anna again and I gently traced her profile with a finger while she slept. Contrary to popular belief, it's not possible to "see" a face by feeling it. The most I could make out when I tried it on my own were a series of bumps— nose, chin, mouth—and most blind people I know would sooner sink into the earth than grope another adult that way. But if Anna's face was, strictly speaking, a blank, the memory it evoked of another sleeping infant was as real to my mind as if I'd traveled back in time and was once again standing beside his crib, watching the moonlight play over his delicate features. Kate seemed glad to be relieved of the isolation of new motherhood, if only for a few hours, and it was nearly three before she made her excuses to leave. When we parted she and I exchanged telephone numbers, even though we knew we would never run across one another again.

When I got home, my place seemed emptier than ever.

I napped for a while in front of the television. When I woke dusk was settling, the room was dark, and I felt stiff and wooly-headed. While I was sleeping I had dreamt of babies and test tubes and crying in the night. And something else too, though I couldn't recall precisely what. It hovered just below the surface of consciousness like a daring housefly, always managing to pull off a last-minute escape. The sense of something urgent eluding me persisted as I went from room to room flicking on lights. I didn't always do this, being well able to navigate my home in the dark. But that evening I was rebelling against a profounder darkness, or maybe needed a symbolic act to chase the shadows away. When the apartment was lit up like a candle I went to the kitchen to heat up a can of soup for dinner.

As I was opening the can it slipped, squirting its contents every-where. I swore and dumped the opener in the sink. I had just twisted the tap to wash it off when I idly recalled what brand it was, one that always made me think of a game of tic-tac-toe. And just like that, I remembered what had come to me in my dream.

Hallie's number was recorded in my cell phone and I nearly tripped over the pile of shoes near the door in my rush to grab it from my coat pocket.

I hadn't expected a warm response. "Oh, it's you," she said, like she had just taken a sip of battery acid.

I went ahead quickly so she wouldn't hang up. "Listen, I just thought of something. Something that may be important."

She cut me off. "Mark, I'm not in the mood for this, not after what happened yesterday."

"Please hear me out. I may be able to prove the paternity test was wrong."

"Sure. And I've just discovered the antidote to world hunger. Speaking of which, my takeout is waiting."

"I'll pay for another delivery if it gets cold. Just be patient for a minute. Charlie may not be the father of that baby."

"That seems farfetched. And how much would you know about paternity tests anyway? I understand you're a doctor, but that doesn't make you an expert on DNA typing."

"I'll admit that, but I've done more than the usual amount of reading on the subject . . . for personal reasons," I added, playing on her sympathy.

Hallie sighed loudly. "You're trying to make me feel like a hard-hearted bitch if I hang up on you."

"Maybe just hard-hearted."

"All right, what is it?"

"It's complicated, but bear with me. Do you remember much biology?"

"Are you kidding?"

"All right. I'll start with my own situation." I still had trouble using the B-word so I had to search for the right way to begin. "This, uh, thing I have . . . well, it's caused by a defect in my DNA. But not the kind of DNA you're probably familiar with."

"There's more than one kind?"

"Yes. Usually when we speak of DNA we're referring to nuclear

DNA, the genetic material that tells a cell how to act, its brain, so to speak. But cells also have another kind of DNA associated with their mitochondria, mini-organisms in the cell that break down food into energy. Think of mitochondria as a kind of powerhouse for the cell. You with me so far?"

"Uh-huh."

"The mutation I have causes the mitochondria to wear out prematurely. The cells run out of juice and stop working."

There was a momentary hush on the other end. "That sounds serious. Does it mean you're slowly dying?"

"We're all slowly dying."

"I didn't mean that in a philosophical sense."

"I didn't either. But don't worry. I won't be disappearing from your life anytime soon. My mutation doesn't affect all cells equally—it mainly shuts down the ones that need a lot of energy to function. In my case, nerve cells in the retinas. What's significant is that in humans mitochondrial DNA is inherited exclusively from the mother. My father couldn't have caused my problem."

"That's interesting, but what does it have to do with Charlie?"

"What Charlie has, Fragile X Syndrome, is similar because of the maternal inheritance pattern. The syndrome is caused by excessive repeats in a gene called the FMR-1 gene. The gene produces a protein that's crucial for intellectual development, though no one knows exactly why. When the defect is present the gene doesn't make enough of the protein to support normal intelligence and the result, depending on the number of repeats, is retardation."

"Go on."

"The syndrome is called Fragile X because the FMR-1 gene is located exclusively on one of two sex-linked chromosomes, the X chromosome. Every child gets two sex-linked chromosomes, one X chromosome from their mother and either an X chromosome or a Y chromosome from their father."

Hallie said, "I remember this now. If you get two X chromosomes you're a girl. Boys have one of each."

"Right," I said. "Charlie has Fragile X because of the X chromosome he inherited from Judith. It couldn't have come from Nate. Even if Nate were a carrier, he could only pass on the mutation to his daughters. The same is true for Charlie. Charlie's male children couldn't inherit the syndrome from him. His female children wouldn't be so lucky."

"Because they would inherit one of their X chromosomes from their father."

"Exactly. Do you recall anyone at the hearing saying what the sex of Shannon's fetus was?"

"No. I don't think it came up."

"Or whether they tested it for Fragile X?"

"I don't remember that being a part of the discussion either."

"Because if it was a girl, the absence of repeats on the FMR-1 gene would be conclusive proof the baby wasn't Charlie's."

"So you're saying the testing lab overlooked something?"

"It depends on what they looked for and how far they went. I don't know whether you're aware of this, but paternity tests are based on averages. A finding of paternity with a 99 percent degree of accuracy only tells you that the alleged father has a DNA profile possessed by one in every hundred males in the general population."

"Meaning?"

"Meaning it identifies someone who *could* be the biological father, but doesn't necessarily prove he is. Charlie has a genetic marker that makes him fairly unique. It should have been part of the lab analysis. Assuming the fetus was a girl."

"And if it wasn't?"

"Then it would be irrelevant. But still worth knowing one way or the other."

Hallie whistled. "Well, that *is* something."

"Can you get a copy of the full lab report?"

"I can subpoena it, but it may take a while."

"What about O'Leary? He doesn't seem entirely comfortable about what's happening to Charlie. Would he give it to you?"

"Maybe. I'll try to get a hold of him tonight or first thing in the morning."

"Will you let me know right away?"

"Of course." She stopped. "Mark," she said, assuming a more conciliatory tone. "I hope we can still be on good terms after yesterday. I'm sorry for what I said to you. I blamed you too quickly. What happened was . . . well, it was my fault too. I forgot one of the first rules of being a trial lawyer: know your own witness. You did better than most laymen faced with that kind of surprise."

"I'm sorry, too," I said, "but not because of what you said. We both screwed up."

"Fair enough. But remember what I said about not getting too involved. Let the legal professionals do their work now. I'll get on that lab report and call you as soon as I know something."

After Hallie rang off I cleaned up the mess the can had made and put the rest of the soup on the burner to heat up. I wasn't very hungry and most of it ended up in the disposal. When I was done I poured myself a glass of bourbon and settled on the couch with a copy of *The Inferno* I had just ordered from an Italian Braille service. It was a mistake. When I came to the lines "I reached a place mute of all light, which bellows as the sea in tempest tossed by conflicting winds," I slammed the book shut in disgust and headed for bed. That night I slept fitfully, passing into real slumber only toward early morning.

At 9:00 a.m. my bedroom phone rang. I had the handset to my ear on the second ring. It was Hallie, but she didn't sound like she'd slept well either.

"I'm impressed," I said, hoping the strain in her voice didn't mean anything. "You work fast."

"It's not that. Are you sitting down?"

"Why do people always ask that?" I was still cranky from lack of rest and alarm bells were going off in my head. "What's going on?"

"It's about Charlie."

"Of course it is, or you wouldn't be calling me."

All of her usual pugnacity was gone. "I don't know how to tell you." She stopped. "He was . . . assaulted." She stopped again, as though she hadn't quite convinced herself of the fact.

I managed to get out, "Where? When?"

"In a corridor last night."

"Was he . . . ?" I couldn't get the word past my lips.

"No, thank God. His pants were down when a guard found him but he understood enough of what was happening to him to scream and kick his attacker where it would do the most good. Apparently he'd been taking some kind of course . . ."

"Fucking Christ!" I cried. "He was supposed to be in protective custody!"

"I know, but it wasn't very protective apparently. I didn't want to tell you. I only got word from the Dickersons a little while ago. I've had the shakes ever since."

"Do they know who . . . went after him?"

"They're holding someone, a gang member who was on a suicide watch. But why does it matter?"

"Because if I ever find the bastard, I'm going to . . ." I disciplined myself to stop. There were no words for what I wanted to do, and it wasn't important. The only important thing was getting Charlie the best possible care so that he wouldn't be permanently scarred. "Where is he now?"

"In the prison clinic. They say he's not talking."

"I'm on my way."

"Mark, you can't—"

"He needs to be counseled by a psychiatrist right away. I'm the best person to do it."

"I don't know."

"Please, Hallie. I can help him. He trusts me and I've dealt with this kind of thing before. It's my specialty."

"Yes, but the Dickersons, well, they're . . . distraught. Saying crazy things. I don't think they'd give permission, is what I'm trying to say."

"Will you ask?"

"I already did."

The universe shrunk to the size of a pinprick. Then it expanded to an enormous space that threatened to collapse and send its atoms hurling in every direction. My skull began to vibrate.

"Mark, what's the matter? Mark?"

I let the handset drop to the floor. Hallie's voice continued to come over the wire, like the whine of an insect. I kicked at the dangling plastic with my foot and missed. I tried to kick it again, but all I met was air. I grabbed for the body of the phone and lifted it high in the air. I brought it down on the nightstand and smashed it into the wood. I didn't stop until the thing was just a piece of mangled wire and circuit board and the shards of the plastic casing were gouging my skin. Then I started on the bedside lamp. The smashing continued until I couldn't find anything else to hurt myself with.

When the tears finally came, they were three years too late . . .

NINE

I'd always been a loner. It was my mother's legacy to me, along with the bad gene I'm glad she never had to know about. Like so much of my life to come, my birth was a mess. Even then I did things my way and entered the world feet first, with my umbilical cord wrapped around my neck. She died not long after, of postpartum hemorrhage. This left me in the care of my father. He was a chemist, one of the few former enemy combatants to secure a visa after the war, and he worked in a research laboratory on Long Island, not far from our home in Queens. He should have remarried, but never did, perhaps out of loyalty to my mother, though I think it had more to do with outlook. I'd therefore grown up one of those rarities among Catholic families in the late sixties: an only child.

You can imagine the pressure this put me under. I wasn't just a male with the responsibility of living up to the family name. I was also on earth to prove myself worthy of my mother's sacrifice. To his credit, my father never openly reminded me of the way I was born. I think he loved me too much for that. But it was love of the controlling, suffocating variety for which Italian paterfamilias are famous, the kind I like to think even Jesus Christ would have fled from.

From an early age I could sense I wasn't meeting expectations. I was a scrawny child who daydreamed at school, didn't appear talented at anything, and had what they called a Mouth. My mouth had a mind of its own. I could never turn it off, least of all when my father was losing his temper. He never subjected me to real abuse, just a stinging slap when I talked back once too often, or time under the belt when I stayed out playing kick the can past curfew, punishment most parents in my neighborhood considered good child-rearing practice.

I didn't thrive under it, though. I was one of those kids who saw massive injustice in my circumstances, reinforced by the weekly torture of confession, where I had to own up anew to the many ways in which I'd disappointed my father—always overestimating them by half a dozen to be on the safe side. As the years went by, I developed a reputation for how much time I spent on my knees afterward, even though I had learned to race through an Act of Contrition like a Formula One driver. Around age ten, I decided that since I was going to stew in hell anyway, I might as well have some fun getting there.

My resistance started out small: lifting five-cent Bazookas from the cigar store on the corner, blowing up cherry bombs in garbage cans in the alley, listening to *avant-garde* music like the Rolling Stones, whose *Sticky Fingers* album, shoplifted from a Crazy Eddie's outlet when I was thirteen, sent my father into a celestial orbit to rival Pluto's. In high school my rebellion blossomed into long hair, more serious acts of theft, and sneaking joints behind the gym, where I was caught more than once by the savvy Jesuit fathers who watched over us. I don't lay claim to being a true outlaw here. In comparison to many teenagers then and now, my antics were tame. But in my particular household they were affronts to authority on the same order as the Budapest uprising. My father reacted with the same heavy-handed tactics as the Kremlin, though since he couldn't actually ship me off to the Soviet Bloc, without the same record of success.

Luckily, I was never caught in the act of doing something really stupid, like setting fire to the chemistry lab or hotwiring a Buick, nor did I ever manage to impregnate Angela Santorini, the local *puttana* in training, though I spent many happy hours in her parents' basement trying. By senior year my grades were abysmal and my disciplinary record worse. When I failed, naturally, to gain admission to a good college, it was clear to my father that I would never amount to anything more than a fast-talking salesman in one of the used-car outlets on Northern Boulevard. He didn't go so far as to disown me, but he made it clear that from then on I was on my own. I reacted the same way I always do when faced with a stiff challenge. Having confirmed every one of his worst fears, I set out to prove him wrong.

Fourteen years later, I had turned myself around and risen to something of a star. I wasn't all that smart, but I'd learned the value of hard work, which in my case consisted mainly of not having to think too much about my many shortcomings as a person. As long as I kept capturing the brass ring, I could reassure myself I wasn't all that bad. My obsession with winning didn't leave much room for relationships, but I told myself I didn't mind. I'd grown used to being alone, especially after my father died of cancer during my second year in medical school. I'd also discovered that women were attracted to success, and even though I only made passing grade in the looks department, I could have the pick of the lot at the Manhattan teaching hospital I'd joined after completing my fellowship: single doctors and nurses themselves just trying to keep pace with the long hours and the mold taking off in their refrigerators. In the years that followed I had a number of flings, none of them ever progressing to the live-in stage. They were good for keeping loneliness in check, but little else; just enough connection to let me continue to claim membership in the human race. I was content, or so I thought, to work and read and ride and fuck, more or less in that order, and occasionally enjoy a good meal out or a visit to my cousins in Italy.

And that's where things stood on the day in my late thirties when Roger Whittaker took me aside and told me it was time to marry.

Roger was my boss, the cold, brilliant offshoot of an old Hudson River clan. Distantly related to the Roosevelts, graduate of Exeter and Yale, inducted into Skull and Bones, the whole nine yards of what still counted as aristocracy in America if you left out the navel gazers in Hollywood. For some reason he didn't mind my outspokenness or my unglamorous family tree, and almost from the day I joined his department began grooming me to take his place when it came time for him to retire to the family's tree-shaded acreage near Poughkeepsie. We weren't close—Roger was too formal for that—but my upbringing had left me vulnerable to friendly attention from father-figure types, and I responded by doing everything I could to live up to his good opinion of me. So when Roger advised me there was a hole in my résumé where a family ought to be, I took him seriously.

Roger had a girl in mind: his fourth child and only daughter. Annie was twenty-nine and worked in a firm that advised the Fortunes on how to select the artwork that graced their executive suites. Roger arranged for us to meet at a cocktail party at the Greenwich Country Club, and right away I came under the spell of Annie's formidable charms. To this day, I don't know why. Before then I'd always shied away from trophy wives in the making, thinking they could have no interest in a sarcastic upstart like me. Annie fit the mold right down to the blonde hair and thoroughbred limbs that were a scarce commodity in the borough I hailed from. After Roger introduced us, we were together all night. I learned that she'd gone to a Seven Sisters school where she'd majored in art history and how to be fascinating to men. Her conversation was light and breezy and touched upon all the usual preoccupations of a Manhattan dweller with means—finding the right prewar apartment, the restoration of Central Park—along with fashion and the arts. Aside from her father, we had almost nothing in common. Yet she seemed to regard me as a potential match, and being flattered, it wasn't long before I started thinking in like terms. We were married in no time in a June ceremony in the same country club.

For a while it was fine. We bought a duplex in the Upper Eighties and a farmhouse near Fairfield for weekends and holidays. As a doctor's daughter, Annie understood the drill and made few demands on my time, filling the hours I was away with her own job, shopping, and a vast circle of friends. She was always impeccably groomed, right down to the last manicured fingernail, and I loved sinking into her honey-toned flesh at the end of a long day, sucking her perfect small breasts, and caressing her smooth thighs before thrusting to blissful release. The sex was so good that for a long time it blotted out everything else. So good, in fact, that I was unprepared for the day, not long after our second anniversary, when the fly in the ointment made its first appearance.

It was a Friday evening, and we'd gone to LeCirce after work to celebrate one of Annie's new accounts. As the waiter was clearing away the remains of our dessert soufflé, I woke up to the sight of Annie fluttering her fingers in my face.

"Mark?"

"Huh?" I said, coming to.

"What's the matter with you tonight? It's like I've been sitting here by myself the whole time."

"Really?" I said. "Do you think anyone's noticed? Maybe we can get a discount on the check."

"Very funny. I bet you can't remember one word I've said."

I couldn't, of course. Nor would I have cared to, being sure it was something I'd already heard a thousand times before and didn't have much interest in to begin with. But I could remember the odd sensation I'd been experiencing earlier, like I was standing across the room watching an undistinguished-looking fellow fiddle with his cutlery while his companion yakked heedlessly away. It didn't hit me like a sledgehammer. It wasn't startling enough for that. But the snapshot left no room for doubt: I had become one of those men who are bored with their wives.

In the months that followed I could only shake my head at my own stupidity. The woman I began seeing clearly for the first time that night was the same person I'd known from the very beginning, but I had been as blind to her as the man I was destined, with exacting fairness, to become. I couldn't excuse my own conduct, nor could I condemn Annie. It would have been easier if I'd been able to say, with any justification, that she was vapid or shallow or materialistic. But she wasn't any of those things. She was simply the uncomplicated daughter of a wealthy man, content to accept her privileged lot in life and not much given over to meditation on fate, or the universe, or the dark workings of the psyche. If I'd expected real companionship from her, I had no one to blame but myself. And I told myself I was asking for too much. The kind of kinship I wanted—that I now realized I'd been aching for my entire life—was granted only to a deserving few, and I wasn't going to be one of them. Meanwhile, it was enough, enviable even, to be hitched to a woman of such breeding and polish, who could look sensational in a cocktail dress and lean and graceful on a tennis court.

The first pregnancy resuscitated our marriage somewhat. There was so much to do and it gave Annie a fresh source of topics to chatter about. We traded our city digs for a shingled Colonial in Cos Cob, decorated a nursery, went to Lamaze classes. I started to commute to work by car. Annie carried the pregnancy well and looked great, hardly more than a bump until she blossomed in her eighth month. Her new proportions revived my interest in her sexually, though I missed the small breasts. It was delicious to press against her aqueous belly while I slid my penis up inside, next to where my son lay dozing in his little sac. For we'd known right away it was a boy; the ultrasound left no doubt. A grandson straight out of the box pleased Roger too and confirmed the wisdom of his choice of son-in-law. When I cut our baby's cord and cradled his tiny, warm head in the palm of my hand, I even allowed myself to think I could be happy with Annie again.

The day we brought Jack home was one of my few experiences of joy. My memories of swinging him over the threshold in his infant seat, of Annie and I laughing together while we tried to solve the Chinese puzzle of his various contraptions, of the rise and fall of his little chest as he lay snuggled between us in bed that night, still bring a knife blade to my chest.

But no advice manual in the world can prepare you for what happens next. There would have been tremendous strain, even if ours had been a good marriage and even if things hadn't gone so badly for us right from the start. Annie was not one of those women who take to birthing like cows or sheep. She'd labored for thirty-six hours before delivering Jack, and his large size required an impressive episiotomy. It was ages before she could sit comfortably without a bucket of ice packs underneath or walk without a sailor's gait. Then she had trouble breastfeeding; for a long time her nipples cracked and bled. Jack's colic started within days of getting him home and quickly built to a nightly ordeal of nonstop wailing. Within a short time we were haggard and snapping at each other. Nine months later we were still at it, and I was flunking Bonding 101.

Infants, I have to confess, have never been all that fascinating to me. Still, I might have developed a stronger attachment to Jack if I'd been allowed to do what came naturally. But even there my luck was off. Once she'd gotten past the initial physical pains, Annie turned to mothering with the fervor of a novitiate. It took her a nanosecond to decide that working again was out of the question, and it was equally plain to her that, biology to one side, parenthood was a calling for which fathers need not apply. Despite years of medical training, I was deemed instantly incompetent, not even trustworthy enough to juggle Jack during his evening squalls or change the occasional diaper. Bottles too were out of the question; they would cause nipple confusion. This left me with little to do but truck to the store when we ran out of Huggies and phone every other evening for Chinese. On the rare days when I was allowed to spend time alone with Jack, he barely seemed to recognize me, brightening only when Annie returned to scoop him up, amid squeals of mutual delight.

But there was more to it than just being left out of the party. I'd become impatient with Annie again. When she wasn't cooing at Jack or waving a developmentally appropriate toy in his face, she was boning up on motherhood like it was a graduate course in quantum physics. Soon my library ended up in boxes in the attic to make way for those best-sellers that equate routine baby care with the operating instructions for a nuclear submarine. Our adult conversation, such as it ever was, dwindled to zero. And forget about sex. Annie's tenderness ruled out even that small consolation for the better part of a year, and she wasn't as appealing anymore. The nursing made it hard to lose those last ten pounds and her swollen, vein-rich breasts were not to my taste, even if I could have brought myself to share them with my son.

I wasn't so shallow that I didn't understand what was happening. Part of what we were undergoing was the great Freudian drama that plays itself out in every family. I was experiencing a father's primitive rage at being displaced in the marital bed. Soon the tables would be turned when Jack started fantasizing my end so he could have Annie all to himself. But that didn't stop me from feeling trapped. Annie had already explained there would have to be more children, three at least, possibly four if the next one wasn't a girl, so I could expect new contenders for the throne to keep arriving every second year. And when I wasn't at work she expected me to be an energetic cheerleader of her love affair with my son. I wasn't allowed to read a book, or work on my bike, or follow the tale of Jack's latest triumph merely by grunting every so often.

I grew even more bored with her. And then bitter. And then disgusted with myself for being so unlike all the other new fathers I was now expected to socialize with, who seemed just as besotted with their offspring as their wives.

Maybe it would have helped if Jack had resembled me. But he was pure Whittaker, large and pale and towheaded. I couldn't find a single point of identification, not even after Jack grew out of infancy, passed his first birthday, and started displaying a personality. By that time Annie had pulled off becoming pregnant again—a feat nearly as miraculous as the Annunciation—meaning Jack had to give up his habit of snacking at her breasts whenever he liked. He reacted to the sudden deprivation by becoming a whiney, overbearing tyrant. I wasn't surprised. Annie couldn't manage the slightest brinkmanship with him, even though she was the one with the arsenal. Jack began refusing to go to sleep at night. I wanted to drop him in his crib and shut the door, figuring he'd eventually get the message, but Annie couldn't sit through ten minutes of his crying. So evenings in our home became a wearying cycle of threats, counterthreats, and ultimatums Jack could see right through—because they were never enforced—until he finally passed out, lathered with sweat and tears, sometime after the eleven o'clock news.

In the time-honored tradition of male absenteeism I fled, throwing myself into work, spending more and more late nights in the city. And though I tried to resist it, the temptation eventually overcame me. I started seeing other women.

Not many, you understand. With my father-in-law right there in the hospital I had to be careful. I didn't do it often either, maybe once or twice a month, with a few women who understood it was for recreation, not for keeps, and who liked me well enough to accept it on those terms. They were as easy to find as in the old days, and because they were now forbidden, more interesting. My liaisons required secrecy, evasion, sometimes even the construction of elaborate falsehoods, and I enjoyed the modest peril this put me in. It dulled my senses to what was going on at home and sharpened my wits at work. If I'd stopped even once to think about what I was doing, or what it was making me into, I would have been able to shrug it off, because by that time the habit of lying to myself had become ingrained.

The day it all ended started innocently enough. It was May and close to the summer solstice, so I'd been able to take my morning ride early. I couldn't leave for work early though, because Jack was running a fever.

"I'm really worried about him," Annie said, as I was knotting my tie in front of the bedroom mirror. The skin under her eyes was puckered and gray from lack of sleep. Annie was always anxious about Jack's health, and even more so lately as she neared her second due date, only three weeks away.

"How high was his fever when you last checked?"

"Hundred and one."

"That's nothing," I said. "Kids his age are always running fevers that high. Probably just a cold. Or teeth. Is he drooling?"

"Yes, but I think it's an ear infection. He never really got over the last one. And he was so cranky last night."

I let that pass and started looking around for my shoes.

"Can't you take him to the pediatrician for me?"

"Right now? I have a consult scheduled at nine." I spotted the heel of a loafer peeking from under the bedclothes and reached down for it.

"Please? Or look at him yourself?"

"OK, OK. Do you know where I left the otoscope last time?"

I didn't see anything amiss when I looked in Jack's ears, and once I'd ruled out an infection I wasn't concerned. The fever wasn't at all high for a toddler and his gums looked sore, so second-year molars were probably the answer. Of course, it was wrong to diagnose my own child, but it was easier than having to haul him to his pediatrician every third day, and I really did need to get to the hospital on time. I told Annie that Jack should have Tylenol every four hours and to call me if his fever climbed much higher. Then I left for work, a good thirty minutes later than usual.

By the time I reached the Henry Hudson the traffic was bumper to bumper. I passed the time in my customary way, with a journal balanced against the steering wheel. It was a dangerous habit but a good antidote to New York road rage, and I did it often. Recently I'd noticed it was getting harder to read small print, which I'd put down to needing reading glasses, so I switched on the lamp over the dashboard to make it easier to see. By the time I got to work I was late for my consult, a bipolar man in his fifties who went into full meltdown halfway through the interview. The rest of the day snowballed from there, and by 6:00 p.m. the back of my neck felt like it had been used to tug merchant vessels up and down the East River. I was looking forward to a date that night with a woman I'd been seeing recently, a whip-thin anesthesiologist with an appetite for ethnic food and athletic lovemaking. I'd already prepared Annie for a late-night arrival, telling her I was trying to catch up on things so I'd be able to spend more time at home when the new baby arrived.

Just as I was walking out the door at 6:45, Annie called.

"Mark, Jack's getting worse."

"How's that?"

"He's crying all the time and I can't get him to stop."

No surprise there. "When did you last check his temperature?"

"Ten minutes ago. It's up to almost a hundred and three."

Once more, I didn't see anything to be worried about, and I was impatient to get to my date. "Annie, I've told you over and over. Fevers in young kids, even high ones, are nothing to get upset about. Put him to bed early—for a change—and he'll be fine in the morning."

"Can't you come home? I've been having contractions all day and I'm exhausted from dealing with him."

It's funny how one moment of selfishness can derail an entire life. I didn't want to do it. I needed time away from Jack and it was just a fever, after all. Annie always overreacted to the slightest sneeze, and it was her fault the kid was such a brat. If she needed a break, she could ask our live-in to watch him. The woman should have been doing something to earn her salary. So I lied and said I was in the middle of an emergency. I told Annie I'd get home as soon as I could, but she shouldn't count on anything earlier than eleven. I said she should continue to administer Tylenol every few hours and to page me if the fever climbed past 104. And then I left to meet my date.

In classic fashion, it wasn't a good time. Rachel had been through a hellish day too, losing a patient on the operating-room table. She was sure it was nobody's fault, but it was always upsetting when it happened. The atmosphere was grim as we slogged through our meal, drinking too much and finding each other's company less inspiring than usual. When we got to her apartment in the West Eighties, I turned off my cell phone and pager, as I always did during sex. Haplessly, afterward, I forgot to turn them back on. And then I did something else I seldom did: I fell asleep.

When I woke a little after ten there was still time to make it home on time if I ignored the speed limit, but when I reached my car the battery was dead. I'd neglected to turn off the dashboard lamp that morning and it had spent the entire day draining my battery. It was forty-five minutes before I could get a jump from the garage attendant, another thirty before I reached the Cross-Westchester and I-95. There I got stuck in a long line of cars behind a semi that had just tipped over outside the Byram exit. By the time they got it cleared, I was already ninety minutes past my deadline. When I walked in the door after midnight, trying to construct an excuse for what had kept me out so late, Annie was beyond hysteria. She'd been trying to reach me for hours. Why hadn't I called? Jack's fever was up to 106. He'd stopped crying an hour ago and was now lying listlessly in his crib. I took one look at his stiff posture and unnatural pallor and knew immediately what it was. I wasted no time getting him to the emergency room, ran every red light on the way, but by the time we got there it was too late for the antibiotics to do much good.

My son was dead, of meningitis, by the following morning.

The next day, while I was packing my suitcase, I told Annie where I'd been that night, and other nights as well. I didn't say I was sorry because I wasn't asking for or expecting any forgiveness. I understood perfectly when she said she never wanted to see me again: I wished that option had been available to me, too. Even at the funeral she hadn't looked at me once, not during the brief ceremony or after, when she walked from Jack's grave on her father's arm with the tears spilling down onto the folds of her black maternity dress. I wasn't able to cry, though there was a moment when they were lowering the tiny coffin into the ground when I felt unsteady and thought I might not be able to keep upright.

I knew better than to expect any mercy from Roger. I'd broken the sacred covenant, failed to protect his daughter and grandson, the most important responsibility I'd been given. It didn't matter that Annie was a competent adult who could have called a doctor, or an ambulance, or even Roger as the evening went on and Jack's condition worsened. Causation was beside the point. We met the afternoon of the funeral, at the offices of the Whittaker family's attorneys in downtown Greenwich. Roger's eyes shone with icy malice from his wing chair across the room while the lawyer laid down my sentence. The divorce would be uncontested in every respect. I could have my own attorney look at the papers if I cared to, but propose no alterations. There would be a small settlement for Annie, a token for appearances' sake, because her trust fund was more than adequate for her needs. I would pay full support for the child soon to be born until he reached his majority. I would relinquish all rights to custody and visitation, save for one annual meeting at a time and place acceptable to Annie. I would leave the hospital where I worked and find new employment out-of-state. Roger would lend his backing to the search and provide appropriate recommendations. Neither side would ever speak of the matters leading to the split.

I agreed to everything. I had proved myself utterly worthless, as both a father and a man, so what did it matter? Ten days later, Annie gave birth to our second son, whom she named Louis. The only time I saw him in person was through the window of the hospital nursery while Annie was napping in her room. I accepted the job from Sep and moved to Chicago. I didn't think it was appropriate to insist on my paternal visit the first year, but Annie sent me a photograph of Louis taken on his first birthday. I still carried it in my wallet. When the second birthday photo arrived, I was already deep into my mobility training with Cherie.

True to my promise to Roger—I owed Annie that much—I never breathed a word about what happened, not to a single soul. No one in Chicago was aware I'd been married, much less buried a child. I think Josh suspected a relationship of some kind, but we'd fallen out of touch after medical school, and he knew me well enough not to pry. Sep had never asked, and my other colleagues probably thought I was gay. If so, I did nothing to correct the misimpression. I wanted no more women in my life and had been celibate since the day I left Annie.

Many hours after I had trashed my bedroom I found myself hugging my knees on the floor of my outdoor terrace, still in my pajamas. There was a gauze bandage pulled tightly around my lower left arm and an old blanket around my shoulders. A bottle of bourbon lay on its side nearby, nearly empty. I vaguely recalled tugging it open with my teeth when I had started drinking late in the morning. My feet were bare and there was a dense fog rolling in from the Lake, pressing against my naked skin like a wet cloth. I was shaking from the damp and the booze and my insides felt as though they had been scoured, wiped clean of everything except a dull, steady ache in the chest.

I know it's been said the unexamined life isn't worth living, but that day I would have given anything to forget mine. For the second time in my sorry existence I had failed someone who was counting on me, an innocent entrusted to my safekeeping, whether I welcomed it or not. I hadn't just broken my Hippocratic Oath, I had annihilated it. First Jack, then Charlie . . . I had let harm come to both, and all because of my lies to myself. Lies that had kept me from ending my marriage to Annie when it was so clearly a failure. Lies that had me thinking I could still do my job after Jack's death finally caught up with me. Lies that had me jumping to meet Di Marco's challenge when I had no business playing courtroom wizard. Lies that, if you went back far enough, had stopped me from returning my father's flawed love.

And then there was the biggest lie of them all.

I couldn't keep the lies up anymore.

Except as they might be needed to save Charlie.

TEN

The next morning I woke at dawn and cleared my head with two hours of riding and a long, scalding shower. If I'd been a real tough-guy detective, I would have followed this with fried green tomatoes and a steak from the meat keeper, washed down by a pot of strong black coffee. But I'd stopped drinking coffee after medical school and meat always spoils in my refrigerator, so I contented myself with tea, some heart-healthy cereal, and a banana that didn't leak when I squeezed it. After breakfast I phoned Yelena and asked her to cancel my appointments for the day. Then I dressed and packed a small backpack with a spare cane and my notetaker, a Braille PDA with wireless capability that I'd nicknamed my Blindberry. By 9:00 a.m. I was in the elevator going down with one of my building's paid dog walkers. One of her charges wrapped his leash around my ankles, but I curbed my hostility and merely wished her a good day.

Down on the street, I hailed a cab and asked to be taken to the station house where Detective O'Leary worked. When we arrived I asked the driver for directions to the front door. "Right there, bud," he said, adding by way of elaboration, "in front." I was weary of explaining that if I was asking for directions to the door it must mean I couldn't see where he was pointing, so I just paid the fare and went out to map the terrain on my own. There were several police cruisers with honking radios in my way, but I banged through a crevice between them, found the sidewalk, and continued up half a dozen steps. A throng of people were milling around at the top. I waited for things to clear before squeezing through the revolving door.

Inside a woman was shouting over the din of ringing phones and clacking keyboards. "You muthafuckas! I gotta see my man right now. He holdin' my check. I got babies to feed."

Someone replied, "Ma'am, his lawyer's on the way. That's all I can say to you."

"His lawyer? Hah! That sonafabitch put a lien on us."

The shouting went on, but at least it told me where the reception desk was. I walked over until my cane hit something solid, and said, "Can someone help me?"

No one answered. I repeated my request, a little louder this time.

"Kelly," a gruff voice said, "you're on Human Affairs duty today. Help out the man in the shades, will you?" The man identified as Kelly came over and asked me what I needed.

"I'd like to see Detective O'Leary," I said.

"You got an appointment with him?"

"No," I said. "But it's urgent."

"How urgent?"

"Well, let me see. A grave injustice has been committed and an innocent man's life hangs in the balance. Is that good enough for you?"

"A wiseass," Kelly commented. "You really blind?"

"No, I'm actually a sociologist conducting field research into attitudes toward the disabled." I lifted my cane. "This is just something I carry around in case I get a sudden urge to shoot a game of pool."

"Plenty of that round the corner, though I wouldn't advise you to go in there without a long session in Tancun. What're you doing in this neighborhood anyway? You gotta death wish?"

"Like I said, I'm here to see Detective O'Leary."

"Well, he's not in. Went out a while back."

"When do you expect him to return?"

"Got me. See, part of being a detective is the hours ain't regular. If you'd phoned ahead, maybe his personal assistant could have told you that."

"Is it OK if I wait for him?"

"Suit yourself. The guest suite's over there."

I followed the sounds coming from the woman who'd been shouting earlier, who was now snuffling and wheezing on a bench to the left of the door.

"You sit down right here, honey," she said when I came up.

"You crazy, lady?" a basso voice next to her said. "There ain't enough room on this bench for a jailhouse shiv."

"Enough room for your nigger ass. Either move or get up. Can't you see this man is blind?"

"That's all right," I said. "If there's no place for me, I can stand."

But my new friend was not to be denied. I heard sounds of shoving and grumbling before I was pulled down onto the seat.

"What's your name?" she asked, when I was at last squeezed into the six-inch space next to her.

"Mark. Yours?"

"Letitia. Letitia Miller. Glad to make your acquaintance."

We shook hands. Letitia's was soft and well-padded, as was her thigh, which was overflowing mine on the hard wooden seating.

"What you here for?"

"My dog's been stolen," I said.

"Your dog! You hear that?" she asked our companions on the bench. "Somebody stole this man's dog. Ain't no civility in the world no more. He gotta name, this dog?" she asked me kindly.

"Trigger," I said.

"Trigger," she repeated. "I like that. Why you name him that?"

"On account of his temper. He's a pit bull."

"You gotta pit bull to take you around? Well I never! But I s'pose a body like you needs protection."

I was about to remark that I also had a guide horse named Silver, when I remembered one of my resolutions from the night before. "Forgive me, Ms. Miller," I said. "I was just pulling your leg. I'm here about a friend. What about you?"

I listened patiently while Letitia told me her life story. How she'd become pregnant at fifteen by a guy who was now in Pontiac doing twenty-five to life for aggravated assault. How his knack for landing in trouble had been passed on to their son, who was now doing a similar spell in the same institution. How this had left Letitia in charge of an extended family consisting of more sons and daughters by various fathers and a flock of grandchildren. How her current beau had just been picked up for trying to fence a carload of stolen auto parts. Letitia was hopping mad about this, having told him she wanted no more truck with the criminal element in her home. I clucked and sympathized at all the right points, wondering when the cycle would end. She seemed like a nice lady whose only sin was wanting to be loved by someone.

Around 11:45 I caught the hint of someone standing over me. "You wanted to see me?" It was Detective O'Leary.

I asked whether there was somewhere we could talk.

"Sure," O'Leary said. "We could go back to my boudoir, or we could do it over food. I've been out all morning and didn't get breakfast. That is, if you don't mind dining with the enemy."

"I'd like to think we weren't enemies. More like fellow truth seekers."

"Truth can be a dangerous thing. Remember what happened to Socrates."

"Am I at risk of being poisoned if I accept?" I asked.

"Only if you chew with your mouth open."

"Don't worry. I'm housebroken," I said. "I can even eat with something besides my fingers."

I gave Letitia one of my cards and told her to call me if there was anything I could do for her. I'd figured O'Leary for an Italian Beef guy, but he drove us to a storefront in Pilsen where they sold homemade tortillas served with *carnitas* ordered by the pound. "I'm addicted to this stuff," he told me, "though it isn't doing my waistline much good. If it weren't for Lipitor my cholesterol would make you cry." We each ordered half a pound. O'Leary was hungry and so was I, so it wasn't until we'd wiped our plates clean that he asked me what I wanted.

"I want to clear Charlie Dickerson," I said.

"And you thought I'd be anxious to tackle such a project, being his arresting officer and such."

"Do you really believe he's guilty?"

O'Leary thought this over before saying, "Doesn't matter what I think. Only thing that matters is the department's clearance rate."

"Don't give me that Claude Rains, round-up-all-the-usual-suspects routine."

"And don't you go thinking this is going to be the start of a beautiful friendship."

"I'd settle for a temporary cessation of hostilities while you hear me out."

"OK," O'Leary said. "I'm listening. But it's gonna have to be something really good to override a videotaped confession and DNA evidence pointing the finger directly at the kid."

"I've listened to the confession. It's garbage and you know it. Charlie hadn't been allowed out of the room for three hours and was frantic he'd wet his pants. It's right there on the tape. I'm told he was squirming in his seat like a fish on dry land."

"I dunno. We'd have let him go to the potty if he insisted."

"But he wouldn't. That's my point. People like Charlie are intimidated by authority figures. By everyone of normal intelligence, for that matter. They've spent their whole lives being told what to do and when to do it. Your guys filled him up with pop until his bladder was ready to detonate and then kept telling him ten more minutes. Just agree to what we're saying, Charlie, and we'll let you pee."

"At least you're not accusing us of withholding food and water."

"That would have been too obvious. But to a boy like Charlie who's been taught that soiling himself is shameful, something *retarded* people do when they haven't been trained properly, your tactics couldn't miss. He didn't stand a chance."

O'Leary said, "Just for the sake of argument, let's say I agree with you. What do you make then of the fact that he was there, covered in the victim's blood?"

"Pure coincidence. Anyone could have killed Shannon Sparrow in that alley and walked off. The fact that Charlie was the first on the scene doesn't prove anything. No one's ever found the murder weapon. You have Charlie's testimony that he didn't understand at first. Her blood was on him because he did what any curious, not very intelligent kid would have done—he reached down to touch it. Then, when it dawned on him what it was, he got scared and tried to wipe it off on his shirt. The stains were consistent with that. And there wasn't any blood spatter."

"So?"

"So how did he knife Shannon in the chest without making a bigger mess?"

"Medical examiner said the blade went in under the sternum and right into the endocardium. Death would have been almost instantaneous and the wound was small enough to internalize most of the blood flow."

"Which by itself is suspicious. They don't give anatomy lessons to kids like Charlie. Whoever did it knew just how to kill Shannon, quickly and efficiently. And why didn't she scream?"

"You saying she was strangled first? Or drugged? ME didn't find any signs of that."

"There are other ways to do it. Like this." I reached both hands across the table until I found his neck. "Don't worry," I said, "I'm not trying to find out what you look like."

"Good," O'Leary said. "'Cause I guarantee you won't like what you see."

I located his carotid arteries just below his ears and pressed down hard. "If I keep this up for thirty seconds you'll pass out." I pressed harder to drive home the point.

"All right, all right," O'Leary said, removing my hands. "I've heard of this. Isn't it a martial-arts move?"

"Yeah. It's called a sleeper hold. But it's something anyone with a medical background would know about. Hell, you could probably find out how to do it on Answers.com. But not Charlie. He wouldn't understand."

"OK, so your theory is someone put the victim under and then knifed her? But why not just slip a blade into her right away? She was a little thing—it's not like she would have been hard to overpower."

"Maybe she knew her assailant and he was trying to keep her from crying out his name."

O'Leary grunted. "Sounds like a stab in the dark, if you'll excuse the expression."

"And why did you change your mind about it being the same person who killed those nurses—the Surgeon?"

"Physical evidence didn't match up. And I'll let you in on a little secret, if you'll promise not to blab it to the reporters. We've been holding something back about those other deaths. We knew all along Dickerson couldn't have done them."

I gaped at him. "That's not what your friend Di Marco said at the bond hearing. Charlie would have been free today if he'd said so. You heard about what happened to him at the jail?"

"Yeah, and I'm none too happy about it myself. If it'd been up to me, I would have let the kid go home with his folks. But Di Marco gets to call the shots in court. There was nothing I could do."

"Tell yourself that often, do you?" I said, not even trying to disguise my anger.

"Don't get pissy with me or this *tête-à-tête* will be over faster than the Cubs can lose a one o'clock start. I'd like to help, but you gotta understand how the system works. I'd be in trouble if anyone knew we were even having this conversation. The only reason I'm here is because I respect you. Can't be easy . . . I mean, with your handicap."

I shook my head with impatience. "Save the sympathy for Charlie. He's the one who needs it. What was different about those other murders?"

"I was being a tease when I brought up Socrates before. The Surgeon left a calling card at his crime scenes—a sprig of hemlock. Probably got it from a cheap thriller. But it makes sense in a screwed-up way. The vics were all hospice workers, and a couple were known to be sympathetic to assisted suicide, may have even helped a few folks along. The prevailing theory is that the Surgeon is some sort of right-to-life advocate. We figure he—or she, since it could be a woman—may be trying to send a message about mercy killing, taking an eye for an eye, if you'll pardon my saying so. Sparrow worked with some pretty messed-up people, but as far as we know she never pulled the plug on anyone."

"And you didn't find any exotic plant matter nearby?"

"No. We took that alley apart and there was nothing like it."

"It could have blown away," I said. "And how do you know it wasn't a copycat killing, someone trying to make it look like the Surgeon's work?"

"I don't for sure. But we couldn't find anyone besides your friend who had a motive to kill her. You're a psychiatrist. You should know that nine times out of ten violent deaths are committed by someone close to the victim."

"OK, but that still doesn't rule out other people. What about her friends and family?"

"We asked around but didn't find much. She lived alone, had a roommate up until December, but they had a falling out and the girl moved away. Most of her family's down in Carbondale. Only one sister lives up here. The two didn't get along, rarely saw one another."

"Would you be willing to give me their names?"

"It's a matter of public record. But what do you think you're going to find out? Hell, man, I hate to point this out, but you can't even see the people you talk to. You think you can spot something we didn't?"

"Maybe I won't just accept the first theory I happen to walk into."

"Are you always this winning? The fact is, I don't have time to chase down every possibility in creation when I've got DNA evidence proving the kid knocked her up. Even you have to admit it looks bad for him that they were sleeping together."

Since we were in such an amicable mode I told him my idea.

O'Leary was sharp. He caught on right away. "Interesting," he said when I'd finished. "You want me to find out if the fetus was a girl?"

"That would be a place to start."

"All right. It's seems like a long shot, but I'll do it, if only to keep you from wasting your time. On one condition."

I nodded.

"After that, you leave this thing alone. If you're right and there's another killer out there—the Surgeon or someone else—he's gonna be none too happy about you sticking your neck out. Last thing I need is some blind shrink screwing up an investigation."

"So you're saying you won't give up—on trying to find the real killer, that is."

"I'm saying that if I find out you've been playing the vigilante Charlie won't be the only one enjoying the hospitality of the taxpayer. Do I make myself clear?"

"Sorry, my lip-reading skills aren't what they used to be."

O'Leary's tone grew cold. "OK, pal, do it your way. Only don't say you weren't warned."

ELEVEN

Shannon's sister lived on the far South Side in a neighborhood called Brainerd. I had the cabbie take me around the block several times before dropping me off in front of the house. I scraped my way up a short concrete walk bordered by a wooden fence. It had warmed up some from the weekend, but the day was still stormy. When I rang the bell there was no one about. Rain pelted the aluminum awning overhead like a sack of loose marbles, and a freight train hooted mournfully in the distance. Inside, something like a vacuum whined steadily. On my third attempt a woman called out, "OK, OK. I heard you. Keep your pants zipped while I shut this thing off."

"You lose your watch or something?" she growled upon opening the door. "What in the hell is wrong with you people? I've been cooped up here all day running low on smokes and no one had the manners to call and tell me you'd be late. Eight to twelve you was supposed to be here. This keeps up and I'm switching to satellite." Her speech had a twang but not full south, and the rasp of a heavy smoker.

"Well, actually—"

"Never mind. You're here now. Come on in. The set's in the den. I hope you brought a new box. I told the fellow was here last month the one we got now is a lemon. My husband had a fit missing the Aaron's 449 on Sunday. Well, whatcha waiting on?" She stomped into the house, apparently expecting me to follow.

I tapped the door frame and stepped over the threshold into a rug that squirted underfoot like it had been used to sponge down a fleet of Freightliners.

"Don't bother to take your shoes off. Your socks will get wet and

I need to give it another once-over anyway. Damn kids treat this place like a barnyard."

I took another tentative step into the room, not sure which way to go.

She must have noticed then.

"Well butter my ass and call me a corncob," she said.

"That's a colorful expression," I said. "Is it regional?"

"Christ almighty!" she said. "I've been waiting four days for a technician to come out and *you're* what they send me?"

"My company has a policy of nondiscrimination."

"I should've guessed from the kind of service I'm getting. Blind leading the blind, if you don't mind me saying so."

I didn't. Based on my own cable reception, it was hard to argue with her.

"Well, I guess I don't care, so long as you know what you're doing."

"Are you Marilyn Sparrow?"

She became mistrustful then. "Say, what is this? You're not the cable man. Who are you? If you're from the collection agency, you can just turn around and go back out the way you came. We're current since April."

"I'm not here about a debt," I said.

She continued without paying attention to me. "And if you're selling magazines I don't need another subscription to *TV Guide*. I still got thirty-six months on the last one you sold me."

"Not that either," I said, reaching in my jacket and getting out one of my cards. "I'm a psychiatrist. I was hoping to talk to you about your sister, Shannon."

She took the card and read it. "A psychiatrist? What do you want to know about Shannon for? She may have been a bitch, but she wasn't crazy."

This wasn't quite the reaction I'd been expecting, but I went on with the tale I'd concocted while my cab was circling the neighborhood. "I read about Shannon's death in the newspapers. I'm working on a study of bereavement in families who've lost their loved ones to violent crime and I'm looking for candidates to include in my research."

"I don't have time for no survey," she said.

"It's not a survey. It's serious academic research, and I'd be grateful for even a few minutes of your time." I was already walking a thin line but added, "Of course, you'd be compensated if you were accepted into the study."

She didn't leap for it immediately, though money was obviously an issue. "I don't know."

"It won't take very long. And I could really use the help." I switched to a confiding tone. "You see, my job's on shaky ground right now owing to my . . . uh, eye problem. I can't afford to be laid off."

That softened her. "I know what that's all about. Randy, that's my husband, was out nine months last year with his gout and the bosses damn near fired him. Bastards always hit you hardest when you're down. And you're legit, right? Not another one of those damn reporters?"

"I'm not a journalist and I guarantee you nothing you tell me will end up in the newspapers. I just want a few words about how your family is handling the loss."

She snorted. "Well, you won't find much grieving going on inside these four walls, I can tell you. I don't like to speak ill of the dead, but that girl had it coming."

"Could we sit down?"

Her Midwestern hospitality came to the fore. "Sure. You want something to drink? I could put some coffee on."

"A glass of water if it's not too much trouble."

She showed me to a stiff sofa covered in a crocheted afghan and went off to the kitchen. From the lightness of her tread I guessed she was lean. The room smelled of stale cigarette smoke, rug cleaner, and vomit.

"Sorry about the smell," she said when she returned with my water. She seated herself in a chair nearby, lit a cigarette with the snap of a lighter, and blew a stream of smoke toward me. "I been working all day to get it out. Teenagers, you know." She lowered her voice and said, "Don't go telling the troopers on me, but I pretend I don't know they drink here. I'd just as soon as have 'em do it at home where it's safe.

Damn country. Kids going off to war and coming back cripples but they can't even take a sip from time to time."

Out of politeness I asked, "How many children do you have?"

"Two. A girl and a boy. Twins. We couldn't manage more on the money we make. Randy, that's my husband, works the night shift at US Steel and I'm a floor manager at Sears. You're lucky I was here when you called. I took a sick day so I could get the TV fixed. They're good kids. I don't know what I'm gonna do when they're gone next year, it'll be so quiet around here. Maggie, that's my girl, is going to Piven Beauty School on the north side so she'll be home weekends, but Shawn just got accepted at SIU."

"Southern Illinois. Isn't that where Shannon went?"

"Yeah. Only one in the family who got to go to college. The rest of us were out chasing a paycheck the day after high-school graduation. Nine kids in all. You don't see that much these days but my parents were raised in the faith. Mama wouldn't even think of taking the pill. Shannon was the youngest. She got a four-year degree and came up here straight away. The rest of the family's still in Carbondale. Getting out of that armpit was the only thing Shannon and I ever had in common. Though I guess I'll be visiting more regular now that Shawn will be down there." She dragged deeply on her cigarette and sent another stream of smoke my way.

"Did you grow up on a farm?"

"Shit no. My dad was a miner. We lived in a little town in the coal belt, DuQuoin is its name, until the mine closed down. Union officials thought they were doing good by the workers, but all they did was give the owner a reason to sell. After he was laid off, only job Dad could get was managing a Clark station in Carbondale so we had to move there. Shannon came along six months later. I was fourteen then."

"So there were a lot of years between you."

"Yeah. When Shannon was born mama was in her late forties. Being a late baby and so on, she was spoiled silly. Some kids brought up that way turn out like saints, but not Shannon. It just gave her airs. Didn't help she was so pretty." Marilyn lit another cigarette and said, "I have a picture of her if you'd like to see it." Then: "Oh. Sorry, I wasn't thinking."

"Actually, I would like a picture if you have one. For the study, that is."

Marilyn slipped out of her seat and went to rummage in a drawer across the room. When she returned, she handed me a three-by-two photo. "Her graduation photo from Southern," she said. "You can keep it," she said.

I pocketed the photo and asked how often she and Shannon saw one another before she died.

"Hardly ever. We weren't good enough for her majesty to visit except on holidays and then all she did was complain about how lousy the food was. Last Thanksgiving my sister Jolene drove all the way up here with a Jello mold, one she'd made herself, shaped like a turkey with colored marshmallows and all. OK, so it wasn't gourmet, but it was cute, you know. Shannon wouldn't even touch it. Said she wasn't gonna eat like trailer trash any more. I told her the only trash was in her mouth."

"Did she ever bring a boyfriend with her?"

"Once. Year before last, I think. Professional type in his thirties. Already bald as an egg, but going places to judge by his clothes. I don't know why she dragged him here, except to show him how low-class we were. I had a good time laying on the country accent for him. Randy said you woulda thought I'd just stepped out of *Coal Miner's Daughter*. I figured I scared him off when he didn't come around again." She cackled, apparently pleased with herself.

"Do you remember his name?"

"Uh-uh."

"Do you know if she had any other relationships?"

"If she did, she didn't tell me about them. But it wouldn't surprise me. Shannon always had some guy in her sights. Only reason she wasn't married already is cause of how picky she was. It wasn't just money she was looking for, though she wanted plenty of that. It was a prestige thing. She wanted to get hitched to somebody important so she could play society wife, show everyone how far she'd come. That's how come I know she didn't do it with that retard."

"Oh?"

"He wouldn't have been good enough for her, even with all the family money. You shoulda heard how she made fun of the people at that place she worked, calling them the Freak Squad and so on. Not much sympathy for the handicapped there, I'll tell you."

This didn't square with what I'd heard about Shannon's affection for her students, but I couldn't let on I knew anything about her.

"It takes a special kind of person to work with the intellectually disabled. You're saying Shannon didn't do it by choice?"

"More like she was forced into it. At school she had ideas of being a great artist. Came up here expecting to be discovered. Caught her up short when nobody wanted to buy her paintings. Wasn't all her fault. I mean, look at what they call art nowadays. Shannon wasn't no Thomas Kinkade, but at least her stuff didn't look like somebody just barfed up their Pizza Hut. Anyway, it wasn't long before she started calling herself an art therapist. Sounded fancier than babysitter I guess, though the pay was just as bad. That's why I was surprised when she started taking all those vacations."

"Vacations?"

"Yeah, weekends to Hawaii, Phoenix, places like that. Had to lord it over us by sending postcards from all the fancy resorts she was staying at. I thought it showed some kind of nerve. Flying all over the damn country and she couldn't even make it down to Dad's funeral last year. Nearly broke my mother's heart when she didn't show. I could have killed her just for that. But it was like I told the police, she wasn't worth the trouble."

I let that slide for the moment. "These vacations, do you know if she was traveling alone?"

"I doubt it. But what does this all have to do with why you're here? I thought we were going to talk about my feelings and all?"

She was sharper than I had given her credit for.

"You'll forgive me for saying so, but you don't sound very broken up over Shannon's death. Was there some other reason besides skipping your father's funeral?"

Marilyn shook another cigarette out of her pack. "Shit," she said, "I'm almost out. You have brothers and sisters?"

I told her no.

"I think there's one in every big family, you know. A kid all the others just can't stand. Shannon was like that. Maybe you'll think it was jealousy, her getting so much more attention than the rest of us. But there was more to it than that. It was like she didn't have proper feelings for other people. Selfish and mean and . . . I can't think of the right word for it, but everything she did had a reason behind it."

"Calculating?"

"Yeah, that's the word. Calculating. Always had what they call a superior motive. 'Course I shed a tear or two when she was killed. Nobody ought to go that young or like she did. But as I said to Randy, there's more going on here than meets the eye." She paused and added, "Sorry, I shouldna said it that way."

"It's all right. What do you think really happened, then?"

"Well, in the first place, like I told you, I don't think she was sleeping with that boy, what's his name?"

"Charlie Dickerson."

"Right. I mean from the pictures in the paper, he's a looker, but they say he's got the mind of a child. And then there was the message she left the day before she died. The one I told that detective about, heavyset guy looks like he oughta be a bouncer."

"Detective O'Leary?" I said before I remembered I wasn't supposed to know who he was. She didn't notice the slip and went on.

"Yeah. Shannon left it on our answering machine here, though Lord knows why she didn't just call me on my cell. All sweet and nice for a change. Said she was going to have a medical procedure and would I mind giving her a ride home afterward? Said it hadn't been scheduled yet, but if I agreed she'd set it up for one of my days off so I wouldn't be put out. Wanted to know what my shifts were like for the next couple weeks."

"Did she say what kind of procedure?"

"No, just that it was nothing serious. Outpatient surgery, but she'd have to go under anesthetic and they wouldn't let her go afterward without someone to take her home. I figured she was getting a boob job, but now I think maybe she was talking about a D and C. Anyhow, knowing Shannon there's a story there. I can't believe she'd get herself pregnant by accident."

I wanted to know more about the exact words Shannon used, but my cover was already wearing perilously thin. "You didn't have a chance to return the call before she died?"

"I was still thinking it over when we got word of what happened. Shannon was never there when I needed her, and I wasn't sure I oughta be wasting a day off chauffeuring her around. If 'twas Jolene or one of my other sisters I'd have been on the phone right away saying 'course I'll do it, but things were that bad between Shannon and me." She paused and said, "I'm not gonna get in the study, am I? I mean, the way I felt about her?"

"There aren't any right or wrong answers in psychiatric research. And I appreciate how forthright you've been with me. One last question. Have you and your family discussed how to dispose of Shannon's belongings?"

"Well that's a funny thing. You know, the police wouldn't give me her keys right away, but when I finally went to her apartment to take a few things all her clothes and such was already packed up in boxes and labeled for storage. Like she was planning on moving away."

I agreed it was odd. "And she didn't mention anything like that to you previously?"

"Not a word, though like I said, we didn't talk much. Stuff's still there if you want to have a look. With all of Shawn's gaming equipment I got no room for it in the basement."

"Hasn't the apartment been rented to someone else?"

"Should be but her landlord says we're on the hook until the lease runs out. Told me 'murder ain't no act of God, lady' and I could sublet if I wanted. Place can stay empty 'til hell freezes over for all I care. Sonofa-bitch wants money outta me he can line up behind all the other people beating on my door."

As if on cue, the doorbell rang. I offered to wait with the technician while Marilyn ran out for fresh cigarettes, and she took me up on the offer. When she returned she told me to take care and to phone her right away if I could use her for my "research."

It was still two hours to my next appointment, so after seeking directions from Marilyn I walked the few blocks east to the Rock Island line and took the next train back to the Loop. On my way down to Marilyn's place I had phoned Shannon's former roommate, Nancy Kim, and made arrangements to meet her after work at a bar in River North. "I don't know that I'll be able to tell you much," Nancy had warned. "Shannon and I hadn't talked in months. But I'm going to need a drink after the day I'm having."

While the local wheezed from station to station I thought over what I had learned. The most useful information I'd come away with were the insights into Shannon's personality. I didn't think her sister's dislike was based purely on resentment of a pampered younger sibling. Shannon sounded like a genuinely unpleasant person, and one with ambitions of landing a wealthy husband. If so, Judith's instincts about her had been right. But they also proved too much: a woman like that would hardly develop a romantic interest in a retarded teenager, however handsome. I was still clinging to the hope that the DNA tests were wrong, that the fetus wasn't really Charlie's, so I regarded the possibility that Shannon had sought an abortion as a neutral fact. And notwithstanding Marilyn's suspicions, I thought it unlikely that Shannon had gotten pregnant deliberately. She might have forgotten to take a pill, or her birth control failed. It happened all the time. The expensive vacations were a point to follow up on, but I had no idea how to go about finding out where Shannon went or with whom. How did real detectives learn these things anyway? Sympathy for the blind might work with someone like Marilyn, but it wasn't going to help me follow a paper trail all over the country. Still, the trips seemed to confirm that there had been another man in Shannon's life, someone with a possible motive to kill her.

The art gallery where Nancy Kim worked was on West Hubbard,

in an area devoted to luxe furniture stores and singles bars. Nancy had asked me to meet her around the corner at one of them, a cocktail lounge called Mojo. I asked a passerby to help me locate the door and entered. The bar was a long, glowing thing set into a floor booby-trapped with irregular tiles. I took the first stool I wandered into and put on my glasses so that Nancy Kim would have an easier time recognizing me.

"Have you made a beverage selection, sir?" the bartender asked. "We have an extensive list of cinema-inspired cocktails."

"Groton?" I inquired.

"Theater major. What can I do you?"

"Is there a house special?"

"That would be the Mozilla. Bombay Sapphire, Chartreuse, and green tea topped with a slice of Granny Smith Apple."

It sounded like Raymond Burr's worst nightmare. "No, thank you. Make it a vodka martini on the rocks with a twist."

"Would you like that shaken or stirred?"

"Stirred, naturally."

Nancy showed up a few minutes later, smelling of Altoid mints and turpentine. "You must be Mark," she said taking the seat next to me and slinging a heavy bag on the floor. "What a day! We're opening a new show tomorrow and I was unpacking canvasses the whole afternoon. Between that and helping unload the floral arrangements I must have set a new world record for power lifting. I've got to be back there in an hour to supervise the last-minute arrangements with the caterer. I'll have the Kimchi," she said to the bartender.

"I'm afraid to ask what that is," I said.

"A martini flavored with chili peppers and pickled cucumber. My homage to ethnicity, I suppose."

"Which is?"

"Korean, of course. Kim is like Smith in Korea."

"Are you the manager of the gallery?"

"No. More like an indentured servant to one of the owners. She's a real horror show. I used to fantasize writing a chic lit novel about her—

The Devil's Own Prado I was going to call it—but someone beat me to the title first. So for much an Art Institute degree. Four years and all it qualifies me to do is sweat like a longshoreman and run out to Starbucks every two hours. Though I guess it's better than working *at* Starbucks. You wanted to talk to me about Shannon?"

"If you don't mind."

She became hesitant. "Can I ask why? Excuse me for saying this, but you don't look like a detective."

"You don't watch enough television. But I'm not a cop. Just a friend of the young man who was arrested for Shannon's death. There are some things about the case against him that don't make sense. I wanted to learn more about Shannon and you seemed like a logical place to start."

Our martinis came and I took a mouthful. It was cold enough to freeze mercury and slipped down my throat like an eel.

"Well, you understand I didn't see her much the last several months. I moved out of the apartment we were sharing in December, the week before Christmas, and only talked to her two or three times since then, mostly about phone bills."

"How long had you lived together?"

"Around a year. I met her just after graduation. We were sharing studio space with five other people in a warehouse up on Ravenswood. I was looking to move out of the dump I was in and Shannon had just found this great apartment in Wrigleyville she couldn't afford on her own—top floor of a three flat and recently renovated. One thing led to another and we ended up splitting the rent."

"Was Shannon working at the New Horizons Center then?"

"No. She was still trying to get by on odd jobs, waitressing and things like that, so she could paint during the day."

"What kind of work did she do?"

"This is going to sound catty, but it was really derivative. All self-portraits in period costumes. Cindy Sherman was doing that eons ago. Still, it was no worse than a lot of the stuff that sells these days and I think Shannon could have gotten some collectors to buy into her premise if she'd stuck with it."

"But she stopped painting?"

"Yeah. After her canvases were turned down by a few galleries, she quit. Just like that. Said she had better things to do than wait 'til her boobs were falling off to be recognized by some gay dealer who only wanted to see pictures of guys fucking. I think she meant it as a put-down of one of our studio mates, Jules, who'd just won a prize for his homoerotic reinterpretation of *The Last Supper*."

I shuddered just thinking about it. "Could this fellow Jules have borne a grudge toward her?"

"I doubt it. I heard another of his canvases just got snatched up by a museum in Cleveland. Anyhow, after she stopped painting she put all her work in storage and as far as I saw never lifted a brush again."

"Was that why she took the job at the center?"

"Yeah. She saw a classified in *The Reader* and used her degree to pass herself off as an art educator. I don't think she liked the job very much, but it paid the bills and freed up her nights so she could party."

"Did she have a lot of boyfriends?"

"Where would you like me to start?"

"I'm mainly interested in serious relationships."

"Well, there was Joel Stern. He's an investment banker in the Loop. I thought he was a real dick, but they were pretty hot and heavy until he got sent off to Hong Kong for six months. At least, that's what Shannon said happened. I think he just got bored with her. And then there was the Invisible Man. I called him that because I never met him."

"Did you know his real name?"

"Nope. Shannon wouldn't tell me. Said the relationship had to be hush-hush because the gossip columnists would be all over the story if they found out. Said a lot about how much she trusted me."

"Do you remember when they started going out?"

"Last spring sometime. I wouldn't even have known she was seeing someone except that she was gone so much. Whoever it was never came up to the apartment and they only got together on weekends, usually on trips out of town. Suited me fine because I could have the place to myself."

This jibed with the vacations Marilyn Sparrow had described. "I don't suppose you ever got a look at him?"

"Uh-uh. He used to phone her a few minutes ahead and she'd go downstairs to wait for him."

"What about his car?"

"That *would* have been hard to miss, even three floors up. A white Jag. But I didn't look at the tag number if that's what you want to know. It wasn't like I was spying on her."

She seemed anxious to convince me of that fact and I wondered why.

"Was she still seeing him when you moved out?"

"I don't think so. It's part of the reason I left. Shannon came home one afternoon in a rage, starting throwing things around. I was pissed because she smashed up a few of my things and didn't even offer to pay for them. After that, I don't think she got out of bed for a week."

"When did this occur exactly?"

"Let's see. It was starting to get cold, so middle to late October."

"And she didn't tell you what had happened?"

"No. Shannon only shared things when she thought she could impress you. All I know is she was really upset that they broke up, like the guy actually meant something to her."

We'd come to the end of our drinks. The martinis packed a wallop and I was feeling the effects.

"Mmmm," Nancy said, clinking the ice in her glass. "That was good."

"Can I buy you another?"

Evidently the drink had loosened her inhibitions. She said coyly, "I think you're trying to get me drunk. How do I know you're not just some pervert on the make?"

"I used to be a Peeping Tom but my career was cut tragically short."

Nancy called the waiter over and ordered a second martini. I decided to play it safe by sticking with what was left of mine.

"What caused you two to finally call it quits?"

Nancy laughed unpleasantly. "It was so stupid. Shannon accused me of reading her diary."

"She kept a diary?"

"At least that's what I think it was. A notebook she wrote in every night before bed."

"A real notebook, not a computer?"

"No, oddly enough, she wasn't very plugged in. I mean, she had a laptop—doesn't everyone?—but she didn't spend much time networking. I think she got turned off when no one wanted to friend her on Facebook. Anyway, the notebook went missing one day and she accused me of taking it. Like I needed to know even more about her. It turned up a week later under her mattress. By that time I'd had enough. I offered to pay all of the December rent if she'd let me out of the lease for the rest of the year."

"And she accepted?"

"Yeah. It surprised me because I didn't see how she could afford the place by herself. It cost nearly four grand a month plus utilities. But she must have found a way because she never got another roommate."

"When did you see her last?"

"Middle of February. We had coffee together, or rather I did. Shannon said she had an upset stomach and the only thing she could keep down was herbal tea. Now that I think of it, it was probably because she was pregnant like the newspapers said."

"Did she mention anything to you about moving away?"

"Moving? No. Why?"

"Something her sister said to me."

"Marilyn, you mean?"

"Yes. Did you two know each other?"

"I met her once or twice. I couldn't believe they were sisters. I mean, Marilyn is so friendly and nice."

"I gather you didn't like Shannon very much."

Nancy giggled. "I guess I should have known better, talking to a psychiatrist. Yes, it's true. I shouldn't speak ill of the dead, but whoever took her out, that retarded kid I mean, was doing humanity a huge favor."

"Did she ever talk about him, mention his name?"

"I don't remember. It's getting late. I should be getting back before the hag starts sharpening her claws. Unless you want to buy me another martini."

I said, amused, "If I do that I won't be the only one having trouble finding the door."

I could feel her eyes on me. "Do you always talk that way?"

"Which way?"

"You know."

I smiled.

Nancy giggled again, tipsily. "You should do that more often, you know. Though it must be really hard."

"Not at all. I just lift the corners of my mouth like this."

"Who's the man behind the glasses?"

"Someone old enough to be your father."

I continued to let Nancy flirt with me until it was time for her to go. Then I walked home. When I got there two messages were waiting on my answering machine. One was from O'Leary saying he'd checked into the DNA lab report. The fetus was a boy. He'd sent a copy of the report over to my office so I could see for myself, but it looked like a dead end.

The other message was from Sep. That afternoon Nate Dickerson had filed an action with the Illinois Department of Professional Regulation seeking to have me relieved of my license to practice medicine.

TWELVE

Sep was going relatively easy on me.

"I've listened to the tape of your session with the young man. I can't say I would have reached a different conclusion, though others will surely find fault with your, ahem, prescription."

That morning there had been a gaggle of reporters on the sidewalk outside my apartment building. I'd been warned to expect them. A hospital public-relations staffer named Tish phoned just before midnight to tell me she'd be at the door with a car to pick me up at 8:00 a.m. It wasn't early enough. They swarmed me the moment I came out the door, dangling microphones and clicking cameras.

"Doctor, is it true Charlie Dickerson was being sexually abused by the woman he killed?"

"Can you confirm that you've been sued by the family for failing to report their relationship to authorities?"

Per Tish's instructions, I kept my mouth zipped. "Let the gentleman through, please," she said as she nudged me ahead. I wondered whether I should have worn a newspaper over my head.

Tish dropped me off at the hospital's main entrance with orders to go straight to the administrative suite where the lawyers were waiting for me. "No detours," she said. I ignored her and made a beeline for Sep's office, stopping only to pick up the package waiting for me at Yelena's desk. The nine-by-twelve envelope was burning a hole in my lap. Despite the trouble I was in, I was more concerned with the DNA report inside it than what might happen to me, and I was anxious to get through with Sep so I could find Josh and have him read it to me.

"What about you?" I asked Sep. "Do you think the advice I gave the Dickersons was wrong?"

"It *was* somewhat unorthodox."

"I see. Charlie Dickerson can be tried for murder, but heaven forbid he should be taught how to take innocent pleasure from his body."

"You know what I mean. The morning papers were already suggesting you may have been responsible, if only indirectly, for that young woman's death. One of them called you 'Dr. Feel Good.'"

Better, I reflected sourly, than Dr. Death.

I waved it off. "I can't be held responsible for people's absurd prejudices. The idea that learning how to masturbate turned Charlie into a depraved killer is laughable, even in our society."

"I agree with you," Sep said. "And based on the tape, no one could claim he was a danger to the young woman. But that's sidestepping the issue. The State Board will want to know whether Charlie was a victim of sexual abuse and if so, why you failed to recognize it. With all that's happened since, I don't see how you can disprove the first point."

"That he was being molested? Come on. Even if they did have sex together, their relationship wasn't necessarily abusive. Charlie's legally an adult. Shannon was only a few years older. I'm told he's very handsome. Is it impossible that a woman of normal intelligence would develop a genuine interest in him?"

I was grasping at straws and Sep knew it.

"Your question is legitimate, but we both know her feelings are only one side of the equation. She was his teacher and an authority figure. Those factors alone create a high risk of undue influence, not unlike the circumstances that resulted in Charlie confessing to something he very likely didn't do. Didn't you testify in court that he is easily led?"

As usual Sep had exposed the weakness in my argument with a logician's skill.

"Still," Sep continued, "I agree we shouldn't jump to conclusions without knowing more. We allow grandfathers to marry teenagers, never mind the intellectual disparity. Is that what you think went on?"

"I have no idea what to think," I said dispiritedly.

I filled him in on some of the things I'd learned the day before, ending with the fact that Shannon may have sought an abortion. "Perhaps she was lonely after the breakup with her mystery lover and fell into a physical relationship with Charlie before she knew what was happening. She certainly had nothing to gain from it, and they'd only need to have sex a few times for her to become pregnant by him. If she was planning on an abortion she may have realized things had gone too far and was trying to do the right thing."

"That's not beyond the realm of possibility, though it sounds out of character for the person you've described. When you interviewed Charlie in prison, did you question him directly about whether they'd had intercourse?"

I shook my head in irritation, mostly with myself. "No. We didn't know about the pregnancy then and . . . well, I confess I was being closed-minded to the idea of a relationship. I was sure his being found by her body was pure happenstance. But even if I'd wanted to ask, I doubt Charlie's lawyer would have let me. It can be a problem when a testifying expert knows too much—as I later learned to my eternal regret."

"Well," Sep said, "there's nothing to do for it now except cooperate with the hospital's lawyers. They're waiting for you upstairs. They'll want to discuss suspension, of course, to protect the institution from liability. I've already told them I won't go along with it, not even on a temporary basis. As far as I'm concerned your conduct was entirely professional. I'm only sorry I got you into this mess."

Without knowing it, Sep had brought up the reason I was there.

"What if I wanted to be suspended?" I asked.

His reaction was swift and cutting. "This isn't the right occasion for one of your witticisms."

I didn't say anything.

"You're serious?"

I nodded.

"That," Sep said, voice rising like a thundercloud, "would be blind folly."

"My specialty these days," I said. "But not right now."

Sep nearly imploded. "I won't entertain it, even for a minute."

"Please, Sep. There are good reasons."

He went on, railing at me. "I can't imagine any. If I suspended you it would be taken as proof you were guilty of malpractice, regardless of the facts. No one would believe me later when I said you did nothing wrong. It would go heavily against you with the Board, never mind what the media would say."

"I know all that, but let me explain—"

But Sep was too wrapped up in his train of thought to pay me any attention.

"It's an insane idea. I'm worried enough as it is about the possibility of some formal action being taken against you. With all the uproar over the murder, there'll be intense pressure to find a scapegoat and the Board won't find it easy to let you off with just a slap to the wrist. Frankly, I don't understand why you'd even suggest it." He caught himself abruptly and stopped. "Unless . . ."

I'd been afraid the conversation would take this turn.

When Sep resumed, he was speaking more to himself than me and his tone had turned rueful. "My God, how could I have missed it? It's what you've wanted all along, isn't it?"

"Wait, Sep, before you—"

"Shame on me for not seeing how much it's affected you. You put up such a good front, I didn't realize . . . it's all there in the literature, the intense mourning for what's been lost—"

"Leave it alone," I said. I could feel myself getting hot, not the best advertisement for proving him wrong.

"—but it's nothing we can't fix with proper attention. You need help and we'll get it for you, the best there is. I know a good man at Rush. Excellent therapist and very discreet. We'll get you in to see him straight away, perhaps start you on a dose of antidepressants at the same time. Trust me. I know it's hard to believe from where you're sitting today, but you *can* feel like a whole man again—"

That was it. I swung my cane down on his desk with all the force I could muster. It cracked the surface like a rifle fired at close range. Some of the papers on Sep's desk scattered and fluttered to the floor. I stood up and turned quickly toward the window so he couldn't read my face.

Stunned, I suppose, by my loss of control, Sep was uncharacteristically wordless.

With my back still to him I said, "I suppose you haven't heard that Charlie was attacked in prison?"

My question had its intended impact. Sep shifted noticeably in his chair and said in a low, grave voice, "No, I hadn't."

"Preventing that from happening again and seeing him home safely to his family is more important to me than . . . well, anything else."

"Yes. I understand why it would be. But you are allowing your anger over a terrible injustice to overwhelm your judgment."

"How is that?"

Sep sighed heavily. "Come back and sit down." He paused and added meekly, "If you don't mind, that is."

I let several moments go by. When I at last reclaimed my seat some of the tension between us had lessened, but I was still shaken.

Sep said in a fatherly way, "Mark, you are clearly capable of a great many things, but do I have to point out the obvious to you?"

I chafed under the reminder. "The only thing that's obvious to me is that if I have to sit in the dark and do nothing while that boy cries himself to sleep every night I *will* end up the cripple everyone thinks I am."

"No one thinks of you as a cripple," Sep said guiltily.

"Really? Forgive me, but only a few moments ago you came close to saying it yourself. You want to know what the hardest part is? I'll tell you. It's not this"—I rapped my cane on his desk again for emphasis—"or some of the restrictions on my freedom, or how much longer it takes to do nearly everything. It's everyone treating me like . . . I've grown a second head. The only thing that's changed about me is that I can't *see*. If I can live with that, why is it so difficult for everyone else?"

"I see," Sep said with unintentional irony.

I shook my head. "I don't think you can." I was sick of trying to prove what no one wanted to believe and also painfully aware of all the things I wasn't telling him.

But if Sep saw through my protest, he decided to give me a pass.

"I apologize. I shouldn't presume to understand what I have no experience of. You were right to call me on it. But I still don't understand what suspending you will accomplish."

"It will give me time to follow up on the things I've learned about Shannon Sparrow and hopefully find out who she was dating. The other man she was involved with had every bit as much motive to kill her as Charlie. The police are done investigating. Detective O'Leary told me his hands are tied and I don't trust Charlie's lawyers not to try to strike a deal with the prosecutor. Hallie Sanchez admitted to me it's the usual way these cases are resolved when there's a question of diminished capacity. Charlie shouldn't have to spend one more day in prison than he deserves."

"And you're willing to risk your livelihood to prove him innocent?"

"Yes."

"Because there's no guarantee I'll be able to reinstate you."

"In that event I'm sure there's a sheltered workshop that would have me."

Sep permitted himself a chuckle. "Pity the institution."

"And all kidding aside, it's also the only way I'm going to get myself out of the mess I'm in. You said it earlier. I'm going to be drawn and quartered in the press before my case even gets to the Board. If I don't find out the truth, there'll be intense pressure for at least a reprimand. You'll have no choice about firing me then. By clearing Charlie I may well clear myself *and* save my job."

"That's a strong argument, but I still don't like it."

"I don't either, but I don't see an alternative."

I knew what I was asking him to accept was a stretch. And he was more right about my emotional state than he knew. I was counting on him coming around so I wouldn't have to take the more drastic step of resigning. He mulled it over for a few minutes.

At last he said, "I suppose if I refused, you'd quit."

I grinned weakly in reply.

"Yes, of course, that's exactly what you'd do. But maybe you won't have to. Maybe there's a way we can both get what we want."

"What do you mean?"

He outlined his plan.

"I'll tell the administration I had doubts all along about your fitness to return to work and that I fear you may now be at risk for a complete breakdown. No, don't make a face, just listen. I'll put in a request for a continuation of your medical leave, ostensibly so you can undergo counseling. You may have to sit through a few sessions later to keep up the subterfuge, but it will be good for your soul. In the mean time, you'll have the freedom you need to investigate." He added wickedly, "And if anyone ever tried to use it against you, you could sue them for discrimination."

"What do I do about the guys waiting for me upstairs?"

"I'll tell them it's my professional opinion you're too distraught to talk right now. That should put them off for the time being."

"Thanks, Sep," I said. The strategy was brilliant and far more clever than my own idea.

"Not so fast. There are two conditions."

I pretended to groan. "Why are there always conditions?" I was relieved there were only two. "Go ahead. Tell me."

"First, no heroics. If there is another murderer out there, he isn't going to welcome your investigation. Keep this O'Leary fellow informed about whatever you find out and be mindful of your own safety."

I nodded. It was more or less what O'Leary had said.

"Second. When this is all over, you'll tell me what's really been going on with you these many months."

"Sep, it's like I've been saying—"

"No arguments. I accept that I was falling prey to stereotypical thinking. But I've been in this business too long to believe I'm completely mistaken. Something is eating at you and I'm not giving up until I find out what it is."

When I left Sep's office, Josh was busy with a patient. I left word with Yelena that he should meet me at the Double L as soon as he could break free.

"Are you in big trouble?" Yelena asked.

"Up to my eyeballs. What does Boris's schedule look like this week?"

Despite the bitter relations between the two, Yelena still managed her ex-husband's books. I gleaned there were two sets of them, one for IRS eyes that assiduously itemized expenses like gas usage and vehicle depreciation, and another that kept track of what Boris actually earned in tips. She punched a few buttons on her keyboard and said:

"Not too bad. The Shriners Convention isn't until Saturday. Would you like me to pencil you in?"

"Not yet. I'm not sure exactly when I'll need him. Just keep your cell phone on."

"Is that a joke?" Yelena said.

I exited my building through a little-used doorway to the rear, wishing I weren't so conspicuous. I was an easy target for a nosy reporter to spot and follow and didn't have a prayer of disguising myself. What could I do—wear an extra hat and dark glasses? Grow a beard? Suddenly I imagined myself being chased down the street by *paparazzi* toting lenses the size of cannon while I frantically swung my cane to escape. It was a relief when I reached the Double L without being accosted by anyone other than the usual complement of busy-bodies telling me when it was safe to cross. After the day I'd had thus far I decided I needed a drink no matter what the hour, so I ordered a double to bide the time while I waited for Josh to show up.

He arrived a little before noon.

"Well, Stan, it's a fine mess we're in," he said brightly when he came up. "I must say you have the David Janssen look down to a T."

"You've heard then."

"Have you lost your mind? Yelena hasn't had this much to talk about since her cousin put dioxin in a rival mobster's vodka. Her phone's been stapled to her ear ever since you left."

"I suppose the whole world knows I'm on leave again."

"The official word is that you're being treated for mild anxiety, but the gossip is you freaked out and tried to commit suicide. Jonathan was telling anyone who'd listen how he saw it coming. He was still shedding crocodile tears in the lounge when I left."

"Suicide, huh? Well, at least I still have my pride to live for."

"Speaking of which, why is there a bandage on your arm?"

"It's nothing. I . . . broke something."

Josh put his hand on my shoulder. "Are you sure? I heard what happened to the kid over the weekend. Maybe we should talk about it."

"Another time. Right now what I really need is food. And I'd like you to read something to me."

We went to another of our usual spots, a Greek diner on Chestnut that aspires to the same lofty standards as the Billy Goat, except that the waitstaff succeeds at being even surlier. I ordered steak and eggs to counteract the effects of the bourbon and sat there aggressively carving the greasy pile on my plate into chunks while Josh read the DNA report, first silently to himself and then aloud to me, making short work of the boilerplate and going carefully over the important parts. When he had finished there didn't seem to be a shred of doubt that Charlie was the father of Shannon's baby.

"They did a combined paternity index, or CPI, of ten thousand," Josh said. "That means the alleles that matched up with Charlie's sample were unlikely to have come from more than one in ten thousand men in the general population. Or, put another way, that there's a 99.9 percent chance he's the father."

I said, "I would have preferred a CPI of one hundred thousand, but they still went farther than most labs do."

"Yeah. It's pretty hard to argue with their finding unless the samples were contaminated or Charlie's got an identical twin we don't know about. So where does that leave you?"

I felt weighed down. I hadn't been gone from Sep's office more than a few hours and already it seemed my chances of proving Shannon wasn't sexually involved with Charlie—which would have helped clear not only him but me—had vanished. Josh saw the expression on my face and tried to cheer me up.

"It still doesn't mean he killed her. Why is everyone so quick to make that leap?"

"Why do you think? Add Charlie's size into the mix and we might as well be facing the lynch mob in *Of Mice and Men*. That's why I'll never be forgiven for my advice to his parents unless I find out what really happened."

"I hadn't thought of that. But now that you say it . . . what can I do to help?"

"Nothing. I don't want you getting sucked into it too. After we pay the check I'm going to go up to the New Horizons Center and nose around, see if I can find out more about Shannon's secret lover. It's the only thing I can think of at the moment."

"All right," Josh said, "but do me a favor, OK?"

"Keep my eyes open wide?"

"No. They wobble enough as it is."

"Go ahead, shore up my fragile ego."

"That's what I was getting at. Somebody needs to be nice to you right now. Might as well be you."

THIRTEEN

"**M**s. Lowe is in a meeting but said she is anxious to meet with you and wondered whether you would mind waiting. She asked that I show you to the garden."

I was speaking to the receptionist at the New Horizons Center.

"Garden?" I said. I hadn't discerned any open spaces when I was coming up on the building.

"Yes, it's one of the center's showcases. Ms. Lowe often brings prospective clients to see it. It's upstairs. May I take you there?"

"No need," I said. "Verbal directions will do."

During the cab ride up I had listened to the center's webpages on my Blindberry. The site seemed to have been designed with disabled access in mind and had none of the tricky menus and dead ends that so often had me pounding my arrow keys in frustration. According to the About Us section, the center was a three-story building that had started out in life as a pickle factory. In keeping with the green craze being spearheaded by the mayor, it relied on solar panels for heating and air-conditioning and was said to be "filled with natural light and the eclectic art works of our clients." Visitors could expect to find a "bright, modern facility light-years distant from the dismal warehouses that housed the intellectually disabled in the past," and a "friendly, inclusive atmosphere built on mutual trust and respect." And they didn't discriminate on the basis of race, gender, or physical handicap, either.

The garden was in a terrace on the roof, through a door to the right of the elevator. I stepped out into neon sunlight and quickly replaced my glasses. A brick walk led away from the door. I caned down it until I came to an obstruction, about waist high. Reaching down, I discovered a planter box, about twelve feet in length and another three in width, bordered with tiles that were cool to my touch despite the heat of the afternoon sun. At the far end, there was a brass sign embossed with Braille that read *Herbs*. Exploring further, I found five other similar boxes radiating from a circular central area, where there was a teak bench in a shaded arbor scented with honeysuckle. Close by insects droned among the blossoms, and farther off, a sprinkler pattered back and forth. I sat down to wait for Ms. Lowe.

About fifteen minutes later the roof door popped open, followed by the click of heels coming down the path. It was a confident walk, purposeful yet unhurried. "Ms. Lowe?" I asked, rising and extending my hand.

The heels stopped a foot away from me. "Yes. Thank you for waiting. I'm afraid my time isn't my own at the moment. My receptionist said you were interested in a possible placement at the center?" She wore no perfume I could smell and her diction had a hint of maturity to it. I guessed her to be near my age, or a little older. I extended my hand farther, but she still didn't respond.

I said, "This is a lovely facility."

"It is nice, isn't it?" she said. Then a touch sadly, "though I don't know how much longer we'll be able to keep it open. I'm surprised at your interest, given all the adverse publicity we're getting. I've been on the phone with our donors all week, and just now another family removed their daughter from the program. May I ask what brought you here? We don't exactly have a truckload of new applicants knocking at the door."

Her demeanor was cordial, but my patience was wearing thin. How much longer would I have to stand there with my hand outstretched before she took it?

"Don't worry, it's not communicable," I said, after a few more seconds had elapsed.

"Communicable?"

"Yes. I've been holding my hand out for several minutes and you haven't taken it."

"Funny," she said. "I was just noticing the same thing."

"That I was waiting for you to shake my hand?"

"No. That you hadn't taken mine."

I was dumbfounded until Alice Lowe began to laugh, a sound like keys jingling. Then I caught on. In my wildest dreams I hadn't anticipated this. I felt myself color rapidly, grateful that it wouldn't be noticed.

"I think I've just been exposed as a blockhead," I said.

"Don't say that," Alice said. "You couldn't have known."

"I didn't think . . . well, I mean, you don't sound like . . ."

"Another blind person? You're right. I don't use a cane at the center. I can see well enough to do without one when I'm here."

"So you're only partially blind," I said.

"Aren't you digging your hole deeper?"

She was right. How many times had I wanted to correct others for making the same assumption—that being blind meant seeing nothing at all?

"I'm sorry," I said. "My foot seems to be permanently stuck in my mouth today. Can we start over?"

"Sure," she said, touching her wrist to mine and then clasping my hand. Her fingers were smooth and slender. "Alice Lowe."

"Mark Angelotti." I fumbled in my jacket pocket for one of my business cards and handed it to her.

"A psychiatrist," she said after perusing it. "Are you here about one of your clients?"

After our opening exchange, the falsehoods I had planned on telling her seemed out of place so I came clean. "Yes," I said. "Charlie Dickerson."

"Are you the doctor who testified at his hearing?"

"Unfortunately, yes."

"Now I understand why your name sounded so familiar."

"You were there?"

"No. But I listened to the news reports. I'm not sure I should be talking to you."

"Why? We're both on the same side."

"And which side is that?" she asked skeptically.

"You spoke of bad publicity. I have to assume the center's fortunes would take a turn for the better if Charlie were cleared."

"And that's what you're trying to do?"

"I believe he's innocent."

"So you're playing detective? Forgive me, but isn't that like a bad Hollywood script? The blind sleuth who 'sees' things no one else can?"

"Now who's being condescending?"

Alice Lowe seemed taken aback, but then recovered and laughed. "Quite right. Come," she said, reaching down and taking my free hand, which she put in the crook of her arm, "let's take a stroll together. This has been an awful day and I need a walk to clear my head."

She showed me around the garden, pointing things out as we went. There was a tactile map near the front that I'd missed, a brass plaque that showed the layout and what was planted in the various beds. "Most of our blind clients have multiple disabilities and lack the motor and intellectual skills to read Braille," Alice explained, "so the signs are a bit of an indulgence on my part. But I wanted the garden to be fully appreciated by all visitors. The beds are at seat height so they can be worked on from a wheelchair, and there are special tools for planting and weeding in the shed. We grow herbs and lettuce and a few vegetables in season, which we use in our kitchen. All of what we raise is organic. Can you guess what this is?" she asked, opening some sort of bin.

"Smells like rotten eggs. Is it compost?"

"Yes," she said. "We have three wet and two dry stacks that we use to recycle food scraps. It's remarkable how quickly they're broken down into fertilizer under the right conditions. Do you know how it works?"

"Not really," I confessed.

"We layer wet and dry material and add an accelerator. Kept moist, the material will break down into usable fertilizer in about a month. Hosing the stacks down during spring and summer is one of our clients' favorite chores."

"Are they all assigned chores?"

"To the extent possible, yes. The ambulatory ones, like Charlie, are obviously able to manage a greater range of tasks, and we encourage them to take part in all of the center's upkeep, not just washing up after meals, but minor maintenance such as changing light bulbs and repairing furniture. We also teach them how to cook and do laundry. Our goal is to give them all the skills they need to live independently."

After the center's website I had been expecting just this sort of idealistic claptrap. "Isn't that unrealistic?"

"For the vast majority of our population, yes. But they take great pride in being able to participate in the same everyday activities as their nondisabled peers. Pride and a sense of purpose. Can you imagine living without that? Despite all the advances we've made as a society, most people still think the lives of the severely disabled aren't worth living. We want to change that perception by example."

"Good luck," I said.

"Well, aren't we bitter. How long have you been blind, if I might ask?"

"Long enough to know how big a hurdle you face. Most people can't fathom why you and I don't just leap off the nearest bridge."

Alice sighed. "I know." I felt her hand begin to tremble on my sleeve. "That's what's made all of this so much worse. I worked so hard to bring the center to where it is, and now . . ."

I realized she had begun to cry.

I did what seemed chivalrous and took her into my arms. She was shapelier than I'd imagined, curves in all the right places, and her hair smelled like ripe currants. She was wearing a lamb's wool sweater and her body felt like a soft bird against my chest. A very nice bird. She shook with muffled sobs while I tried to comfort her with ineffectual pats to the back.

After a long while Alice stopped and I handed her my handkerchief.

"I'm sorry," she said, taking it from me. "That was very unprofessional of me. It's just that I've been under such strain lately and I can't help feeling that it's all my fault. Maybe if I'd been able to see what was going on . . ."

"Don't think like that," I said, imagining myself in her place and coming rapidly to her defense.

"But it's unavoidable," she said. "I'd been warned about Shannon and of course I tried to observe her behavior myself, but there are just some things I can't do as well as a sighted supervisor. And now I'm afraid that my mistake will be seen as further proof that blind people . . . that *we* shouldn't be placed in positions of responsibility. The newspapers haven't come out and said it point-blank—that would be too politically incorrect—but every article goes on and on about how many of the staff members here are disabled too, as though it explains everything that happened. That's why I was surprised you didn't know."

"I've been ignoring the papers recently. I don't think either one of us is going to be nominated for Blind Role Model of the Year. But you say you were warned about Shannon?"

"Yes. Regina Best, our speech therapist, came to me last summer and expressed concerns about how Shannon was interacting with our clients. Regina thought she was too physically affectionate with them, but when I asked her to be more specific she could only point to the type of behavior I would expect from any trained caregiver. Many of our clients are easily distracted and don't always understand verbal instructions. A gentle touch to the arm or the cheek is often necessary to help them to focus on what the speaker is saying. And hugs are a means of providing positive reinforcement, as a well as a way of celebrating their victories."

"But Ms. Best didn't see it that way?"

"Regina tends to view everything in black and white. She's an active member of the disability-rights movement and always on the lookout for what she regards as patronizing behavior on the part of 'ableists.' She has a valid point, to a degree. Unsolicited touching *can* be humiliating, as I'm sure you've experienced when someone has insisted on pulling you across a street. But Regina takes it too far, likening pats on the head to how plantation owners treated slaves in the South, or how pet owners treat dogs and cats. That's not the way we think of our clients here. Still, in light of what's happened, perhaps we ought to have had a strict policy against any physical contact, the way they do in almost all public schools nowadays. It makes you wonder what our society is coming to when we can't allow *any* displays of affection for fear it will pave the way for abuse."

"Do you think Shannon was abusing Charlie?"

Alice sighed uncomfortably. "The conclusion seems inescapable, doesn't it? He fathered her baby."

"I'll grant that, but it doesn't mean Charlie killed her. You said you tried to observe Shannon with her students. Did you notice anything unusual about her relationship with Charlie?"

"I sat in on some of her classes, of course, especially in the fall of last year, when we were preparing annual performance evaluations. I should delegate more, but I like to know everything that's going on at the center. With the benefit of hindsight, I think Shannon may have been more attentive to Charlie than some of her other students. He's such a sweet boy, it's hard not to respond to him."

"You were working here the morning of the murder. You didn't hear anything out of the ordinary?"

"No. I always arrive here around seven o'clock on weekdays. But since I don't drive, I enter by the front door. My office is also at the front of the building, on the third floor, so I doubt I would have noticed anything happening in the alley."

"The rear entrance is unsupervised?"

"Yes. We don't have the resources for more than one security guard and it always seemed unnecessary until now. The door to the alley is kept locked, naturally. Employees access the building using key cards, and there's a motion sensor that turns a light on when the entranceway is approached. Most of the staff park their cars in the lot where Shannon's body was found."

"Does the system record who comes in and out?"

"It's not that sophisticated, I'm afraid. Why? Do you think a staff member could be responsible for Shannon's death?"

"It's a possibility that should be explored. Did she have any enemies you were aware of?"

"Well, I couldn't say she and Regina were on the best of terms, but Regina's above suspicion. She's a wheelchair user and I doubt she can lift her arms above her head. The police thought so too, apparently. They didn't spend more than five minutes questioning her, though that may have been the result of subtle prejudice. Regina is very seriously disabled and, sadly, some people find her appearance disconcerting. It's a shame because she's a very shrewd observer."

"Would you mind if I spoke to her?"

"That's up to Regina, but I'd be glad to show you to her classroom when we're finished."

"Is there anyone else who may have harbored a grudge against Shannon?"

"A grudge? I'm afraid I can't help you there, Doctor, even if I were the type to dwell on petty disputes among my staff. I knew Shannon wasn't universally liked, but almost everyone rubs others the wrong way sometimes. Shannon was a bit immature, but also young in years. I thought she could grow out of it. It's what I kept telling Regina."

"What about friends at the center, someone she might have confided in?"

"Dean Parsons, maybe. Or Leslie Sherman. I think they went out for drinks together sometimes after hours."

I pulled out my Blindberry and made a note of these names. "Do you think they would talk to me?"

"Perhaps," Alice said. "But you might stand a better chance of getting them to open up if I asked the questions first. What are you interested in finding out?"

"I have reason to believe Shannon was in a relationship with someone that ended a few months before she died. Did you know anything about it?"

"No. As I said, I try to stay out of the personal lives of my staff. Shannon came alone to the last holiday party, but that's all I can tell you."

"When was that?"

"In December, the week before Christmas."

"Did she seem depressed then, upset?"

"Not that I noticed."

"How about later in the spring, before she was killed?"

"I didn't notice anything different about her then, either. But I was somewhat distracted. We were overwhelmed with a major grant application, one that would have enabled us to expand our home care program significantly. If you work in a hospital, you know what that process is like."

All this time we had been standing two feet from one another. I wasn't sure why, but I sensed there was something else she wanted to say to me. All of a sudden she answered my question by touching my sleeve. "Thank you for letting me cry on your shoulder. I didn't realize how much I had been bottling up inside until then."

"It's what I'm supposed to be good at—getting people to unlock their feelings. I just hope I'll be able to continue doing it."

"Oh." Alice jerked her hand away as if suddenly chagrined. "I didn't . . . how inconsiderate of me. Here I am so focused on my own troubles I didn't even think that you might be under siege too."

"I'll survive."

"I will too. I always have. But it's nice to have someone to talk to, someone I don't need to explain everything to."

I knew what she meant. "I'd be glad to offer my shoulder again if you need it. Or better yet, buy you dinner sometime."

"Thank you," Alice said. "I'd like that. And I won't forget to ask around about boyfriends. Just give me a day or two." I heard a faint click as she opened the crystal on her watch. "Shall we go see Regina then?" she asked. "I hate to cut our conversation short, but I have another appointment in ten minutes' time."

I left her feeling like I'd gained an ally.

Regina Best stooped to receive me. At least that's how it felt, though it was I who had to stoop to take her frail hand. It was as insubstantial as straw but there was a defiance in the way she returned my grasp that challenged me to pity her. Alice had told me she had a degenerative disorder that, starting in late childhood, had gradually twisted her body into a grotesque shape, eventually robbing her of the ability to move all but her head and shoulders. Independent breathing would go next, and then speech. I felt like an arriviste in comparison.

"It's always refreshing to talk to someone who doesn't shudder and look away when they first see me," she explained casually as she led me into the empty classroom. I followed the hum of her motorized wheelchair to an arrangement of table and chairs. "Sit down," she said in a reedy but commanding voice. "There's a seat directly to your left. But be warned, it's a little lower than you're used to."

I appreciated the precise directions until I realized what she meant. The chair she'd indicated was kindergarten sized and forced my knees practically to my chin. Seated this way, Regina Best's head was only a few inches away from mine. Her breath exuded a medicinal scent, like a dentist's.

"That's better," she said. "Now I won't have to twist up to look at you. My spine is curved and I can't sit up straight, so I ask visitors to come down to my level. I'm sure they think it's a terrible imposition—like all those handicapped parking spaces."

I couldn't argue with her. I'd often felt a wave of annoyance when I was in a hurry to park and there were three or four reserved spaces standing empty. Besides, the seat I was in right then was damned uncomfortable.

"Are you active in our movement?" she asked straightaway.

"I'm not much of a joiner."

"You should be, you know. Our fight is every bit as important as the civil-rights movement in the sixties. It enrages me that the same so-called liberals who see racism and sexism everywhere refuse to acknowledge the persistent discrimination we face. We don't want handouts, just the right to be treated with dignity. When a person with disabilities can't get through a restaurant door that's too narrow for a wheelchair it's the same as saying 'we don't serve coloreds.'"

"Well, maybe a little different," I offered foolishly.

"How? Don't you feel deliberately excluded when you come across a doorway that isn't signed in Braille?"

I felt compelled to explain that Braille signage was a convenience, but apart from restroom doors and elevator buttons, not something I strictly needed. "I can always ask for directions."

"But that's exactly my point. You shouldn't *have* to ask. Disability is purely a social construct. If we lived in a barrier-free society you wouldn't be '*dis*abled' anymore. You'd be just like everyone else."

Everyone except people who could see. "Maybe, but not all things that would make life easier for me are worth the cost."

Regina sniffed dismissively. "How expensive can it be to put Braille on signs?"

"I wasn't talking only of dollars."

"Or to install audible traffic signals?"

"Now that you say it, beeping traffic lights are a good example of what I mean. They cover up the sound of traffic and make blind pedestrians seem more helpless than they really are. I'll allow there's a much stronger argument in favor of wheelchair ramps in public places." I was hoping to end the discussion there.

Regina, however, wasn't giving up. "So you don't think access is important?"

"No, but you can't ask for special accommodations all the time *and* expect to fit in."

"You care too much about that. It shouldn't be our job to fit in. It should be society's job to integrate *us*."

I should have just agreed, for the sake of moving on, but I didn't like what she was saying. "I thought you weren't asking for special favors. Doesn't everyone have to respect some social norms if they don't want to live alone?"

Regina sidestepped that. "I can tell you're a clever man," she said. "But you're not fooling me. I see it all the time. You hate yourself, don't you?"

"What makes you say that?"

"I noticed it right away when you sat down, how you threw your cane on the floor like you couldn't get away from it fast enough." I wondered where else she expected me to store a five-foot pole while stuffed into my miniature chair. "You despise it and everything it implies."

It seemed to be my day for being on the receiving end of opinions about my mental health. Was there anyone who didn't think I was a self-loathing candidate for electric shock therapy?

"The only thing it implies," I said resignedly, "is that I'm not fond of dogs."

"I'll prove it to you," Regina went on, undeterred. "Answer this—if there were an operation to restore your sight, would you do it?"

"It's a moot question, because there isn't any," I said.

"But what if there were? The medical profession is always trying to come up with new ways to 'cure' us. Why, I read just the other day about a microchip that can be inserted in the brain and hooked up to a camera small enough to fit onto a pair of glasses. Would you undergo a procedure like that just to be quote-unquote *normal* again?"

"If you're asking whether I'd do something that would make me look like a crew member on the Borg ship, the answer is no. But if someone offered me a safe, noninvasive way to see again, I wouldn't turn them down just to keep up my club membership."

"I knew it!" Regina cried triumphantly.

"You think there's something wrong with that?"

"Yes. You're just buying into the whole idea of disability as pathology. The majority wants to stamp us out so they won't have to be disturbed by our wheelchairs and crutches and canes. Prenatal testing, euthanasia—they're just another form of genocide. But disability doesn't have to be looked upon as a diseased state."

"If you say so."

"I do. Our blind members often remark on how they would never want to become 'sighties.' Once you come to see it that way—as a different but deeply satisfying experience—you'll never want to go back."

Words failed me.

"Will you think about it?" Regina said. "I could send you some material. In Braille, of course."

"No thanks. It would be a waste of postage."

"But it's free—all our mailings to blind members are. It's the law."

"Sure," I said, giving up. "Could we talk about Shannon Sparrow for a bit?"

"Why not? I expect Alice told you I hated her."

"She put it more diplomatically, but I gathered you didn't get along. May I ask why?"

Regina paused. Then she surprised me by reaching out and grasping my right knee with her claw-like fingers. "You're strong, aren't you, for your size? How old are you?"

"Forty-eight."

"I would have thought younger. Does it disturb you to be touched by me?"

"No."

"It would be if you weren't VI. I'm not going to live very much longer, did you know that?"

I'd surmised it from what Alice Lowe told me.

"I won't live to be your age," she continued. "I probably won't make it much past my thirtieth birthday."

I frowned.

"You needn't pretend to be saddened. It's a fact and I accept it. The conventional wisdom is that living so close to death makes a person more . . . saintly, let's say. But it hasn't done that to me. If anything it's made me more resentful of what I'll never have. I wouldn't want to be anyone else, but that doesn't mean I have to like people who are smug about their own good fortune."

"Is that what Shannon was like?"

"Mmm. Not just beautiful and healthy, but certain she deserved to be, as though it were a privilege bestowed on her specially for being . . . I don't know, singled out in some way. The way she looked at me . . . It wasn't pity. I'm used to that. Or even revulsion. It was as if I didn't even exist, except as a contrast to her own glaring superiority. She regarded our clients the same way. Not as people, but as things so beneath her they might as well have been under a microscope."

It was the same egoism Shannon's sister had described. I said, "And yet I'm told she was physically affectionate toward her students. Didn't you complain about that to Alice?"

"Shannon did pander toward her pupils, but it was just an act. That's another reason I found her so objectionable. She treated them like little pets. Her students didn't understand how offensive her behavior was. I felt someone should stand up for them."

"So you spoke to Alice?"

"I did. But Alice never wants to see the bad in people. She told me I was over-dramatizing the situation. Personally, I think Alice was a little afraid of her."

"Why would Alice be afraid of Shannon?"

"Alice likes harmony. She prefers smoothing over differences to confronting obnoxious behavior, and Shannon was one of those difficult employees who's always picking fights."

"What sort of fights?"

"Well, over hours for instance. Several staff members here are on flexible schedules because of medical issues, like dialysis. I'm at my least fatigued early in the day so I typically leave at two, though I'm paid as though I work a full day. It's not unfair because I make up for it by taking fewer breaks and catching up on paperwork when I'm at home in bed. Shannon disagreed and kept raising 'unequal treatment' during staff meetings. Alice should have stood up to her, but she eventually gave in and let Shannon set her own hours. I think she was concerned Shannon would lodge a reverse-discrimination complaint. Then there was that ridiculous issue over Shannon's allergies."

"What was she allergic to?"

"Work, mainly, if you ask me. It started around November. Shannon suddenly discovered she had food 'sensitivities'—to gluten, lactose, what have you. Up until then, all staff members had been required to eat lunch together in the cafeteria. Alice believed it was important to maintaining community. Typically she'd invite three or four of our clients to join the faculty. The food here is very good—not the usual institutional fare, plenty of salad and fresh fruit—but Shannon claimed she could only eat what she'd prepared herself at home."

"Couldn't she have done that and still joined you for lunch?"

"That's what I said. But apparently her 'sensitivities' also included dining with people whose table manners aren't always ideal, so Alice allowed her to eat alone in her classroom. She said we had to respect Shannon's need for a calm atmosphere during mealtimes. Shannon started bringing all these containers of strange things to work and had a fit if anyone touched or moved them. One day one of her thermoses was accidentally shoved to the back of the refrigerator and she accused me of taking it."

"Why did she accuse you in particular?"

"We'd run into each other a few minutes before when I was coming out of the kitchen. I'd gone there to refill a water bottle and didn't even go near her things, but she stormed into my classroom, all indignant, asking what I'd done with it. I didn't know what she was talking about and told her I had better ways to spend my time than sampling her beauty potions. She called me a 'deformed little bitch' and said I was jealous of her because the only thing that would ever get close to my cunt was a catheter."

I recoiled from such overt nastiness. "That was . . . an ugly thing to say."

Regina chuckled. "I told her she was sorely mistaken if she thought I was a virgin. *That* shut her up fast."

"What happened then?"

"She hissed at me like a cobra and left. I was still laughing about it when I saw her pass my open door a few minutes later with the stupid thermos clasped to her chest like a baby."

"Did you have any other run-ins?"

"We exchanged words here and there. Shannon was always making spiteful remarks and I wasn't about to forego the pleasure of playing tit for tat with her. By the way, aren't you going to ask whether I have an alibi?"

"I'm sure the police already covered that with you."

Regina let out a bitter little snort. "Don't be naive. The officer who came to question me couldn't wait to get the interview over. I was here, you know, right in this room when Shannon died, but he didn't want to know about it. All he asked me was whether I'd seen poor Charlie Dickerson that morning. If I'd been able-bodied I would have been a prime suspect—don't they always want to know whether the victim had enemies?—but he just assumed I was incapable of it."

I thought about that. If one were strong enough it might be possible to inflict the wound that killed Shannon from a sitting position.

"What about you?" Regina asked when I didn't speak right away. "Do you think I could have killed her?"

I thought she was being deliberately provocative, but I played along. "Did you?"

She didn't answer.

After a moment of silence I heard the click of a button and her machine stirred to life. She moved off slowly in the direction of the door, and said over her shoulder, "You're trying to humor me, Doctor."

"Are you going to answer my question?"

"No," she said. "I'm tired now and I want to go home. Maybe some other time."

And like an automated hummingbird, she was gone.

FOURTEEN

It was still light when I reached home. I didn't feel like going inside yet, so I walked the half block to the esplanade beside the Chicago River. From there you can stroll east to the Lake and, with a brief detour north, continue out onto Navy Pier. During the day the pier is jammed with day-trippers, drawn to its popular blend of scenery and kitsch. But at that hour the excursion boats would be sighing at their moorings, the trinket merchants would be collapsing their stalls for the night, and the sightseers would be making for their cars. I knew if I hiked the quarter mile to the end I could have the place to myself.

I skirted the cotton candy and popcorn booths near the Ferris wheel, threaded through the emptying beer gardens and cafés, and went on to where the only sounds were the clap of the chop and the mawkish cries of the gulls overhead. At the easternmost point of the pier I took a seat on a bench facing out, remembering how the Lake used to look bathed in the rosy wash of twilight. A faint pulse to my right betrayed the presence of the Chicago Harbor Lighthouse. I breathed in the Lake's saltless odor, still a novelty to someone raised on the East Coast. Unlike the Atlantic, the Lake's tides are barely noticeable. But it has the same brooding presence as an ocean, the same implacable moods, and being by its side could usually be counted on to bring me peace.

I needed some peace then.

My conversation with Regina Best had unsettled me, and not simply because I felt compelled to defend my principles to someone who had a far greater right to view the world with hostility. I felt threatened by our discussion, forced to consider that I might be changing in more ways than I wanted to admit. I was far from liking my handicap, but I could tolerate it reasonably well so long as I thought of myself as essentially the same as other people. A few missed signals were all that separated me from the rest of humanity, a few minor deviations in the way I did things. But what if there was more to it than that?

It was different, I thought, for those blind from birth. How could you miss something you'd never experienced? But just as I didn't spend every waking moment longing to see again, neither did I want to believe the visual world was gradually losing appeal for me. Research had shown that the brain compensates for blindness by shifting functions to other capabilities. My remaining senses, hearing, touch, smell, *did* seem sharper than they were before. But I told myself it was simply because I relied on them more. If—when—the opportunity arose, I could easily go back.

Unless it was too late.

With some difficulty I forced my thoughts back to Charlie. The day hadn't been a complete failure, though it hadn't added much to my inventory of facts. I was still close to where I had started, with only the hunch that Shannon's anonymous lover had played a role in her death. The DNA report had been a disappointment, but it meant one less thing to follow up on. It was a virtual certainty Charlie had fathered Shannon's baby. The only question now was how he and Shannon had become intimate. I thought about what Alice Lowe had said about the extra attention Shannon gave Charlie and what it might mean.

As a psychiatrist I knew that people sometimes sought unequal relationships to fill an inner emotional void. And though child sexual abuse by women was considered rare, it did occur, and probably more often than the reported statistics indicated. Some call it the ultimate taboo, so deeply ingrained is the belief that women are incapable of molesting children. Their sexual passivity and maternal instincts are presumed to block such impulses, making the act too shocking for most people to accept as real. And yet there were well-documented cases of mothers having intercourse with their sons, of babysitters seducing their young charges . . .

As she had been described to me, Shannon didn't fit the profile of a typical abuser, a person with few educational attainments reared in a chaotic home. They were different from pedophiles, who are sexually attracted to children but don't always act on their desires. Child sexual abusers tend to be poor, to have difficulty holding down a job, and to have themselves been sexually abused as children. Frequently they are socially isolated, driven to forbidden relationships to compensate for overwhelming feelings of inferiority. Though I knew little about Shannon's upbringing, the portrait that had been painted of her was of a young woman raised in comfortable circumstances—too comfortable, if you believed her sister—and at least outwardly confident and secure.

But as I sat there analyzing the information I'd gathered, I began to recognize a different pattern, something that might also have been rooted in Shannon's childhood. From what I'd been told, Shannon had received excessive praise and attention as a child. She had grandiose views of herself, an inflated sense of entitlement, and little, if any, empathy for others. She was demanding and manipulative, treating personal relationships as simply a means to an end. In Marilyn Sparrow's words, she didn't have "normal feelings for people." These were classic symptoms of narcissistic personality disorder. And though NPDs often appeared to others as confident, successful people, inwardly they suffered from crippling feelings of low self-worth. The recent loss of a relationship that was important to her could have underscored those feelings in Shannon, driving her to seduce someone unlikely to reject her advances.

Did Shannon initiate a sexual liaison with Charlie to prove that she was still sexually desirable?

It was possible, I decided, likely even. I realized then how clouded my judgment had been up until that point. As a newly disabled man I had projected my fears about my own diminished appeal onto Charlie, subconsciously rejecting the idea that a normal woman would reject him as a sexual partner out of hand. And I'd desperately wanted to believe my original diagnosis was right. I couldn't fool myself any longer. It now seemed abundantly clear that Shannon was abusing Charlie. I simply hadn't spotted it.

I was so caught up in self-recrimination that I didn't even realize someone had come up to my bench until he spoke in my ear.

"Mistuh Mark?"

I recognized the voice at once. It was Mike, the *Streetwise* seller.

"Mistuh Mark? You OK? I apologize for botherin' you, but when I saw you sittin' out here all by yourself I thought maybe you was lost and could use a hand home."

"Thanks, but I'm not lost—not in the way you meant, anyway. Have a seat."

"No, no. I see now you was just sittin', enjoying the beautiful evening." He sounded embarrassed to have approached me.

"I was, but there's plenty of room on this bench for two of us. Do you come here much?"

"Some. I live right over there."

I couldn't see the gesture, but assumed he was pointing back toward the mouth of the pier. I hoped it didn't mean he was one of the legions of homeless people typically camped out on Lower Wacker Drive.

"We're neighbors then," I said. "Where exactly do you, uh . . . hang out?"

"Here and there," he said. "Around the water. I like it better than the shelter, especially when the weather is warm like this. I got me an old surplus tent, and nights when I don't get chased I find a place on the south side of the river. It's peaceful there, and I can watch the ships traveling by."

I nodded. I lived almost directly opposite the place he was talking about. "Please," I said. "Sit down and join me."

He did, leaning a stick of some sort against the bench between us.

"I was just doing some fishing," he explained. "They say the yellow perch is back so I come out here to try my luck."

"Did you catch any?"

"Some shorties is all. Thought I had a bass on the line, but he got away. Gotta get me a better pole to be landing one of those. I been saving for it with my paper money."

"How's that work? You get a percentage of what you sell?"

"Yessir. I buy the paper for ninety cents and sell if for two dollars, keep the difference. Some months I make three hundred dollars."

I internally calculated what that meant—less than $4,000 per year.

I said, "I sure wish you'd let me be one of your customers again." It still stung that he had turned me down that day the previous fall and I hadn't tried to buy a paper from him since.

"You got me wrong, Mistuh Mark. I ain't no charity. I'm a businessman."

A businessman selling a product. A product he naturally assumed I couldn't use.

I suddenly realized how wrong I'd been.

"Will you be working tomorrow?" I asked.

"If I still be standing."

"Good. Look for me early in the morning. There's something I want to show you."

The next day, bright and early so I wouldn't be seen by my colleagues—I was supposed to be closeted with my therapist, after all—I stopped by my building and took Mike upstairs to show him my scanner. I placed one of my journals on the screen and he and I listened behind a closed door while it read a page of the article back to us.

"Well, I'll be," he said when the machine had finished.

"I can use it to read almost anything printed, newspapers and popular magazines too, but I mostly get those off my computer. It's faster if I read them this way," I said, showing him the refreshable Braille display next to my keyboard. "But you see I *could* read your paper if I wanted to."

"I didn't know they made things like that. How much it cost you?"

"You don't want to know."

When we parted a little later on the street I was the proud purchaser of the latest *Streetwise* edition.

I spent the rest of the morning working off the list of Shannon's friends and acquaintances I had gleaned from the newspapers. Most were semiemployed artists she'd hooked up with in Chicago, but a few had known her when she was a student in Carbondale, and one, a young woman named Beth Andrews, who worked at an accounting firm in the Loop, had known Shannon since childhood. She agreed to meet with me at a coffee shop during her morning break.

"How did Shannon get along with her parents?" I asked her.

"As well as any of us, I suppose. You know how it is when you're a kid. You'll do almost anything not to be like them."

I could relate to that. "Were they close?"

"Not really. Shannon's mom was one of those nervous, prying types, you know, the kind that would read your diary to find out whether you were screwing your boyfriend. And her father . . ."

"Yes?" I prompted.

She lowered her voice to a conspiratorial whisper. "Big drinking problem. The kind where even your aftershave smells like whisky. I don't think I ever saw him sober. I heard it caught up with him last year. Had a stroke brought on by liver disease. Even then Sue—that's Shannon's mom—was smuggling six-packs into his hospital room. She was one of those, whaddya call them—"

"Enablers?"

"Yeah, that's it. Enablers. But he wasn't a mean drunk. More like one of those who's just sad all the time. Shannon was embarrassed by him, thought he was a loser."

"Was he ever violent toward her?" I asked, thinking this might have explained her absence at his funeral.

"No. She was his favorite. Couldn't turn down anything she asked for. It made the others so angry, seeing all the things she got that they didn't. Marilyn especially. I remember Marilyn taking a hairbrush to her once, just before she moved up here to get married to Randy. Shannon had borrowed a dress of hers without asking, and Marilyn had a fit. Shannon just laughed at her, said she wouldn't let herself get pawed by some hillbilly who'd probably end up in an I-beam someday. It made Marilyn so mad I thought she'd rip Shannon's hair out." She chuckled at the memory. "And then there was that business about the twins."

"What business?" I asked.

"Marilyn's twins. Randy had a problem, came down with the mumps when he was in the service, and Marilyn had to go to one of those sperm outfits to get pregnant. It was supposed to be a big dark secret, but Marilyn told Sue and she let on about it to Shannon last fall. Shannon went around telling everyone from Carbondale like it was a big joke. Even I had it out with Shannon then, telling her it was a mean thing to do."

"Do the twins know?"

"They do now. They're nice kids, I don't think they care much, but Marilyn was furious when it got back to them, afraid they'd think less of Randy as a father. That's when Marilyn stopped talking to Shannon. Some soap opera, huh?"

I agreed with her, remembering the phone call to Marilyn and wondering why Shannon had sought her sister's help if they weren't on speaking terms. Could Shannon have intended to lord her pregnancy over her sibling? It seemed to fit in with everything else I had learned about her, casting her in an even worse light.

My next stop was to see Joel Stern, the investment banker Nancy Kim had told me about. He worked in one of the big towers on Dearborn, forty floors up. When I arrived in his office he was packing for a move and I had to maneuver around several Humvee-sized boxes to take a seat.

"My bank's been taken over," he explained, "so my group's being moved to New York. It's just as well. Chicago's fucking dead as far as the markets are concerned. All the big deals are in London now. I'm hoping to get a transfer there one of these days, or if I'm lucky, Dubai. Expensive, but the lifestyle's good. What I wouldn't give for a steady supply of Cuban cigars."

I pictured him wearing a starched Thomas Pink shirt and patterned braces to go along with the flowery cologne I smelled when I shook his hand.

He went on in his Gatling gun style. "What did you want to know about Shannon? I already told the police all about her. *Corinne!*" he bellowed abruptly. "Would you please move some of these fucking boxes out of here? And bring me another Diet Coke. Don't forget the ice." He remembered he had company and asked, "You want one?"

"No, thank you. About Shannon—"

"I've gotta shed some of this fucking weight. It's the meetings. I can't help myself when they bring out the snacks. You look like you're in good shape. I know a blind guy who's a fund manager at Harris. Goes out running with his dog every day. I don't know how he does it."

"Why, are his legs affected too?"

"I mean keeps on top of things. Me, I can't go twenty seconds without checking the screens." To illustrate the point, he clacked a few keys on his computer and said, "Fucking Fed. One of my clients is waiting for the rate to come down so we can announce a reverse swap. *Corinne!*" he roared again impatiently. "I'm gonna start pissing sand if I don't get that pop."

Corinne came in and set down a glass on his desk. She began tugging at one of the cartons to my right. "Thanks, hon," he said to her. "When you've finished with that one you can start on the tombstones. Just the deals over a hundred mil, OK? I won't have room for the others. Fucking Manhattan real estate." He turned his attention back to me. "What was I saying?

Not a whole fucking lot. "We were talking about your former girlfriend. The one who was slashed to death."

"Oh, yeah. Shannon. Nice-looking broad, but not the kind you'd get serious about."

"Why was that?"

He gargled a mouthful of his soft drink. "Well, not exactly the classy type. Dressed like a Rush Street whore. Didn't matter to me, I was just in it for the sex. Shannon was a real acrobat in bed. It's hard to get action like that these days, especially from the skirts around here. If they sleep with you at all, it's just to move ahead, right? And as soon as you pull out they're back tapping on the Blackberry. Not that I don't take a peek afterwards too. Fucking things are like heroin."

I wondered whether he kept steering the conversation away from

Shannon on purpose. "Did Shannon have any . . . er . . . unusual sexual interests?"

"Like being tied up, you mean? Nah. If she had, I would have dumped her right away. I don't go in for that kind of thing. Well, maybe a little doggie style. And some of that Victoria's Secret merchandise is a real turn-on. You know, the push-up bras and garter straps. I really admire what they did with that brand. Practically owned the market for tramp wear until the other retailers got wise to their act. Too bad about that last quarter, though. Luckily I'd already shifted most of my portfolio to derivatives. You invest much?"

Maybe he'd like to take me on as a client. "You mentioned 'dumping' Shannon. Does that mean you broke it off?"

"Yeah. I didn't like all the hints she was dropping about a commitment. We'd only been dating for six months for Chrissake, and already the girl was planning the fucking engagement party. I could just imagine what it would be like introducing her relatives to my folks. Like that scene in the beginning of *Deliverance*, know what I mean? So I stopped calling."

I thought Marilyn Sparrow would enjoy knowing her act had paid off. "When was this?"

He swilled some more of his soda and belched. "More than a year ago now, I'd guess."

"How'd she take it?"

"Pissed, of course. In my experience, they always are. But she got over it. Last time I saw her she was with another guy, older fellow and by the looks of him, rolling in it. It was at Charlie Trotter's, last September I think. I was there for a business meeting and she caught my eye on the way out the door. Looked pretty pleased with herself."

"Did you get a close look at the man?"

"Uh-uh. They were across the room and I was with clients so I didn't stop to say hi. Plus, to tell the truth, I was a little tipsy. We must have polished off six bottles of Bordeaux. Clients were French and they expect that sort of thing. Set my expense account back two g's. Fucking incredible, though. Went down like a call girl on a john. Are we getting close to being done here? I've got a hundred messages and the day's not getting any younger."

"One last question," I said, figuring he couldn't resist the urge to brag some more. "Do you mind telling me what kind of car you drive?"

"Sure. It's a BMW 5 Series Sedan with a bronze finish. Got it two years ago when I was doing a deal over in Germany. You can buy them there, you know, and have them shipped back. The savings are fucking unreal and you get a big discount on the luxury tax and import duties. If you're interested, I could get you set up with a dealer . . ."

Fifteen minutes later I was back on the street feeling no wiser about Shannon than before. Joel Stern may have been a master of misdirection, but I doubted it. He seemed as genuinely removed from reality as anyone in his line of work.

By this time it was close to noon. The day was fair for May in Chicago, neither bone-chilling nor drenched with humidity, and the streets were beginning to fill up with office workers in search of natural light. I picked up a couple of Red Hots at an Irving's outlet and walked over to the Exelon Plaza on Madison, where stairs lead down from the street to a sunken plaza with a jet fountain in its center. It was tricky getting past all the sun worshippers lounging on the steps and I poked more than one limb on the way down, feeling like a nuisance each time. When I reached the bottom a man with a West Indian accent offered to help me find a seat and I gratefully accepted.

While I ate I listened to the gushing water and thought about what to do next. I'd almost exhausted my list of names and was no closer to learning the identity of Shannon's secret lover than when I'd started out. And even if I found him, what if that too proved to be a dead end? I had no suspect and no motive. True, the more I learned about Shannon the more unpleasant she sounded. But was a malignant personality enough reason to kill? O'Leary had been right. I was getting nowhere by going over the same ground as the police. I needed a fresh approach.

After a while I had an idea and phoned Yelena on my cell.

Astoundingly, she picked up right away.

"*Borya?*" came a voice that could have splintered wood. It was followed by a spate of Slavic I didn't need a translator to get the gist of.

"No. Your other true love."

"Oh."

"Try not to sound so elated. Listen, I need you to do something for me."

I explained what I wanted.

"You're asking me to spy?" Yelena said when I finished. I didn't take the offended tone seriously. Judging by the amount of inside dope Yelena had on everyone else in the office she was well-versed in the type of espionage I had in mind.

"Isn't that what you people are good at? Besides, it's not spying. The woman is dead, so she can't complain. And if anyone asks, I'll take responsibility. Call me back on my cell when you have the information."

"Where are you anyway? It sounds like a beach."

"Doctor's orders. Sunlight and plenty of Vitamin D to help counteract my suicidal depression. Will you do it right away?"

"I have a report to bind for Doctor Goldman."

"Threaten him with a different kind of bondage if he objects. It'll only take a few minutes."

I rang off and waited. With a national medical database still a few years away, my hospital, like many others, had set up its own system, which was linked to the offices of private practitioners throughout the city. My fingers were crossed that Shannon's name would turn up in its records, saving me a lot of digging. For once, the dice obeyed me. A few minutes later Yelena called back with a name and address. I phoned ahead to see whether I could be seen that afternoon. When I heard it could be done, albeit with difficulty, I dumped the remains of my lunch in a trash can and hopped a Brown Line train headed north.

That spring, the century-old 'L' lines were disintegrating from lack of funding while the lawmakers in Springfield fought with the governor over increases to their pay packages. The result was a nightmare of service interruptions and snail-paced trains, with dire warnings of worse to come. Though it was only one in the afternoon, it might as

well have been rush hour. I didn't mind since it meant I wouldn't have
to engage in a debate with someone who insisted on giving up their pri-
ority seating for me. No one moved an inch as I shouldered through the
packed flesh, eventually ending up jackknifed against a woman rustling
a paper bag. The sweet-acrid odor of rhubarb and strawberries wafted
up from it, filling my nose with spring. "I bought them at the farmer's
market at the Daley Center," she explained when I remarked upon how
good it smelled.

When the loudspeaker announced Belmont, I fought my way off
the train and followed the steps of the other departing passengers down
to the exit turnstile, blinking as I left the station and came out into the
bright sunlight. I dug my glasses out of my pocket, pulled my hat brim
down low, and set out east in the direction of the Lake.

Within a block I had hit my stride, holding my cane at waist level
and tapping it back and forth in an arc slightly wider than my shoulders. I used a rigid fiberglass cane without one of those silly red stripes.
Early on, I'd decided if I was going to use a cane at all, it wasn't going to
be a pretend one with a silver handle and an ebony finish. White-cane
laws exist for a reason, and I was more concerned about being mowed
down by an unsuspecting motorist than looking like Fred Astaire. The
aluminum tip looked like a flying saucer and made a racket like a dying
Chevy, but if I paid attention to the sound I could make out some of
the things I was passing: a vacant lot, a brick wall. And my cane's long
length—it rounded off just at the tip of my nose—allowed me to move
as quickly as I wanted to without risk of impaling myself on an unex-
pected obstacle.

I was moving along at a brisk speed when in between the sound
of my taps I noticed someone walking not far behind me. Whoever
it was had a distinctive squeak to their shoe, like the sole had been
worn down from a fallen arch. It seemed familiar, something I'd heard
recently, though I couldn't remember when. The squeak went on for
several blocks, never more than five or ten feet away, slowing when I
slowed and speeding up when I quickened my step. I began to think
I was being followed. The sensation grew stronger and stronger until

the hairs on my neck were standing up as stiffly as a marine squad. At Clark I stopped and pretended to consult my wristwatch to see what my shadow would do. He or she passed by and kept going without a pause. I mocked myself for my paranoia and went on.

Dr. Terry Garland belonged to a group practice called Women's Wellness Associates on the corner of Belmont and Broadway, smack in the middle of the neighborhood known as Boystown. I didn't think they got a lot of walk-ins.

I liked Dr. Garland almost at once. She didn't sputter and lose the power of speech when I introduced myself, but simply asked if she might show me to her office, and then steered me there with a subtle touch to the small of my back. She had a deep, rich voice tone, bordering on a baritone, and a powerful, spicy scent that made me think of pumpkin pie. We passed down a corridor where doors were being repeatedly opened and shut. Behind one of them an infant was wailing like a bagpipe.

"I don't have much time to spare, I'm afraid," Terry said, after we'd seated ourselves in her cramped office. "You wanted to know about Shannon Sparrow?"

"Yes," I said. "You were her obstetrician?"

"I guess you could call me that, though I saw her only once. It was an accident that I saw her at all—my practice has been closed to new patients for some time—but one of my partners had a family crisis that day and I took over her appointments for her." Terry rummaged around in her desk drawer, removed something, and asked, "Want one?"

"Depends on what you're offering."

"Sorry. That was dumb of me. Piece of gum," she explained.

"Sure." I held out my hand, and she deposited a foil-wrapped stick into it.

"I should warn you, the flavor's clove. I got addicted to it after I stopped smoking."

I bit into the gum and had an instant recollection of a college girl-friend with a fondness for Doc Martens and D. H. Lawrence.

I said, "I didn't know they made this stuff anymore. Where did you get it?"

"There's a shop up the street that specializes in sixties novelties. They even have Trolls. I used to love those things, had dozens of them." She laughed, self-deprecatingly. "I know I'm dating myself."

It sounded like my kind of store. But I was anxious to get on to what she had to say about Shannon.

"So Shannon wasn't a long-term patient of yours, then?"

"No. Apparently she'd called us as an emergency referral, thought she was miscarrying."

"Do you know who referred her?"

"You'd have to ask my partner. When I heard what had happened to her, I thought about calling the police but I wasn't sure I was ethically permitted to disclose she was a patient. And, well, I'm always so busy. I'm a single mother myself, and some days it's all I can do to find time to brush my teeth. But you're here now, and really how much harm can it cause?"

"Cavities, mainly."

She laughed again. "You're funny. Were you treating her, too?"

"No. The boy who's been accused of her murder. I'm being sued for malpractice for failing to realize she was . . . er, involved with him. That's why I'm here. I was hoping you could help me out with a little information."

"Oh," she said sympathetically. "I know what you're going through. You're not safe these days unless you order every possible test, whether or not it's necessary, and even when you do, heaven help you if the baby comes out with a problem. I had a mom not long ago, two older boys with autism and ADHD. I deliver the third by emergency C-section, and guess what? He's autistic too. Except this time it's *my* fault. I can only imagine what it's going to do to my premiums."

I commiserated with her and then steered the subject back to Shannon.

"It's nothing earth-shattering," she said. "Just that some of her behavior was odd. It made me wonder, especially later when I heard she'd been killed."

"Odd in what way?"

"Inconsistent. It started on the day she came in."

"Which was when, exactly?"

"Let me see." She fiddled with her keyboard for a moment and said, "February 14. How appropriate. Valentine's Day. She was about six weeks pregnant then."

"So that would place conception around the end of December?"

"That's right. Apparently she didn't realize she was pregnant right away, because she had what she thought was a light period in January. Then, when another one didn't come, she took a home test and panicked, thinking the earlier bleeding meant she was going to miscarry. She was pretty upset about it."

"Did you think that was unusual?"

"A little. Usually when I see patients like Shannon—single women who haven't been trying to conceive—they're not too thrilled about being pregnant in the first place. Miscarriage isn't pleasant, but a lot easier to handle emotionally than abortion."

I nodded. "But she wasn't miscarrying?"

"Uh-uh. I gave her a pelvic and asked her some questions. She said the blood flow had stopped only a day or two after it started and she hadn't experienced any cramping. When I heard that, I suspected post-implantation bleeding. Many women spot a bit around the time the embryo leaves the fallopian tube. Based on what she was describing, I told her she probably had nothing to worry about. She seemed so relieved I thought she was going to cry."

That was surprising, given what Shannon's sister had told me about a possible abortion.

"So as far as you knew, she was planning on keeping the baby?"

"That's what I thought—at least initially. It struck me because she admitted she wasn't in a relationship with anyone. It's no easy thing to raise a child alone and I was a bit surprised she wasn't asking me about other options. I assumed it was a religious issue."

"Did she say who the father was?"

"No. And I don't ask unless the patient volunteers the information. I did confirm that she wasn't having sex with multiple partners to lessen the possibility of an STD. Shannon said there had been only one man, that she'd broken up with him after New Year, and that she wasn't planning to tell him about the child. Later, when I read in the papers who he was, it surprised me. I mean, here she was, a teacher who'd had sex with one of her students. Didn't she realize what kind of trouble she'd be in if she carried the baby to term? You remember the story about that high-school teacher, the one who got pregnant by a seventeen-year-old. Didn't she go to jail?"

"Yes. But Charlie Dickerson is legally an adult. Maybe that's why Shannon thought she could get away with it, especially if she wasn't planning to say whose baby it was."

Terry said, "Fair enough. But if she was sure it was his, I don't understand why she didn't want to have the fetus tested."

"You discussed that with her?"

"At length. I always bring it up, regardless of the mother's age. The American College now recommends preliminary screening for trisomies in all pregnancies. A simple blood test is all that's needed, and a detailed ultrasound is usually sufficient to confirm a positive result. It's become so routine in my practice, we don't even think about *not* doing it. But Shannon turned me down flat."

"Did she say why?"

"She seemed to be morbidly afraid of doing anything that might cause harm to the fetus. I explained we weren't talking about CVS or amniocentesis, which do carry a risk of fetal death, however slight. But she wouldn't even hear of it. She told me that she worked with intellectually disabled adults, thought they were lovely people, and was sure a positive result wouldn't alter her plans. I couldn't argue with that, so I let it drop."

"How were things left between you two?"

"Pretty standard. I prescribed prenatal vitamins and asked her come back in a month's time. I advised her to get plenty of rest and to take it easy for a while and to call me if she started to spot again. I could have handed her back to my partner, but being a single mom myself I felt some sympathy for her. I remember thinking I didn't like her all that much, but maybe I would warm to her over time, and she was going to need a lot of support over the next months."

"Was that all you were going to tell the police?" I asked, disappointed. I had gotten my hopes up there would be more.

"No, wait. About two weeks later Shannon called back asking about a paternity test."

I cocked my head in Terry's direction. "You mean a DNA test?"

"Right," she said. "I asked the reason and she told me she was no longer sure who the father was, that she'd lied to me when she said there was only one. I wasn't too happy about that, but it happens. Many women have trouble admitting to sex with multiple partners, especially to a doctor they've just met. It's one of the reasons I don't like seeing new OB patients. I like to have an established relationship with someone whose baby I'm going to deliver, so they trust me and I trust them. With the malpractice situation, you can't be too careful. Anyway, Shannon told me she'd been having second thoughts about not informing the baby's father, there were money issues involved, and she needed to be absolutely certain who he was before she went ahead."

So Shannon hadn't been sure the fetus was Charlie's. Or had she?

"That's interesting," I said. "What did you tell her?"

"I told her yes, prenatal paternity testing was available. But it requires a fetal tissue sample. The only way to get one is by doing CVS or amniocentesis. I was remembering her earlier objections to testing, you see—the fears she'd expressed. I advised her to wait until the baby was born, when she could get the results in as little as two weeks."

"What did she say?"

"She did a complete about-face about the baby's safety. Told me she didn't care what happened to the child. She had a decision to make and 'obviously'—to use her words—couldn't wait nine months to find out. She demanded that I schedule the procedure as soon as possible. Was pretty snotty about it, actually."

"Did you go along?" I asked.

"Are you kidding? You can imagine the warning bells going off in my head. Here was a woman I barely knew who'd first turned down a completely innocuous blood test and now wanted me to plunge a six-inch needle into her abdomen. I was worried about what would happen if I did what she asked and—God forbid—something happened to her baby. All I needed was another lawsuit. So I told her I first wanted to do the blood work and a Level II ultrasound. If one or both indicated a higher than normal risk for a birth defect we could consider a more invasive procedure that would also tell her who the father was. Otherwise, I couldn't in good conscience agree."

"What was her response?"

"She said something I won't repeat and hung up on me."

"What did you make of it?"

"I don't know. Something in her manner made me feel she wasn't telling the truth. To be charitable, given what we now know about the baby's father, she may have started to think about what it would be like to raise a retarded son or daughter."

"Not a son," I said.

"Why?" Then she thought about it and said, "Oh, yes of course. Fragile X. How clever of you."

"So you think the sudden concern about who fathered her baby was manufactured, a way of getting genetic testing without coming right out and asking for it?"

"You're the psychiatrist, you tell me. To tell the truth, I don't know what to think, except that something must have happened in those two weeks to make her think less fondly about the baby she was carrying. It would explain what she meant by not having nine months to make a decision."

"Earlier you mentioned her reaction when she found out she wasn't miscarrying. Could that have been faked?"

Terry thought about this before answering. "I don't think so. We were sitting face to face in my examination room. I've been doing this a long time and I'm certain I would have known. I've never seen anyone so overjoyed."

"You also said something about the pregnancy being unplanned. How did you know that? Did she tell you?"

Terry paused before answering. "Now that you mention it, no. I just assumed it was because she was young and single. What are you thinking?"

"Just that she might have conceived intentionally."

Terry snorted. "You don't think she actually wanted to marry that boy, do you?"

I winced.

Terry must have noticed my expression and hurried to say, "I'm sorry, that didn't come out the way I intended. Of course, if he were of normal intelligence . . . ," she trailed off.

Which only made it worse.

FIFTEEN

When I got back to the street, I was tired and confused. The sun was drilling holes in my eyes again, so I crossed over to the shady side of Broadway and began walking south. I remembered the area well from the long walks I had taken after moving to Chicago, seeking out the attractions of my new home and trying to forget why I had one. The strip I was on winds past some of the most desirable addresses in the city, but it hardly resembles a shopping magnet for the wealthy. Used-clothing emporiums and acupuncturists share frontage with hardware outlets and insurance agencies, and the antique stores lean more toward Fiesta Ware than Chippendale. It has an unpretentious Midwestern feel to it, as far removed from Madison Avenue as Cape Town is from the North Pole.

At Fullerton, I stopped at a coffee shop, ordered myself a rare espresso as a treat, and phoned Alice Lowe.

"I'm glad you called," she said. "I asked around like you wanted and found out a few things."

"I'm in your neighborhood now. Would it be all right if I stopped by in a little while?"

"I have a staff meeting starting in a few minutes. But if you're free, perhaps we could have that dinner you promised me?"

It sounded like a swell idea to me.

We agreed to meet at the New Horizons Center at 6:30. I had a few hours to kill, so I walked the few blocks over to the Lincoln Park Zoo. The baby giraffe had drawn a crowd and the pathways were thick with strollers and baby joggers and nannies chatting in Spanish and Tagalog and Polish. It was easy to tell them apart from the biological mothers, whose conversation tended toward the didactic. "No, Taylor, that's not a bear. It's a koala. Can you say K-O-A-L-A? What letter does *koala* begin with?" I thought of my own son, Louis, now coming up on his third birthday. I wondered if we would ever visit a zoo together and what he would make of a father who always needed to have sights pointed out for him. As if reading my mind, a docent stopped me and offered me a Braille guide to the exhibits, and I wandered around identifying lions, and tigers, and bears until nearly closing time.

When I tapped up to the center a little later, Alice was waiting for me at the door. "Here," she called when I came up. It suddenly struck me that I hadn't been on a date with a woman since the night Jack died. I quickly shoved aside the thought.

"How's everything?" I asked awkwardly. "Another rough day?"

"Impossible," she said. "That's why I was so forward about asking you to dinner. I could really use a hiatus for a few hours. How about you? Any success?"

"I'll tell you while we eat. Where are we going?"

"A neighborhood place called LaScala that's supposed to be good. It's within walking distance. I looked up the menu on line. Shall I describe it to you?"

Alice locked her arm in mine and highlighted the house offerings while we strolled over to the restaurant, housed in a Victorian on Southport. When we arrived, "Nessun Dorma" was playing quietly on the sound system, pans were being rattled in the kitchen, and wood smoke was drifting from an oven in the rear. Tables lit with votive candles winked like a field of fireflies at dusk. The hostess showed us to the one Alice had reserved, in a corner where I could stow my cane upright. Alice carried a folding model that she collapsed before sitting down.

"I'm sure we're creating quite a scene," she said after we'd gotten settled. "Two blind people eating out without a sighted keeper."

"Should I knock over my water glass to liven things up even more?" Alice giggled.

"Or accidentally set fire to my tie?"

"Might be wise to reverse the order," Alice said.

After the waiter announced the daily specials and we'd ordered food and a bottle of wine, I asked Alice what she had learned.

"It's not much. I asked around about whether Shannon was dating someone. No one had seen the man, but it seemed she did have a beau."

"Did you find out his name?"

"No. As you mentioned, Shannon was being very secretive about it. Mmmm, that smells good."

The waiter had whisked over our first course, fried artichokes *alla giudia*—in the Jewish style—and we dipped in. Between mouthfuls, Alice told me that around February of the preceding year, Shannon had come back from a long weekend with a tan and told one of her coworkers, Dean Parsons, that she'd been to Hawaii. This was followed by half a dozen other weekend trips, including one to Arizona in March, and another to San Francisco in April. The frequent travel continued until the fall, when Shannon abruptly stopped mentioning it. All of this squared with what Marilyn Sparrow had told me.

"Did Parsons know who she was vacationing with?" I asked.

"No. Just that she wasn't by herself."

"She could have taken those trips with a female friend," I said, playing devil's advocate. The artichokes were just right, crisp but not chewy, and I suspected the chef had been trained abroad.

"I don't think so. That's a lot of money to spend on airfare. Shannon's salary, unfortunately, was barely above minimum wage. But there's more. Around June, she received a package by special delivery with a turquoise box in it. I assume you know where those come from."

I did. It was Annie's favorite jeweler, and I'd purchased many a peace offering there.

"Tiffany," I said. "Did anyone catch the name of the sender?"

"Nellie, our receptionist, said it came directly from a store on Michigan Avenue."

"Did Nellie watch her open it?"

"No. But later that day she was seen wearing a necklace, an expensive-looking one. After that she wore it every day."

"Did you get a description?"

"Yes. It was silver or white gold with a teardrop-shaped diamond pendant."

I made a mental note to ask O'Leary whether such an item had been found on Shannon's body. "That could be important. I doubt Charlie could have purchased an expensive gift like that on his own."

"True, but all the necklace shows is that there *was* someone else in the picture," Alice said. "We don't know if he was involved in Shannon's death."

Our *primi piatti* had come. I twisted a strand of homemade *chitarra* onto my fork and tasted it. It too was perfect, bathed in a clam and garlic sauce. I probed my plate with my fork and found one tucked into its shell. It was as fresh and sweet as any I'd tasted in Italy.

"This place is amazing," I said appreciatively.

"I'm glad you like it. I was worried it would be one of those dreadful rubber cheese and Ragu joints."

"Properly speaking, *ragù* just means sauce. It doesn't have to resemble watered-down tomato paste."

"Spoken like a true Son of Italy. Now it's your turn."

"Sorry. I don't cook."

"Silly. I meant for you to tell me what you found out today."

I filled her in on my visit to Shannon's gynecologist while I emptied my plate and swabbed up the remains of the sauce with a chunk of crusty bread. When I mentioned my idea that Shannon might have become pregnant with Charlie's child on purpose, Alice grew quiet and asked me to pour her another glass of wine.

"But why . . . why would she do something like that?"

"I can think of only one reason."

"Which is?"

"Blackmail."

The word cast a pall over the table.

"That's . . . plausible," Alice said, after a moment. "But do you really think Shannon intended to go to this . . . boyfriend of hers, demand some kind of payment? It sounds so nineteenth century."

"I know, but look at the lengths she took to conceal the affair. I'm thinking it was someone important, a politician maybe. Her former roommate said they broke up sometime last fall. Maybe Shannon was trying to salvage something from the relationship, even though it was over. Maybe she was using Charlie to get pregnant. She'd have to move quickly to pass the child off as the other fellow's. Charlie happened to be available and was unlikely to raise an objection."

"But wouldn't a paternity test eventually prove who the real father was?"

"I think she never intended it to get that far. She'd offer to have an abortion in return for some kind of payoff and then disappear. According to Shannon's sister, her place was packed up, like she was planning to move, and she'd scheduled some kind of medical procedure, one that involved anesthesia."

"All right," Alice said. "I'm with you so far. But then why the sudden desire to have the baby tested?"

"That's the part I don't get. Unless she thought there was a chance she was mistaken. Maybe mystery man called her bluff and she got desperate. We know now that the baby was Charlie's. But that doesn't mean she was sure it was."

"There's no doubt about the accuracy of the DNA test—I mean that Charlie was the father?"

"I had a friend read it to me. The alleles of Shannon's fetus matched up almost perfectly with Charlie's. If there's one thing I've learned in life, it's that genes don't lie."

Alice chewed on this a bit before replying. "You say that like it means something special to you."

I stiffened. I didn't like being asked about how I went blind, but it was my fault for leading the conversation in that direction. And Alice wasn't being morbidly curious in the manner of strangers who thought it appropriate to ask me how I dressed myself while I was standing on line at the grocery store. So I told her about it while we ate our main course, a melt-in-your-mouth veal *saltimbocca*.

"That's tough," she said when I'd finished. "I've often asked myself whether it's better to go blind gradually or all at once. You seem to have had the worst of both worlds."

"What about you?"

"Car accident," she said. "My fiancé—his name was Ted—and I were returning from a weekend at a friend's cottage in Delavan. It was Labor Day and we'd both had too much to drink. Ted lost control of the car going up a ramp. We plowed into a bus and Ted was killed instantly. I should have died too, but I woke up a week later in intensive care with massive head injuries. It took months to learn how to walk again. I've been legally blind ever since. I was twenty-five when it happened."

I wanted to know how old she was now, but thought it impolite to ask. "What did you do before?"

"I was a nurse. Naturally, I couldn't continue working in a hospital, so when I was up and about again I went back for my master's degree in Rehabilitation Counseling. I'm forty-two now, in case you were wondering."

I smiled at how easily she had read me. "I confess the question had occurred to me. Is this the part where we're supposed to describe what we look like?"

"I already know."

"Yeah. How so?"

"George Clooney. I'd know that voice anywhere. Perhaps not as tall."

I laughed. "It's a good thing you *can't* see me."

"What about me?" Alice asked playfully.

"Diane Keaton."

After we'd finished with coffee and I was paying the check, Alice asked if I'd like to stop by her place. "It's only a few minutes away and we could open a bottle of Armagnac I bought in France."

"That's a bit rich for me, but I'll take bourbon if you've got any."

Alice lived in a two-flat on Altgeld in the upper unit. "I bought it for the sunlight," she said as she unlocked the door and let us in. "We're in the living room, couch on your left. I'm going to freshen up a minute. Feel free to look around."

That was a nice touch, if you'll excuse the poor pun. Coming upon an unfamiliar room always presented a social dilemma, a Hobson's choice between asking for a sketch of the floor plan or creating suspense for my onlookers by feeling experimentally ahead. Often I took the coward's approach and waited by the door until someone caught on and came to my rescue. It was childish, but I hated feeling like I was on the wrong side of a two-way mirror with the rest of the world looking in. There was no danger of that with Alice, so I accepted her invitation to explore.

I made a few passes around the perimeter before tackling the center. The apartment was an older one with hardwood floors and a fireplace flanking the left wall. Facing it were a couch and glass-topped coffee table with a vase of tulips in its center that I paused over. On a set of bookshelves to the side of the mantle I located Alice's sound system and CD collection, neatly organized in cubbyholes according to type—opera, jazz, etc.—with Braille labels above each section and on the individual covers. Her taste was much classier than mine, which tended toward the sort of music that can be heard on 97.1 The Drive. I picked out a jazz album I was familiar with and put it in the player while I continued my inspection of the shelves. They contained many books, both Braille and standard, and more than a few plaques with what I guessed was Alice's name on them.

Beyond the living area I found a door leading to a small galley kitchen. The appliances were newer, and like mine, equipped with blind-friendly controls. Everything was as neat and orderly as a cross-stitch. Evidently Alice didn't share my predilection for household sloth. I washed my hands and dried them on a towel and took a sip of water from the tap. Back in the living room I noticed a stand near the window with some ceramic pieces on it. They were the shape and size of nautilus shells, with long, looping whorls etched into the surface like the patterns waves leave on a beach. I traced them with my fingers until Alice returned, some long minutes later.

"Do you make these?" I asked her as she was pouring our drinks nearby.

"The ceramics? Yes, a hobby of mine." Alice touched a tumbler to my hand and we went to sit on the couch.

"I forgot to ask you whether you wanted ice," Alice said, "but I pegged you for a straight man."

"Is that a veiled slight to my conversational skills?"

"I was thinking more of sexual orientation. You are, aren't you?"

"Straight?" I wasn't bothered by the question, though I was curious about what prompted it.

"I'm sorry. It's just so rare to find an unmarried man your age who is."

"How do you know I'm unmarried?" I tested.

"I don't know. I suppose I would have expected you to mention it by now if you were."

I surprised myself by telling her I was divorced, though I didn't supply any of the details. "And you? I mean, after your fiancé was killed, you never found someone else?"

Alice sighed. "I had a few relationships, but none I cared enough about to continue. And I've been so busy the last ten years getting the center established. It's been my whole life. It's difficult to sustain relationships when you're working so hard for what you believe in."

"Uh-oh," I said. "An idealist."

"You're not, I take it."

"Everyone has an angle, even when they claim to be motivated by altruism."

"What's yours then?"

"Filthy lucre," I said.

We talked of many things while the bourbon and the strains of Miles Davis's trumpet lit a glow in my limbs. I was feeling guilty about enjoying myself so much while Charlie was still locked up in a cell, but I had been without any break for so very long. And more than that, I was experiencing an odd sensation, something I had once taken for granted but seemed to have forgotten lately. It confused me at first, until I sorted it out. For the first time in over a year, more than that if you counted the months I spent locked up in my apartment, I was completely at ease in the company of another human being.

Up until then, I'd gone out of my way to avoid other blind people, thinking we could have little in common. I told myself blindness was just a random physical trait, like being left-handed or having red hair, not a basis for companionship. And to me, "blind" still summoned childhood memories of Mr. Cosenza, the unmarried neighbor who sat on his porch all day chain-smoking and threatening to call the cops on our games. He frightened me, and after I wound up in the same boat, gave me another reason to pry myself out of the house. But as I sat there warming to Alice's conversation, I realized what a hypocrite I'd been, buying into all the stereotypes I fought so hard not to have applied to me. Sure, Alice lived alone, but it wasn't because she was cranky or a misfit. She went everywhere and did everything and was as cultured and interesting a person as I'd ever met.

But that was only half of it. During my relatively short stint as a blind man I'd lost track of all the strategies I used to appear as normal as possible. Turning my head at loud noises, "looking" at people when they spoke to me, relaxing my eyes when I sensed them wandering. These and other behaviors had become almost as repetitive as breathing, yet never entirely effortless. I knew my facial expressions still reflected what I was thinking, that I hadn't forgotten how to smile or frown, but all the same I periodically checked them to be sure. The Regina Bests of the world would have chastised me for trying so hard, but I could no more allow myself to develop a zombie stare than I would have stopped combing my hair or brushing my teeth. What I hadn't considered up until then was how exhausting it all was. With Alice I could let go—be as blind as a post if I liked—and not have her think any worse of me. It was like finding family.

"Where were you?" Alice asked. "I think I lost you for a moment."

"Just how nice it is to be here—with you. Sort of like being at a drive-in movie. Alone in the dark where no one can see us."

"Oh dear," she said in mock alarm. "You're not going to grope me, are you?"

"Only if you promise to grope me back."

"I was hoping you would say that."

I moved in closer and let my lips find hers. We stayed that way for a long while, kissing and exploring each other shyly. Alice's cheekbones were high and she had a lovely curve to her jaw. She wore no jewelry except for a pair of small pearl earrings. I traced my fingers over them and down her smooth neck to her breastbone. Alice began to breathe more rapidly and gave me permission to continue by placing a hand in my lap. My penis leaped at her touch. *Whoa, buddy*, I recall thinking. I hadn't anticipated us ending up like this, wasn't sure we should be moving so quickly, but my misgivings were quickly scuttled by her apparent willingness and my own overpowering need. My hands shook as I loosed the buttons of her blouse. Alice undid her bra and guided me to her breasts. I felt her nipples come erect, as soft as doeskin in the quick of my palms. When I put my head down to take one in my mouth she shuddered and said, "Perhaps we should continue this in my bedroom."

Of course I came too quickly, it had been that long.

But Alice didn't seem to mind, saying only that I'd flattered her. After I'd recovered from the shock, Alice refreshed our drinks and we made love a second time, very slowly, to the strains of the jazz still drifting in from the other room. When we were done, I lay with my head on Alice's chest, listening to the stronger music of another beating heart while she rubbed little circles into my scalp.

"A man with a full head of hair," she observed. "I like that. Are you gray?"

"A little, when I last looked. Probably more now. I suppose it's one of the few advantages. I don't have to be confronted each day with how rapidly I'm aging. And you?" I provoked.

"You should know better than to ask a woman that."

"You could lie to me, you know. I wouldn't know the difference."

"No. But I wouldn't like myself for it. What was it you said earlier about genes?"

"That they're the only things in this world that don't lie."

"That speaks volumes about your sense of trust. Are you really that jaded?"

"Only when I'm not being cynical. But you're welcome to keep working on me."

"I might just do that," Alice said, laughing and pulling me atop her once more.

SIXTEEN

Dean Parsons had a clean, male odor and a frank, open air. "Alice told me what you were trying to do, and I want to help," he said to me. "This job's the only thing standing between me and the soup kitchen right now. I've been putting out feelers here and there, what with the center in so much trouble, but I haven't come up with anything. There aren't a lot of openings for physical therapists with only a bachelor's degree. I should have gone on for my master's, but I was already up to my neck in debt. I've been paying off my student loans for ten years and I'm still way in the hole. Costs me $900 a month with no end in sight. I would've been better off becoming a plumber, like my old man. But I like helping people. Mind if I do a few stretches while we talk?"

I said I didn't. We were in the center's physical recreation room, a sunlit space at the rear of the facility. I heard him lower himself to a floor mat and begin grunting, while my thoughts drifted back to earlier that morning.

It had been close to dawn when Alice and I finally dozed off, cradled in each other's arms. I awoke alone a little after 8:30 to the sound and smell of bacon frying. "I need protein after all that exercise," Alice said when I had dressed and followed my nose to her kitchen. "Coffee?"

"Tea, if you have it, with milk and sugar. God, I'm sore," I said, drawing my shoulder blades together and rolling them back to ease the crick.

Alice set a tea kettle on the burner. "Hopefully not on my account."

I realized my mistake and apologized. "I didn't mean that the way it sounded. I'm a little out of practice sharing a bed."

"I thought so. Why? Surely you haven't been holding back because you think less of yourself as a lover?"

In reality, the worry had been there, and I'd almost welcomed my history as an excuse for not testing the situation. But I couldn't tell her that. Despite the closeness that was developing between us, I wasn't ready to disclose my fears about my weakened sex appeal, much less reveal my shady past. I didn't think someone as upright as Alice would react positively to learning I was a serial adulterer with a son's death on his conscience. I wasn't even sure how I was going to make good on my promise to tell Sep and not have it permanently ruin his opinion of me. "It's not that," I prevaricated. "It's just that I've been preoccupied with . . . so many other issues. And now there's this problem with Charlie."

"Yes. I shouldn't have distracted you from that. Or myself from the center, for that matter. I'm dreading what new woes today will bring."

"It's that bad?"

"Yes. I've been putting off meeting with our lenders, but with families bolting left and right . . ." The tremor in her voice was wrenching and I wondered how it felt to be facing the destruction of her lifelong work. "Do you think we've been fooling ourselves, thinking there's a way out of this?"

"I'm not ready to give up yet," I said.

But I didn't feel at all confident about our chances.

We talked about our plans for the day over breakfast, and I told her I wanted to stop by the center before going home, to talk to Parsons and Shannon's other friend, Leslie Sherman. After Alice had showered and dressed, we walked to the center holding hands but saying little, each preoccupied with our own thoughts. When we parted a block from the front door she asked "Will I see you again?" I answered, "Unless you're blind." She laughed and pecked my cheek. "You're a good man. Call me if you learn anything new." The sound of her receding steps filled my ears until they were swallowed by the blare of a truck horn half a block away. I let a respectable interval pass and then went over and entered the center myself.

"It's hard work," Parsons was now explaining between puffs of breath, "lifting clients in and out of wheelchairs all day long, helping them with their range-of-motion exercises. It really messes up my back if I don't watch my core. The ambulatory ones, like Charlie, are easier. We used to play ball, things like that. Before he got arrested, I was teaching Charlie how to bench press. He's a great kid, you know."

I agreed.

"I could probably land work as a home aide, but the pay's even worse and, I mean, who wants to be wiping up somebody else's piss and shit all day long? At least here, I didn't have to do diaper duty and I felt like I was putting some of my schooling to use. I'll probably end up in a health club. Got a friend who's a personal trainer at Windy City Athletics, said he'd put in a good word for me. Funny world, isn't it, when there's more money to be had helping rich folk trim their guts than working with people who are happy just to be able sit up? You should count yourself lucky." He stopped abruptly. "Sorry, that was a bit presumptuous of me. But working for Alice . . . I guess I don't think of being blind as such a big a deal anymore. If it wasn't for the cane you wouldn't even know."

I asked him if he could shed any further light on who Shannon's boyfriend had been.

"Rich dude is all I can tell you. Had to be, with the places he was taking her to. That place in Phoenix, what's it called? The Biltmore. Shannon brought back pictures. You've never seen anything like it. Looks like an Arabian palace. Probably costs more to stay one night there than I pay a month in rent. And that necklace he gave her. It was worth so much Shannon had to have it insured. Or so she said."

"You didn't believe her?"

Parsons had moved on to a nearby weight machine and was energetically clanking a barbell up and down. "Shannon bragged a lot. Couldn't help herself, I think . . ." *Clank* . . . "It's part of why she wasn't liked around here, that and the fact that she was, you know, so into herself. I didn't mind. Most folks are just as self-centered. They only do a better job of pretending that they give a damn about other people . . ." *Clank* . . . "I can tell when it's genuine. Alice, for example. That woman's a saint. Sorry I keep going on about her. You'll think I have a crush on her. But she really cares. That's why this thing with the center is killing her . . ." *Clank* . . .

I steered him back to Shannon again, but he didn't have much else to tell me. Neither did Leslie Sherman, the center's occupational therapist, though she confirmed what Parsons had said about the necklace being insured.

"Came with some kind of legal appraisal. Shannon showed it to me. I thought it was tacky, her boyfriend letting her see how much it was worth. Guy must have been some kind of jerk. I told her she would have been better off with Dean. Poor boy had a real crush on her."

"Dean?"

"Yeah. If you asked him, he'd deny it, but it was clear as day, the way he always hung around her classroom after hours, offering to help her clean up and stuff. Followed her around like a puppy. Shannon called him 'hound dog' behind his back."

"Did it ever lead to anything, you think?"

"No way. Shannon finally had it out with him, told him she'd complain to Alice about sexual harassment if he didn't back off. That was enough for him. Dean worships Alice. It's a mother thing, I think. Dean's took off when he was just a kid. Alice appeals to guys like that, the ones who missed out on all the milk and cookies when they came home from school. Not that Alice isn't attractive too, but . . ."

I didn't like discussing someone I'd slept with the night before, never mind what the conversation suggested about my own vulnerabilities. I guided us on to a different topic.

"What about Charlie Dickerson? Did he hang around Shannon too?"

"No more than any of the other kids. That's why I couldn't believe that story about the baby. I mean, it's not like our clients just roam around the halls all day. You should have seen my schedule before all the bad publicity. Back-to-back sessions all day long. And Shannon ran a group class. She couldn't just sneak off in a corner with Charlie while everyone else was coloring. It would have been easier for someone like me, who worked with them one-on-one."

"Maybe they met in the proverbial broom closet. And I was told Shannon was allowed to lunch in her classroom alone."

"Right. But the classroom doors are always open during the day.

It's a state requirement. And forget about the closets. They're always locked during school hours to prevent accidents. Some of the kids here will eat anything."

"She could have borrowed a key."

"And what, pushed Charlie up against the wall? Do you realize how big he is? I don't want to sound crass, but it would have taken some kind of *Kama Sutra* pose for them to get it on that way."

"So where could she have taken him then?"

"I don't know. All I know is that it couldn't have happened the way everyone thinks. Not around here, anyway."

On my way out of the center, I was almost through the door when I heard the sound of a motorized wheelchair bearing down on me like a Panzer division.

"Doctor," Regina Best called out imperiously. "I need to talk to you. Will you stop for a moment?"

I turned.

"Still gathering clues, I presume," she said, scooting the chair to within a foot of me.

I dug my glasses and hat out of my pocket and put them on. I was feeling naked in front of this odd, belligerent woman and wanted something to hide behind. "Is there something else you wanted to tell me? I'm in a bit of a hurry."

"Yes. You look like you need a shower and a shave." She lowered her voice to a whisper. In Regina's case this was barely louder than a squeak and I had to strain to catch her words. "I saw you walking to the center this morning through the window upstairs. It's obvious what you and Alice were up to last night. But don't worry—I won't broadcast it."

"That's well, because I don't see how it's any of your business."

"Of course, who *you* sleep with is no concern of mine. It's Alice's choice of partner I find interesting."

"I thought you believed in cripples banding together."

"Oh, but Alice isn't like that. She's beautiful, you know. Though far too modest to tell you so herself."

Not again, I thought. "Is there another point to this conversation? Because I really have to be on my way."

"There is. I thought of something else that might interest you. If you'll accompany me I'll show you."

I didn't want to have to spend any more time in Regina's company than I had to. I thought she was just playing games with me, daring me to take her seriously as a suspect. "Can't you just describe it? You'll have to do it when we're there anyway," I complained.

"I think it's better if I show you."

Without asking my permission, Regina took my hand and began leading me back through the center. She pulled me along rapidly on smooth, polished floors, through a series of corridors, up one ramp and down another, until we reached a door. There she pushed a button, taking us out into a small, dank space outside. From the muffled sound of traffic I surmised we were in a sheltered vestibule below street level. Regina explained we were now at the center's rear entrance, near the parking lot where Shannon Sparrow was killed.

"You can't see the parking lot from down here," Regina said, "unless you are very tall, but it's directly across the alley from us."

She described the steps leading up to the alley, which were out-fitted with a mechanized wheelchair lift on one side.

"I don't like these things," she said to me as she maneuvered her chair onto the lift. "I don't think they're safe. But Alice said there wasn't enough money or space to construct a ramp like the one in the front. You can take the stairs while I go up." She punched another button and the mechanism began its slow, jerky ascent. I climbed next to her until we were at the top. Regina stopped us there.

"We're facing west. Right ahead of us, about twenty feet away, is the parking lot where Shannon's body was found. It's across a narrow alley, in poor repair. You'll have to watch your step as we cross."

The alley was gravel covered and pitted with holes. "This way,"

Regina said, "and watch the crater on your right." Ahead of me I could discern an open space delineated by the shadows of two larger buildings on either side. A stiff breeze was blowing through it, and it lifted the brim of my hat, almost taking it off.

The parking lot was a smoother surface that felt like it had recently received a fresh coat of asphalt. When we were in its center Regina said, "There are twelve spaces, arranged in three rows of four. There aren't enough to accommodate all the center's employees, but we were lucky to have this much. The spaces are all assigned to specific employees, except for two that are reserved for visitors."

"Which one was Shannon's?" I asked, visualizing what Regina had described.

"She didn't have one. It was another item on her list of complaints. But Alice assigned them based on need and seniority, and there weren't enough for Shannon. That's the first thing I wanted to tell you. I thought it was curious that she was found here, almost where you're standing."

The reality of being so close to the place Shannon had died came over me then and I could almost see the body with Charlie huddled next to it. "How far away from the center are we right now?" I asked, trying to fill in the mental picture I was constructing.

"No more than twenty-five feet."

"And the alley—is it open at both ends?"

"Yes. The south end, to our left, opens onto Fullerton, and the north onto Montana. We're roughly in the middle of the block." That fit in with the traffic sounds I could hear coming from Fullerton, one of Chicago's main east–west thoroughfares.

"All right," I said. "So you're saying she shouldn't have been parked here that morning. What would have happened if she was found using someone else's space? Does the center employ a towing service?"

"Of course not. I suggested it, but Alice said she could never allow anything so mean-spirited. But there would have been a row, another dust-up involving Shannon."

"From what you've told me there was nothing unusual about that."

"But there's more. My space is over there . . . sorry, at the north end of the lot, right next to the alley so I don't have to travel far to get to the door. I have a van, with hand controls. The morning it happened, I happened to be here early. Lately it's becoming more and more difficult for me to sleep at night, and I woke that day at five. I decided I'd have better luck taking a nap later on, so I called my attendant and asked her to come get me ready. She got me dressed and I drove down here myself. I arrived just after six thirty."

"Was the lot empty then?" According to the medical examiner's report, Shannon had been killed sometime between 7:00 and 7:30.

"Yes. But as I was leaving my van, a car came through the alley, going south. I didn't get much of a look at it the first time, but it was a tan compact and the driver sped up when he saw me."

"You're sure of that—that the driver was a man?"

"Not entirely. Whoever it was went by very quickly and was wearing a hooded jacket. I can't say for sure, but I think he was trying not to be recognized. I didn't have time to catch the license number, but it wasn't something easy to remember, like vanity plates."

"And you say you saw the car more than once?"

"Yes. Not long after I'd gotten myself upstairs and settled in, I realized I had left some papers I needed in my van. I came back down and was almost at the top of the lift I showed you when I saw the same car again. I didn't get as good a look the second time because my head had just cleared street level, but I was sure it was the same one, speeding past. I was irritated because the tires spit up gravel in my face. You see why this is so important?"

"I don't know," I said. "It could have been anyone." I didn't want her to know how significant I thought it really was.

Regina clucked in irritation. "Why would the driver keep circling through the alley at that time of day if he wasn't up to something?"

"Maybe he was lost. Or looking for a place to park on the street and came through here to avoid having to stop at a light. Drivers take those kinds of shortcuts all the time."

"You're not much of a detective," Regina scoffed.

"Who do you think it was then?"

"It must have been that man—the one the newspapers are calling the Surgeon. Only the police were too stupid to see it."

"Nice theory. But no one knows whether the Surgeon even exists. That's just press speculation."

"The method used to kill Shannon was the same," Regina countered. "As well as the location and the time of day. If it wasn't the same killer, someone went to a lot of trouble to make it look that way. Even you can see that."

"Yes, but you're forgetting about the hemlock," I retorted, before I could stop myself.

"Hemlock?" she said quickly.

I went on, enjoying her surprise. "Yes. The Surgeon always leaves a calling card with his victims. The police have kept the information from the papers so they'll be able to tell if some crackpot comes forward claiming credit for the murders. They didn't find any near Shannon's body, so it couldn't have been the same man."

"I had no idea . . ." Regina said meditatively.

"And while we're on the topic, I'd appreciate it if you kept that tidbit to yourself." I was now chagrined that I'd had blurted out O'Leary's secret so easily. Why did this woman always bring out the worst in me?

Regina said, "Of course. But if it wasn't the Surgeon, who was it?"

"I haven't the vaguest idea. Unless there's something else you've been holding back from the authorities."

"It's not holding back if they don't ask."

I remembered Charlie then and changed my tone. "Regina," I said pleadingly, "if there's anything else, something you haven't told me . . ."

"I've said everything I'm going to say to you. Now it's up to you to put the clues together, Doctor. Or should I say, Sherlock?"

SEVENTEEN

In the cab going home, I put aside my irritation with Regina and thought about what to do next. I briefly considered contacting O'Leary again. Sep had warned me to be mindful of my limitations and not to take chances with my safety. But the real murderer—whoever he was—couldn't possibly be threatened by my stumbling efforts so far. My theory that Shannon had become pregnant on purpose was pure conjecture. I still didn't understand why, much less how it might exonerate Charlie. Regina's sighting of the strange driver could be important, but I didn't see any way to follow it up. There must be a million beige compacts in the city. Without tag numbers the car would be impossible to trace. I thought back to my dinner with Alice, the expensive necklace that had to be insured. Maybe there was another way to go about this.

I got back to my place around eleven and went about tidying myself up. I considered leaving my day-old beard in place, but ditched the idea as overkill. I still shaved the way I'd always done, in the shower without a mirror. It's not at all difficult, and I rarely cut myself. But that morning I purposely nicked my chin twice and didn't put as much effort into taming my hair, so that a few of the livelier cowlicks still stuck out when it was dry. Using a handheld color identifier I selected a blue shirt and a loud tie to wear with a brown tweed jacket, along with mismatched socks and a pair of scuffed loafers. I replaced my regular cane with an old one that was patched up with a piece of electrical tape after an unfortunate run-in with a ComEd construction site. Just before leaving I scooped up my keys and change, and checked to be sure my bank card was in my wallet.

At the ATM on the corner I put on my ear buds and listened while the machine took me through the menu. I selected my savings account and made a withdrawal of a thousand dollars, which I inserted into my money clip. It's heavy and gold and looks like something J. P. Morgan might have pulled from his frock coat when he wanted to reward the help, a long-ago gift from Annie that I never liked and seldom used. The wad of bills did a jig in my pocket as I trotted west on Grand and up the staircase to Michigan Avenue.

I felt excited, pumped up with nervous energy and wondering whether I could carry off the bit of theater I was planning. So I didn't notice immediately when the squeaky-soled person showed up again. I had just emerged onto Michigan when I first heard the sound behind me. Once again it seemed to match its pace to mine. But the sidewalks were swimming with pedestrians. It could have been anyone with a pair of worn-down shoes. I told myself I was just dreaming and continued on.

The Chicago flagship of Tiffany & Co. has all the cool elegance typical of the chain, though it isn't quite as large as the Manhattan outlet I once frequented. The catering to the poorer classes was instantly apparent from the thickness of the pile beneath my feet and the hushed silence of the room as I entered, broken only by the whispers of the sales staff hovering to the right of the door. One of these gatekeepers was on me the second I poked my way through the armor-plated entranceway.

"Are you lost, sir? Perhaps I can direct you to another establishment?" Central casting couldn't have done better with the accent. He sounded like Basil Rathbone swallowing his *r*'s.

"Why I don't know," I replied, wagging my head from side to side like Ray Charles in the middle of a hot R&B number. "Is this the Tiffany store on Michigan?"

It was excruciating to be unable to observe him as he took in my hair, the Band-Aid I'd stuck on my cheek as a last-minute inspiration, the uncoordinated clothing, and bedraggled cane.

"Why yes, yes it is!" He said it as though the thought had only just occurred to him.

"Thank goodness," I said, trying to look relieved. "Usually I have my dog to take me places, but he's ill. Cancer, I'm afraid. I should have him put down, but I just don't have the heart to do it. He's been such a loyal friend for so many years. I asked my housekeeper to write down your address on this piece of paper here"—I reached into my pants pocket and pretended to wrestle with something—"but no one would stop to read it to me and I couldn't remember whether you were on Michigan between Superior and Walton or Walton and Huron . . ."

While I was removing my hand from my trousers I hooked the money clip with my forefinger and let it drop to the ground. "Oh, dear," I said, feigning surprise. "What did I just do? Did I lose something?" I moved into a squat, holding my cane with my left hand and feeling about with the right.

"Please, sir—" the salesman said. I noticed he made no move to help me, as though I might be infected with Ebola.

"No, no," I said loudly. "Don't put yourself out. I can do things for myself. Just give me a minute or two." I moved onto hands and knees and began groping the floor confusedly. "It has to be here somewhere," I said, looking up with a daft smile. I continued kneading the carpet until I encountered a hard object, which turned out to be the salesman's shoe. One of his coworkers stifled a cough and a woman at the back of the store stage-whispered, "Jesus, will you look at that? Why aren't they helping him?" This was too much for my new friend and I found myself being pulled up by the armpits and held none too gently while someone else retrieved the money and my cane.

"Thanks," I said apologetically when they were unceremoniously handed back to me. "I'm not usually this clumsy. Do you mind if I count it to see if it's all there? Not that I think anyone here is out to cheat me, but a man in my position can't be too careful." The salesman agreed tepidly and stood by while I moistened my fingers with my tongue and slowly counted off fifty twenty-dollar bills.

"Did you wish to purchase something?" he asked when I'd finished, no doubt hoping to salvage something from the situation. I may have been an eyesore, but I was carrying around enough cash to boost somebody's monthly commission.

"Yes, if it wouldn't be too much trouble. It's my wife, you see. She had this really nice necklace and I lost it and . . ."

He stopped me peremptorily. "Allow me to have one of our junior assistants help you. We maintain a lounge to the rear for serving our better patrons." He barked over my shoulder, "Tanya? Can you take this gentleman there? *Now*, please?"

Tanya came at once and he handed me off to her like I was a vial of nitroglycerin.

Tanya proved to be less squeamish than her superior, helping me back to a comfortable seat and offering me a cup of tea. "That's so sad about your dog," she said.

"Thank you. He and my wife are all I have in this world. She's a wonderful woman, stood by me through all of this"—I pointed at my eyes—"even though it's been so difficult for her. She never complains and always treats me like a real man. Lets me open doors for her and everything. That's why what happened with the necklace is so upsetting." It occurred to me that I might be laying it on too thick, but she swallowed it like a peach smoothie.

"What was it?" she asked, laying her hand on my arm sympathetically.

"Well, I was washing the dishes one night last week—I always do the washing up because it's one of the few things I can still do around the home—and I didn't realize she'd left the necklace on the counter near the sink. I must have knocked it into the disposal because there was this horrible grinding noise when I turned it on and the next day my wife said the necklace was lost. I couldn't tell her what I thought had happened, it was too embarrassing. So I lied and pretended to search all over for it. Still, I think she suspects something and . . . well, I just can't tell her, that's all. I thought if I replaced it with a new one I could hide it under a pillow somewhere and . . . You don't have to tell me how cowardly that sounds, but I hate it when I can't do things as well as other people."

Tanya said soothingly, "It doesn't sound cowardly to me. It sounds sweet. What kind of necklace was it, do you know?"

"Just what the saleswoman described when I first bought it—platinum with a diamond-studded pendent in the shape of a heart. I know that doesn't help much, but I can only see what my fingers tell me," I said, assuming a sorrowful expression.

"That's no problem," Tanya said. "We keep records of what our customers have purchased going five years back. If you'll just give me your credit card number, I can look it up."

I'd been expecting this and had another story made up. "That's a problem too. I don't use credit cards. I'm always worried someone will take advantage of me. Identity theft is a real problem for the handicapped, you know." This was true, but mostly for the elderly and housebound, and I had fraud monitoring on my cards like everyone else. "That's why I always pay in cash," I added.

"Well," Tanya said thoughtfully, "if it was delivered somewhere, we would have kept the shipping records."

I pretended to brighten. "Really? I was hoping that. I did have it delivered—to my wife's place of work." I gave her the address of the New Horizons Center.

"Let me see what I can find in our system. What's your name?"

I surreptitiously crossed my fingers before replying, "My wife's name is Shannon Sparrow."

"Why, what a pretty name!" Tanya exclaimed right away, not noticing that I hadn't really answered her question.

"Yes," I went on boldly. "It's why she didn't change it when we were married."

"With a distinctive name like that it shouldn't take long to find her in our records. Give me a minute to look and I'll be right back."

I waited anxiously, at once thrilled that my subterfuge seemed to be working and fearful that Tanya would yet catch me in a fraud. A fluorescent light overhead sputtered, counting off the seconds like sand in an hour glass. When enough had fallen to fill Jones Beach, Tanya returned.

"Found it!" she declared in triumph. "It's one of our signature pieces. We don't have it in stock, but I can have it ordered for you. And guess what? A copy of the original appraisal was there too, so you can submit an insurance claim."

"I don't know about that," I said. "My wife might find out."

"We can send it directly to the insurer, if you prefer. You should, you know, Mr. Dickerson. An expensive piece like that . . ."

I was momentarily stunned, not sure my hearing hadn't gone the way of my sight. "What did you just say?"

"Mr. Dickerson. That is your name, isn't it? Nathanial Dickerson is what we have in our records. They say you purchased a diamond pendant necklace valued at $4,500 for a Ms. Shannon Sparrow on June 16 of last year. You paid for it with cash, just like you said. Is there something wrong? You look ill all of a sudden."

Later, I wasn't sure how I got out of there without giving myself away. My hands were shaking like an old drunk and I could barely control them long enough to put down a cash deposit on the necklace and sign the order form. It would be waiting for me at the store in a week's time. "Call ahead, just to be sure it's come in," Tanya warbled as she escorted me to the door. "I hope it turns out all right. I would never have said this before, but your wife is a very fortunate woman." I muttered a weak thank you and stumbled out into the daylight. Somehow I managed to get back to my place without being flattened by someone's Ford Explorer, my thoughts racing ahead of me like wildfire.

Nate? Nate was Shannon's lover? It seemed fantastic and yet it fit, starting with Judith's suspicion that Shannon was molesting her son. Judith's instincts had been good. Shannon *was* sexually involved with a male family member—Judith just hadn't latched onto the right one. And it explained the DNA results, too. I remembered suddenly what Josh had said about Charlie having an identical twin. I had been so focused on the fact that only one in ten thousand men could have fathered Shannon's child I had overlooked the obvious. As father and son, Nate and

Charlie's genetic profiles would resemble one another closely. Even if the testing lab had been alerted to look for such a match, the statistical nature of the analysis might have precluded saying with certainty which of the two it was. And the affair with Shannon left no doubt in my mind. I hadn't been wrong about Charlie and Shannon after all.

But with my relief at not having screwed up came another, ugly, realization. Nate had stood by while Charlie was accused of murder and withheld information that almost certainly would have exonerated his son. As a doctor, Nate must have known what the DNA results really meant. Yet he had remained silent, and even gone so far as to sue me for a faulty diagnosis. What kind of man would send his child— *any* child for that matter—to prison to cover up an adulterous affair? Did Nate care so little for Charlie that he would allow the boy's life to be destroyed simply to avoid a confrontation with Judith? The idea sickened me, and all the more so because it recalled all my own lies to Annie and their fatal consequences for Jack.

Unless . . . unless there was more to it than just concealing an extramarital fling. As O'Leary had reminded me, it was textbook knowledge that most violent deaths are caused by a person close to the victim. It was the reason I had been so fixated on finding out the identity of Shannon's lover. I thought back again to my lunch with O'Leary, my speculation then that the killer had been someone with a medical background. Nate was a surgeon. He would have known how to silence Shannon quickly, before she had a chance to cry out. He also would have heard about the Surgeon murders, which were all over the news. He was clever enough to have planned Shannon's death so it would look like another in the same string of killings.

What he couldn't have anticipated was Charlie stumbling onto Shannon after he had left her for dead. I imagined the dilemma this must have created for Nate—his life or the life of his son. Perhaps he had been able to rationalize putting his own interests first because in his innermost reaches he was ashamed of Charlie. During our first interview, Judith said Nate never spent any time with the boy and Nate went out of his way to emphasize Charlie's limited intellect. I'd thought it was just an overreaction to Judith's fanatical boosterism, but it might have been a sign of deeply conflicted feelings about Charlie. Nate's anger toward me after the hearing also fit the pattern of a man unable to square his conscience with his conduct. He was projecting his guilt onto me, finding a scapegoat for the hideous injustice he was inflicting on his own child.

The more I thought about it, the more sense it made. I had a theory, more plausible than any I had come up with before. Now I just needed to prove it.

I spent the rest of the day on my desktop computer. My excitement had proved inspiring and I thought I had another way of connecting Shannon to Nate. Virtually every state requires doctors, as well as lawyers and accountants, to complete a certain number of continuing professional education hours each year. It's a win-win for everyone—except the Treasury Department. Lawmakers appear virtuous by holding licensees to strict standards, the CPE programs get rich selling them to a captive audience, and the participants can deduct the tuition as a business expense when it comes time to pay their taxes. To further lessen the pain, CPE is usually offered at luxury resorts so that the attendees can unwind on the ski slopes or lounge by a pool after dozing through an hour or so of lectures in the morning. Annie had accompanied me on many such excursions, and I was betting that Nate, a frequent speaker on the CPE circuit, had used them as a means of treating Shannon to expensive trips courtesy of his employers.

It took a few hours of searching and listening, but by late afternoon I had compiled a list of Nate's appearances at such seminars during the preceding year. I understood Judith's complaint that he was always away. Given Nate's travel schedule I was surprised he found room to operate, let alone spend time with his family. Altogether, he had taken twenty-two trips in the previous twelve months. A few were short hops to places like Detroit or Indianapolis. But the majority were weeklong stays in resort areas with a healthy ratio of golf course to regular acreage. When I finished, the beginning of my list looked like this:

January 12 to 26	Ritz Carlton, Palm Beach
February 6 to 12	Mandarin Oriental, Honolulu
March 12 to 14	Biltmore Hotel, Phoenix
April 23 to 28	Grand Hyatt, San Francisco
May 9 to 11	The Westin, Miami

And so on, for a total of two dozen hotel stays in all.

It was a start, but now I needed to prove Nate had taken Shannon with him. I got nowhere with phone calls to the first three hotels on my list—they didn't give out information about guest stays, not even to someone claiming to be the guest's husband. Hotel number four required the guest's credit card and Social Security number before they would check. The clerk at hotel number five put me on hold until the Muzak—a salsa-inspired rendition of the "1812 Overture"—finally drove me off the line. On my sixth try I got lucky. A sympathetic clerk bought my story that Shannon was taking me to the cleaners in a divorce settlement and agreed to see whether she'd stayed there in March, but there was no record of her having registered under her own name. Ditto with the seventh and eighth calls. I was beginning to feel despondent again until I hit on another idea, one more likely to succeed with an official-looking caller ID. It was a quarter to five, so I paged Yelena on her cell.

"What's going on with you?" she asked me when she rang back, already on the way home, judging from the highway noise I could hear in the background.

"The straight jacket's a little tight, but I'm beginning to see some advantages to padded surfaces."

"Dr. Frain has started a pool on whether you'll be coming back."

"That was thoughtful of him. Which side are you in on?"

"It wouldn't be polite to say. What do you want now?"

I outlined what I needed her to do in the morning.

"Is that legal?" Yelena asked when I was through giving her the script.

"Since when has that ever bothered you?"

"They're sending my cousin back to Murmansk on Tuesday. It's warmer here."

I sighed. "How does two days off next month sound? I'll tell everyone you came down with a case of shingles."

"Make it a week, and I'll think about it."

Good ol' Yelena, always upping the ante.

"That's too bad. I heard Dr. Brennan say he'll be looking for a new assistant when Brenda retires next month. He mentioned you for the job if I can't come back." Sep was an unapologetic secretarial slave-driver; it was widely believed that Brenda had made it to retirement only by faking advancing deafness.

"Twist my arm, why don't you?" Yelena said.

I told Yelena I would e-mail her a list of telephone numbers. Before she rang off, I also secured her promise to call the hospital garage to find out whether Nate Dickerson drove a white Jaguar to work.

By the time I'd finished the e-mail to Yelena it was close to 5:30 and a long evening with nothing to do loomed ahead of me. On impulse, I called Alice and asked if she'd like to come over.

"I meant it when I said I'm no cook, but we could order in. And I need to talk to someone about what I found out today," I told her.

"What is it? You sound almost . . . breathless."

"I don't want to tell you over the phone. It'll take too long to explain."

"I'll be there," Alice said.

I spent an hour or so making my apartment less of a minefield for the low of vision. Then I called Hallie Sanchez.

"I'm glad you called," she said. "I heard about the complaint Nate Dickerson filed against you. I want you to know I had nothing to do with it. He acted rashly, against my advice. It doesn't help Charlie's case and it's just plain wrong. That's off the record, of course."

Of course. But I couldn't blame Hallie. She had a client to represent—a client whose father might be the real murderer. I couldn't tell her what I knew; it would put her in an awkward position. But I could try to buy some more time for Charlie.

"How is he?" I asked, not especially keen to know the answer.

"He's . . . well, he's still very quiet, not talking about what happened. But he's in the prison hospital and I arranged for visits by a private psychiatrist." She gave the name of a doctor I knew, a woman reputed to be excellent, and my fears eased somewhat. "She says we need to take it slowly."

"Has a trial date been set?"

"Not yet, but there may not be one."

"Hallie," I said. "Please tell me you haven't agreed to a deal. Not that quickly." It hadn't even been a week since the preliminary hearing.

"Not yet. But Di Marco called, asking for a meeting next week. I'll listen to what he has to say. I'll have no choice. And it may be the best thing for Charlie. The judge denied our motion to suppress the confession, as I knew she would after the DNA evidence came in."

DNA evidence that only I knew might be flawed. I again fought off a desire to tell her. I had to go slowly if I was going to prove it was Nate, not his son, who had killed Shannon.

Hallie was saying, "With the charge reduced to manslaughter, and given Charlie's special circumstances, we may be able to get a sentence that would allow him to serve his time in a minimum-security prison."

"How much time?"

"I don't think they'll agree to anything less than ten to fifteen. That's too long, I know, but his life wouldn't be over. He'd get out when he was in his thirties, maybe sooner."

"You can't agree to that."

"I won't like it, but my job is to obtain the best possible result for him. His parents, Nate especially, want this over with. Nate said prison might even be good for Charlie, teach him a job he could do. He was only joking, of course. He's still very upset about what's happened and wants to do what's best for the boy. It's plain he loves his son very much."

I had to swallow hard to keep the bile down my throat.

"Hallie," I said. "I know what I have to say carries zero weight, but please don't rush into anything. There can't be that much urgency and . . . I've found out some things that may change your mind."

"What things?" Hallie said sharply.

"I can't tell you just yet."

"Playing detective now, huh? Come on, Mark, listen to yourself. Who do you think you are? This isn't a parlor game for amateurs. This is the real world, where people get sent to death row for crimes they didn't commit. If the best I can do is spare Charlie a life sentence, I'll do it. You're only a psychiatrist. What makes you think you can keep Charlie from going to prison if I can't?"

Her words echoed my own doubts and put me on the defensive.

"I'm trying," I said heatedly, "which is more than I can say for you."

"Trying to prove something to yourself, is what I think. Charlie's well-being has nothing to do with it."

It was too much for me to hear and I lashed back.

"Why don't you just say it," I said, becoming shrill. "You think Charlie's life is worthless, or close to it. One day he'll end up in an institution anyway, so what difference does it make if it's one with bars on the windows? If he were a teenage boy of normal intelligence, a kid with a bright future ahead of him, you'd be fighting tooth and nail for him. You're giving up because he's retarded. You probably even think he did it."

Hallie spit back, "That's a contemptible thing to say."

"Is it? A year or two ago I wouldn't have thought it possible, but my own experience has opened my eyes to the way people like Charlie . . . the way *we're* looked upon. Wouldn't it be nice if we could all be shipped off to another planet so nobody would have to rub shoulders with us? You're just like all the rest."

"You don't know what you're talking about."

"Give me a reason to think I'm wrong."

"All right. I wasn't going to mention it because I thought it was irrelevant but now that you've accused me of being some kind of Hitler Youth you might as well know."

"Let me guess," I said. "You once befriended a little crippled kid at school."

"You can be a real asshole, you know that? No, it's my brother. He has ROP."

Retinopathy of prematurity—like Stevie Wonder. That jarred me. I thought back to that day in the Double L when Jesus wanted to introduce me to his cousin. *Hallie couldn't be . . . ?*

Hallie continued, "We were always taught to treat him just like anyone else. He's a computer engineer now, with a great wife and three kids. It wouldn't even occur to me that his life isn't worth living. In fact, in many ways I envy him. I've always wanted a marriage like his. As far as I'm concerned, there isn't anything he can't do. And not just because he's my brother. I gave you a chance, didn't I? Now maybe I think I shouldn't have. I don't need *you* to remind me that I failed Charlie at that hearing—or that I might be failing him again if I cop a plea."

Tears were pooling in her voice and I instantly regretted my stupid outburst.

"Excuse me a minute," Hallie said abruptly.

I felt like a genuine heel.

When she returned to the line I said, "Don't worry. It's off now."

"What's off?" Hallie said through a tissue.

"That gigantic chip on my shoulder. I'm sorry. I didn't really mean what I said—about you not trying hard enough. It's just this whole situation . . . it cuts too close to home." This had to qualify as the understatement of the century. Hallie blew her nose. "Just do one thing for me—hold off making a deal with Di Marco right away. There are things you don't know, things I can't tell you about yet, but if I'm right they change everything."

"When will you be able to tell me this big secret?" Hallie asked, still not fully recovered.

"I don't know. Soon, I hope. If it turns out to be nothing, I'll support you in whatever you think is best for Charlie."

"Well that's certainly a comfort."

"At least you're back to being snotty with me."

Hallie said, "I wish . . . well let's just say that when this is all over I'd like us to be friends."

"Me too," I admitted.

After I rang off I wondered about this sudden influx of women into my life. I hadn't realized it before, but I was attracted to Hallie. Not in the same way I was attracted to Alice, but I liked the way Hallie was always so direct with me, questioning my motives. Alice challenged me too, but in a different way. I'd always found pure intentions hard to swallow. It threatened my jaundiced view of the world to think that Alice might be the real thing, that rare sort of person who really *did* care deeply about other people and wanted to improve their lives. I felt drawn to her self-lessness, but it also made me uneasy. Could two so fundamentally different people find contentment with one another for very long?

Alice arrived at seven, with a bottle of Bordeaux and a roast chicken from Fox & Obel. While the food warmed up in the oven we went out to my terrace, where we sat sipping the wine in the gentle evening breeze. Not far away, traffic thrummed on the Drive and a merchant ship chugged slowly up the river, accompanied by a flock of chattering gulls.

"That's awful," she chastised after I'd described the incident in the Tiffany store.

"All right, so I'm not much of an actor."

"No. I meant something different. You played the clown, used blindness as a club to beat those people with."

"I was simply taking advantage of their prejudices. What's wrong with that? It got me what I wanted, didn't it?"

"But at what price? You confirmed every stereotype of us there is. What are they going to think of the next blind person who walks into that store?"

"So you're saying the end can never justify the means? I was trying to get at the truth, to help Charlie," I said. What I had thought of as a brilliant ploy earlier in the day now seemed shameful in the face of Alice's disapproval. "OK. So maybe I went a tad overboard."

Alice reached over and took my hand. Hers was soft in mine and I raised it to my lips in a conciliatory gesture. "Will you be able to forgive me?" I said.

"I understand what you were doing. I just wish you could have gotten the information some other way. Did you like lying like that?"

"A little," I conceded. "It was like . . . I was turning the tables on them. I felt in control, something I don't get to experience much lately."

"You underestimate how much in control you really are. Of course I'll forgive you. Anyway, the real villain here is Nate, isn't it? How could he fail to come forward about the affair? Didn't he think it was significant?"

"It was only significant if he had something more serious to hide." I told her my theory that Nate was the murderer. "He had the right knowledge. Pressure on the carotid arteries here and here"—I showed Alice how it could be done—"would put Shannon under in thirty seconds or less, and then all he had to do was slip a scalpel under her rib cage. A quick thrust upward to pierce the cardiac sac and he was finished. It would only have taken a few minutes. I'm not saying only a doctor could have done it, but it's not possible Charlie would have known how to kill so cleanly."

Alice shifted disquietly next to me. "That's . . . so horrible. I can understand a murder committed in the heat of passion, but to lay in wait for someone like that. How could anyone live with that on their conscience? And if you're right about the baby being his, why wasn't he worried about discovery?"

"I think he was counting on Shannon's murder being seen as just another one of the Surgeon killings. If Charlie hadn't shown up accidentally, he might have gotten away with it."

"That's what I really can't forgive. Allowing his own son to take the blame. I never had children of my own, but I think of my clients at the center in much the same way as a parent. I could never allow harm to come to them just to fulfill a selfish need of my own. What he did was monstrous."

I wondered again how I was ever going to tell her about Jack.

"What are you planning to do? Have you told the police yet?" Alice asked.

"No. I'm still trying to nail down a few more facts. If Nate's as cold-blooded as I think he is, he's not going to roll over just because I ask him to. If only I could get my hands on that diary."

"Which diary?" Alice asked, puzzled.

"Something Shannon's roommate told me about. A notebook she wrote in every day. I'm sure Nate figured prominently in it, along with anyone else who ever crossed her."

"Do you know where she kept it?"

"No, but it's probably packed up with the rest of her things in her apartment. Her sister gave me permission to go through them, but I don't know if the offer is still open."

"You're not thinking of going there by yourself?" Alice said, with amusement.

I laughed. "And risk getting you sore at me again? Besides, even if I did I wouldn't know where to look or how to read a diary if I found it. As you know, scanners aren't much help with handwriting."

"Nor, am I, sadly. You should have picked a better accomplice."

"I don't know about that," I said, pulling her in for a kiss. "If you didn't have so many scruples you'd make a fine coconspirator."

After dinner I gave Alice a tour of my place. She was delighted when I placed her hand over mine and showed her how to do "walk the dog" with one of my yo-yos.

"When you've got it right, you can feel it tug on the string a certain way."

"I think I see," Alice said. "This is fun."

"Watch out. If you're not careful I'll feel encouraged to bring out my Batttleship board next," I said.

"I believe I had another sort of game in mind."

"Oh?"

"Something closer to Twister."

I gladly obliged and we spent the rest of the evening engaged in decidedly adult pursuits.

EIGHTEEN

I slept dreamlessly and when I woke the next day Alice was gone. She'd left a message on my cell phone apologizing for having to be at an early-morning meeting. I brewed a cup of Constant Comment and listened to the weather forecast and the morning headlines. Peace talks in the Middle East had stalled, another mayoral aide had been indicted for bid-rigging, the economy was dragging like a wet sail. Change the date and it could have been last week's news, or the following month's. The only cheery item was that the Mets had taken the first in a three-game series against the Cubs, prompting resurrection of an old joke. Question: "What did Jesus say to the Cubs?" Answer: "Wait 'til I come back." After I'd chuckled over that one a bit I put on padded shorts and a jersey and clipped onto my bike. I was feeling slack around the middle, so I did a series of intense intervals for an hour, pushing my heart rate up until the sweat was pooling in my eyelids and my quads were groaning. Then I showered and dressed in a suit, chased a frozen waffle with some orange juice, and went over to my office to see what Yelena had been able to dig up for me.

An hour or so later found me stepping off the elevator into the waiting area of the Cardiac and Thoracic Surgery Group. I'd been there once before and remembered it as a large, open space reminiscent of a coral reef. Furniture groupings in bleached wood rose from a deep blue carpet beneath pastel artworks with splashy themes. My mental map of the room was pretty good and I would have negotiated it smoothly had it not been for a palm tree that materialized out of nowhere, whipping me in the face with its fronds. I swore and detoured past it, wishing that for once Rentokil would live up to its name. At the reception desk, I waited while a pleasant-sounding woman finished chatting with a patient about his forthcoming angiogram.

"You're in the wrong place," she said to me when she was through. "Ophthalmology is one floor down, on nine."

"Eight, actually," I said, rubbing my cheek to ease the sting from the tree. "I'm one of their better customers."

"So I guessed. I'm sorry about that plant. I should ask the service to trim it. Can I help you with something?"

"It depends. Is there a doctor in the house?"

"One or two," she said. "Do you have a heart problem?"

"Only when I wear it on my sleeve."

She chuckled. "Don't tell me—a sensitive type."

"Goes with the territory." I had decided in advance to flirt with her—assuming she was, in fact, a *she*—thinking it might help my chances of getting in to see Nate. "Tell me, are you as beautiful as you sound?"

She chuckled again, mirthfully. "Honey," she said, "I'm fifty-four years old. I've got more gray in my hair than McDonald's has trans fats and an ass you couldn't lift out of this chair with a back hoe. Still, it's nice of you to try."

"To me the only thing that matters is what's on the inside."

"What is this, the Hallmark channel?"

I could worship this woman. "What's your name?"

"Denise. Did you know you have a scratch on your face?" I took the tissue she offered me. "It's over more to the left. Now down a little. There, you've got it now."

I showed Denise my hospital ID and told her whom I wanted to talk to. "It's a personal matter. I don't have an appointment, but he'll know what it's about."

Denise punched a few buttons and spoke to a functionary on the other end of the line, who put her on hold. I waited, shifting from foot to foot. Since following Nate wasn't exactly an option, I wasn't sure what I was going to do if he refused to see me. A few seconds later, the answer came back. I was buzzed through a security door and Denise came around and nudged me down the corridor to an office at its far end. "Thanks," I said as we came up to the closed door. "I've always relied on the kindness of strangers." Denise straightened my lapel and gave me a friendly pat on the arm. "Come back and see us again some time," she said. "We could use more gentlemen callers like you."

I paused a moment before knocking, going over once more what I planned to say.

I had been counting on Yelena's flare for duplicity, and she hadn't let me down. Claiming to be Nate's assistant, she had spent the morning calling the hotels on my list and telling them the story I'd cooked up about a flooded basement and a skeptical IRS auditor. Hostility toward the taxman being what it is, most of them had been glad to help out by e-mailing duplicate expense statements. When I got to my office, the PDFs were waiting in a stack on my desk, neatly clipped together. Yelena had read them to me one by one. In each case, Nate had been traveling with a woman identified as Mrs. Dickerson and had squandered impressive sums on spa appointments and room service, including midnight deliveries of sevruga and Veuve Clicquot. It was a sure bet he hadn't shared them with Judith.

But that wasn't all. Acting on my instructions, Yelena had also confirmed Nate's ownership of a white Jaguar. According to the Ukrainian garage attendant Yelena had befriended with promises of helping him secure a chauffeur's license, Nate had driven the Jaguar until January, when he had traded it in for a new silver Mercedes CL Class. Warming to her task, Yelena had even secured a further piece of information that I hadn't thought to ask about. When she finished I gave her a bear hug and said, "*Ty moyo solnyshko!*" She shoved me away like I had just stepped out of the reactor chamber at Chernobyl. "Your sunshine? Some compliment coming from you," she said. "And your accent stinks." But she was obviously pleased.

None of what I had was proof positive that Nate had murdered Shannon. But it was enough to confront him with. Or so I believed.

I knocked and entered Nate's office.

"I probably shouldn't be talking to you," Nate said immediately, lumbering up from his chair. "My lawyers said not to. What are you doing here? If it's about getting permission to see Charlie, you can forget it. We've had more than enough of your quack remedies."

"I have some information that could help your son. I thought you might like to hear it."

"I can't imagine what it might be," Nate said.

"May I sit down?" I asked.

Nate came around his desk and led me to a seating arrangement near a window. He towered over me like an ancient redwood. I wondered if there were photographs of Charlie nearby, and if so, how Nate could stand to look at them. The chair he showed me to was low-slung and covered in the sort of antique leather that felt like it had once been tossed around by the Gipper. I misjudged the seat height going down and landed with a creaky plop. "If you're trying to make me feel sorry for you, it won't work," Nate said, planting himself opposite me.

I wished I could see something more than the vague mountain a few feet away. "There's nothing to feel sorry about—except what's happening to Charlie," I said.

"For which I hold you fully responsible. I should have listened to Judith. She said you weren't fit to take someone's temperature."

"I'm surprised you can say that with a straight face."

"The facts don't lie."

"Which facts are those?" I said.

"The DNA test, to start with. That woman was sleeping with my son as sure as I'm sitting here."

"She was sleeping with someone."

"What's that supposed to be, some kind of joke? I've checked into you, you know. I hear you regard yourself as a wit. But clever talk isn't going to help you with the State Board."

"Let's skip it, then. You and I both know Charlie wasn't the father of that baby."

"Really? Where did you go to medical school—Grenada?"

"There was ivy on the walls, if that's important to you."

"Well, I'm surprised. I would have thought they'd taught you a course or two in genetics. But maybe you were sleeping in class. It wouldn't surprise me."

"Save the *ad hominem* attacks. My credentials aren't at issue here."

"Then what is?"

"Some information I intend to make available to Detective O'Leary. Want to hear it, or shall we just go on with all the back-thumping?"

"Go ahead, if you think it will change anything."

"It changes everything. I know about your affair—with Shannon."

I had been expecting hasty denials and protestations of innocence. But Nate didn't jump up and gasp in surprise. He didn't weep or beg for understanding. He simply went quiet and stayed that way for several long minutes. His silence put me at a disadvantage. I tried to maintain a steady gaze in his direction while I waited for a response.

"So you found out," he said tonelessly after a while. He didn't seem that all that concerned.

"It wasn't very hard," I said. Oddly, it angered me even more that he wasn't denying it.

"Don't congratulate yourself. I'm just curious about how much snooping you've been doing."

"I heard about the necklace Shannon was wearing and traced it back to you. You were sleeping with her last September when you and Judith came to see me with Charlie. Judith must have known subconsciously what was going on. When you saw how close she was to guessing the truth, you decided to break things off."

Nate laughed, a savage throaty sound. His next statement caught me off guard. "Have you ever been married?"

I told him just to keep him talking. "Once."

"Divorced?"

I nodded.

He turned reflective then. "You're fortunate. I was never able to break free, myself. As you probably suspect, Judith isn't an easy person to live with. You wonder why I stay with her."

"The thought had crossed my mind. Is it because of Charlie?"

"Oh, nothing quite that simple. I always knew about her insecurities, her fears. It's what attracted me to her in the beginning, that she needed my protection. And the money played a role too, I won't deny it. When I met her I was young and ambitious. Judith had social connections it would have taken me years to establish. I never stopped to consider what it would be like living with her day in and day out, the constant drama and near hysteria. And then we had Charlie and she couldn't forgive herself for making him the way he is. She grew even worse. After a time I couldn't stand being home, but I didn't think I could walk out on her and not have it ruin my reputation. And she would have fallen to pieces without me. That's the irony—I stayed for her, not for him."

"So you started having affairs," I said.

"Yes. It's funny isn't it? How much easier it is to face being a liar and a cheat than desert someone you once cared about. Shannon wasn't the first. I met her at the center one day when I was picking up Charlie. She was very attractive and came on to me right away. I knew it was risky but I couldn't help myself."

"How long had it been going on when you and Judith came to see me?"

"A little over seven months. That's why I thought Judith's fears were ridiculous. I knew Shannon didn't have any interest in Charlie. By that time I'd figured out what she was—a cold little thing and an expert manipulator. You're right. When I saw how spiteful Judith had become toward her I thought I'd just be asking for trouble if I let the relationship continue. So I told Shannon I couldn't see her anymore."

"When was this?"

"Late October."

"How did she react?"

"In a way I'd never anticipated. I thought Shannon understood it wasn't serious. But she apparently thought I was in love with her. She became enraged, all red-faced and spitting, spouted the most theatrical nonsense. I laughed when I heard it. She'd even entertained notions of us getting married and starting a family. I knew then what a mistake it had been."

"Did Judith ever find out?"

"No, and I made sure she wouldn't. It wasn't so much that I was afraid of exposure—Judith would never have the guts to leave me. The uproar would be too much for her. I just didn't want to live with all the recriminations. And after Charlie was arrested, telling her would only have upset her more."

"And you didn't think about telling anyone else—the police, for instance?"

"What was the point? All it would have done is bring down suspicion on me."

So there was the proof of Nate's towering indifference toward his son. A voice at the back of my head reminded me of all the things I hadn't done to save Jack. But I was only a murderer in my own estimation.

I said, "And the DNA evidence coming to light—that didn't change your mind either?"

"I admit I was enraged when I learned, but it was more anger about how Shannon had used Charlie. She came to me, you know, not long before she died, claiming the baby was mine. She thought it would be enough to make me divorce Judith—my last chance to have a 'normal' family was how she explained it to me. Stupid girl. It apparently hadn't occurred to her that any offspring of Charlie's would have a 50–50 chance of inheriting Fragile X from his father. If I had known then what she was up to, I probably *would* have killed her."

Something in his answer was off. But I was so sure his words amounted to a confession that I pressed ahead. "So you admit you did it?"

"Did what?"

"Murdered Shannon," I said.

Nate seemed startled for a fraction of a second, then recovered and chuckled nastily. "That's your theory, is it? I should have guessed. And now you've come here to trade."

I wanted to reach out and throttle him. Did Nate really think I'd strike a bargain with him, cover up a murder in exchange for having the charges against me dropped? That my license was more important to me than Charlie's well-being?

"My information's not for sale," I said harshly.

"Good. Because you're barking up the wrong tree."

"Am I? I'm sure the police won't think so. You killed Shannon and

let your son take the blame for it. After you found out about the pregnancy. You knew the baby was yours. You've admitted to me how Judith
would have reacted if she found out. I'm betting Shannon threatened to
tell her. Or go through with the pregnancy unless you agreed to marry
her. The only way you could get rid of both problems was to kill her."

"You're dreaming," Nate said with amusement. "Next thing you
know you'll have me standing on the grassy knoll."

I continued on, unwarned by the mockery in his tone. "I have a
witness who saw a man driving through the parking lot early on the
morning Shannon was murdered. You arranged to meet her there,
didn't you? You probably offered to pay her off and came prepared.
Shannon was murdered by someone with medical knowledge and a
surgeon's skill. Who better at locating a victim's heart than you? And
you won't be able to produce an alibi. I had my assistant check with the
hospital garage. They keep videotapes of cars coming in and out, for
insurance purposes. Your arrival that morning will be on film. That and
the fact that you used the valet service that morning, probably because
you were already late. Their records show you dropped off your car
at 7:45. You had just enough time to kill Shannon and make it to the
operating room on time."

Nate said, "So now you've been using hospital personnel to spy on
me. You're even more imprudent than I thought."

"The police will be able to subpoena the videotapes. And I'm told
Shannon kept a diary she wrote in every day. Your name and all the
details will be in it."

"So what?" he said, dripping contempt like an IV line. "Your only
evidence is that I was involved with the woman."

"And had the best reason to kill her."

"Hardly. I've already told you Judith would have overlooked the
indiscretion—she's done so before."

"Maybe she wouldn't have found it as easy to overlook an illegiti-
mate child."

"Oh, that," Nate dismissed.

"Genes don't lie," I said.

"They do when they're the wrong genes," Nate said. "I can prove I wasn't the father. You can confirm it too with a little more prying into the hospital's records. For that matter, I'll give my doctor permission to talk to you so you won't be tempted to commit another ethics violation."

I suddenly remembered that first day in my office, Nate's speedy response when I offered to refer him to an urologist.

"It was after Charlie was born. Judith wanted more children, but I just couldn't face the idea of another one like Charlie. I didn't trust her to stay with birth control. It's what I told Shannon when she came to me claiming the baby was mine."

The back of my neck began to smolder.

"I had a vasectomy. Fifteen years ago."

I blinked and turned my face away.

"I'm sterile. Completely sterile. Now get out of here before I call security."

I desperately wished there was a hole I could crawl into.

So I did the next best thing and went to the Double L. It was still early in the afternoon, but Jesus was already on duty, apparently filling in for one of his fellow barkeeps. I clambered clumsily onto a bar stool and he poured me a double without my even having to ask.

"*Perdoname*, homeboy," he said, "but you look like somebody whose best friend just got run over by a truck."

"More like the wheels of justice."

"Anything I can do to help?"

I took a swig from the tumbler he passed me. "Sure. Is there a newspaper around? I need someone to read the employment section to me."

"Job trouble?"

"Let's just say I may soon be in the market for an opening as a hermit."

"Can't be that bad. Always plenty of *locos* out there."

"Unfortunately, the State of Illinois can be picky about the people it allows to practice medicine. The odds are I won't be one of them soon."

"That *is* bad."

I rested my chin in my hand. "Oh well, there's always Social Security to fall back on. While it's still around."

Jesus grew thoughtful. "Have you considered . . . ? I mean, there was this guy from my neighborhood growing up, got his legs blown off in Vietnam. Used to work the corner of Madison and Wells on one of those little wooden carts. People said he went home every night to a penthouse on the Lake. With the right getup you could be just as affecting."

I gulped another mouthful of bourbon. "Thanks for cheering me up. Hey, this stuff's good."

Jesus had begun wiping down the bar next to me. "It's my special stash. Twenty-year-old Maker's Mark. I only give it to customers who look like they really need a lift. Maybe you could use some late-night companionship, too. For you it would be at a discount."

"I appreciate the offer, but I'm in a relationship right now."

"Someone you're serious about?"

"Maybe. It's too early to tell. While we're on the subject, do you have a cousin named Hallie?"

"Yeah. Hallie Sanchez. Why, you know her?"

"We've been working on a case together. It's part of the reason I'm in so much trouble. If you see her it would be best not mention my name. We're not exactly on good terms right now."

"That's too bad. It's funny, but I had the idea of introducing you two. She hasn't had a lot of luck with men and I was thinking you might be her type."

"What type is that, I'm afraid to ask."

"Reasonable. She's had it up to her *ojos* with Latino guys. Too many hang-ups about their mothers. And every girl's either a madonna or a whore."

"Plenty of that where I come from, too," I said.

Jesus went on, "Trouble is most Anglos bore her to death. Lately she's been panicking about not finding somebody to settle down with, worried her biological clock is running out. I told her she should chill. '*Chica*,' I said, 'you wanna be a mother, *no problema*.' Nowadays, you don't need a steady man to get knocked up, you don't even have to sleep with him. Look at all the lesbos doing it. 'Course it would totally freak out my aunt—"

I stopped him suddenly. "What did you just say?"

"About my *tía* getting upset?"

"No, before that."

"I was saying how a girl doesn't need to have sex with a guy to have his baby."

"Jesus," I said, "don't take this the wrong way, but I could kiss you."

Boris arrived with the car a little before 10:00 p.m. I was waiting for him outside my building dressed in dark slacks and a windbreaker, my Mets cap on my head and my backpack on my shoulders. The air was chilly and the streets hushed, the city beginning to hunker down for the night. I heard the engine purr to a halt and the door latch snap as Boris came around from the driver's side to get me.

"Which one did you bring?" I asked. "Not the stretch, I hope?"

"You say you don't want be noticing. So I bring the Lincoln." Unlike Yelena, whose English is flawless, Boris speaks with a thick accent and often garbles his syntax. "Is black car with frosty windows."

"Great. That's perfect."

Boris believes in the little touches that keep customers returning. The town car smelled as though it had just left the showroom and its bar was freshly stocked. There was a television console in my armrest and several magazines spread on the seat in a fan. Lord knows what Boris expected me to do with them. "Try some of the vodka," Boris urged. "Is premium." A drink sounded good, but I couldn't afford to be fuzzy-headed. "Another time," I replied. I gave him an address in Wrigleyville and we swung onto Lake Shore Drive, picking up speed. I sat back and watched the intermittent flash of street lights over the windshield. Boris tuned into a talk radio program and I paid attention to the debate for a while—should the latest kleptomaniac starlet be returned to prison?—until I despaired of hearing an intelligent remark. There was nothing to do but cross and recross my legs and listen to the hum of the roadway beneath the wheels while we made the twenty-minute drive north.

Marilyn Sparrow had been happy to hear from me, though she couldn't offer much in the way of help.

"Apartment's been rented," she said, when I'd phoned to ask whether her offer to look through Shannon's things was still open. "Asshole landlord finally got wise that I wasn't handing over a check without a fight. I sent the key back yesterday. By regular mail."

"And the boxes with Shannon's stuff—where are they now?"

"Still there, as far as I know. New tenant's moving in on Monday. I spoke to him this morning—nice fellow if you're not bothered by faggots. Told him to put the boxes in the basement and I'd come get them my next day off. How's the study going? You got any news for me?"

"Er . . . it's going pretty well. I'll know in a few days whether you'll be selected. Do you think the landlord might let me in if I said I had your permission?"

"If you can find him on a Friday night. But what's your rush? I'll have them back in a week or so. You can just come by then. What is it you want, anyhow?"

"Someone, a friend of Shannon's, mentioned she kept a diary. I thought it might shed light on her feelings around the time of the murder."

"Well, like I said, you're welcome to whatever you find. But how will you be able to read her papers?"

"I'll, uh, be bringing a fellow researcher."

I didn't think I had a week to spare, so after I rang off with Marilyn I called Nancy Kim at her gallery. Then I did a couple of Internet searches to see if my idea was feasible. When that was done I phoned Regina Best and asked her for a description of the thermos she'd mentioned.

"Big, small? Anything you can remember. Except that I'm not interested in what color it was."

"Half-size I believe. And wide-mouthed, like the kind you would carry soup in."

"Did you ever see her eating from it?"

"Why? She didn't die of food poisoning, you know. No, as I told you, Shannon always ate by herself. What are you up to?" she asked suspiciously.

"Just following up on a theory."

Now arrived at our destination, Boris was concerned about leaving me.

"All you have to do is point me to the bottom stair. I'll be fine," I said.

"You are sure?"

I hastened to assure him I would be. In truth, it would have been helpful to have a pair of watchful eyes along, but I didn't want to risk getting Boris in trouble with the authorities. I was feeling guilty enough about involving Yelena in potential wire fraud earlier in the day. Besides, I figured if I was caught alone I could always pretend I had simply wandered up there by mistake.

"No cabs soon," Boris persisted. What he meant was that the Cubs' seven o'clock start was still underway, having apparently made it into extra innings. From the groans of despair pouring forth from the ballpark several blocks away, it sounded like defeat was imminent. The streets would soon be filling with angry fans in various stages of inebriation.

I said, "All the more reason for you to get out of here. As soon as the game lets out, this area will be crawling with cops."

In the end, I only got him to leave by promising to page him when I was through.

A fixture of the Windy City, 3-flats are found in almost every neighborhood but are especially plentiful in the area around Wrigley Field. Their rental units are never on the market long. Picture windows, twelve-foot ceilings, and prices so reasonable they would make a New Yorker weep are the main selling points, along with rear porches that are a prime venue for social gatherings on game days. These impromptu bleachers are not without risk. Some years earlier one of them had collapsed during a Friday-night mixer, plunging a dozen partygoers to their deaths. In the wake of the tragedy, the city had begun a crackdown on landlords that must have doubled the price of Wolmanized lumber in the region, not to mention the unreported income of Chicago building inspectors.

They are also a burglar's best friend.

As I'd confirmed earlier with Nancy Kim, Shannon's apartment had one of these wooden terraces, accessed via a staircase leading up from the back alley. I was fortunate it had been repaired recently, as I discovered after I finally shooed Boris off and tested the first step. It was as solid as a scaffold, as was the railing, which had the telltale roughness and odor of new pine. I was also lucky the night was too cool for sitting out. When I listened at the foot of the stairs there seemed to be no one above me following the Cubs' progress in the open air. I could proceed without being seen and hopefully without being heard.

I went up, tapping the risers ahead of me with care. When I reached the first landing I halted briefly, listening for signs of activity in the adjacent apartments, but they were quiet. I probed ahead carefully in case one of the tenants had left something lying around—empty beer bottles or a rusty lawn chair—that would have made a ruckus if I bumped into them. Nothing. I kept on going. Midway up the next set of stairs I heard a scuttling sound and felt something warm graze my leg. I almost cried out, thinking it was a rat, but when it returned again, rubbing my shins and mewing, I realized it was only a cat. The last thing I needed, but I hadn't thought to bring raw hamburger with me to distract the animal sentries. "Get lost, Simba," I hissed. "Outta here." The cat paid me no heed and followed me eagerly up.

The door was at the far end of the third-floor landing, next to a window. The knob was old-fashioned, with a decorative filigree covering its surface. I squeezed it gently in both directions, but it was locked tight. No matter. I'd come prepared for this.

The convenience of the Internet cannot be overstated. When I decided there was no alternative to searching Shannon's apartment, I had counted on being able to gather the information I needed quickly, and sure enough, there were web tutorials for the novice housebreaker everywhere. I found a site with more verbal description than diagrams, and memorized the pages by sending them to my Braille printer and reading the text aloud to myself several times. It wasn't as foolproof as my old photographic memory, but it did the job. Half an hour later I had a solid mental picture of a standard deadbolt lock, and a reasonably firm grasp of how to manipulate it without a key.

Lock picking is uncomplicated in theory. In the most common variety, the bolt is held in place by a spring cylinder, or "plug," controlled by pins aligned with hollow shafts in the lock's housing. The trick is to apply reverse pressure to the plug while easing the pins into their slots. When this is done correctly, you can hear or feel a slight click as each pin is released. A set of professional lock picks—only $19.95 with free shipping, I discovered—will do the job nicely, but I didn't have time for that. Once I understood how the mechanism worked, I locked myself out of my apartment with only my universal bike-repair tool and surprised myself by pulling off a practice round in less than five minutes. After I'd managed this feat several times I felt confident I could gain entry to Shannon's apartment without having to smash a window, but just in case I packed a glass cutter, a hand towel and some Band-Aids. Surgical gloves, Ziploc bags in various sizes, and an old stadium blanket also went in my bag. There was no need to bring a flashlight.

Shannon's door turned out to be no problem—apart from the safety chain I discovered after I'd performed my new stunt. But years of bicycle repair had also taught me how to free the most awkwardly positioned nuts and screws, and despite sweaty palms and a ravenous feline milling about my ankles, a few minutes with the Phillips head were all

I needed to tease the chain from the door frame. I pushed the cat away and slipped into the apartment, only then noticing that my heart was pounding like an oil rig. I was in. Now what?

I first needed an idea of the apartment's layout. Starting in the kitchen, I rounded the walls, locating cabinets, an aluminum sink, an electric stove, and a refrigerator, which had been turned off and emitted the stale odor of takeout. There was nothing in it but various sticky substances I chose not to explore and an open box of baking soda. The kitchen led to a dining room and, following that, to a living area. The minute I turned into it, I realized something was wrong.

I'd expected to find Shannon's belongings neatly packed away in boxes in the center of the room. I'd remove the contents from the boxes one by one and place them on the blanket, to be returned to their original location before starting on the next. If all went according to plan, I wouldn't overlook what I'd come for and could leave the place as tidy as I'd found it. Two steps into the living room were all it took to send my scheme—or rather, my feet—flying. Expecting a more or less clear path, I was startled when my cane immediately encountered a large, soft mass. I took a quick step backward, only to catch my heel on something smooth and slippery. I lost my balance and crashed wildly to the floor, landing on my back amid a sea of debris.

For a few minutes, all I did was lay there, breathing hard. After the shock had receded, I made a snow angel motion with my arms, locating my cane a few feet away. I retrieved it and pulled myself to a sitting position. With my legs splayed out on the floor, I tapped out a half circle in front of me. It took only seconds to realize that what I'd tripped over wasn't an aberration. I was sitting on the edge of disaster zone. Books, papers, plastic and metal items, smashed crockery, clothing, tangled-up bedclothes, scores of smaller items I couldn't begin to identify, were lying in every direction as if churned up by a tornado. And broken glass, lots of it, judging by the crunching sound. Someone had gotten there before me. Someone in a hurry—or with an ax to grind.

I stopped and sat there thinking. Having come this far, I didn't want to give up, but the fall and the chaos in which I'd found the place had put a major dent in my plans. I hadn't anticipated feeling my way through a garbage dump, let alone one filled with so many jagged edges. Searching Shannon's things now would be like investigating a sunken ship without a wetsuit. Or breathing gear. With only my hands to guide me, I could probably count on multiple stab wounds. And there were even bigger safety issues to worry about. Whoever had wrecked the place might still be there, possibly in the same room. Watching and waiting for the right moment to crush my skull from behind.

Feeling like a clown with a bulls-eye on his back, I pushed myself cautiously to my feet and made my way back to the kitchen. My temples were humming and my face burned. I turned on the faucet and splashed water on it, before resting my head against the wall. Forgetting that I'd managed to pick the door lock only ten minutes before, I allowed a wave of helplessness and self-pity to wash over me. In real life, blind people didn't scale walls or steal precious contraband from well-guarded castles. They stayed at home, minding their own business and playing Braille Scrabble. If they were very adventurous, they ran marathons or competed in beep baseball. They didn't fool themselves into acting like ninjas.

It was time, I thought defeatedly, to concede what everyone had been saying to me all along. I was hopeless as an investigator and probably finished as a doctor. When the authorities got through with me, I'd be lucky if I could land a job as a research assistant at one of the big drug companies. In the worst-case scenario, I'd end up on the street, selling newspapers like Mike or pushing a supermarket cart filled with unwashed blankets and empty return bottles. Or locked up in an asylum.

I'm not sure what finally brought me back to my senses: the picture created by my overheated imagination, or that the situation I was in suddenly reminded me of George.

For the first few months after my illness, I'd stubbornly turned down Felicity's repeated advice that I subscribe to a course in home management. But midway into Marta's annual visit to her grandchildren in Caracas, I acceded to a one-day session with a vision-rehabilitation specialist. I was tired of playing *Let's Make a Deal* with the contents of my pantry, and figured if nothing else he could help me label my canned goods. George was a semiretired sexagenarian who had previously worked for the Veteran's Administration. His first piece of advice was not to waste my time on things I wouldn't have bothered with before, like fixing drains or whipping up soufflés.

"Stick with what you already know and like to do," he told me. "Then figure out an alternate way of doing it."

"What if I liked painting beautiful landscapes?"

"Then go on painting them. You think there's such a thing as an insurmountable problem? The client I had before you was an architect."

"What's he doing now? Modeling clay?"

"No. The last I heard he'd been picked to design the new children's museum."

I admit I was impressed. George explained how his client now used computer software to create tactile blueprints for his projects. It took more time, and he had to rely on his mental skills for three-dimensional images, but he was back at his job and being well paid for it.

"Look, sonny," George said. He called me "sonny," even though I was more than half his age. Or maybe it was his way of implying I should be more upbeat. "I'm not going to tell you to go out and climb Mount Everest, though it's been done. Just keep an open mind and stop crying over spilled milk. Here, I'll give you a demonstration."

We were standing in my kitchen. George removed a bottle of beer from my refrigerator and casually dropped it on the floor. It shattered, sending shards of glass and a stream of frothy liquid across the tiles and onto my stocking feet.

I felt more surprised than offended. "I hope that wasn't the '56 Dom Perignon. I was saving it for better company. Wait, I know. It *is* the Vitamin D stuff."

"If only milk smelled that good. Don't worry. I'll spring for another six-pack when we're through."

I hoped that didn't mean we would be breaking another five bottles. It worked, though. A stupid, insignificant thing, but it worked. By the time I had finished sweeping up the glass and mopping the floor, without any assistance from George and in pretty much the same way I would have when I could see what I was doing—though I did put on a pair of shoes—I felt more in charge of my situation than at any other time since the lights had gone out.

What I was dealing with now wasn't all that different. It was just a bigger mess.

I went back to the other room, stuck my tongue out at whoever might be lurking in the shadows, and began cleaning up, using the ripped-off side of one of the boxes as a combination shovel-finder. It took a while, but when I was finished, most of the broken things were safely pushed aside to one corner. I then attacked the bedclothes and linens, fishing them up with my cane and giving them a good shaking before tossing them atop the heap. Shannon's books and papers went in another corner, for O'Leary to go through later if my hunch panned out. Though I itched to know whether Shannon's diary was among them, I fought off the urge to look. There was no point in wasting time on something I didn't have a prayer of recognizing.

When I'd reduced the mound in the center to a pile of smaller, mostly non-threatening objects, I began examining them by hand, a task made more difficult by the surgical gloves I'd put on, which decreased the sensitivity in my fingertips but prevented contamination of the evidence. At times it was easy to figure out what I was holding; at others all I could do was guess. An alarm clock, a hair dryer, a picture frame, a stuffed animal. I found a plastic bag holding jewelry and other bric-a-brac that I went through carefully, along with a small suitcase holding nightgowns and lingerie. If I felt uneasy about pawing through the dead woman's things, I told myself that what I was doing was no more invasive than carving up cadavers in medical school, a procedure that always left me desperate for a hot shower. Still, the scent of Shannon's perfume was everywhere, and it rose up to fill my nostrils like decomposing flesh.

When I finally found what I was looking for it was near the bottom of the pile, among an assortment of toiletries and other bathroom supplies. There was no mistaking the slim plastic tube with the rubber bulb on one end. I handled it like a baby, placing it and the gloves I had been wearing in one of the plastic bags, on which I also wrote the date and time with a marker. CSI *here I come*, I thought happily.

Having secured this trophy, I still kept going, half-expecting to be charged any moment by a madman wearing a wig and wielding a huge kitchen knife. But Mrs. Bates failed to materialize, and I was able to finish my search without interruption—also, without opening an artery. My only other prize was the small thermos that I discovered when I went back to the kitchen to check the cabinets. I was getting tired and would have skipped the room entirely but for an instinct that told me I couldn't quit until I had looked everywhere. The thermos smelled like dish detergent and had probably been washed thoroughly, but I tucked it inside a plastic bag all the same, labeling it with the date and time as I'd done previously.

When I was finally finished, the two plastic bags went in my backpack with the gloves and my tools. I washed my hands thoroughly and checked to be sure the lights were still off. Then I let myself out of the apartment, pulling the back door shut firmly behind me.

It was then a little after 2:00 a.m.

NINETEEN

The streets outside were deserted, the Cubs fans having long departed for home. It had turned into a cloudy, moonless night. A warm front had come through while I was in Shannon's apartment, bringing light rain and a loamy fragrance to the air. I decided it was too late to bother Boris, so after listening in the alley to confirm I hadn't been seen, I set out on foot. Earlier that evening I'd used Mapquest to plot a route from Shannon's place to the 'L' station on Addison, only a few blocks away. Even at such a late hour taxis were likely to be idling there, and if all else failed, I'd just take the train home.

The damp air muffled the sounds of my taps as I set off down the street. Tree branches overhead dripped like leaky faucets and sent streams running off the brim of my hat. I heard faint laughter from behind a closed door and the yipping of a terrier, but otherwise the neighborhood was quiet. I concentrated on avoiding the puddles on the uneven sidewalk and keeping track of my position.

Chicago streets are laid out in a precise grid dating from the era after the Great Fire. One of its features is that city blocks are of almost even length—every eight blocks covers a mile—and I'd learned to estimate when I would get to the next corner by keeping a vague count of my steps. The system is also ideal for finding street addresses, since the numbering system corresponds exactly to the distance from an axis formed by the intersection of Madison and State, increasing in increments of one hundred with each block. It's a blind person's dream, the only exception being avenues like Clark and Lincoln that cut through the grid at an angle, creating scissored junctions with multiple corners and an array of confusing crosswalks.

It was one of these that tripped me up.

My original plan was to go south to Grace and then east three blocks to Clark. A right turn there would eventually bring me to Wrigley Field, on the opposite side of the street. The Red Line stop was immediately adjacent to the ballpark's southeast corner, so once there I couldn't miss it. But the directions I'd listened to neglected to mention that Clark passes through Racine at a sharp angle about forty feet after the turn off from Grace. When I got to the intersection I thought I was crossing Clark when in fact I was crossing Racine, and I didn't realize I'd taken a wrong turn until I'd gone on several more blocks without finding a hint of a baseball field. Confused, I'd retraced my steps, missing Clark altogether on the return journey and finally concluding I was lost when I found myself in a cul-de-sac blocked by a cement wall and a tall chain-link fence.

It was hardly the first time this had happened to me. By then I'd come to view it as inevitable that I would occasionally have to stop a passerby to ascertain exactly what corner I was facing, or go back and forth several times before I recognized a place I'd been to a dozen times before. I won't say I always dealt with the situation with aplomb, but neither did it send me into fits, and usually I was able to shrug it off as another one of the minor annoyances I was used to.

But that night was different. By the time I found myself (literally) up against a wall, it was nearing 3:00 a.m. I was exhausted, worried about getting my cache safely home, and thoroughly disoriented. My usual tricks for estimating location were of no use because there was no moon. Of course, if I'd known I was on Racine a few blocks north of Addison I could have just headed south and found the 'L' station in no time, but it wasn't until I revisited the episode later that I understood where I'd gone off course. I couldn't call a cab on my cell because I didn't know where to tell the dispatcher to send it, and I was too embarrassed to start knocking on doors. There was nothing to do but strike out in a random direction and hope I ran into a friendly stranger or late-night establishment hospitable to drunks and stray blind men.

I found a stranger. But he wasn't friendly.

As I turned to exit the cul-de-sac, I realized with an alarming sensation that I wasn't alone. A crunch of gravel at the entrance to the street. The faint click of moving parts settling into gear. A forward rush of air. But no engine throttle. Under ordinary circumstances I should have heard it coming. Through the many long months of training with Cherie, I'd learned to approximate the distance of moving vehicles, the relative speed at which they were approaching. It was what gave me the confidence to go anywhere I wanted, in or out of familiar territory. But this time there was no warning sound. Before I even knew what was happening, something large, cold and metallic exploded into my midsection.

The force of the blow sent me flying into the air. I immediately lost control of my cane, which clattered to the ground like a dropped spoon. I bounced onto the hood and over the windshield, frantically grabbing for something to hold onto. Sliding and spinning, I managed to latch onto a wiper before I was sent hurtling over the roof. I hung there for a moment, swinging wildly back and forth while the brakes screeched to a halt. The sudden shift in velocity did nothing to slow my forward momentum. The wiper came loose in my hand and I went tumbling over the side.

Sooner or later, every cyclist goes headfirst over their handlebars, and I'd been in enough serious collisions to know how to minimize the damage, tucking my chin and bringing my elbows to my chest just before I crashed to the ground. I landed hard on my side and rolled several times before skidding to a stop at the foot of what I guessed to be the fence. For a while I didn't move, assessing my level of injury. My face was lacerated and I felt pain in my rib cage, but my wrists and ankles weren't broken and I could wiggle my toes. My ears were ringing but my head was clear. The car hadn't been moving that fast and my backpack, still attached to my shoulders, seemed to have absorbed a fair amount of the blow.

The smell of burnt rubber filled the air and I could feel the heat of the engine some yards away. The lights were off and it was idling almost silently. The driver seemed to be waiting, deciding something.

I didn't know whether to lie still or call for help. If it had only been an accident, the driver might be scared. The cul-de-sac wasn't well lit.

Maybe he hadn't seen me until just before the car struck and was unsure of his best move. Take off on the assumption I couldn't identify him or face added penalties for running down a blind man. Unless hitting me was deliberate. But that was absurd. I was letting all this cloak and dagger stuff get to me. I moved painfully into a crouch and then a standing position, feeling for the chain-link fence behind me. "Hey," I called out experimentally. "Anybody there?"

The window on the driver's side came down. Was he checking to see whether I was injured? I waved at him and said, "It's OK. I'm not hurt, just a little shaken."

I got no answer. The car's headlights came on and its wheels began to turn, spitting spray onto the wet pavement. Was he backing up or moving forward? The car began to roll again, picking up speed. Heading forward and straight at me. "Please!" I yelled one last time before I gathered he wasn't stopping. I reversed in a hurry and started to climb, tearing at the diamond-shaped wire above my head. As the car accelerated further, the engine finally sprang to life, roaring like a jet engine in the narrow confines of the alley.

The first time the front end struck, it missed me by only inches. The impact caused the fence to fold inward like a slat on a venetian blind and I lost my footing. Dangling there like a piñata, I heard the car moving in reverse toward the street. Twenty yards. Fifty. It squealed to a stop before churning its wheels and speeding back in my direction. With a sickened feeling, I realized he really did mean to kill me. The sweat was slicking my fingers as I searched for a toehold. All at once, I remembered the maneuver I used to mount fences when I was caught trespassing as a teenager. I started to swing, using the weight of my lower body like a pendulum until my right foot connected with something solid. I forced the toe of my sneaker into a hole half its size and heaved myself up.

The second time the car hit the fence swayed like a dancer. Perched precariously on the crossbar with only one leg over the top, I didn't stand a chance. The last thing I remember was hurtling head forward into nothingness.

When I woke I was lying in someone's flower bed. There was mud on my face and vegetation in my teeth. My left eye was swollen shut and my rib cage felt as though it had been through the spin cycle of a washing machine. I picked out the plant matter with one hand while I felt with the other for my things. My hat was long gone, but my backpack, with my cell phone and the finds from Shannon's apartment, was still hanging by one of its straps from my shoulder. I shook my head from side to side, ignoring the chimes going off between my ears. *Stupid, stupid, stupid.* As if failing to page Boris and becoming lost weren't enough, I had to go and get myself in a cat-and-mouse game with a demonically possessed vehicle. Was there no end to my hubris?

When the 911 operator came on the line, I told her I'd just been the victim of a hit and run.

"All right, sir," she said. "Try to remain calm. Just tell me where you are and we'll have a squad car there in a jiffy."

"That's going to be a problem," I said. "I don't know where I am, except that it's in somebody's yard in Wrigleyville."

"You can't be more specific than that?" she asked skeptically.

"No. I'm, uh . . . blind," I said.

"Uh-huh. Can you give me your location before the attack?"

"I don't know that either."

"How can you not know where you were?" she chided me.

"I was lost."

"All right then. Look around you. Is there a house nearby?"

"I think so. But I can't really see it."

"Were you hit on the head?"

"Yes, but that's not why . . ."

"No lights on in the house?"

"Please," I almost sobbed. "It's like I told you. I'm *blind*. Blind as in not able to see."

"Oh!" she exclaimed. She continued as though this was nothing out of the ordinary. "Well, don't worry. You probably have a concussion. I'm sure your vision will clear up soon. Give me a moment while I put a trace on your call."

The squad car arrived several minutes later, siren whining and lights flashing, looking like a burst of antiaircraft fire in an old war movie. By that time the owner of the yard had come out with a flashlight, and after ascertaining I wasn't wielding a shotgun, taken me out to the street. Two cops walked up and introduced themselves.

"You the accident victim?" one of the officers asked me.

"You might call it that."

"Dispatcher said you were having some trouble with your eyes."

"No more than usual."

"Well, try not to panic. An ambulance is on its way."

"I don't need an ambulance," I said impatiently. "And please stop waving your fingers in my face. What I need is to see one of your officers right away—Detective O'Leary from the Fourth. Can you get hold of him on your radio? And then maybe one of you can help me find my cane."

"I oughta have you arrested," O Leary said to me, after I had finished telling him everything. "Or committed. I can't decide which. Why didn't you just ask me to send some of the boys to look through her stuff?"

"I thought you'd laugh at me. It was just a suspicion after all. Ouch!" I said involuntarily. A resident was pulling a suture through my forehead while I sat in a paper gown with my knees hanging off a gurney. We were in the curtained-off partition where the other cops had taken my statement a few hours earlier. It being early on a Saturday morning the emergency room was doing a brisk trade, and since I wasn't coding when they brought me in, I had to wait a long time to be attended to by the resident, whose name was Tim and who reminded me of myself at that age. Considering what had occurred, I'd gotten off easy—a few cracked ribs and a gash above my eye that only needed eight stitches.

"Two more," Tim said. "Then we're done. But if you don't keep still I can't guarantee you won't cause a riot among the villagers when you lurch out the door."

"Thank you, Doctor Frankenstein."

"Frankensteen to you," Tim said.

"While you're at it, do you think you could lift me a new pair of retinas from one of the accident victims in the fridge?"

"Sure thing. Any other areas of your anatomy you'd like me to augment?"

"That part of me was still functioning when I last checked."

"Sorry, I forgot you can't see it when somebody winks."

"Are you medical types always this jovial?" O'Leary asked.

"Occupational hazard," Tim replied.

"Yeah, for us too I guess. And that's another thing," O'Leary said to me. "What the hell were you doing roaming around on foot in the middle of the night? You forget how to call a cab? You're lucky you didn't end up in the fridge yourself. Or maybe that's what you wanted. I heard they put you on leave."

"Is that why you were following me?" I asked, to change the subject.

"Say what?"

"Following me. As in violating the privacy rights of an unsuspecting citizen. I apologize for being such a poor challenge, by the way."

"How'd you . . . ?"

"You should buy a new pair of shoes. Or get those fixed. I may not have amazing superhero powers, but I can recognize a sound when I hear it often enough." Tim had finished and I ran my fingers over the stitches. It was a neat job and probably wouldn't leave much of a scar.

"No feeling the artwork," Tim admonished.

"I thought there might be a hidden message for me there. How about it, O'Leary, are you going to fess up?"

"I admit I was worried about you getting yourself killed. So yeah, when I had time I kept tabs on you. I would have been there last night if I hadn't credited you with more intelligence."

"Can you find out who hit me?"

"Not unless you got his plate numbers."

I gave him an exasperated look. "I was thinking of witnesses. Neighbors who happened to peek through their curtains while I was being run down."

"We'll check, but folks in that area are used to late-night disturbances. Especially after the Cubs have gone down in flames. And while we're on the subject, you could do with some wardrobe changes yourself."

I assumed he was referring to my Mets cap, which had been found covered with tire marks not too far from my cane. The latter had also been run over several times and reduced more or less to splinters.

"So your theory is that it was just a deranged fan?"

"For now, at least. Who knew you were going to be at Sparrow's apartment last night?"

It was a good question. I thought back to my preparations the day before. Marilyn Sparrow could have guessed where I'd be. And Nancy Kim and Regina Best. I gave O'Leary their names.

Tim helped me ease my arms out of the paper gown and passed me my pants and shirt. My ribs ached and my left eye felt like someone had pasted two halves of a lemon there. It was still leaking and already half-crusted over like a pastry tart. "I want you in to see your ophthalmologist first thing Monday morning," he said. "Normally, I'd tell a patient to watch out for blurred vision, but that's not feasible in your case and I don't want to see you ending up with a prosthetic eye. You never know—maybe they can fix what you have someday. You can have the stitches removed in a week or so. Until then, just watch for signs of infection. You want a scrip for Vicodin?"

"No, the amber stuff in a bottle will do just fine."

After we left the hospital, O'Leary offered me a lift home and I was more than happy to accept. O'Leary had sent the items I'd borrowed from Shannon's apartment to the police lab for testing. The results wouldn't be ready for another forty-eight hours, but I was pretty confident of what they would show.

"Go over this again with me," O'Leary said in the car. "You think she got pregnant on purpose?"

"That's what her sister suggested. She said Shannon wasn't the type to mess up and get pregnant accidentally. The more I thought about it, the more it fit. I think she stumbled on Charlie while he was masturbating at the center—having just learned how much fun it was, he was probably doing it whenever he had the chance—and got the idea of using the pregnancy to get back at Nate. She must have talked Charlie into using a paper cup and handing it over to her. It would be easy to concoct some story he'd believe, or else she threatened to tell on him if he didn't do what she wanted. The thermos was to keep the stuff warm until she could get home and use the turkey baster."

"And all this so she could blackmail Nate?"

"Not initially. I think she believed she could pass the child off as his. A paternity test would have a hard time distinguishing between the baby's father and its grandfather. Shannon was arrogant and self-centered enough to think Nate would come running back to her if she was pregnant with a so-called normal child. She showed some insight into his psychology in that respect. It doesn't take a psychiatrist to see that Nate is deeply embarrassed by his only son. Shannon was banking on him wanting another pass at fatherhood, this time with a child he could raise in his own image. She didn't realize the whole plan was flawed from the start because Nate would know immediately the baby wasn't his."

"Or that she was running the risk of producing another kid like Charlie, if I understand what you told me about Fragile X Syndrome."

"That too. She probably got far enough in the literature to find out about the maternal inheritance pattern, but didn't understand how it plays out in the second generation. Since Shannon herself wasn't affected, she thought her baby would be safe."

"So you think she wanted to keep it?"

"Yes, but not from any deep maternal feeling. From what everyone's told me, Shannon was hell-bent on landing a trophy husband.

Even for his age, Nate fit the profile. He's prominent socially as well as professionally and brings home a pretty penny. The baby could be cared for by nannies, and Shannon could play the rich doctor's wife. She couldn't have done much better. And I think getting Nate to marry her was a psychological imperative for Shannon. Her ego couldn't live with rejection. She would have done anything to win him back."

"This disease you told me about—"

"Narcissistic personality disorder?"

"Yeah, that one. You're pretty sure Shannon had it?"

"It's only a supposition. I can't be certain, but it explains many of her actions and how she thought she could get away with them. Most normal people wouldn't have had the audacity to conceive such a plan, let alone carry it to fruition."

"OK," O'Leary said. "But if we assume that's what she was up to, where does it take us in terms of the murder? You're saying the father killed her. I agree with you he had the means to do it, but what was his motive? He slept with her, so what? It had to be kept such a deep, dark secret that he killed Sparrow to keep his wife from knowing?"

"That's the part I haven't figured out yet. But I'm guessing Shannon came back to him with some kind of monetary demand. After all, we only have it on Nate's word that Judith would have looked the other way if she found out about their affair. Maybe Nate is attached to all that trust-fund income. Or maybe she threatened to go through with the pregnancy if he didn't pay her."

"Fair enough. So you think he arranged to meet Shannon in the alley behind the New Horizons Center, and when she showed up he killed her and took off, never imagining that his own kid would end up tripping over the corpse."

"Something like that. Remember, Regina Best said she saw someone drive through the alley several times that morning, like they were waiting for Shannon to show up. By the way, please do me the courtesy of taking that woman seriously. She's got a few issues, but being in a wheelchair doesn't make her an imbecile. Your guys missed some useful information by not treating her like a real person."

"I take the point. Was there anything else?" O'Leary had slowed his car and stopped in front of my building.

"One more thing. The necklace. Was it found on Shannon's body, do you remember?"

"I'll go back and double check the stuff she was wearing, but I don't think so."

"I was told she never took it off."

"Meaning if it wasn't on her when she was found, the killer took it."

"That's what I'm thinking."

"What difference does it make? It's probably in the Chicago River by now."

"Maybe, but it wouldn't hurt to look. Can you search the home?"

"What kind of a moron do you take me for? We already did once, after the kid was taken into custody. I don't know whether Di Marco would give me permission to go back, but I'll ask. Meanwhile, we'll find out what those lab tests have to say. And I'll have a look at the girl's place. Will you be around later?"

"Yeah."

"Don't make any plans until you hear from me."

After O'Leary drove away I went upstairs and downed a shot of bourbon and four acetaminophen tablets. Then I fell on my bed and slept for the better part of the day.

When I dreamt, I was never blind. People had faces and I could perceive objects from far away. Often I found myself in foreign places I'd once traveled to, marveling at the sensation of moving through space as easily as an antelope or a gazelle. I climbed mountains through tall stands of pine, tramped white sand beaches under a cerulean sky. I crossed cityscapes glittering with cathedrals and skyscrapers. It was always an odd transition waking from these vivid images to a different experience of reality, the texture of the blanket under my fingers, the clicking of my bedside clock. Freud said most nocturnal dreaming is a form of wish fulfillment. I don't think this is why I dreamed of myself as a sighted person. I think it was just what my mind was more used to.

That afternoon I dreamed I was with Alice. We were sharing a picnic on a blanket laid out in the shade of a tree, surrounded by a field of wildflowers. My head was in her lap and I was reading poetry aloud from a book, and when she leaned down to brush her lips on my forehead I saw her as clearly as I've ever seen anyone. She wasn't beautiful in a classic way, but I liked her small snub of a nose and generous, laughing mouth. Her eyes were light brown and her hair was chestnut-colored, falling from the crown of her head in waves. She was wearing a necklace I'd bought her and the diamond pendant caught a shaft of sun that sent rainbows in every direction. I returned her caress and told her how much I cared for her.

Then the sky darkened and a flock of crows came careening down. I knew at once why they had come. I looked up at the tree branches above us and they were everywhere, black and full of menace. "Run, Alice," I shouted. "Hide. They've come for you." But it was too late. The crows were swarming her. "No!" I screamed, "Leave her alone!" She tried to shield her face, but it was no good. I wanted to go to her, to stop them, but I was frozen in place. The crows were all over her, pecking at her cheeks, destroying those beautiful hazel eyes. I screamed again uselessly . . .

Somewhere in the distance a phone was ringing.

I came to abruptly in my wrinkled, blood-stained clothing and jumped up to wrestle the receiver from its hook.

It was Alice.

"Mark? Where have you been? I've been trying you all day," she said after I'd mumbled a greeting. It was disconcerting to hear her voice so soon after the dream and I was breathing heavily. "Have you been exercising?" she asked. "You sound like you just finished a race."

"It's nothing," I said. "Just a bad dream."

"Why were you asleep in the middle of the afternoon?"

"I . . . uh . . . had a little adventure last night."

I gave her a vague outline of what had happened, omitting the details and making it seem as though it was just an accident. Alice knew I was leaving things out, but chose not to question me too thoroughly, thereby leaving a shred of my dignity intact.

"That's horrifying. What was that driver thinking of? Even if he didn't know you were blind, he should never have driven away."

"I admit I sent a few choice epithets in his direction."

"Did you report the incident to the police?"

"Yeah, but there's only so much they can do. He's probably scared shitless right now, worrying whether he'll be caught."

"That's not much of a consolation. You could have been seriously hurt. Or killed." There was more than the usual amount of concern in her voice, which pleased me.

"About the black eye—does it hurt much?" Alice asked. "I could come over and take care of you. You've heard of the Florence Nightingale effect, I assume?"

"You mean when nurses develop an erotic interest in their patients? Sounds like an attractive proposition. But not tonight if you don't mind. I'm beat and I don't think I'd be very good company." It was true, to a degree. My sides had grown even stiffer while I was napping and I could barely move without feeling a sharp, stabbing pain in my midsection. Alice would be sure to notice. But mostly I wanted to be ready if O'Leary called.

As if reading my thoughts, Alice said, "There's something else you're not telling me. Is it about Charlie?"

"Mmmm. But I don't know yet how it will pan out. Why don't we plan on having dinner tomorrow night? I can fill you in then."

"I'd love to, but I can't. I'm going to a play with a friend."

I surprised myself by feeling a stab of envy. "A male friend?"

"Yes. But don't be jealous. He's my former boss, directs the state rehabilitation counseling agency where I used to work before I left to head the center. He heard about the trouble I was having and offered to try to take my mind off things for a few hours. And I thought it wouldn't be a bad idea to start hitting up some of my old contacts. I'm going to be needing a new job soon."

"I'm sorry," I sympathized. "Truly sorry. But don't do anything precipitous—the center may not be over yet."

"I'd like to believe that. And please watch yourself. I won't force you to tell me what really happened last night, but I don't want you taking any risks on my behalf."

I rang off feeling warmer toward Alice than ever.

A little after ten o'clock found me sitting in an unmarked car with O'Leary on the nine hundred block of West Belden. O'Leary had explained we were facing east, with a view into the alley behind a row of graystone mansions on North Dayton. Another unmarked car was stationed on Webster, keeping watch over the alley's south entrance.

"So how do you like surveillance work?" O'Leary asked.

"Not bad. Do you think I'm cut out for it?"

"I don't know. Patience might be an issue."

I stifled my jerking knee. "I admit I'm finding the scenery a little dull, but can you blame me?"

O'Leary had called at six with news both positive and negative. Preliminary results had confirmed traces of Charlie's DNA in the turkey baster, but it wasn't enough to convince Di Marco. The prosecutor had flatly turned down O'Leary's request for a second search warrant. And if Shannon's diary still existed, it was nowhere to be found in her apartment. It was therefore up to us to find definitive proof of Nate's guilt.

After O'Leary picked me up at my building we swung by Bari Foods on West Grand, where two other plainclothesmen were waiting for us. O'Leary introduced me to them, a fellow named Monaghan who smelled like Brylcreem and a younger one named Jimenez who gave me a ghetto handshake. From there we drove north to Lincoln Park and found a space in a DePaul campus parking lot. After plotting logistics and gorging on subs stuffed with prosciutto, mortadella, and provolone, Monaghan and Jimenez went off for a smoke while I put in a call to Hallie.

"This is starting to become a bad habit, you calling me on a Saturday night," she said when she heard my voice. "Especially when I'm alone and staring at another long night with only a DVD and takeout to keep me company."

"I know the feeling," I said.

She hesitated a fraction before asking, "Would you like to come over?"

"I can't tonight, but I'll take a rain check if you'll let me."

The police radio on the dashboard crackled to life and O'Leary hastened to still it.

"What was that noise?" Hallie asked quickly.

"Uh . . . my pager just went off," I lied. "A patient of mine is being admitted tonight. I've got to head over to the hospital in a few minutes."

That seemed to satisfy her. "So why are you calling? Do you have some news for me?"

I told her about the necklace. And about Nate's affair with Shannon. And about the forensic analysis. She wasn't exactly thrilled.

"Well, that's just peachy," she said when I'd finished. "What the hell am I supposed to do now?"

"I thought maybe you could make a motion or something to get Charlie released."

Her exasperation was plain. "You don't understand. Nate's been paying for Charlie's defense. Technically that makes him my client too. What you just told me creates a conflict of interest. I'll have to disclose it to Nate immediately."

"You'll have to tell him the police are on to him? Hallie don't, not yet!"

"There's something else you're not telling me. What is it? What are they planning?"

"I'm not sure, but O'Leary mentioned the possibility of another warrant."

"You realize I'll have to warn Nate about that too?"

"You wouldn't!" I said, winking over at O'Leary.

"I'm afraid I don't have a choice." She exhaled loudly. "Didn't I tell you to leave criminal law to the professionals? What you've done simply complicates the situation even more."

"I thought I was helping Charlie."

"Oh, Mark," she said, "I like you, but you are so . . . impossible."

"I guess I do keep messing things up," I agreed shamefacedly. "Will you have to tell Nate tonight?"

"As soon as I get off with you."

"Nice work," O'Leary said when I'd ended the call.

O'Leary and I passed the next several hours staked out on Belden nursing tall cups of coffee with the windows rolled up. It was a steamy night and the car soon became stifling, choking with the aroma of the sandwich leftovers on the back seat. There was a small rotating fan on the dashboard and O'Leary switched it on. I rolled up my shirtsleeves and tried to keep from fidgeting while we made small talk.

"You any relation to the lady with the cow?"

"You know, I've spent half my life trying to come up with a good comeback to that question," O'Leary said. "But no, my relatives were still eating grass on the far side of the pond when the city went up. Must have been some party."

"South Sider?"

"Born and bred. How about you? You don't sound like you're from around here."

"Queens. I spent my formative years lolling around Shea Stadium."

"I wouldn't go bragging about that, if I were you."

"I guess I shouldn't need to be reminded," I said, rubbing my stitches.

The time passed slowly, one hour grinding into the next. I learned that O'Leary had gone to college at Holy Cross and been in the seminary a while before concluding his true vocation lay on the other side of the wire grill. We shared anecdotes about the terrors of a Catholic education and growing up at the tail end of the baby boom. O'Leary was a few years older than I and a Midwesterner, but our experiences were remarkably similar. We were both only children. O'Leary's father had been on the front lines when police were stoned by rioters at the

'68 Democratic Convention. Half a year later, just after being pro-
moted to detective, he was gunned down in a suspected Outfit hit at
a warehouse on the Northwest Side. O'Leary's mother had remarried
but died shortly afterward, the victim of a botched cesarean. After that,
O'Leary had been raised by his stepfather, another cop. O'Leary had
been married to the same woman for twenty-five years, but seemed
touchy about the subject so I let it drop.

A little after 12:30 O'Leary's radio did its Rice Krispies number
and Monaghan came on.

"Party just popped his garage door. Exiting now in a silver Mercedes, license plate KAP-1088. He's coming your way."

"Here we go," O'Leary said, keying the ignition.

I buckled my seatbelt and waited, feeling an adrenaline rush as we
pulled out of the space and began to pick up speed. O'Leary continued
to exchange cop pidgin with his colleagues in the other car, which
allowed me to follow our progress.

"Going code nine with the vehicle at Belden and Halsted. Left turn
signal."

"You want us to take the lead?"

"No. Just bring up the rear, code four."

"Copy. We'll swing around and follow."

Traffic seemed light, and we cruised along at a leisurely pace.

"Can you see the driver?" I asked anxiously.

"From this far back? Not a chance."

The Mercedes proceeded two blocks to the intersection of Halsted
and Fullerton, where it made a right. We took the same turn, heading
east. The city blocks whooshed by in the dark while I chewed my
knuckles. O'Leary, in contrast, was deathly calm at the wheel beside
me. I wondered what Nate had planned when he got to Lake Shore
Drive. If it were me, I would have gone south past the city limits to Lake
Calumet, a wetland aside I-94 where only the most intrepid sportsman
still fished. It was the kind of graveyard that beckoned those with something to hide, the same swamp where Leopold and Loeb had dumped
the body of little Bobby Franks. Or else I would have gone north to

Waukegan Harbor, a body of water containing enough PCBs to cool greater Los Angeles and correspondingly inhospitable to search divers.

As it turned out, the driver of the car had something less elaborate in mind.

Still going east, we passed Clark and down a small incline that told me we were coming up on Lincoln Park.

"Party has moved into the left-turn lane at Stockton, slowing for a red light." O'Leary told his colleagues.

"He's not getting onto the Drive, then?" I asked.

"Doesn't look like it. Turning left now," O'Leary informed them.

"Copy. What'd you think he's got in mind?"

"Dunno. Hold on . . . party's slowing, looking for a space to park. I don't think he's made us, but I don't want to take any chances. We'll go on ahead and come around again. You do the pick up."

"Copy."

"And don't let him throw anything in the water. I don't want to spend the rest of the night up to my chin in duck shit."

"Might I ask exactly where we are?" I said when they were finished.

"North Pond. You know it?"

I remembered the lagoon at the north end of Lincoln Park, a migration point for Canadian geese and all-year home to various species of local waterfowl. It was shallow but brackish, fringed with cattails and tall weeds, and often covered by a low-lying mist. It would have made a decent dumping ground if you didn't know you were being tailed by the police.

The minutes dragged like a truant on his way to detention. We stayed on Stockton until it ended at the top of the park and took a left and then another, making a semi-circle around the park's west end. By the time we were getting near to where we'd started, I was gouging jack-o'-lanterns into the sides of my seat.

"You're murdering me," I said, when I couldn't stand the suspense any longer. "What's going on?"

"You think I got eyes like a hawk? Give us a few minutes to get closer."

"We're coming up on them now," he told me fifteen seconds later. "When I stop you stay put, but you can roll down the window and listen."

O'Leary pulled up to the curb and jolted us to a halt. He squeaked the emergency brake into place and heaved himself out of with the motor still running. I hastily searched my armrest for the window button and pushed the small lever as far as it would go. A quick inrush of humid air followed. I thrust my chin out and scanned from side to side. There was a street lamp several yards off, bathing the area in harsh light. By holding my head at a certain angle I could just make out the three people silhouetted against sky: Monaghan and Jimenez and a taller figure between them. I strained for more but it was like trying to glimpse a shadow puppet through a sheet of moving water. I gave up and listened to what my ears had to tell me. There were no sounds of struggle, only someone whimpering softly. Like a coward.

O'Leary had finally reached the grass verge. The soft earth swallowed his footfalls as he approached the group waiting for him. I heard him chuckle softly and say, "Well, well, well. Not quite what we were expecting, but I'll take it." Then to the other cops: "You find any of the items we were after?"

"In here," Monaghan replied.

O'Leary took a bag of some sort and rustled its contents.

"Nice-looking. OK. Put the bracelets on and read her her rights."

Her? I didn't understand until Monaghan spoke again.

"Judith Dickerson, you have the right to remain silent . . ."

TWENTY

O'Leary kept busy the rest of the weekend. When he finally returned my calls on Monday there was a lot to tell me.

"She's not talking—the family lawyers have her sewed up tighter than a Muslim bride—but we've got enough to file charges. It's what you thought. Sparrow was blackmailing her."

"Why are you sure it was Judith and not Nate?"

"Circumstantial evidence, but it all adds up. Remember how she was supposed to be away at the family vacation home in Michigan when Sparrow was killed?"

I remembered. "New Buffalo, wasn't it?"

"Yeah. Except that an EZ-Pass camera on the Skyway caught her driving back into the city at 6:15 that morning."

"Car?"

"A bronze Lexus sedan."

I whistled.

"And that's not all. She claimed her cell phone was missing, but we pulled the paper records from her carrier. She placed two calls to Sparrow the night before the murder, one right after she'd purchased a handgun from a dealer outside Bridgewater."

"Interesting."

"But that's not all. We had your friend Regina Best try to pick her out of a lineup. Best couldn't make the ID but she's now positive the person cruising the alley that morning was a woman. We also checked out the family bank accounts. Before she left for Michigan, Judith had a fifty-thousand-dollar cashier's check drawn on her trust fund at the Northern."

"Fifty, huh? I'm surprised that's all that Shannon asked for."

"Probably just the first installment. The way I see it, once Sparrow figured out she wasn't going to get anywhere with the husband, she decided to hit up the wife. Judith went along with the blackmail at first, but then changed her mind, probably not trusting Sparrow to follow through on her promise to get an abortion. That's when she decided to kill her."

"Have you found the murder weapon?"

"Uh-uh. But we're getting ready to dredge the Lake near the New Buffalo cottage. According to the surveillance cameras, Judith ran straight back there after the murder, and I have a hunch we'll find it underwater with the gun. We've also impounded her car. If she was there and had contact with Sparrow, the forensic analysis should turn it up."

"How long will it take to find out?"

"A couple of days. I'll phone you as soon as the results are in."

"Where's Judith now?"

"Out. She posted bail on an evidence-tampering charge this morning. Which reminds me. It's time for you to give this case a rest. I'm too busy to watch your back any longer and if you're right about being deliberately attacked, somebody out there doesn't like you. Practice your swordsmanship, pilot a speedboat—do whatever it is you people do for a challenge. Just stay away from law enforcement. *Capisce*?"

For once, I intended to follow his advice.

Not long afterward, I was being sternly dressed down by Hallie for feeding her the story about the phony police search.

"You didn't think to enlist my help? How am I supposed to trust you again? And don't give me that doe-eyed look. You deliberately lied to me."

We were in her office, one of the coffin-sized spaces allocated to Wentworth, Feinstein's associates and furnished with little more than a modular desk and two hard chairs. Hallie sat in the one across from me, presumably glowering. She hadn't even offered me a refreshment when I came in, brusquely pushing me toward the guest seat with a shove to my back. Except for the fact I was pretty sure I would be spared corporal punishment, I felt like I was back in my high-school principal's office again.

"Does it make a difference that it was in a good cause?"

"Oh, so you're falling back on situational ethics."

"Professional ones, too. Didn't you tell me that disclosing what I knew about Nate and Shannon put you in a conflict of interest? Short of advising one of the senior Dickersons to give themselves up, what could you have done anyway?"

"I don't know. But I would have appreciated the opportunity to decide for myself. Instead, you hoodwinked me."

"All I did was inform you that the police were thinking of conducting a second search of the Dickerson house." Which was technically true, even if it was about as convincing as telling Monsignor O'Donnell it was only a Turkish cigarette.

"And hadn't even taken one step toward obtaining a search warrant," Hallie said, not in the least mollified. "Assuming, which I find highly unlikely, Di Marco would have allowed them to."

"Would you have, if you'd been in his shoes?"

She was quiet just long enough to concede the point. But not the match. "Tell me this—what would you have done if I hadn't taken the bait? Gone on another breaking-and-entering spree?"

I reached up to rub my stitches, which were starting to itch. "No, I think my days as a cat burglar are over."

"What on earth prompted you to pull that stunt, anyway?"

"Something your cousin said." Against my better judgment I told her the story.

Hallie wasn't pleased that I knew Jesus and even less happy that we'd been discussing her. "I wish Jesus would keep his big trap shut. Sometimes I'm embarrassed to admit we come from the same gene pool. You know about his 'business,' don't you?"

"He's, uh, offered to put me in touch with some of his lady friends." I decided against telling her she was one of them. "I hope I'm not that desperate—yet."

"Spare me the false modesty. If you weren't such a magnet for trouble, I might even consider dating you. So you think the two incidents are connected?"

"Unless Cubs fans really *are* that insane."

"It was probably a mistake. Someone who had too much to drink."

"In a blind cul-de-sac? I don't think so. And I was carrying my street cane—the big tall one. Even if you were drunk, you couldn't miss it. Whoever it was knew I couldn't see them and was trying to kill me."

"Or less dramatically, warn you off the case. So who do you think it was?"

"I'm not sure, but I've been thinking a lot about that night. That car, the way it seemed to come out of nowhere. It must have been a hybrid. They're so quiet when they're coasting you can barely hear them."

"What does Judith drive?"

"I checked with O'Leary. A Lexus with a standard transmission. Besides, I don't see her as the killer."

"Why not?" Hallie asked. "It sure looks like Shannon was blackmailing her. Isn't that a good enough reason for Judith to want her—and possibly you—out of the way?"

"Think about it. Let's say it's true Shannon approached Judith with a demand for money. Why didn't she just report Shannon to the authorities for abusing Charlie? It's not like she had something to hide."

"Maybe Shannon threatened to go through with the pregnancy if she didn't get paid and Judith didn't want another mentally disabled child in the family."

I shook my head. "I don't think Judith would have cared about that. It doesn't seem to have affected her love for Charlie."

"But from what we know of her she certainly would have minded Shannon becoming her daughter-in-law. Remember, Judith didn't know Shannon had impregnated herself with Charlie's sperm artificially. Shannon easily could have manipulated Judith into thinking that Charlie slept with her out of love. It's what Judith was so afraid of to begin with."

"True," I replied. "But then why the sudden decision to kill her? To someone as wealthy as Judith, the money would have been meaningless. And why purchase a gun if she didn't intend to use it?"

"So you're still putting your money on Nate."

"I'm saying that between the two of them, Nate had the better motive. After he spurned her marriage offer, Shannon would have done anything to destroy him. He knew it, and he knew he'd never be free of her. Even if the child wasn't his, she could have caused a major scandal. Nate admitted to me Shannon wasn't his first. A few more extramarital flings coming to light and who knows? He might even have been forced from his job." I kept the irony of my saying so out of the discussion. "And unlike Judith, Nate wouldn't have been able to stomach another retarded offspring."

"So you're saying by killing Shannon, he solved two problems. All right, I buy that. But then why was Judith trying to get rid of that necklace?"

"She must have been protecting someone."

"Who? Nate?"

"Charlie, more likely."

"What are you saying? That Charlie did it?"

"No, of course not. Only that Judith may have thought so."

"All right, but I'll thank you to keep that theory to yourself. It's not going to help me tomorrow when I move to get Charlie out of jail."

All at once, I felt uneasy. "I thought that would happen automatically."

"Shows how little you know. Right now, the case against Judith is almost entirely circumstantial. It wouldn't surprise me at all if Di Marco decided to stick with what he's got."

"Are you saying . . . ?"

"That Charlie's not out of the woods yet? I'm sorry to be the bearer of bad tidings, but that's right."

At eleven the next day we were back in Judge La Font's courtroom, waiting for a break in the case she was trying. Ordinarily it would have produced a yawn: an elite squad of Chicago police accused of shaking down drug dealers for a share of the profits, except that the cops had mistaken a seventeen-year-old honor student at Walter Payton for one of their targets. After hearing testimony from the boy's mother, who had been handcuffed to a radiator while the cops worked him over with a tire iron, the judge sent the jury out and called an hour's recess. Hallie said this was to give her time to light up in the judges-only smoking area on the roof. It was one of the few perks that came with the job.

The news that Charlie's case was on the call had traveled quickly, and most of the fourth estate decided to stick around for a possible scoop. Hallie hadn't requested that Charlie be present, but Nate and Judith were there, seated in the front row with Judith's new lawyers. After finding room for me in the opposite bank of seats, Hallie left to take up a position at counsel table and I did my best to pretend I wasn't on the receiving end of a battery of hostile looks. The journalists must have been gleeful taking it all in. A few minutes went by before the one next to me said:

"You can relax now. The boy's parents are making a big show of not looking this way, and everyone else is back to playing with their iPhones."

It was kind of him, but it only confirmed what I'd been thinking. "Thanks," I said. "Is there an app for avoiding socially awkward occasions?"

He laughed and nudged my forearm. "If there was, it wouldn't be free. Tom Klutsky, I cover legal affairs for the *Sun-Times*." The paw he slid into mine was as meaty as a stockyard.

We shook and I introduced myself.

"I know who you are. I was here a month ago when you were on the stand."

"Not my finest hour," I said, wishing he hadn't brought it up. "I've been trying my best to forget it."

"Are you kidding? I thought you were outstanding."

My jaw dropped a foot or two. I couldn't have been more surprised if Clarence Darrow had suddenly descended from the heavens and fist-bumped me.

"What, Hallie the handsome didn't tell you? I guess not," he said, seeing my asinine expression. "Well, let me explain it to you. Any witness can be surprised. Happens all the time, especially with a shark like Di Marco. It's how they deal with the grenade that's just been tossed in their lap that singles out the pros from the wannabes."

"The only thing I recall wanting to be was a hundred miles away."

"Sure you did. But you did a good job of hiding it. I've been covering this beat for a long time, and I've never seen anyone hold up so well under a tough cross. Cooler than the Lake in February. I was impressed. The other regulars were, too."

Until then, it hadn't occurred to me that my performance was anything but laughable. "That's not what you guys said in the papers," I complained. "I was under the impression that my approval rating was hovering slightly below the Vatican's."

"Aw shucks," Klutsky replied. "You know what they say about not believing everything you read in the papers. Especially these days, when we're all looking over our shoulders to see if our jobs are still there. And you gotta admit, the advice you gave the boy's folks made for juicy copy. But you stuck to your guns. I thought it was admirable, even if my editor wouldn't let me say so."

"I can't wait to read what you write about my license hearing."

"That's still on?"

I nodded glumly.

"Well, I'll see what I can do. In the meantime, you ought to look into getting yourself certified."

"I don't think an insanity defense will impress them."

Klutsky laughed again. "No. What I meant was as a forensic psychiatrist."

I stared straight at him. "You must be out of your mind."

"I'm serious. Do you know what those guys make in a year?"

"A lot more than I do, I'm sure. But I'm not interested in the money."

"Then do it for humanitarian reasons. You strike me as the type who wouldn't give an opinion he didn't believe in 100 percent. That's a rare commodity in an expert, and juries can sense it. You'd be passing up the opportunity to help out a lot of folks, and I'm not talking about our friends in the thousand-dollar suits."

"I doubt any of them would want to take a chance on me."

"You've got it all wrong. You remember that scene in *To Kill a Mockingbird* when Atticus Finch cross-examines Mayella? He has to tread very carefully because if he comes on too strong about her being poor white trash the jury will start rooting for her. Rape victims with a sexual history present a similar problem. Di Marco to one side, I have a hunch most opposing counsel would shy away from criticizing you too harshly for fear of looking like an asshole."

"Thanks," I said, "but being an object of pity isn't my idea of how to supplement my income."

"Suit yourself," Klutsky said, "but don't be surprised when they start calling. Speaking of which, do you mind if I get in touch with you when this is all over?"

"Why? So I can sell you my life story?"

Klutsky leaned in next to my ear. "To be truthful, I was hoping for an exclusive. It would make a great human-interest story. Justice isn't blind to this psychiatrist, or words to that effect."

I knew it. But the temptation to fix some of the unflattering portraits that had been painted of me was strong. "I'll think about it. But only on certain terms."

"Short of writing outright fiction, I'll do anything you ask."

"I get to kill the story if I don't like how it turns out. No cute puns. No dwelling on the fact that I can manage on my own. And none of the usual 'living in darkness' bullshit. I have enough on my hands without everyone wondering whether I'm going to burst into tears."

Klutsky said, "I promise I'll make it sound no more serious than a hemorrhoid. Which, if I have to sit on this bench any longer—"

His words were cut off by the clerk's voice booming, "All rise."

Hallie didn't waste much time on the preliminaries. "Your Honor, I have with me this morning a motion for the immediate release of my client from custody and the entry of an order acquitting him of all charges. Two new developments prove beyond a reasonable doubt what we have contended all along—that Charles Dickerson did not murder Shannon Sparrow, and indeed, was the innocent victim in this matter."

Hallie paused for dramatic effect.

"Go on," Judge La Font said. "I'm listening."

"First, according to newly discovered evidence, which forensic analysis has confirmed, it is now abundantly clear that Ms. Sparrow was not sleeping with my client when she became pregnant with his child. Rather, she stole his ejaculate in an effort to create the appearance that they were sexually intimate. Why the prosecution did not uncover this evidence earlier is a mystery, but it demolishes the argument that my client killed Ms. Sparrow out of jealousy. Put simply, they weren't lovers. They never even held hands."

"Possibly because his were otherwise occupied," Di Marco put in, drawing scattered chuckles from seating area.

"Quiet," Judge La Font barked. "You too, Mr. Di Marco. What are you saying, that she took his sperm?"

"That's how it appears. Traces of Mr. Dickerson's DNA were discovered in a turkey baster located in Ms. Sparrow's apartment. The only logical inference is that she was using it to impregnate herself artificially."

"Why on earth would she do that?" Judge La Font asked.

"For purposes of blackmail. Following upon this new evidence I was informed over the weekend that the authorities had taken another suspect into custody—namely Judith Dickerson, my client's mother, who appears to have been the target of the blackmail scheme. Mrs. Dickerson was caught trying to dispose of an item of Ms. Sparrow's jewelry that was taken from her body at the time of the murder."

"Is this true, Mr. Di Marco?" Judge La Font asked, showing interest. "Has Mrs. Dickerson been charged?"

"Only with obstruction of justice," Di Marco answered. "She was released yesterday after posting bail."

"Bail in the amount of half a million dollars, Judge," Hallie put in quickly. "If that doesn't speak volumes about my client's innocence I don't know what else does. I would also remind the court of the state's refusal to afford the same treatment to my client, a mentally disabled youth with no history of violence, who has been detained in prison for more than a month, suffering untold psychological harm. All because his caretaker set out to kidnap his unborn child."

"Does either of these developments bear on the admissibility of the defendant's confession?" Judge La Font asked, predictably concerned that her ruling might come under criticism.

"Certainly, as they demonstrate, yet again, that my client was tricked into admitting culpability for a crime he did not commit," Hallie replied. "It's obvious that the police had no interest in pursuing other theories after Mr. Dickerson was arrested. They didn't even search Ms. Sparrow's apartment until last week. I'm asking that this travesty be ended now. If nothing else, my client should be committed to home custody while the prosecution continues to spin its wheels."

"Do you have a response to that, Mr. Di Marco?"

"Sure," Di Marco said, seeming unworried. "Nothing Ms. Sanchez has offered proves a thing. Suppose they never had intercourse. So what? If the defendant was as badly abused as his counsel claims, he still had a motive to kill her, possibly even a better one. And the other suspect is the boy's mother, who was captured attempting to dispose of evidence that would have further tied the noose around his neck. The fact that he didn't mention Mommy during his confession is irrelevant.

I would have done the same thing if my mother had helped me murder my girlfriend."

"She wasn't his girlfriend," Hallie shot back heatedly. "Your Honor has viewed the videotape of the confession. There was no mention of an accomplice at any point during the interrogation. Indeed, the prosecution's entire theory at preliminary hearing was that Mr. Dickerson acted alone in retaliation for the withdrawal of Ms. Sparrow's sexual favors. We now know that was a lie. Frankly, I'm surprised the prosecution hasn't already agreed to drop the charges against him."

"That's her theory," Di Marco rejoined. "I have a different one. The victim asked the defendant to masturbate because she liked it that way. Or maybe she couldn't stand to be touched by him. He got angry after being denied the real thing, so he killed her. He was found alone so he probably acted alone, but maybe Mommy was there to cheer him on. In either case, that's for the jury to decide. As for the confession, Your Honor has already ruled it to be both competent and admissible. Nothing has come to light to alter that opinion. Frankly, *I'm* surprised Ms. Sanchez would engage in such a transparent attempt to influence public opinion before jury selection."

Hallie's response was cut short by the judge. "I tend to agree with Mr. Di Marco. You're just arguing the evidence, Counsel. You can make the same points in front of the jury when we try the case. Which will be soon, unless the defense is willing to waive speedy trial."

"We're not waiving, Your Honor," Hallie said strongly. "Not while my client remains locked up behind bars."

"Then let's get a date on my calendar."

That was all it took.

I heard a shocked "*No!*" followed by sounds of a scuffle. "No, no, I won't have it," Judith's voice rang out. "I listened to you before and this is what it's brought. I will speak. I demand the right to speak." She was standing, almost shouting, struggling bodily with someone I took to be Nate. He implored her to sit back down.

"Please, darling. This is craziness. You won't be doing him any good. I'll . . ." I waited anxiously for him to complete the phrase.

"What is this disturbance?" Judge La Font demanded before he could finish.

"I'm his mother. I have a right to say what I know," Judith wailed to the now utterly still courtroom. She was weeping openly, filling the air with ragged sobs. Even Judge La Font seemed at a loss to know what to do. "Will someone, anyone, please tell me what is going on?" she cried in frustration.

"May I have the court's indulgence?" came a deep voice I didn't recognize. "It will only take a few moments." Judge La Font assented and Judith was persuaded to sit down. A round of spirited whispering ensued, followed a few minutes later by footsteps moving toward the podium.

"Your Honor, I sincerely apologize for the interruption. My name is Matthew Fenton. I was retained last week to represent Judith Dickerson, the mother of the accused. My client apparently desires to make a statement in open court. I realize such a request is highly irregular and I wish to be on record that I have counseled her in the strongest possible terms to refrain from such a course of action. However, Mrs. Dickerson will not be persuaded. Frankly, I fear I lack the means to stop her." He seemed to be begging Judge La Font to do it for him.

Di Marco jumped in before the judge had a chance to respond. "I'd like to hear what she has to say, Judge. It might spare the court a great deal of time—especially since Mrs. Dickerson is here right now and apparently anxious to tell us." What he meant was, before her lawyers had another opportunity to clamp the lid on her.

"If it would speed my client's release, I'd like to hear it too," Hallie said, reminding the judge that another life was at stake here.

"Counsel, approach the bench," Judge La Font ordered. "You too, Mr. Fenton." Since there was no jury present, I assumed the sidebar was to give herself time to think. Several minutes went by while the judge debated which was worse—sanctioning a procedural anomaly or having the hearing end on a huge question mark. In the end, according to Hallie, what appeared to sway her was the risk to her own reputation if she cut the inquiry short.

The attorneys resumed their positions and Judge La Font asked Judith to rise.

"Mrs. Dickerson, you are neither a party to this proceeding nor an officer of the court. Because of that, I cannot allow you to take the podium. However, if you are willing to be placed under oath as a witness, the court will hear your testimony. I must warn you that if you take the stand you will be waiving your constitutional rights against self-incrimination, as well as subjecting yourself to possible penalties for perjury. Do you understand these admonitions?"

"Yes," Judith said in a firm voice.

"And you wish to proceed despite them and against the advice of your counsel?"

"Yes," she said, even more firmly.

"Then I will ask the bailiff to swear you in. Mr. Di Marco will handle the questioning."

Di Marco began quietly, even sympathetically.

"Mrs. Dickerson, I take it you have something to tell us. Does it have to do with the morning the victim was murdered?"

"Yes. I was there. I saw her. Where we had arranged to meet. It was early. Before Charlie was up."

"Can you be more specific about the time?"

"Sometime between seven and seven thirty."

"Where were you when you saw Ms. Sparrow?"

"At the New Horizons Center. In the alley behind the school. It was where she said I should come."

"And what was the reason for your meeting Ms. Sparrow there?"

"I was to bring the money. It was what she demanded to leave Charlie alone. She told me they were in love."

"You believed her?"

"I did then. Now I know it wasn't true."

"You say Ms. Sparrow asked you to bring money. Was she blackmailing you?"

"Yes."

"And what precisely were you paying Ms. Sparrow to do?"

Judith was confused by the question. "I don't understand."

"Were you paying her to have an abortion?"

Judith took sharp offense at this. "Certainly not. Even if she were the mother, I could never have allowed it to be murdered. It would have been Charlie's child, my *grandchild*."

Di Marco seemed surprised by her answer. "Then what *was* your arrangement?"

"She was to live at a home for unwed mothers I support charitably. Until the baby was born. So that she and the child would have the best possible care. Afterward I would pay her the rest of the money to leave it there and go away."

"And after that, what did you envision happening to the child?"

"I was going to adopt it. To love it and raise it as my own. That is why I had to allow *her* to live. Even though she'd taken advantage of Charlie."

"I see," Di Marco said, although it was plain he was having trouble following. "Did anyone else know of this plan? Your husband, for example."

There was a long pause before Judith answered, as though she were debating something internally.

"No. If the baby were a girl she would have been like Charlie and he wouldn't have wanted it. No one else would have, either. I know because my work involves counseling families with genetically abnormal fetuses. They almost always choose to abort the child."

"I see," Di Marco said again, before resuming. "Let's get back to the day Ms. Sparrow was killed. How did you arrange to meet?"

"By phone, the night before. I was supposed to call her to find out where to go. She wouldn't tell me beforehand. When I heard it was to be at the New Horizons Center I protested. I was worried someone— Charlie or one of his teachers—might see us there. I asked if there wasn't somewhere else we could go, but she told me to shut up. I was afraid she would change her mind about having the baby, so I agreed."

"Is that when you purchased the gun?"

"Yes. I wasn't thinking clearly. It was foolish, of course. I couldn't shoot her without harming the baby."

"Was that the only time you spoke to Ms. Sparrow that night?"

"No. I called her again later, after I'd become calm again, to confirm that I was still coming."

Di Marco apparently liked this answer well enough to move on. "Where were you when you first saw Ms. Sparrow the next day?"

"In my car. I had just pulled up to the parking lot when I spotted her."

"Did you exchange any words?"

"Words? No. Of course not," Judith said as though it were a stupid question.

"You didn't say anything to her or she to you?" Di Marco tried again.

"How could I have done that?"

Di Marco said patiently, "Mrs. Dickerson, I'm trying to understand what happened after you met Ms. Sparrow in the alley. You testified that you saw her there sometime shortly after seven. What happened next?"

"Why, I took the necklace and left. Isn't that what you wanted to know? I took the necklace so no one would think Charlie had given it to her."

"Why would someone think that?"

"Because I thought it was mine. Charlie always liked it so. I thought he must have borrowed it and given it to her as a present. That's why I didn't throw it in the Lake with the gun. I thought it would look suspicious if it disappeared. I didn't find out until later that there were two of them."

"Let me see if I can get this straight," Marco said, struggling to keep up. "You took the necklace to protect your son?"

"Yes."

"So that he wouldn't be blamed for murdering Ms. Sparrow?"

"Yes, yes of course."

"But it wasn't your son who killed her."

"I've told you before. He couldn't have done it."

"And why is that Mrs. Dickerson?"

"Because she was already dead when I got there."

"That's not saying a lot. He could have killed her before you showed up."

"But I know he didn't. He was at home, like I told you. And she was waiting for someone else."

"What makes you say that?"

"Because she was holding this."

Hallie later told me that Judith's expression was one of pure malice as she removed something from her handbag and passed it to Di Marco.

Di Marco took it and studied it for a moment. "Your Honor, the witness has just handed me what appears to be a handwritten note addressed to the victim. Subject to its being properly authenticated at a later time, may I read the contents into the record?"

There was no one to object. Judge La Font signaled he could go ahead.

He read it aloud slowly, extracting every ounce of the suspense. *"Baby—your demands are becoming impossible. Daddy has a surprise for you. Wait for me outside the center and be prepared for a long vacation."*

The signature at the bottom was Nate's.

TWENTY-ONE

Nate's arraignment set off a media frenzy that didn't die down until a week later, when it was overshadowed by the indictment of another alderman on bribery charges. The police were releasing few details, but in the absence of hard fact the local news outlets had worked overtime at rumor and innuendo, stopping just short of stating that Nate was the still-at-large Surgeon. A Streets and San worker who moonlighted for Lincoln Park Towing suddenly remembered spotting a silver Mercedes C-class idling on the same street where the Surgeon had last struck. Coworkers of Nate's, speaking on strict anonymity, had mentioned his "God complex" and "excessive good spirits" in the operating room, where he bandied wisecracks and tapped his foot to selections from Wagner and Liszt. Somehow news of the Surgeon's signature had finally leaked out, and a landscape contractor for the Dickersons solemnly led a Channel 2 video crew to the ornamental hemlock he had planted in the couple's front yard the previous spring.

Throughout it, Judith maintained a dignity worthy of the Windsors, decamping to her parents' penthouse atop the Powhatan shortly after transporting Charlie from prison in a shaded limousine. Taub family retainers, including a virtual army of lawyers and advisors, were observed going in and out of the building's art deco lobby, but kept a tight-lipped silence, declining to comment even after the divorce papers were filed in a no-fault proceeding at the Daley Center. If the tabloids were hoping for a celebrity-style showdown, simmering with accusations of domestic abuse and child neglect, they were sorely disappointed. Having finally secured her son's freedom, Judith seemed content to nurse her wounds in private and away from the cameras' glare.

"I thought wives weren't allowed to testify against their husbands," I said when I phoned Hallie to ask how Charlie was doing.

"You didn't think of that before now?" she said, her patience with my armchair lawyering clearly exhausted. "It's a common misconception. The spousal privilege only covers communications from one spouse to the other, not things they become aware of independently."

"So if Nate had admitted the affair to Judith she couldn't have said a thing. It's only because she got her hands on that note that she was able to implicate him."

"Very good. But why do you care?"

Watching Nate's public flogging had made me more grateful than ever for the secrecy pact with Annie, even if it underscored the similarity between our positions. "I was just wondering, that's all. By the way, did anyone ever find Shannon's diary?"

"You're still thinking about who tried to run you over."

"Wouldn't you?"

"Well, if it was Nate, you have nothing to worry about now. Without access to Judith's funds he couldn't make bail. I heard he was blubbering like a baby after his first night with the general population. Aren't you going to ask me why Judith didn't come forward with the note sooner?"

"The question had crossed my feeble little mind."

"Well, there's a lot more to the story than what came out in court. Now that Di Marco needs my cooperation to get access to Charlie, he's sharing like a Girl Scout. Remember how Judith testified that she made two phone calls to Shannon, the night before the murder?"

I remembered.

"The second was after she purchased the gun, when she'd had some time to cool down and think. After the first conversation she started to worry that Shannon might renege on her promise not to come near Charlie again. Judith decided she wanted something she could use with Charlie if Shannon came back asking for a wedding ring. Of course, the marriage plans were all made up, but Judith didn't know that. In the second call, she asked Shannon to write a Dear John letter to Charlie explaining that while she cared for him, she could never marry him without his parents' permission, etcetera, etcetera. Not terribly persuasive, but it might have convinced Charlie."

"But Shannon didn't write any such letter."

"Exactly. Her parting shot was to put the note from Nate in a sealed envelope for Judith to find later."

"So Judith would know just how badly she'd been treated. Nice. But then why didn't Judith use it to exonerate Charlie earlier?"

"Because she forgot about it. After Judith found Shannon's body, she panicked and ran, or rather drove, all the way back to Michigan. Along the way, she was so focused on not being found with the gun that she completely overlooked the envelope, which she'd shoved into the glove box and didn't remember until you tricked me into warning her about another search. That's when she looked inside."

"Only to discover that her husband was a cheat as well as a possible murderer. Ouch."

"She didn't make the second leap, not right away. Not knowing about the artificial insemination, she still believed Charlie had been romantically involved with Shannon. But she was now suspicious enough about Nate to go looking for evidence of an affair. That's when she discovered her own necklace still lying in its box in her jewelry drawer. Apparently, Nate doesn't have much imagination when it comes to buying presents for his lady friends. He'd purchased a nearly identical piece for Judith for their last anniversary. At that point, Judith's options were to hang onto both of them and hope the police didn't draw the obvious conclusion or dump the one belonging to Shannon."

"Why didn't she come forward with the note when she was arrested?"

"Her lawyers urged her not to. Remember, their duty was protect Judith, not secure Charlie's freedom. The note would have complicated her defense by suggesting another motive for Shannon's murder. Like you, she thought Charlie would be released as a matter of course. It was only when she saw that Judge La Font wasn't going along that she decided to ignore them. In a twisted way, I've got to hand it to Di

Marco. If he wasn't such a jerk we might never have learned what really happened."

"Can they prove when the note was written?"

Hallie was pleased with my ignorance. "You mean can it be carbon dated, or something like that? No, forensic science isn't that sophisticated. The best an expert will be able to say is that it was written in Nate's hand sometime in the last year or so, which will allow Nate's lawyers to argue it's not proof of murder, only the sort of embarrassing thing a middle-aged man might send to his much younger lover."

I don't know why this made me uncomfortable. Charlie was safe, wasn't he? "How do you rate his chances?"

"Nate's, you mean? If he were my client, I'd advise him to cut the best deal he can get. For starters, a wealthy surgeon who cheated on his wife multiple times isn't going to be too sympathetic to the average juror. Add in the fact that there's a direct line from Nate's philandering to Shannon's manipulation of his disabled son, and he starts to look like a real swine. The way the murder was committed rules out a heat-of-passion defense, and Di Marco will be all over the fact that it was done with so little fuss—just the way a heart surgeon would set out to dispose of his victim. And, not surprisingly, Shannon's DNA was found all over his car. In the absence of another viable suspect, I'd say he hasn't a prayer."

"Won't his lawyers be able to say it was that other killer, the Surgeon?"

"And risk having the jury think they're the same person? I wouldn't touch it in a fireproof suit. No, at this point, I'd say finding the Surgeon—or the murder weapon—is about the only thing that *could* save Nate."

After Hallie and I said our good-byes, I walked over to my office building. I wasn't ready to return to work yet—there was a trip I was debating taking and I needed to serve my sentence with the therapist

Sep had arranged for me to see—but I thought I ought to follow Tim's advice and have Bob Turner look at my eye. It felt better, but it was still swollen and tender to the touch and I didn't want to take any chances with it. Also, something else was on my mind that I wanted to discuss with him.

"Nice color," Turner said, after he had probed my socket and tortured me with a penlight for several minutes. "You could pass for a beautiful sunset. But your pupilary response is good. And I don't see any signs of corneal swelling. I could put a protective patch over it, but I trust you to stay away from stock cars for a week or so. Have you been experiencing any other problems?"

"No, and that's the other reason I wanted to see you. It's the opposite. I could be imagining it, but the sight in my right eye seems to have gotten a little better lately, especially around the periphery."

"I'm eager to hear about it."

"It's subtle and I don't know quite how to describe it, but to give you an example, a little while ago I was following you around the room with more than just my ears."

Turner was sitting on a small rolling stool. He pulled it forward to face me and positioned a slender object a few inches away from my eyes. "It may not be your imagination. It's not uncommon for Leber's patients to rebound a little after the first phase has run its course." He began moving the object slowly across my field of vision. "Hmmm, looks like you're tracking this."

"Yes. A pencil, isn't it?"

He slid back a few feet. "How about now?"

"Harder, but I can still see something."

He moved in closer again. "How many fingers am I holding up?"

"Three."

"And now?"

"Just the one."

"CF at five feet." He flipped through the pages of my patient folder. "Slightly better than the four feet last time. Have you noticed anything else?"

"Certain light sources seem warmer, in a way."

"So some color perception, too."

I said, feeling rash, "Do you think there's a chance . . . ?"

Turner let a long moment pass before replying. "I can't lie to you, Mark. With your mutation the odds are . . . well, let's just say it's unlikely you'll experience a significant improvement and leave it at that. But if you're interested, I could run some more tests."

I shook my head. "That won't be necessary."

Turner misinterpreted my answer. "But that doesn't mean you should give up all hope. There's a lot we don't understand about your disease. In some ways the damage you've suffered is similar to the effects of a brain injury. I had a patient last week who was shot in the head in a hunting accident in his teens. Total cortical blindness. Woke up one day in his thirties and saw his wife's face for the first time."

"I hope he liked what he saw."

"All I know is he cried for over an hour."

"So things like that really happen, huh?"

"It's rare, but not unheard of. And who knows? With stem-cell research we could be only a few years away from new treatment options, maybe even able to regenerate severed spinal cords."

"I won't go shopping for a new car."

Turner said, "I wouldn't advise it. Not unless it can steer itself."

I smiled painfully, remembering my encounter with the mad driver.

Turner, apparently thinking this meant my morale needed boosting, said, "I'm sure the last year has been hard on you. You can't blame yourself for seeing things that may not be there."

"So you *do* think it's my imagination."

"I didn't say that. I'm just cautioning you to take things slowly."

I didn't even know why I'd asked.

But Turner wasn't finished giving advice. "You've made it through the worst part. Maybe it's time to ask yourself whether your life would really be all that different if you *could* see again. It doesn't seem to be holding you back from anything."

It was, but I wasn't going to tell him about it.

That exchange stayed at the back of my mind all day while I busied myself with overdue chores. On my way home from Turner's office, I stopped by the Lighthouse to pick up a new straight cane, not liking the feel of the collapsible one I'd been using since my regular job had been turned into toothpicks. My closet was ripe with dirty laundry, so when I got back to my apartment I threw a load in the basement machine and phoned to have my dry cleaning picked up. I retrieved the mail from my lobby inbox and sorted it into smaller piles, setting aside what I needed my reader's help with and writing checks for utility bills that were about to come due. I cleared out the spoiled food in my refrigerator and walked over to the White Hen on the corner to pick up fresh milk, eggs, and bread. Feeling virtuous for having achieved so much in a single afternoon, I had just paid the clerk and was replacing my credit card in my wallet when I remembered something else prudence would dictate I take care of soon, so when I got back upstairs I called the Secretary of State's office in the Thompson Building and asked to be connected to the license bureau.

"Depends on what kind of card you're looking for," the official said after I'd put my question to him. "For the basic, non-driver ID, all you'll need is a birth certificate and proof of residency. If you want the special ID you'll need a statement from your doctor certifying that you are a disabled person within the meaning of section 4A of the Illinois Identification Card Act and stating what your classification is."

"My classification?"

"Yes. Don't you know it?"

"I didn't even know there was such a thing."

"Are you able to be gainfully employed?"

"Yes."

"Live independently?"

"I should hope so."

"Then you're a 1. Unless you can't walk two hundred feet without assistance. Then you'd be a 1A. If you couldn't work or live alone you'd be a 2."

I wondered what a 3 was. A vegetable, maybe. Or one of the stiffs they resurrected to round out the polls on Election Day.

I said, "Just out of curiosity, what's the reason for putting that kind of information on an ID card?"

"You'll have to ask someone else that question. I can switch you over to the Disability Advocate at the attorney general's office if you'd like."

"That won't be necessary. The non-driver ID will work just fine."

"Are you sure? The disabled ID is free of charge. The fee for the non-driver card is twenty-five dollars."

I wanted to tell him no price was too great to pay to avoid the equivalent of wearing a big red *D* on my shirt, but held my tongue.

"When can I come in to do this?"

"Any weekday, from nine to five."

"Will there be someone there who can assist me in filling out the forms?"

"Yeah, but if you're smart you'll bring a friend. It will help pass the time while you wait. Could take a few hours to get to the head of the line."

I was getting antsy just thinking about it.

"And don't forget to bring your driver's license so we can cancel it."

I'm not sure what made me ask the next question.

"About that. Once I've officially given up my license, would I need some kind of special clearance to get it back again? I mean, supposing my eyesight suddenly returned to normal?"

"Nope. All you need to do is take the eye exam. Pass that and nobody here will care if you've got ten Seeing Eye dogs."

I thanked him and hung up and thought about what he said for a very long time.

I'd arranged to have dinner with Alice that evening in a restaurant on Randolph, just west of the Loop. I set out walking there a little before six, in time to stop in at the Tiffany store before it closed. Tanya had left several messages on my answering machine telling me that the necklace I'd ordered had arrived and was waiting to be picked up. I thought it was only fair that I pay for it and I wanted to correct the bad impression I left there the first time. When I sailed through the door and made it without mishap to the service desk at the rear, I was wearing the smart sport jacket I'd bought at Mark Shale the previous January with the assistance of a gay salesperson. It was chestnut, *GQ*'s "must have" color that year, and coordinated nicely with the fawn slacks and cream silk tee he'd suggested to go with it. *Queer eye for the blind guy*, I recalled thinking as he rang up my purchases.

It certainly impressed Tanya. "Wow. Is this a new look?"

"Only my hairdresser knows for sure. You look pretty swell yourself this evening."

"Oh, but you can't . . ."

On impulse I decided to test something.

"How do you know?" I asked. "How do you know I can't see you?"

"Well, you've got that cane, for one thing."

"But if I didn't, what would you think then?"

"I don't know. Your eyes do seem a little unfocused sometimes, but when you're looking straight at me like now . . ." She cut off abruptly. "This is awkward."

I apologized and told her to forget it.

"No, no. I can understand why you'd want to know. I guess I'd have to say I couldn't be sure one way or the other."

"So I might fool you if I were only pretending to be blind."

"I think so. But why would you do that? Why would anyone?"

Why indeed, I thought.

Alice had arrived at the restaurant before I did and was already seated when I came up to the table I'd reserved near the window. It was one of those chic establishments where the food makes up for cramped seating and self-conscious minimalism. The chilly décor didn't bother us. Our table was covered in a cloth so stiffly starched it could have done extra duty as sheet metal, but there was a hyacinth in a vase between us, sending off shivers of musk. I've always loved the smell of hyacinths, and I said so.

"Me too," Alice said. "Do you think it's blue?"

I fingered its waxy petals. "Like your eyes?" I said.

"I was wondering when you would to get around to asking that. No, they're an undistinguished brown. Mud brown, my mother used to say."

"And your hair?"

"Brown too, I'm afraid."

I noted she hadn't exhibited the same curiosity towards me. She waited until we had ordered and the waiter had brought our aperitifs to bring up Nate's arrest again.

"I don't know how to thank you."

"I don't know there's anything you should thank me for. Do you think the outcome will make much of a difference to the center's survival?"

"Maybe not. I still have the fact that I didn't supervise Shannon adequately to deal with. But at least Charlie's been cleared. You did a wonderful thing for that boy."

I shrugged.

"Will you be able to see him?"

"If Judith had her way, I wouldn't still be in the same galaxy."

"What about the case against you? Will the charges be dropped?"

I said, "Let's not talk about that. I don't want to think about anything else except being with you tonight."

We spent the rest of dinner immersed in more pleasant topics. Our likes and dislikes in literature, places we'd traveled to, her upbringing and mine. I amused her to no end with tales of my vainglorious deeds as a teenager and the lengths my father had to go to keep me out of reform school. Toward the end, she asked me what his name was.

"Same as mine. Dante."

"Really? So that's what the initial *D* on your card stands for. How beautiful! Why don't you use it?"

"Be serious."

"Were you and your father named after the famous one?"

"Family lore has it that we're distantly related. My father was extremely proud of the connection, and like many Italians his age, could recite large portions of the *Commedia* by heart. He wanted the same for me. Every day after school I had to get through at least one canto in Italian before I could escape outside to play. You can see how it shaped my personality—all that emphasis on sin and punishment."

"But isn't it also about salvation, too?"

"Yes, but I always sided with the sinners, the less repentant the better. It's funny, but I've been thinking a lot about that work lately. That Dante wrote it while he was living in exile, at a time when his life couldn't have seemed bleaker."

"What was the name of the woman he loved?"

"Beatrice."

"Were they ever together?"

"No. She married someone else. After Dante was driven from Florence he died alone in Ravenna. I visited his tomb once. It's a surprisingly simple monument for someone the Italians revere as their greatest poet."

The waiter interrupted us then, bringing dessert.

When we were finished with our meal, I asked Alice if she'd like to walk home with me. "It's a quarter after eight," I said. "If we walk quickly, we'll get back in time to listen to the Water Arc."

The Water Arc is a Chicago novelty. In the warmer months it goes off hourly, thrusting a majestic geyser hundreds of feet in the air over the Chicago River. When I was sighted I used to enjoy the spectacle from my terrace, pausing from whatever I was reading to watch the water take off like a silver jet in flight. After I became blind I tended to observe the Arc closer by, either near its source in Centennial Fountain or, when I wanted a real treat, crossing over to the river's south bank where I could listen to the cascade raining down on the pavement like a liquid "Ode to Joy." Though intended primarily as a visible monument, I liked to think the Arc was also designed with someone like me in mind: a spectacle every bit as thrilling to the ears as fireworks are to the eyes.

Alice evidently shared my fondness for it. "That would be delightful," she said.

We took our time strolling back, crossing over the Adams Street Bridge and following the river past its T-shaped fork and over to its mouth at the lakefront. It was one of those spring evenings when the lingering daylight and the languid air come together in a state of atmospheric perfection. I couldn't actually see the sunset, but I could sense its splendor, the ribbons of vermillion and gold to our backs casting long forward shadows in our path. It seemed a shame to spoil it, but during dinner I had made up my mind.

So when we were halfway back, I told Alice about Jack.

She was unusually quiet when I finished. By that time we had stopped near where the Arc would soon strike up its symphony of sound. We rested against the railing beside the swirling currents of the river, as dark and tangled as my history. The breeze had picked up and a lock of Alice's hair brushed my cheek. Across the water I could just make out my apartment building silhouetted against the sky like a specter in the dusk. I wondered whether it would ever feel like a home to me and whether, like my namesake, I would reach the end of my life still in exile, still alone. It didn't make what I had to do next any easier.

"I'm not sure what reaction you were expecting from me," Alice said after what seemed like an eternity. I tried to read her voice for a signal, but none came to me.

"I was hoping only for an honest one."

"You blame yourself for your son's death."

I nodded.

Alice sighed. "You shouldn't punish yourself so much. He might have died anyway, even if you had been there. But I suppose that's the worst part—not knowing one way or the other."

"That and knowing I didn't love him enough."

"Someone, I think it was Maimonides, said that every man is half guilty and half innocent. Each of us is capable, through even the smallest of acts, of tipping the scales of the universe toward righteousness. You did that by helping Charlie."

"It doesn't make up for what I did to my son."

"I think you're wrong. You risked your career to save that boy. That has to count for something."

"So you think there's some sort of cosmic ledger out there, where credits for good deeds offset the bad?"

"I'm not that simplistic, but surely a lifetime of good works can make up for one moment of weakness." She took my hand and squeezed it. "I want you to know it doesn't alter my opinion of you. You inflicted a terrible wrong on your wife and child, but you paid a price no one should ever have to pay."

And would continue paying for the rest of my life.

"I'm sorry then," I said, throwing her hand off. "I was hoping you would see it differently. I thought it might make it easier."

"Easier?"

"Saying good-bye."

"Good-bye? Why? Are you going away?"

"Now that you bring it up, I've been thinking I should."

"I don't understand."

"Don't you? But before I go, there's something I want you to have."

"This conversation isn't making any sense," Alice said. But doubt had overtaken her voice. Doubt and the onset of fear.

"Here," I said, taking the slender box from my jacket. I held it out to her. "I looked up the arrangements online. They'll let you have one item of jewelry besides a watch."

Alice just stood there.

"Take it," I said angrily, pushing it forward.

She did as I asked. I could feel her hand shaking. "It's a box of some sort. Held together by a ribbon. Satin, I think, and very soft." Alice lifted the cover from the box and removed the velvet case inside. I heard the lid snap open.

"A necklace. It's beautiful. But it looks just like . . ." She caught herself and said, "I meant that figuratively, of course."

"You needn't pretend any longer," I said, more bitterly than I intended to.

I reached into my breast pocket and pulled out my cell phone.

"I'm going to call Detective O'Leary now. We can listen to the Arc until he gets here. Or rather, I'll be the one just listening. You can watch and tell me whether there are any rainbows."

"Wait, Mark. Don't make any calls yet. Let me explain . . ."

"What is there to explain?"

"I wasn't trying to trick you."

"Oh really? I'm sure it was a piece of cake. All you had to do was mimic me. Now we're tapping with our canes, now we're feeling for our chairs, now we're fucking with the lights turned off. Did it make you feel superior knowing you could stop anytime you wanted to? Or did you just enjoy the fact I couldn't see the look of amusement on your face?"

"Don't. For God's sake don't. It was never like that. I wasn't lying when I told you about my accident. I know how it feels to be in your shoes. I *remember*. The awkward silence when I entered a room, the way everyone treated me like a piece of glass. I was still the same person, but everyone acted as though I were a walking tragedy. It's one of the reasons I was so devoted to the center."

"Devoted enough to kill to keep it going."

"When I couldn't see any other way out, yes. Charlie, the others . . . I was trying to make a difference in their lives."

I remembered then what she had said about the center's clients being like her children and some of my anger toward her lessened.

Still, I couldn't keep myself from asking, "And the sex, was that an act too?"

"Never. You have no idea how attractive you are."

She didn't need to add the caveat.

"I know what you're thinking," Alice said, "but you're wrong."

I didn't reply.

Alice said, "Will you let me show you before you make your phone call?"

Before I could consider my answer, Alice reached up and cupped my face in her hands. Then she touched her lips gently to mine, letting them linger there.

It was only as she began to disengage that I felt the pressure below my ears and realized what she was doing.

I don't know how long I was unconscious, only that when I came to again I was stretched out on the pavement with a cloth stuffed in my mouth. I couldn't see a thing. My wrists were lashed tightly above my head, held fast to something cold and wet. The ground under my back was damp too, as though it had taken a recent soaking. Several feet below me I made out what sounded like waves lapping against a wall and, from a greater distance, the sound of cars passing on a roadway overhead. Other than that the night was completely still, wrapped around me like a thick comforter.

With some difficulty I made out that I was tied to the railing where Alice and I had been standing when she knocked me out.

I tested my bindings by flexing them. My wrists felt like they were being held in place by a large rubber band. It bit into my skin when I moved them, hastening the numbness that was beginning to creep up into my fingers. A stick of some sort was wedged between my upended elbows and my chin, preventing me from turning my head to either side. My legs and torso were free, but I was trussed so tightly I could only angle my body a foot in either direction. Whenever I did it set off a sharp protest in my still-mending ribs. My lips were dry and my mouth raw from the cloth, which was lodged dangerously close to my windpipe.

While my head continued to clear, I ran through my options. Shouting for help seemed unwise. It might make the cloth slip farther, cutting off my air supply. My cell phone was in my jacket pocket, but too far from my hands to get at. I could kick at the ground, but the noise was unlikely to attract attention. On the south side of the river at this hour there would be little traffic. Only a fool would risk its shadowy footpaths after nightfall. The far bank was usually better lit, but it was at least thirty yards off. At that distance I doubted I would be noticed by a stroller, and even then I would probably be mistaken for a vagrant sleeping it off. I'd be lucky to be freed any time before morning.

I wondered what Alice had used to tie me down. When I caught on, I very nearly laughed.

Folding canes are sold in many different configurations and lengths, but have one thing in common: a strong elastic cord that runs from the top of the cane through its hollow sections to the tip. The cord is taut enough to hold the sections in place when the cane is distended, but also flexible enough to permit it to be folded up accordion style when it's not in use. A plastic cap in the handle opens to allow the cord to be tightened when it becomes loose by tying off a simple knot. I surmised that Alice had opened up the cane she was carrying and removed several of its sections, leaving one in place in the middle. This would have given her several feet of cord to work with, and further explained the "stick" wedged beneath my chin. The cloth in my mouth was no doubt the ribbon from the box I had given her.

I had to admire her ingenuity. Even at this time of night, planes left O'Hare every fifteen minutes. In a rental car Alice could be over the Canadian border before the police even knew to look for her. In the meantime I wasn't in any particular danger. Though the pressure on my wrists was painful, the circulation to my hands wasn't completely cut off. If I lay there quietly I could make it to dawn unharmed, with no more serious injury than my tattered pride.

Though I felt every bit the fool I began to relax some.

Until a gurgling noise from across the river told me what I was really up against.

I barely had time to prepare before the Arc went off. It lifted high into the sky and hissed there a moment or two before gathering speed. The first drops caught me on the forehead. I heard them hit the pavement with a popping sound. I gulped a lungful of air and clamped my jaw shut.

When the first wave hit, it was like being struck by a torpedo. In a split second the area around me imploded. The roar in my ears was deafening. Instinctively, I arched my hips and tried to turn away, but it was no good. With my shoulders locked firmly in place, all I could do was thrash uselessly from side to side. I squeezed my eyes shut against the spray coming at me from all angles. It felt like a hail of darts. At two thousand gallons a minute, there was never any letup. The water quickly soaked my clothing, turning my skin to ice. If I didn't drown first, I'd probably die of hypothermia.

My doctor's training was no help. I knew the Arc went on for roughly ten minutes, too long for me to survive without fresh oxygen. And that was the least of my problems. Somehow I had managed to keep my mouth shut during the first impact, but the Arc was lashing my exposed face like a monsoon. It was only a matter of time before the water filled my open nostrils, then my sinuses. With the ribbon stuffed down my throat my gag reflex would fail and I wouldn't be able to cough up enough liquid to keep it from leaking farther down. It would pool in my trachea, then my lungs . . .

The Arc continued its pounding assault.

I've since heard it said that drowning is the worst kind of death. That those who manage to survive it are left with scars more emotional than physical. That the last seconds before the airways collapse produce a terror like no other. Maybe. Being burned at the stake sounds worse. But all the same, I wanted to weep. I remembered the other times in my life when I'd been this afraid: when I was rushing Jack to the hospital, when the blood tests came back, when the second spot made its inevitable debut. Stumbling helplessly around my apartment not long after its arrival, paralyzed with dread and wondering whether I really *was* paying for my sins, I returned to the theory I'd seized upon when

Turner was delivering his prognosis. It wasn't risk-free. A crazy shrink posed as many problems as a blind one. But if I could just keep my colleagues from finding out, hold onto my wits until the crisis passed, my vision would eventually return. Or so the textbooks said.

It may be pushing several metaphors at once to say that I had to drown before the scales were lifted from my eyes, though at the time I did happen to be flopping on the ground like a hooked fish. And as epiphanies go, it was almost an anticlimax. I was too good a psychiatrist not to have noticed that as the months went by, my sight wasn't improving. That even in moments of forgetfulness, when I was absorbed by problems other than my own, the blockage stubbornly refused to clear. It was easier to put off the day of reckoning than to face up to the truth. In reality, the lie I had fashioned as a lifeline was steadily pulling me under, as surely as if I were being sucked under the tsunami of my own towering deceit.

But trapped beneath the Arc that night I knew.

And oddly enough, I stopped giving a fuck.

By this time the shivering in my limbs had turned to near convulsions and it was only through sheer will that I wasn't coughing up the water now steadily seeping into my esophagus. I knew that if I tried to breathe, even for a second, it would all be over. The bands of hot steel around my chest were growing tighter and tighter. Soon my lungs would burst from the strain. I thought of Jack and Annie and my fatherless son, Louis. I still hated myself for everything I had done to them and always would, but there was yet a possibility, however slim, that I could make amends. Find a path out of the dark wilderness where I was lost. So while the water raged around me, clawing at my sides like the vines and branches of Dante's wood, I fought. I fought even though it was hopeless, even though my insides were on fire, even though if I did manage to survive, I would never look upon their faces again. I fought for that last chance to see another day. And when I couldn't fight any longer, I cried out.

A sort of giddiness came over me then, followed by the sensation that I was dreaming. It wasn't such a bad dream. A ghostly figure appeared and called my name. A shade, I decided. Just like in mythology. There would be a dog, too, a nasty three-headed thing, slavering and snapping at my heels. But my guide would steer me past the monster, help me safely across the river. My very own Beatrice. Whoever it was was removing my bindings, plucking at them as easily as a harp string. I was gathered up and carried off, laid down in a meadow of incredible softness. The apparition stood over me, beckoning me to rise. I smiled at her as she bent down to kiss me.

Except that the lips kissing mine weren't soft. They were pointed like a shark's snout and concealed a row of sharp teeth. And they weren't kissing either. They were pushing and pulling, gnawing at my lips. The gnawing grew more insistent until it felt like my tongue was being ripped out. I wanted to scream but I couldn't make any sound. And then the fire in my chest returned, filling my mouth with smoke. It tasted like a campfire and I had to spit it out . . .

"Mistuh Mark?"

I rolled onto my side and vomited.

"Mistuh Mark, are you OK?"

TWENTY-TWO

The weapon was where I told O'Leary he would find it, at the bottom of the rooftop compost bin Alice had shown me on my first visit to the New Horizons Center. It was a stainless-steel tool normally used for sculpting ceramics, slender but sharp enough to carve a hole in someone's aorta if you knew what you were doing. Alice's fingerprints were on it, along with traces of Shannon's blood. It was wrapped in a hooded parka next to the charred remains of a ruled notebook presumed to be Shannon's missing diary. A check with the secretary of state confirmed Alice's ownership of a tan Civic hybrid with recent repairs to its front bumper. Further investigation uncovered a pattern of regular transfers from the center's bank account to an art-supply firm in Carbondale later revealed to be a shell licensed in Shannon's name.

"I'm glad you weren't hurt," Alice said. We were sitting across from one another in the Cook County jail, separated by half an inch of Plexiglas.

"I wish you'd considered that before you tried to waterboard me," I replied, only partly in jest.

"Yes. It was generous of you to come."

My eye was healed and other than a few scrapes and bruises, my near-death experience had left me largely unscathed, except for an irrational fear of the shower. I'd bathed at the sink that morning and put on a freshly pressed suit, thinking it would be the last time we ever met. It had been an ordeal getting in. The guards had declared my cane to be contraband and I had to be led by the hand by a puffing matron who acted like a blind visitor was an affront to prison regulations. "I'll be back when your thirty minutes is up," she said, dumping me into a cubicle that smelled like a lavatory stall. I had to put my lips up to a mouthpiece in the center to make myself understood, and hold my ear to its scratched surface to hear Alice's replies.

"Are they treating you all right?" I asked.

"Not as badly as I treated you."

"We don't have a lot of time," I pointed out.

"I know. When . . . how . . . did you figure it out?"

"I'm not entirely sure, but I think it began with Nate's note to Shannon, the one Judith produced in court. It was too convenient, and the timing was ambiguous. The note could have been written months earlier, an invitation to one of their out-of-town flings, but as Hallie explained the science to me, Nate would never be able to prove it. It started me questioning my own motives. Had I pursued Nate to the exclusion of other suspects because of a subconscious need to see him—and by extension, myself—punished? What if I was guilty of the same rush to judgment that put Charlie behind bars?"

"And your self-doubt ultimately led to me?"

"Not at first. I hardly wanted to think I was sleeping with a killer. But I did go back over some of the things I'd learned about you. Like Regina's observation that you were always kowtowing to Shannon, as though you were afraid of her. I couldn't imagine why. It seemed inconsistent with the strong, confident woman I was getting to know. You were also the person who had the most to lose if anything questionable came to light about the center, and of course, you'd once been a nurse. Still, I didn't see how it was possible until I visited my eye doctor."

I told her about my conversations with Turner and the clerk from the DMV. "I recalled then that you'd lost your sight to a head injury and the other pieces started falling into place. Little things, like how quickly you caught on when we were first introducing ourselves. And that night in your apartment, how long you left me by myself. It was like you wanted to me to find all the things that would normally show up in a blind person's living quarters. Except for the tulips on your coffee table, everything was as it should be. Tulips are beautiful, but they have almost no scent, not the first flower of choice for someone who can't see."

"You *are* dangerous. But then, why didn't you turn me in before we had dinner?"

"I wanted to be wrong. And it wasn't until you made that mistake about my name that I knew for certain."

"What mistake?"

"At the restaurant. You asked me what the initial *D* on my business card stood for. You'd only know there was one if you could read the printed inscription. I didn't have them include it in the Braille overlay because there wasn't enough room."

"And yet you calmly sat there eating with me as though nothing had happened."

I grinned crookedly at her. "A fellow's entitled to a nice night out before he turns his girl in for murder."

"I'm glad we had that last time together. If it means anything, I was having trouble reconciling what I had done with my feelings for you."

"Do you know where they'll be sending you?" I asked, to move us off the subject again.

"To the Lincoln Correctional Facility, a medium-security facility for women. With credit for community service and good behavior I could be paroled before I'm ready for a cane again. I've offered to teach classes on living skills to senior inmates who are losing their sight."

"I can't imagine a better teacher."

"You're being kind again. Tell me, what brought you here?"

"I wanted to ask you something. Not about the murder—something else." I stopped, unsure now whether I had made a mistake in coming.

Alice read my mind. "You want to know what it was like."

It made no sense, but I had to find out. "Yes," I said hesitating, then with more conviction. "Yes, I think I do."

Alice chose her words carefully. "Terrifying in the beginning. I know, I'm supposed to say I was positively leaping with joy. But it wasn't like that. I hadn't been unhappy living as a blind person. When I thought about it at all, it was just another part of who I was. What I couldn't face was another setback. Becoming attached again to things I no longer missed. Does that seem strange?"

It didn't. Not any longer. "Did it happen all at once?"

"You mean like in the movies, when the heroine's bandages are lifted and her doctor's face swims slowly into view?"

"You've left out the part where her fiancé shouts 'It's a miracle! Now we can be a real family!'"

Alice nearly choked laughing. "No, nothing like that. It was so gradual I didn't even notice at first. But after a few months I couldn't deny what was happening. I was in line to get the job at the state agency I mentioned to you. I knew they couldn't hire someone able-bodied when there were so many other deserving candidates vying for the position, and I wanted to be chosen more than anything else. You know what those agencies are like—half the time the employees are just as bigoted about the people they're supposed to be helping as the rest of the world. I thought I could change things from the inside. So I didn't tell anyone my sight was getting better."

"And kept it a secret even after it returned to normal."

"It was almost too easy. And it enabled me to set an example as a capable, independent blind person succeeding in a position of responsibility. I bought contact lenses that were too powerful for what I needed and wore them at work, so I wouldn't be tempted to use my eyes when others might notice. No one did. All they ever saw was the cane."

"That first night we were together, in your apartment . . . you took your contacts out while I was exploring."

"I wanted to get a good look at you. My vision's not perfect, not by a long shot, but at close range not far from what it was before my accident."

"And while you were checking me out you looked to see if I was wearing a wedding ring."

"Yes. That was another mistake. I was worried you'd catch on there and then."

I didn't comment on how she'd distracted me. "And you cheated on other occasions as well."

"I couldn't help it. It was so glorious, so liberating to be able to see again. As you guessed, I had my driver's license reinstated and bought a car so I could take long rides in the country on weekends. North to Door County, east to the Michigan shore. And that's how the game finally caught up with me. I was stopped at a gas station on the toll road in Indiana when Shannon pulled up behind me. I was by myself so she figured it out instantly."

"And began blackmailing you."

"Yes. She cleaned out all of my savings. But that wasn't enough for her. I had to start embezzling from the center to keep up with her demands. I was living in constant fear that someone—Regina especially—would become suspicious about why I was always giving in to her. And then I found them—Shannon and Charlie—together."

"Where?"

"In my office. I noticed Charlie was absent during lunch one day and went looking for him. When I opened the door Charlie was stretched out on the couch. It was horrible, she was standing over him . . . urging him on. Charlie, the poor dear, he didn't understand. But Shannon . . . I can still see the expression on her face, the look of obscene triumph. I shut the door and waited outside. When Charlie came out I told him he was a good boy and asked him to help himself to a snack. Then I went inside and confronted Shannon. I said what she had done could never happen again. She just laughed and said she'd see me arrested and the center closed if I tried to interfere. I knew then there was only one way to stop her."

"How did you get her into the alley that morning?"

"I knew she'd been using the parking lot when she wasn't supposed to. I made a point of mentioning at a staff meeting that I expected one of the spaces to be available that week. I drove around every day waiting to see if she'd take the bait. I knew it was my only opportunity to make it look like a random killing . . . like those other poor women who died. I'd almost given up hope when she showed up that morning. I didn't know she and Judith had arranged specifically to meet there."

"It's a wonder you two didn't bump into one another."

"Yes. Or Charlie. You can imagine how I felt when he was arrested. I was debating what to do when you showed up at the center. When I saw how determined you were to find the real killer, I thought there might be a chance of casting the blame on someone else. So I took it."

"And me in the process."

"You say that so easily now."

"I've had time to get over myself. I know it wasn't all pretend—for either of us."

"If you can believe it, I never really meant to cause you harm. That first time, in the car, was only to keep you from suspecting me."

"And the second time?"

"To give myself room to get away. And yes, to punish you a little. For turning up in my life when you did. For letting me see what might have been."

What could I say? That we were both sinners? That she had taught me a valuable lesson? That while I'd never be able to explain it, I forgave her?

Alice let a few moments of silence pass before asking, "What will you do now?"

"Go back to my job. I have to put food on my table. And I've been thinking about trying to do more courtroom work. I seem to have a knack for it. And . . . well, maybe it would help change some of those perceptions you were talking about earlier."

Alice said, "I like that idea, but I was referring to other unfinished business."

I looked down at the table, traced its grimy surface with a finger. "I haven't made any decisions about that."

"What's holding you back? Your son needs you in his life."

"I know. It's . . . more complicated than you think. My wife—my *ex* wife—doesn't know . . . about *this*."

Alice sounded shocked. "You never told her?"

"I'm not supposed to communicate with her, except in writing through our lawyers. I don't know what to put in a letter. 'Dear Annie, I am pleased to inform you that the bastard you wished dead—or worse—has received his just reward. P.S. You don't owe him a thing.'"

"Why not just explain the facts? Are you worried that she'll pity you?"

I shook my head. "Not that."

"What then?"

"That she'll forgive me when she shouldn't."

Alice's jailor was back, telling me it was time to leave.

"Is there anything I can do for you while you're away?" I asked.

"Write to me once in a while. And send me any Braille books you don't need. I'm sure we'll be able to use them in the prison library. And Mark . . ."

"Yes?" I said, rising to go.

"If it's not too hard, find a way to forgive yourself."

"I can see why you were concerned," Sep was saying.

We were in his office and I had just finished telling him about the day I found out I was losing my sight. As promised, I had come completely clean with him. I had left nothing out, starting with my father and continuing right on up until the day Jack died. Told him of the shattering guilt I had suppressed for so long after. The guilt that allowed me to think I was losing my mind.

"Unilateral presentation is one of the classic symptoms. It was entirely rational for you to suspect a conversion disorder—hysterical blindness."

"I thought so, too. I couldn't stop remembering what Annie told me when I explained where I'd been that night. She said she never wanted to see me again. In Turner's office that afternoon I realized I had been hoping for the same thing, wishing there was some way I wouldn't ever have to look at myself again. It seemed like too much of a coincidence."

Sep said quietly, "And perhaps still does. Are you sure your first instinct wasn't right?"

I wrinkled my nose in displeasure. "You mean that I've been making it up all along?"

"'Making it up' is the wrong way of putting it. You've undergone a terrible loss, not just your child but your faith in your ability to heal others. It can take the psyche years to recover from such an event. There may yet be a possibility, however remote, that your vision will improve someday."

I shook my head. "You're not saying anything I haven't wished a thousand times. But genes don't lie—even when they don't tell the whole story. I've had a time bomb ticking inside me my entire life. It was bound to go off sooner or later. I'm just lucky it happened as late as it did."

"But to play devil's advocate, as you've explained to me, not all people with your mutation lose their sight. Some never develop any symptoms at all."

"True, but it's been almost two years. I have to accept that it's here to stay." I shrugged and added, "If only to keep from truly driving myself crazy."

"I'm sorry, then."

"Me, too. Meanwhile, there are plenty of other issues to keep me occupied."

"Our colleague may be able to help you there."

"If only he'd stop thinking my hearing was suspect too. I'm considering wearing ear plugs to our next session."

"Go easy on him. It takes time to get used to your sense of humor. And what of Charlie?"

"He's doing much better now that he's home. Judith has given me permission to see him while she's at work. In fact, I'm going over there after we're finished."

"I'm glad to hear it. Shall we set a date for your return then?"

"Only if I can be forgiven for feeling a profound sense of *déjà vu*."

When I arrived at his home, Charlie was waiting for me on the front steps. He jumped up to give me a bear hug. I was carrying an overnight bag and he asked me if I was going on a trip.

"I'm taking a plane to New York City."

"That's where the Mets live," he said excitedly. "In Shea Stadium."

I didn't have the heart to correct him. And to my way of seeing, it would always be Shea.

"Are you going to see them?" Charlie asked.

"I'd like to, but I won't have time this trip."

Charlie took me inside and showed me his room and his collection of action figures. Afterwards we played video games on the floor of the family den, Charlie beating me handily every time.

"You're even worse than Dad," he told me.

"Give me some time," I said. "I'm still getting used to this."

I stayed until it was almost time for Charlie's dinner, when Boris appeared on schedule with the town car. I said good-bye to Charlie with promises to return soon.

The ride out to O'Hare was the usual conga line, compounded by a sudden thunderstorm that pummeled the town car's roof like a percussionist gone amok. But when we pulled up to the departures level forty minutes later the squall was beginning to let up, and from the corner of my right eye I glimpsed a pale glimmer of sunshine peaking from behind the clouds.

I tipped Boris a C-note and asked him to treat Yelena to a nice night out.

And then I boarded a plane headed east, to where Louis would be waiting with his mother to meet me.

ACKNOWLEDGMENTS

To give proper credit to all those who aided and abetted this book, I should start with my mother, Janice Raimondo, who instilled in me the love of words that led to my first career as a lawyer, and then to the not-unrelated job of writing fiction. I wish she were here to share this achievement.

A close second place goes to my sister, Sandra Berg, MD, my ideal reader, scientific consultant, and volunteer proofreader, who was always there to cheer me on when it seemed as though I should have heeded the warning above those famous gates to hell.

I also owe an enormous debt of gratitude to all my other early readers and cheerleaders—Caryn Jacobs, Julia Parzen, Brian Massengill, Jill Martensen, Blair Wellensieck, Mike Feagley, John and Denise Noell, Melissa Widen, and Debra de Hoyos—for their candid, insightful, and generous support.

To my agent, Kate Folkers, who rescued me from the slush pile and gave me invaluable suggestions for the novel's improvement.

To my editor, Dan Mayer, and all the folks at Seventh Street Books, for taking a chance on a first-time author and for all the things, big and small, that went into the book's publication. A special thanks also to my copy editor, Ian Birnbaum, my proofreader, Jade Zora Ballard, and my cover designer, Jackie Cooke.

To my wonderful children, Kendra, Jacob, and Tamsin Parzen, for putting up with late dinners, missed pick-ups, and a semideranged parent while it was being written. You are my constant joy and inspiration.

And last, but not least, to my husband, Stanley Parzen, whose incurable optimism has always been the lifeline keeping me afloat. It is no cliché to say I couldn't have done it without you.

A portion of the proceeds of this book will be donated to IFOND, the International Foundation for Optic Nerve Disease. To learn more about the foundation's work, please visit its website at www.ifond.org.